taylor
made

kj lewis

Cover Design by Regina Wamba at maeidesign.com
Interior Design by Champagne Formats

dedication

To Rachel – the first to say I should, could and did.

ch♥pter
one

Breathe in. Breathe out. *Fuck me.*

How do I get myself into these situations?

For the normal person, flying would not warrant a "fuck me," but when it comes to flying, I am not normal. I have issues. Control issues. Control is my security blanket. I don't like to give it to others. If I cling to it, I know I am going to land on my feet.

The practical side of me understands flying is a safe way to travel, but I've never understood asking someone to put their trust in a tin can, flown by someone they've never met, whose sole intention is to hurtle them down a runway at a ridiculous velocity and propel them into the air. Seriously, what sense does this make to the average person? What person wants to give this kind of control to someone? I barely tolerate being driven by others. But, like always, the convenience of the tin-can of death wins out when it comes to travel, and I subject myself to the emotional torture.

My best friend Jules would call this propensity toward hyperbole "dramatic." Not really a word I would use to describe myself. Drama is for girly girls or bitchy girls. I am certainly not a girly girl. I admit there is a version of me that can be a bitchy girl—a trait the airline employee behind the desk in Memphis is well acquainted with.

The day from hell ended with me running towards my gate, only to watch the airline employee close the door as I was yelling that I was almost there. She had just clicked the door closed when I arrived in front of her, out of breath and barely able to stand. I could see people in the gateway still waiting to board and she refused to open the door. It was the only remaining direct flight. What's more is she appeared to enjoy my frustration. A conversation with her manager, a bump up to first class, a three-hour delay, one layover later, and I am finally on the last leg of my journey.

Feeling my anxiety flare, I take a deep breath and try to focus on what I can control. From the small window on my row, I see the ground crew prepare the plane for our flight. I cannot wait to be home. Funny, I used to say that about Memphis, but if home is where family is, Memphis stopped being home long ago. New York is my home now. I was born and raised a Memphian, but I have become a New Yorker at heart.

I heart New York. I have a true love for my city. Not always an easy love, mind you. New York is a demanding love. New York makes you need it. Want it. Have to have it. New York makes you work for it, and I like the work. I get it. It's something I've never held against it.

With a three a.m. start, my day has been hectic with travel, a missed appointment, more angry and agitated people than I care to count, and, eventually, a missed flight, which is how I find myself in Chicago's O'Hare airport. The only plus to today was being bumped up to First Class. I'd hoped it would tame the growing fear of another flight, an added takeoff and landing. Regrettably, I am sitting here wearing the same fears, wondering the same thing I do every time I fly: *why* and *how the hell?*

I've never flown first class before. I've always been the cattle they march past the people at the front of the plane. A social-caste processional. The airlines have first-class fliers sit first so they can provide them with refreshments to watch from their oversized seats while the cattle herd by to get to their undersized ones. Some don't look at you, like they're embarrassed for you. Others seem irritated that they have to endure this cattle call of people moving by them, as if your presence as you stand there waiting for the line to move is an inconvenience to them personally.

I had decided earlier I wasn't going to give into the classicism I judged the airlines for. I was going to board and be seated after everyone else. But I needed a Diet Coke. Honorable of me, I know. As I sit here watching the procession, waiting impatiently for my Diet Coke, I find I don't like to look at the cattle passing me, not because I am embarrassed for them. But I'm embarrassed the herd might mistakenly think I am part of this first-class caste.

Once everyone is seated, the stewardess returns and, with a smile, picks up my Diet Coke and the orange juice of the little girl across the aisle from me. She can't be more than five. I watched as her mom reluctantly entrusted her daughter to the stewardess and kissed her with a promise her grandmother would be waiting for her when she landed. She's a beautiful little girl with curly light brown hair and dark eyes.

She has her coloring to keep her attention and a stuffed bear that she loyally introduced as her best friend, Walter. Walter wears a blue and green striped tie and has a monocle that makes him look older and wiser than his years. She introduced us when I commented that I liked his tie. I'm pretty sure Walter and his monocle are silently judging me and my nervous foot fidgeting at the thought of taking off.

The door closes and the plane starts to back away from the gate when the familiar panic creeps into my chest. Just as I seek out my happy place, I am granted a short reprieve when the attendant announces overhead that we are delayed for a few minutes and will be returning to the gate. The catastrophe of today replays in my mind. These trips are getting harder and harder. I'm not sure how much fight I have left in me. The selfishness of that statement leaves me frustrated and angry with myself.

I grab a barf bag to keep handy. As I try to concentrate on keeping my breathing steady, my eye lands on the multi-colored circles that make up the pattern on the carpet. My mind moves to my to-do list for work tomorrow. I don't have any clients to meet with, but my team has a lot of shopping to accomplish to ready our client's closets with the latest fall fashions. Mentally cataloging what needs to be done, a pair of brown Berluti shoes come to a stop in my line of vision.

Scanning my eyes up, I process the vision of the man attached to the shoes. His handmade gray suit is tailored to perfection. His legs long and lean. The jacket is buttoned while one hand rests in his pocket. He has on a blue and green stripped tie with a simple silver bar tie clip and a crisp white shirt. I know that the suit he is wearing cost more than I make in a month. His cuff links are small, round, blue dots that look like sapphires with silver around the edges. Actually, based on the fact that I price the ensemble he is wearing at least fifteen grand, my guess is they are platinum. His copper and caramel-brown hair is askew, like his hands have been giving it a workout. His chin is angular and sporting an evening shadow. Impressive. Powerful. I have seen a lot of stunning men in my line of work, but this…this is another level.

"Sorry to inconvenience you, but I believe that's my seat," he points to the empty one next to me.

I run my fingers over my bottom lip to make sure I'm not drooling and to help close my mouth that seems to have unhinged at the sight in front of me. My voice and manners kick in, and I manage a coherent response.

"No problem. I'll move over so you can have more head room. Unless you prefer the window?"

"No. Thank you," he says.

I settle into the window seat, my eyes meeting his as I reply, "My pleasure." Something in my response causes his blue eyes to skip, halting my breathing. They are striking. A medium blue with specks of silver dusted in. Commanding. Illimitable.

A flight attendant makes an announcement that once again the door has been closed, and we are to prepare for departure. He must have been the reason we were delayed. I couldn't get through the door for a plane that was still loading, but this guy gets the entire plane returned to the gate for him?

He punches a number on his phone and announces to the person on the other end that he made the flight they held for him and what time he is expected in New York.

"You know. If you are responsible for delaying an entire flight, I don't think I would broadcast it over a phone call." I unload my misguided frustration out on him.

The plane backs away from the gate as the attendant reviews the safety features of the Boeing 737 we are on. While I am certain most people ignore her, I pull the card out of the pocket attached to the wall in front of me and follow along, determined that, if nothing else, the headlines will read that I, and hopefully others near me, survived whatever catastrophe happens. I count how many rows there are between us and the exits behind us. I make note that the door has a pull handle and that the closest exits to me are in front of me and have handles located at the bottom right-hand side that activates the safety slides. Placing the card back in its pouch, I can never decide if it's better to have the window shade open to see my life flash before my eyes, or to close it for ignorant bliss. Ignorant bliss wins out, and the shade comes down.

"My apologies if I've offended you." His apology is not really an apology. In fact, he seems rather surprised that I said something to him.

"You haven't. But I'm sweeter than most people on this plane." I offer my go-to southern smile to make amends, causing him to cock his head in thought. "Honestly it's not a big deal. Misguided frustration. I'm just over this day."

"I'm having a bit of a day myself." He says absently looking forward, folding one leg over the other and smoothing his tie down his torso. My eyes follow on instinct.

"I'm sorry," I say sincerely with a pat to his arm. Because I am. I am not arrogant enough to think I am the only one who could be having a terrible day. "Anything I can do to make it better?" I offer empathetically. If he's had a day worse than mine, he can use it.

He doesn't respond but gauges me, when the captain announces that we are next in line for takeoff. I remind myself to breathe as my head hits the headrest from the force of the plane propelling itself down the runway. White-knuckling the armrest, a light dew settles over my skin. My eyes close just as the front of the plane comes off the ground. Within seconds, the back of the plane is airborne, and we take that little dip every plane makes once it leaves the ground. *Fuck me.*

A chuckle reaches my ears, and I cautiously open one eye to see him watching me. It becomes clear that I said that expletive out loud and not just to myself.

"Sorry. I don't usually use such colorful language," I blush.

"No worries. Are you ill?" He eyes the barf bag in my lap.

"Severe fear can have a not-so-pleasant effect on my stomach." When we take another slight dip in our climb, my breath catches and my grip tightens. I sip in a deeper breath and then release slowly. I know only a handful of ways to calm myself. That is one. Sometimes it works.

Leaning forward, I check on the little girl and her buddy Walter, only to find they are better than I ever hope to be. She looks at me and I wink at her. Her smile reminds me of wildflowers and fireflies in a mason jar. Sweet. Innocent. Unadulterated. Oh, to be five again.

"Is this your daughter?" he asks.

"No. She is traveling unaccompanied to her grandmother's." It hits me that I am giving information about a little girl to a total stranger, but something about him feels familiar and safe—and dangerous at the same time. I can't put my finger on it…

He greets her with a nod and a hello. She gives him a full-on mega-watt smile that lets me know, even to a five-year-old, this man is handsome. She responds with a small wave, and he leans over the aisle to better hear her.

"This is Walter. Your ties match," she says.

"Walter, you have impeccable taste," he replies. She proudly accepts this as a compliment to herself.

"She seems fine" he says turning back to me.

"I'm sorry?" In the confusion of my anxiety, I'm only half listening.

"You appeared to be checking on her. I was just saying she seems fine. Better than you actually." His tone is one of frustration, as though I should easily be following the conversation. I'm not sure if I want to smack or lick the smirk off his face.

"Yep. She is taking this flying adventure like a boss." Steady as a rock. Her five years, light-years ahead of my twenty-five. I release another long breath.

"Did you tell her you were afraid to fly?" he asks.

"Previous exception aside, I don't make a practice of telling people my fears."

"Because?"

"Because telling someone what you're afraid of is like handing them a playbook on how to defeat you." And, for some reason, without prompting, I add, "And I don't like to be defeated."

As soon as the words leave my mouth, I regret them. The expression on his face tells me I revealed more than I intended. He looks at me for what feels like a full minute, only turning away when the attendant walks up.

"Another Diet Coke?" She hands me the drink. I smile and nod my thanks.

"May I bring you something to drink, sir? Wine? Cocktail?" She looks at him longer than necessary, her expression changing, as if to say, "Mother, may I?" I recognize the symptoms. I, too, am suffering from the same ailment.

"Bottle of water, thank you." His reply is perfunctory and dismissing.

I search my bag and locate my iPod, placing it and my earbuds on the small tray table that is shared between the middle armrests. My iPod has seen better days. Some days I feel like my iPod, being held together by duct tape. The screen cracked a couple of years ago, but this iPod takes a licking and keeps on ticking. Also like me, I muse to myself.

"Your iPod appears to be in the need of repair."

I nod in acknowledgement. "I've had it for about 10 years." I pick it up and look at each side. "I think it's a 3rd generation. I don't really know. I bought it used when I was in high school. It has been a good friend. It still works." With the screen so cracked, I struggle sometimes to read what songs I'm pulling up, but it plays. I run my thumb over my cherished friend.

"Maybe it's time for a new one?" He picks up my iPod and turns it over again. A label with my first name and a pink heart is on the back. "Emme."

"Not in the budget. Besides, they don't make the Classic anymore, and I don't really want another version. I like the Classic. Holds more music without all the bells and whistles. Just a good, sturdy, hard-working iPod. All I need."

He nods and takes a drink of water.

"Do you like music?" I ask.

"I do. All kinds." He pauses like he is trying to decide something. He then asks, "What brings you to New York, Emme?"

Distracted by the way his tongue massages my name, I catch myself looking at his mouth, envisioning other things his tongue could be massaging. I'm caught off guard that my thoughts have gone to such a foreign place. *Why is this stranger having such an effect on me?*

"I live there," I stutter, realizing he has caught me staring. Again!

"You? You live in New York?" His incredulous eyes sweep over me, landing a little too long on my chest.

I can't determine if it is a question meant to keep the polite conversation going, or a question of judgement. Like I'm an outsider who doesn't belong. I concede that I am not dressed my best today. It's the middle of August, and I've been in three different cities, with three very different climates, all in one day.

The cuffed skinny jeans I'm wearing are a little too snug for my ample hips and ass, a gift from my mother. The ass not the jeans. Thankfully, she gifted me with a flat stomach and smaller waist to offset the other two. A white tank top and my grandfather's thread-bare, oversized navy blue cardigan pushed up to my elbows round out my travel attire. I know it's only my imagination, but I can still smell my grandfather when I wear it, even though it has been washed a thousand times since I took it as my own. It's my comfort piece. It makes me feel like I am wearing a hug. And after spending the day in Satan's lair, I need all the hugs I can get, even if it's only in the form of a cardigan that's more than forty years old.

Other than a soft-pink matte lip gloss, I am wearing no makeup. I have large, cocoa-brown eyes. The front of my light-blonde hair is braided on one side. It is held together by bobby pins and a tiny, blue metal flower that turns my side part into a messy bun. The only jewelry I am wearing is a long artsy necklace and my grandparents' white-gold wedding bands on my right middle finger. My wrist dons the Rolex that belonged to the father we never knew. It has a black leather band with a white mother of pearl face.

"Yes, I live in New York," I reply with bite. "Does that surprise you? I have lived in the city for seven years now. Moved there when I was seventeen."

A look creeps across his face that leaves me feeling like I've been warned about my tone.

"I was taken by your accent," he says slowly as if to clarify. "Where are you from, originally?"

"Memphis. Born and raised."

"Ah," he says, like a piece of a puzzle has fallen into place. I have long become used to comments and occasional snares concerning my southern accent. Despite my time away from Memphis, I still have it. Truthfully, I wouldn't have it any other way. You can take the girl out of Memphis, but you can't take Memphis out of the girl. Memphians are proud of our southern roots. I don't notice my accent, but rarely a day goes by without someone commenting on it. You would think I was transplanted from another country.

The attendant makes another stop to replace my now empty Diet Coke, halting when he positions his hand to stop her from placing the new glass on the tray table.

"Could you bring her a bottled water instead?" He directs more than he asks.

"Certainly, sir" She retreats without even looking to me for approval. *What the…?* I'm so dumbfounded by the whole encounter that I find myself speechless, and only a small noise of protest escapes my throat when he looks at me. I know by the look on his face that there must be one of shock and confusion on mine.

"That would have been your third Diet Coke since boarding," he says, in a voice that denotes his irritation at having to explain himself. Is he monitoring my alcohol consumption or something? Am I in Diet Coke's Anonymous? Is he my sponsor? "You need to drink water. Flying can dehydrate you, and you stated you've been on a plane more than once already today."

"You do know I'm grown right?" My tone is sharp. His eyes deliberately land on my chest before crawling their way up to my mine. There's a heat in them.

"I'm aware."

"I've been on my own since I was sixteen. I think I can handle a drink selection. In fact, I'm certain of it." My indignant manor is interrupted when the attendant drops off my bottle of water and two freshly baked chocolate chip cookies. I don't know if she intends it to make amends, but they are deliciously warm and gooey. He declines his.

"Actually. I'll take his." I smile sweetly at the stewardess before looking defiantly at him. Two extra cookies almost offset my lack of Diet Coke.

Sitting back, I realize he is watching me. He looks like he is having a conversation in his head and needs no one else to participate or give feedback. Rotating the cap back on his water, I find my ire dissipating and my mind wandering again, wondering what it would feel like to be beneath those strong hands. I like men with strong, firm hands. It's often one of the first things I notice about a man. It is a testament to his striking looks that his hands weren't the first thing I noticed about him.

"What do you do in New York?" He distracts my wayward thoughts. I have to remind myself he's had a crummy day and give him props for attempting polite conversation.

"I work for Jackson Hollingsworth. Are you familiar with him?"

"Not personally, but I know of his business and I'm sure I know many of his clients. What do you do there?"

"I am the styling and personal analyst for his company."

"How long have you worked for Mr. Hollingsworth?"

"We met my first year in New York. I was leaving class one day and ran into *Grays Papaya* to grab a hot dog. He was on the Upper West Side to see a client. I made an unfortunate comment about the shape of my hotdog, and we have been close ever since." I smile just thinking of Jackson.

Like Jules, Jackson Hollingsworth is my life line. I was drowning when he rescued me back to land. He is the successful owner of a very prestigious brand imaging company. He is beautiful in his own right with ebony skin, hair trimmed close to his scalp, broad shoulders, and a sculpted body. He is the epitome of masculinity. Jackson draws the attention of women everywhere we go, disappointing them when they learn he is engaged. To Patrick.

"So you attended Columbia?" His eyes lose a little of their warmth. Why, I am not sure.

"No." Where did that come from?

As if to answer my unspoken confusion, he explained, "You said you were leaving class on the upper west side. I assumed, based on the fact that you work for Mr. Hollingsworth, that you were referring to Columbia."

"Oh, no. Right. Sorry. No, Julliard. I was attending Julliard.

"You went to Julliard?"

"Yes. Then NYU."

"You went to Julliard, NYU, and worked for Jackson Hollingsworth? In seven years, that's quite a resume."

"If that were true, it would be," I laugh and clarify. "I accepted a scholarship to Julliard before my financial responsibilities changed. Once there, I realized that, between required practices and performances, the time frame was too stringent to allow me to work. So, I left Julliard after one semester and went to NYU. Unfortunately, I had to put it on hold, too. I couldn't give school and studying the time required *and* take care of my responsibilities. I've been with Jackson ever since. What do you do?"

"I work in acquisitions." He seems annoyed that I have directed the conversation back to him.

"If finances had not been an obstacle, would you have stayed at Julliard? I thought their scholarship program was competitive and covered all school and living expenses?"

While I don't enjoy talking about myself, I also don't shy away from answering easy questions. It gives people a false sense that I'm an open book. I am transparent about things most people might not comment on, but I hold close the things that matter the most to me. Share my thoughts, not my feelings, a lesson learned in deflection that has served me well.

"You know, I'm okay. Really. You don't have to distract me with questions. I am sure you have more important things to tend to."

"I don't ask frivolous questions Emme, and I never ask a question I don't want the answer to," he pauses. "Expect it actually." His tone is imperious, authoritative, but his eyes are kind and inquiring. "If finances had not been an obstacle, would you have stayed at Julliard?" he repeats. Something I also get the feeling he doesn't do often.

I nebulously wonder how the questions have turned back to me so quickly but find myself compelled to answer him, for reasons I'm not sure I want to analyze. Is it because he is kind, or is it because he demands it? Either way, I wasn't prepared for the question. No one has ever questioned my answer before. They have always accepted my reasoning that money was the issue, and it was. But the larger part was that I had lost my love for playing. Now, holding a cello was like holding a lifeless creature. It has been six years since I picked one up. I doubt I ever will again.

Taken aback by the direction of my thinking and the depth of my feelings in front of a perfect stranger, I opt for a fact that played a far less significant role in my decision to leave Julliard and give him my "blind date" answer to what, at that time, was an easy choice.

"No. I came to realize I didn't want the life of a concert cellist. I didn't want to travel eleven months out of the year. I wanted more roots than that life would give me."

He stares at me with a long canyon of silence that I feel the need to fill with…I don't know—something. But my mind can't seem to form a sentence. I'm not comfortable with him looking at me like I'm a puzzle where the pieces don't match up. It's like he knows and is waiting for the real story. Side-stepping that mine field, I look forward and take a break to gather my wits about me. It's been a long time since I have even looked at a man this way. Actually, I never have. I have never looked at a man this way, much less someone I only met forty-five minutes ago.

It's in that moment of space that my terror comes roaring back, angry at being ignored. The plane hits an air pocket and drops what feels like a thousand feet, eliciting screams from the rear of the plane. The captain announces overhead that he is turning back on the seatbelt light and asks passengers to be seated. We are beginning to encounter some turbulence from a storm. I hate his calm voice that has no feeling, no un-derstanding that I am being tormented. I know it is meant to soothe us, but I'd rather hear panic and determination, like he is going to fly this plane as if his life depends on it. His calm voice makes me think he has his head back, chillin', and not correctly assessing the death-con level we are clearly experi-encing.

He instructs us to stow belongings, put seats in the up-right position, and close tray tables, while the attendants come around to clear trash before taking their seats. I close my eyes and concentrate on not needing my barf bag. My hands take a death grip on the armrests while my mind tries to control the pace my heart is beating. I'm stuck in this small space with nowhere to go, forced to endure whatever happens. I have no control. None. My breathing is coming faster now, and I realize if I don't figure out a way to self-soothe, I'm going to hyperventilate and have a full-on panic attack. Every time the plane takes another dip, people cry out. *Why the fuck doesn't someone knock them out? Their screaming is only making it worse.* Just when I have reached the height of powerlessness, I feel it: A calm. An equanimity. My fear is still there, but my breathing comes in deeper droves. My heart slows from a full-on gallop to a survivable canter.

I open my eyes to see him calmly sitting with one leg draped over the other. His suit is still perfectly pressed, as if he has no concerns in the world. Like we are sitting stationary and not about to meet an untimely death. He watches me, and I distantly process that it's not his demeanor that is placating me, but it's his hand—the one that has taken mine as he slowly and repeatedly moves his thumb across my knuckles in a circular motion.

"You're safe." His eye contact offers an assurance that I am far from feeling, but at the same time holds power over my fear. It is such a simple statement. A statement I have not felt or heard since I can remember.

"How much longer?" I whisper.

"How much longer?"

"How much longer till we land?"

"We'll start our decent in about twenty minutes," he assures me.

Twenty minutes. Twenty minutes. It might as well be a life sentence.

The captain, who I am sure has heard the cries of his passengers, comes back on over the intercom in his same steady voice, informing us that he has been unable to find a smooth patch of air to fly in and to expect rough turbulence until we land. All along, he continues to console me by steadying my hand with his. Another dip, another group screaming. Another jostle and crash accompanied by more screams. The fear I think I am doing so well to contain must be showing on my face, because he quickly explains that some overhead compartments have come open, emptying their contents on some of the passengers. It's in that moment that I remember the little girl.

I always thought I would be heroic if the need ever presented itself. I would be Wonder Woman, wearing the stars and stripes, my metal-covered wrists ricocheting bullets. People would tell stories of my heroism and bravery. Yeah, no one will be writing that about me if we die tonight. I kick myself for being so selfish. Shaking my head in frustration, I whisper, "What a dick." My comment stops the traipse of his thumb across my knuckles.

"Excuse me?" he asks with a dip in his eyebrows.

"Sorry, not you. I mean me." I lean forward and ask the little girl if she's ok, her face a mirror of my feelings. She looks at me with big, round eyes, and I have to strain to hear her small voice.

"I'm scared."

Right then and there, I know I need to lock my shit down.

"Come sit with me. It's ok," I say at her hesitation. Regrettably, I squeeze his hand before removing mine to reach across him, making sure she isn't knocked down as we continue to bounce. In a blink, she is in my lap. I undo my buckle, pull the belt around us both, and click it back in place. Wrapping my arms around her, I smile as she lays her head against my chest. Her face towards him.

"You have nothing to worry about," I assure her.

Thunder booms around us, and I see an acknowledgment from him that we are having a rough ride.

"One of my favorite movies is *Sound of Music*. Have you seen it?" She nods while holding tighter to Walter.

"You remember the part where it's storming and they're in Fräulein Maria's bed, scared, and she sings to them? Well that song has always made me feel better. Whether I'm happy or sad or scared."

Softly, I begin singing "Raindrops on roses and whiskers on kittens…" as I unwind my earbuds from my iPod and pull up "A Few of My Favorite Things" on my cracked screen. I place buds in her ears and hit play. She closes her eyes and listens as I softly rock her side to side, rubbing her back in a comforting repetitive pattern that mimics the one across my knuckles minutes ago.

Still bouncing like a rock skipping across the water, we begin our descent into LaGuardia. Landing. I think I hate it more than take off. One runs a close second to the other. I glance to my right with a smile, to say a thank you for his kindness, and I am met with a heat-filled look.

"What?" I mouth with an inquisitive slope of my eyebrows.

"You." He answers simply and follows with a glance from the little girl to me as clarification. I blush—not a response that is common for me.

I hear the landing gear lowering and feel the grinding of its machinations. I realize we have said fewer than three words to each other in the last twenty minutes of the flight, but I feel like we have had one of those high-school conversations where you talk all night long with your crush.

It feels like the pilot is working overtime to control the plane when the wheels finally hit the ground with a thud. The flaps shoot up with a roar to bring us to a crawl, and the plane erupts in an applause so joyous, you would think we just witnessed a miracle. Maybe we did.

The captain welcomes us to New York and doesn't hide the appreciation in his voice that we have landed. Releasing the breath I was holding all this time, I say to the girl, pulling the earbuds from her ears, "We're safe and we're here!" She throws her arms around my neck and leans up for a kiss before making her way back to her seat. I remind her to stay put until everyone gets off the plane and then the attendant will take her to her grandmother.

We stand when the door opens and he takes a slight step back, motioning me in front of him. I move into the aisle and with a placement of his hand at the small of my back, he ushers me forward.

Walking up the short ramp, it dawns on me that we will be saying good-bye. It unsettles me for reasons I am not sure I want to understand. Deflecting my feelings for light conversation, I declare how happy I am to be on land.

"If I didn't think security would detain me, I would kiss the ground right here," I laugh.

We walk side-by-side to the escalator that moves from the terminal down to baggage claim and transportation. A feeling of sadness and loss lingers around us.

"Do you need help with your luggage?" he offers as we step off the moving stairs.

"Thanks, but it was a there-and-back trip, so I don't have any."

Missing my original flight has me getting home later than anticipated. It's August, and even though its ten thirty at night, it's stifling. I stop to place my oversized Louis Vuitton bag, a vintage that was my mom's, between my feet, freeing my hands to remove my cardigan and knot it around my hips. I watch his eyes canvas my body, finally moving up to my face with no remorse at being caught. A smile plays across his lips.

"What part of the city do you live in? Can I provide your transportation? My driver is here."

Provide my transportation? Why not just say "Can I give you a lift?" It doesn't surprise me that he has a driver. Some of the most influential and powerful men in the city are my clients. I am used to being around wealth, and he exudes it.

"I live in SoHo, but I'll just take a taxi. I don't want to inconvenience you."

He gives a shake to his head "It's not an inconv…"

"James!" I turn towards the familiar sound and two of my dwarfs, Drew and Russ, walk up each pulling me into their arms, planting a loud, wet kiss on me.

"What are y'all doing here?" I ask, surprised to see them.

"You're in Memphis less than twelve hours and your accent is even thicker." Drew mimics a ridiculous southern accent. Why can't people learn to do a true southern accent? Must everyone make all southerners sound like we are missing four teeth and had a baby with Cousin Earl?

"We were at Kyle's parents' house in Queens for dinner, so we hung around to pick you up," he explains. "You ready? No luggage, right?"

Deep down in a place I shouldn't explore, I am disappointed. I wanted to see where this ride would take me.

"Sure," I say with a smile I am not feeling. "I was just about to catch a ride. We were seated next to each other on the plane." They look quizzically between me and my new friend. "I was bumped up to first class," I clarify.

"Well good thing we caught you before you left. Save him an extra drop." Drew gives him a direct look and then drapes an arm over my shoulders. "Thanks for looking out for James. We'll take her from here."

What the fuck? I look at him like he has lost his mind. *Take me from here. What the hell does that mean?* Like I'm suddenly the unaccompanied minor. *I'm a fucking adult!* I hand them my bag.

"I'll be right there," I say, dismissing them in irritation before turning my attention back to him.

"Thank you for the offer. I should probably go before security makes them move."

"James?"

"Huh? Oh, yeah, Emme James. James is one of the names people call me."

"You live with three men?"

"Actually, I live with six. One more and I'm Snow White. Although we don't have space for one more, so alas, I'll never make princess status. I call the boys my dwarfs, anyway. As a consolation prize," I smile. "Thanks again for the offer."

"Goodnight," he nods to me.

In a move of showing him my true appreciation for his kindness during the flight, I wrap him into a strong hug before he has a chance to respond or anticipate my actions. It's a one-sided hug for what feels like a very long minute. I feel his resolve finally snap, and his arms fold around me. Leaning my head against his chest, I squeeze and breathe him in. *He smells divine, like...him.* Releasing him I reach up and place my palm to his cheek. Idly, I register that he has leaned into my touch.

"Thank you. You are very kind."

His eyes unreadable and jaw rigid, he nods in acknowledgement before watching me walk away.

ch♥pter
two

"What was that all about?" I ask harshly while closing the leather-clad door to Kyle's BMW.

"Uh, you're welcome," Drew replies, like they were doing me a solid.

"I'm welcome? I'm welcome?" My sheer disbelief in Drew's statement has me repeating myself.

"Yes, you are welcome!"

I glare at Russ next to me in the back seat. Then I direct my glare back to the front passenger seat.

"Seriously, Drew! He was completely nice, and you basically peed on me right in front of him!"

We pull onto the Queens expressway, and I catch Kyle's eyes bounce from me in the rearview to Drew sitting next to him, a confused look in his eyes like he's trying to catch up.

"What is she talking about? What did you do Drew?" Kyle asks like he's talking to a child.

"I didn't do anything. I simply thanked the guy and told him we had her from here."

"What guy?"

"The plane guy."

"What?" Kyle inquires in an exasperated "help me understand" tone, looking at Russ next to me.

"This guy that was on James' flight was being a little too possessive, so we took care of it," he explains without prejudice and a shrug of his shoulders, like he's speaking only the truth, and I or anyone else would be irrational to think any differently.

"That is ridiculous!" I say with enough feeling for the both of us, since they want to play this one off like I'm the idiot for being mad. "He was very kind and very polite. His intentions were..."

"To get into your pants," Drew speaks over me.

"You're ridiculous."

"I'm ridiculous?"

"You're ridiculous!" I state with more force.

"I'm ridiculous?" He's riled up now.

"Yes! What are you a parrot? Did you fall down today and smack your head on the pavement? I don't need you, or any of the dwarfs for that matter, to step in and pee on me in public."

"What does that even mean, James?" Drew grunts, unable to hide his irritation.

"It means, Drew, that I don't need y'all to stake claim to me like I'm something that needs protecting."

"You guys know James doesn't like to be handled," Kyle interjects, trying to contain the situation.

"We *didn't* handle her Kyle," he argues. "We showed her the same courtesy we'd show our sisters. And stop calling us dwarfs James. It's not very manly."

With a deep sigh of frustration, I shake my head and lay it against the head rest. "I am living with baboons."

We're coming across the Williamsburg Bridge now, and the exhaustion of the day has taken the fight out of me.

"It doesn't matter. It's not like I'll see him again. I don't even know his name. I'm just ready to be home," I say a little deflated. Even with my eyes now closed, I can feel them watching me. Drew's the first to break. He always is.

"How was your trip?"

"Long and stressful."

"Want to talk about it?"

"Nope."

"How about some Doughnut Plant?" Kyle always knows the way to my heart. Food. Especially my favorite doughnut place in the city.

"Crème Brulee and Manhattan Cream. Your favorites," he entices. Not that I really need it. I love all things food.

A dozen shared doughnuts later, we are finally home. Home is a classic, white cast-iron facade building, typical of the area. Our apartment is a three-bedroom, one-bath, fifth-floor walkup on Greene St.

Matt, the head dwarf, has been renting this apartment for a few years now. He lived here with his wife while finishing medical school at Columbia, and she was in her first-year internship at New York Presbyterian Hospital. Becca is now an attending physician in Boston, while Matt is in his last year of residency. When he's finished, he will be moving to Boston. Actually, all six of my roommates are doctors at New York Presbyterian. Matt kept the apartment and took on five roommates for extra income.

By Manhattan standards, our apartment is large, at a little over a thousand square-feet. The entry is a small hallway leading into an open kitchen, dining, and living area. The bones are what you would expect from a SoHo apartment. High, open ceilings with cased windows across the front. I place the mail I grabbed on the way up on the kitchen counter as I make my way to my alcove.

Off of the living area are two bedrooms with our only bath in between. On the other side is the larger bedroom and a small, three-sided alcove, two inches smaller than a twin bed. It opens to the living room. The guys stay two to a room, and I sleep on the couch.

The alcove is all mine. I have smartly utilized the square footage to get the most out of the space. Sliding back the curtain I installed, I turn on the small table lamp that sits on the four-drawer teal dresser I found at the Chelsea Antiques Garage for a steal. Its slim profile made it the perfect piece for the space. The back wall houses my closet. It's only three-feet wide, but the shelves above the rod extend the entire height of the twelve-foot wall, some holding clothes, others with decorative boxes, framed pictures, and items from my childhood. A full-length mirror hangs on the wall between the dresser and the closet. Opposite the dresser and mirror is an overstuffed, comfy, white cotton chair, large enough for me to curl into, with a soft, colorful throw across the back. It sits at an angle, leaving just enough floor space to maneuver the closet and get dressed.

I come in here to read and have some alone time when I need it. Even though the curtain doesn't block out noise, the visual barrier is really all I need. I like to still hear the guys. It reminds me that I'm not alone, that I have loved ones near.

Matt and Russ are both married to wonderfully strong women whom I adore. Tim is engaged, Kyle is one step away from engagement, while Drew and Ryan have made an art form out of being single. All six men are smart, capable, and sexy as hell. It's like living in a GQ magazine. Except that the place was a hazard area, and their living habits were atrocious. How they made it before I moved in, I'll never know.

I am closest with Matt. We met at Junior's in Brooklyn

during my third year living in the city. We were sitting next to each other, waiting for our cheesecakes, and struck up a conversation. His wife Becca and I became fast friends. At the time, I was living in the Bronx, and Becca always thought I should be somewhere safer and actually in Manhattan. But living in the Bronx was all I could afford, and I was having a hard enough time making ends meet.

Jackson has always paid me a generous salary and would pay me more if I would let him, but I won't take what I don't earn. So, I picked up a couple of night jobs and with my financial responsibilities in Memphis, I was still struggling to make ends meet.

After Becca moved to Boston and the dwarfs were on their own, she called me and asked me if I would move in, rent-free, in exchange for "overseeing" the apartment, make sure it stayed livable and the guys actually ate a green vegetable at least once a week. She felt like it was the best of both worlds. It's been the seven of us ever since. Some days are more trying than others, but mostly it's like living with six brothers. I get a free place to live, and they get a wife/mother/sister/friend in exchange. The day and need dictate which hat I wear for each of them.

Grateful that it was a one-day trip and I don't have a bag to unpack, I throw on a tank and some sleep shorts and make my way to the kitchen. One of the ways I earn my keep is making sure they each have a healthy meal. I look at the calendar on the fridge and see that four of the guys are working tomorrow. Their shifts are a minimum of sixteen hours. Grabbing the Sharpie, I write their names on their individual brown paper lunch bag with twine handles. I make each of them two healthy meals and a snack to take to work. I put a little note in each bag. I am adding the last orange to the bags when Kyle comes in for a snack.

"The guys picked up an extra shift, so they won't be in tonight. You should crash in a bed instead of the couch."

"I think I will. It's been a long day and I am bone tired."

"Sweet dreams, James," he says as he kisses me on the forehead.

"Thanks. Love you." I start the nightly John-Boy ritual with whomever is awake. Experience has taught me to never miss an opportunity to tell the ones you love that you love them.

"...love you, too," he slurps biting into an apple.

Pulling the covers over me, I sink in and think about the day from hell. I feel like each trip to Memphis is the same. I'm not accomplishing anything. I have the same arguments with the same people. I'm just not sure what the next step is and how much fight I have left in me. My mind moves to the stranger on the plane tonight, and how out of character our conversation was for me. Was it because the day was so horrible that my mind needed idle conversation to decompress? Even as I wonder, I know it was more than that. It was him. Conversation felt easy and safe with him, but also necessary. Like it was expected.

Morning comes earlier than I had hoped and based on his language and the pillow Drew throws at my head, I must have slept through my alarm going off. God bless whoever put the old car horn alarm on cell phones. It's the only noise that wakes me. So maybe it takes a while for me to hear, but what can you do?

I sit on the edge of the bed, allowing my body time to

acclimate to my mind giving it commands. I hate mornings. I am not a morning person.

Grabbing a Diet Coke, my first thought is of him. I wonder what his mornings are like, who he spends them with, what it would feel like waking up next to him? I start the coffee for the group, and the carousel begins. Food, coffee, and an endless stream of people in and out of our only bathroom. We have our routine worked out pretty well. If you get up when I do, you get breakfast. While I cook and clean, the guys start their shower rotation. Once food goes on the table, each person is responsible for loading his dishes in the dishwasher and I'm free to take my shower.

Sharing a bathroom with six guys is pretty interesting. I have learned that they care not if they smell like peaches and cream. If it's in the shower and it looks like something to clean yourself with, they will use it. It's a running joke at the hospital that my guys are the best smelling residents there. I have trained them well. Their wives, current or future, all owe me a debt of gratitude for teaching these men to put the seat down. Now, if I could only teach them to replace the empty roll on the toilet paper holder, I might feel I've accomplished something.

The bathroom is a decent size with a glass shower, a toilet, and, thankfully, a double vanity. We installed a curtain over the outside of the shower door, so one person could be taking a shower in private while others use the bathroom or the sinks. Not ideal, but necessary when sharing a bathroom with seven people.

As I said before, I am not a girly girl. It doesn't take me a long time to get ready. This morning is holding true to the routine. I'm bathing to The Killers, when a movement catches my eye from the corner of the shower. A water bug. Also known as a cockroach. Also known as my arch enemy. My kryptonite. I can pick up a snake, hold a mouse, bait a hook, but do not put a roach anywhere in my radius. Slowly, I start backing up to the shower door never taking my eyes off it. I can hear my heart beating in my ears, my stomach starting to churn. This is worse than flying. This is a full-on panic attack of fear.

Three things happen at once. It shoots towards me at lightning speed. I scream like Norman Bates has thrown back the shower curtain. I run. One second I was in the shower, and the next I am in the living room. Thankfully, somewhere in between my subconscious grabbed a towel.

Matt comes out of his bedroom, walks to the bathroom, and closes the door, like he is out for a morning stroll. Kyle is at my side telling me to take a deep breath and slow my breathing. The door opens and Matt comes out.

"Taken care of."

I can count on one hand how many bugs I have found in our apartment, but the guys know the scream. They don't understand the rationale or the reasoning behind my fears, but they realize the seriousness of it. The first time they encountered what they thought was just a girl being a girl over a bug, they did what guys do. Tease. Act like they are going to toss it on you or run their fingers over your arm like it's crawling on you. One complete meltdown and brown-bag hyperventilation later, they learned I am not that girl. Since then, they have only been my white knights when I encounter a bug.

"Jesus, James. You scare the shit out of me every time." Drew pulls me back into the present when he enters the living room. "You ever going to tell us why?"

"Why what?"

"No one has that kind of reaction without a story."

"There's nothing to tell. It's just an irrational fear." As I say it, I know they aren't buying it, but I am grateful when they let it drop.

Matt touches my shoulder forcing my eyes to him. "You're ok."

I let out a long deep breath. "I'm ok," I affirm.

"Actually I don't think you are," Drew says, turning me around and looking me over. "You're bleeding."

"What?" Matt asks, taking a step back and looking me over.

"She's bleeding. There's blood on the floor." Drew points down at the red spots.

"Here." Kyle points to the back side of my hip. Sure enough, there's a coffee-can size circle of blood on my towel and drops on the floor. "Let me see." He begins to pull the towel back.

"I don't think so," I say dubiously.

"James, you're bleeding. We're surgeons. We've seen it all. Now, let us look."

I roll my eyes and turn my towel so the opening is in that area and pull back the edge just enough for them to see where the blood is coming from while keeping all my girly bits covered.

"Damn, James! You sliced it open. It's deep, too. Didn't you feel that? Wonder what she cut it on?" Kyle checks out the damage while Drew looks around the bathroom.

"She caught it on this metal piece." He points to the strike plate that is connected to the door jam.

Matt is holding the towel to the cut, absorbing the blood. "She's gonna need stitches. Who has their work bag here? Anyone have a suture kit?"

"Really? Stiches? Is that necessary?" I ask.

"Yep," Matt nods once in confirmation. "When was your last tetanus shot?"

"Two years ago."

"At least you won't need that," he says grabbing a sealed tray from Drew.

"Lay down on the couch," he instructs as he drapes a blanket across it, "and I'll suture you up." The living room has two club chairs that are anchored by a couch on each side. The rectangular coffee table in the middle is currently housing three laptops and bag of chips that, most likely, is empty and needs to be thrown away.

Me and my stupid fears. How do I get myself into these messes? I lay on the couch with the cut side closest to him. Matt leaves the room and comes back with a towel for my dripping hair and one that he later uses to cover me as much as possible while he begins prepping me.

The guys were right. They could care less who is attached to the ass or what the ass looks like, they are have a pissing competition over who is the best man for the job.

"Let me do it," Drew insists.

"You're Ortho. You don't care what scars look like," Kyle says.

"That's true, man," Matt agrees.

"Dude, you're trauma," Kyle says to Matt, like it's a no brainer. "I'm Neuro. I stitch up brains. I should do it."

"I did a stint in Plastics. I'm doing it," Matt argues. He is already gloved and ready to go.

"Now, you're going to feel a little pinch, Emme." Matt puts on his doctor tone. "This will numb the area. After that takes effect, we can have you done in no time."

Twenty minutes later, he's done.

"Hell, Matt. That took fucking forever!" Both of the guys

lay into him.

"Well, it took twelve stitches, and I don't want her to have a scar," he pushes back.

"That's true," Drew says. "I'd hate to mess up that luscious ass. My God, James. Your ass…" he trails off. "I can't believe I've been living in the same apartment as that all this time".

Matt and Kyle both slap him across the head as I tighten the towel around me and make my way to my closet to get dressed. "Dude, not cool." I hear them chastising Drew as I close the curtain. The wound is tender to the touch, so I opt for cotton underwear to let it breathe a little.

Every Friday I bring home my outfits for the following week. One of the perks of working with Jackson is the wardrobe he provides. He expects his employees to represent the image of his company. Instead of a clothing allowance, we have a closet of designers that we have full access to. It's the most amazing closet I have ever seen, and I have been in some pretty spectacular closets.

This whole fiasco has me running late, so I go for the easiest outfit: a Missoni Mare striped one-piece. I've wanted to wear these adorable shorts since summer started, and the wound gives me a practical reason. Since the back is cut out in the jumpsuit, I grab a blazer to complete the ensemble. I throw on my favorite long necklace I picked up at a street fair and slide on a pair of Louboutin pumps. I put my hair into a messy bun, add a little mascara and some lip gloss, and I am out the door in less than ten minutes.

Sliding on my sunglasses as I exit our building, ready to haul tail to the subway, I am pleasantly surprised to see Jackson standing with a coffee in one hand and a Diet Coke in the other.

"Hello, beautiful." He kisses me while handing me my

drink.

"Hello, beautiful." I return his greeting and his kiss. He twirls me around looking at the day's chosen outfit.

"Love it," he says. "I can't believe it's long enough in the back. It looks great."

I was equally surprised given the hem is sitting an inch higher than what I usually wear.

"I swear your legs look a mile long."

"Pretty sure it has something to do with the four inch heels I am wearing," I smirk.

"Thank God I came to pick you up on my way in. I can't imagine you taking the subway in those."

"Thank you for the Diet Coke," I say, getting into the back of his car and greeting his driver.

"You're welcome. I wanted to make sure you were in one piece after your trip home yesterday. Thought you might need my undivided attention for a few minutes."

"You're sweet, but I'm fine. Tired, but fine." If I say it enough times, will it be true?

"I'll let you get by with that lie for as long as you want to keep it up. When you're ready to talk, you'll talk," he shrugs. "And since when aren't you tired? I don't know how you keep the pace you keep and accomplish all you do. I'm exhausted just thinking about your daily schedule. Today is not going to be any different. I have a full day's session for you. Blaine Moore is coming in today for a new image. The label wants him to be edgier in his personal style and more confident in his interviews. I want you to take the lead. He was runner up for "Sexiest Man Alive," and the label wants him on the cover next year. Start with your questionnaire, but don't let him know you're rating him. The label wants a read on him by end of day. They're about to drop millions on him, and they want to know that he has the goods to go the distance."

"No problem. But I won't do the questions without him knowing it's a rating system. That's the only way my system works. I have to be honest with them so they will be honest with me. If the label wants to know the real deal, they have to let me do it my way."

Jackson ponders this as we pull up to our building across from Bryant Park.

"Okay, I trust you. Don't get it wrong. This is a huge account for us."

"Got it, Boss."

"You know what it does to me when you call me 'Boss.'" His wink turns into a smile.

I give him my best "why, I can't possibly know what you're talking about" innocent smile that I know tickles him. "Get out of the car, Romeo. We're here."

From the car to the elevator, Jackson draws the attention of almost every woman we pass. He is formidable in his stature and appearance. At a muscular six-foot-five, his clothes fit his body like a glove. Jackson is a man who is comfortable in his own skin. Who can blame him when that man is a modern day Frank Sinatra with a slightly edgier style and has the moves of a young Sammy Davis, Jr. He really is beautiful, inside and out.

We exit the elevator on the twenty-first floor. Our receptionist, Amanda, buzzes us through the half-opaque, half-clear glass doors that have "Hollingsworth Imaging" etched out of the frosted area.

Amanda's simple, black desk is situated in front of a seating area comprised of two white leather chairs with a round table between them. Behind Amanda hangs a large, colorful art piece by a local artist. Like the rest of the office, the area is clean-lined and understated. It reflects the same mix of contemporary chic and mid-century modern that Jackson, himself, conveys in his personal style. After a warm welcome from Amanda. Jackson heads to his office, while I head into the workroom.

The workroom is a large, open space that houses my team, Joy and Henry. Their desks are on opposite sides of the room. My office is across the back. In the center of the room is my team's worktable surrounded by six chairs. Behind Joy's desk is a large door that leads to our styling closet. The facing wall, behind Henry's desk displays our image boards. Next to the boards is a platform surrounded by a five-way wrap-around mirror.

"Good morning, team. Let's take five and group before we start our day," I say pulling up a chair to our work table.

"We have Blaine Moore coming in today. Joy, I'd like you to pull three everyday looks, and Henry I would like you to pull three event looks. Make sure to include the Saint Laurent studded boots that I picked up at Barney's last week. Those will be perfect for him. I'll work on our image board. You have an hour to put looks together while I get to know him. After that, we'll do the first run through, then I'll take him to lunch while you each pull ten looks. The afternoon will finish with the last run-through and the cherry. Sound good?"

"Yes," they answer in unison.

When I style someone, I'm always looking for the one thing that makes each person unique, or "the cherry." It's the "cherry on top", so to speak. My questionnaire and our "cherry" technique is what sets our team and Jackson's company apart from any other. Other companies only see dollar signs and mold the person to some pre-fab image that the client—or the client's company—thinks they want, or need, to sell their product. We mold the image around the person.

"Emme, Blaine Moore is here to see you," Amanda announces through the speaker.

"Show time," I say to Joy and Henry. I make my way to the reception area.

"Hi, Blaine. I'm Emme James. Nice to meet you." My brown eyes meet his grey, and they are congenial and welcoming. How did I get so lucky? I am surrounded by beauty. *Smoke and mirrors,* I remind myself.

"Nice to meet you," he shakes my hand. "Sorry I'm running late. Honestly, I'm sorry to be doing this at all. This is the label's doing, not mine."

"Well, hopefully we can make this as painless as possible, please come with me." An edge enters his eyes at my request and a slow, almost wicked, smile sweeps across his face.

"Ladies first," he says pruriently.

I know then that I am in the presence of a player. I give him my best stern-but-amused look, and he throws his head back and laughs a deep, sexy, throaty laugh. I shake my head, "It's going to be a long day," I quip and show him to my office.

My office is in keeping with the look that Jackson has for his company but is also uniquely me. My desk sits to the left. Behind it is a row of floating shelves flanked by two large photos. To the right of the door is a dark purple modern couch and chair with a natural wood coffee table that looks like it was cut straight from the tree.

Above the couch, I have a painting that my grandmother gave me right before she passed away. Other than my father's watch, it is the only thing of value that I didn't sell. It's by a local Memphis artist Paul Edelstein, from his *Lost in Love* collection. This painting has people standing in a group, composed of mostly bright colors, while black- and brown-tinted greys are layered in. Offset to the right is a dark-haired girl in a white dress holding bright blue flowers. Even though the faces are abstract and not defined, to me each one conveys an emotion. I see happiness and sorrow wrapped in what I imagine is a celebration. I love it.

"Please, have a seat," I motion to the couch. I sit on the opposite end and relax into the cushions. I have found in the past that a casual stance helps put my clients at ease. Amanda enters and asks what Blaine would like to drink. She brings him water and me a Diet Coke. Standing there a little longer than necessary, my "thank you" brings her back to the present, and she leaves blushing.

"I imagine that's the effect you have on all women."

"Apparently, not *all* women," he teases.

I give him my best no-nonsense look again, and change the subject back to business.

"So, your label wants to up your image. We are just the people to make that happen. I have a particular way I like to work with a client. I have a set of questions that I would like you to answer so that I can learn a little about you. This will help me not only guide your style, but direct the label in how to best present and represent you. I am being paid by the label for my services, but you are my client. Not them. That's the only way this works. We're a team. Got it?"

"I'm intrigued," he acquiesces.

"Great. Let's get started. Tell me a little about your parents?"

"Your first question is about my parents?"

"Yes."

"Not, how do I see myself, or what is my favorite color?"

"Nope."

"Hmm. Why not?" he cocks his head to the side. Curious.

"Because you don't know the answer to that question, so how can I expect you to convey it to me?"

"I know my favorite color is green."

"As do I. It was in an interview you did as a favor for a teen reporter."

"My niece"

"Now I'm the one interested. Tell me about her after you talk about your parents."

An hour later, Joy enters the room to notify me they have their looks pulled together. We enter the workroom, and I introduce him to Joy and Henry. Joy and Henry are seasoned veterans with my processes and take control of making small talk to allow me a minute to review their pulls while making several notes.

"Okay, Joy. Why don't you walk us through the everyday looks first, then Henry can do the public event looks. Blaine, I would like you to hold all comments until the end."

My team takes twenty minutes each to introduce their looks and a quick review of their reasoning behind why they made the pull.

The next twenty minutes are really the sum and substance of our meeting. It's where the client responds to the looks, and then, as a team, we review the notes I made on their pulls before their presentation. The idea is to see how well I am matching up with my client. Can I know their response before I take cues from their facial, behavioral, and verbal feedback? If I missed the mark, I have to go back to the question session and ask different ones. In the four years I have been using my system, I have only had to go back twice. I've never had to do a third round, and frankly, if I did, I would release them as a client. I am clearly not the right fit for them.

"Blaine, tell me what you like and dislike about each look

and why. Then I want you to tell me your favorite of all six looks and what it reminds you of. Got it?" I cross my legs and his eyes follow.

"Eyes up," I say with the same no-nonsense look I have given him twice already. He responds with a sly smile and moves into his thoughts on each look. He finishes with his favorite look and what it reminds him of.

Every client's favorite look evokes a memory that he is tied to. Something that reminds them where they were, who they were with, and how they felt at a special moment, whether it was a sweet or angry moment with someone or a moment of rebellion. Clients always remember what they were wearing. That is the beginning of helping them understand their image, who they want to be. I never know what it's going to be for that person until I ask my trademark questions. When Blaine finishes, I announce that I am nine-for-nine.

Henry nods, "Let's get busy then, Joy."

I smile at Blaine, and he looks perplexed.

"Why don't we walk over to the grill and get some lunch while they do the next pull. This time it will be twenty looks. You will leave with fifteen today."

"Just like that?"

"Just like that."

"How can you know that you'll have 15 looks for me today?"

"Because I am nine-for-nine. I wrote down nine comments about the looks when I reviewed them this morning, and they matched your nine responses just now. I know that we are on track. I wrote down the direction I wanted them to take in their next pull based off what I thought you would choose as your favorite look, about which I was right again."

"You were nine-for-nine," he says in a supercilious tone.

"Actually, I was ten-for-ten if you count that I matched your favorite look. See for yourself." I hand him my notepad as I stand.

"Wow."

"You're very articulate," I tease.

"Smart-ass."

I shrug with a smile that has him laughing, when Amanda enters and brings me a package.

"This just arrived via courier for you. You have to sign for it directly."

I apply my signature to the line she points me to and hand her back the pen. The package is wrapped in brown craft paper with a string tied around it. "Emelia James" is written on top.

"I wonder what this could be? I didn't order anything." I frown and shake it for clues.

Joy's and Henry's curiosities pique, and they congregate around me and Blaine at the worktable. I open the package and pull out the telltale Apple box.

"I didn't think they sold the Classic anymore?" Blaine muses.

"They don't."

It is a brand-new 160GB iPod Classic. Speechless, something I am often not, I remove it from its plastic covering. Turning over the iPod, I notice an inscription on the back: *Someone told me there's a girl out there with love in her eyes and flowers in her hair.*

"Zeppelin," Blaine says just behind my shoulder.

"Going to California." I add.

"Why not send the Touch?"

"I don't like the Touch. It doesn't have the memory and it has too many other things than just music. I'm a fan of the

Classic. Simple."

I look through the paper it was wrapped in, not really expecting to find a note, but already knowing it is from him. The thought of him makes my pulse jump, as it has done no less than twenty times since our flight last night.

"Who's it from?" Jackson has entered the workroom.

"An acquaintance. Blaine, I would like to introduce you to Jackson Hollingsworth." I sidestep the question and find my footing again.

Jackson gives his firm handshake and greetings to Blaine, engaging him in conversation over his experience so far, but not without first giving me a glance that I know means "this conversation is not finished."

Jackson has a previously scheduled meeting he has to prep for, so he declines the invitation to lunch. He assures us he will be back in the office for our end of day wrap up.

I grab the envelope clutch I'm carrying today. "Ready?"

"Ladies first," he says with that same sexy, slow smile.

"Really? Is this going to be our thing now?"

"Oh, I hope so," Blaine smiles, entering the elevator.

The day is sunny and beautiful, but the summer heat has me removing my blazer. We cross 42nd Street, making our way to the upper terrace at the back of the New York Public Library to the Bryant Park Grill. Our office frequents Bryant Park, whether we are eating at the Grill or grabbing some food from one of the kiosks by the fountain. We enter the iconic restaurant and are seated upstairs on the rooftop so that we have a view of the park and the surrounding city. This is one of my most loved areas in the city.

The waiter comes to take our drink order.

"Blaine Moore. I'm a big fan," says the waiter as he shakes Blaine's hand. "*Sex with You* is my favorite." My laughter cues a redness that rises to his cheeks when he realizes how his statement sounded.

"No worries, man. You'd be surprised how often that happens." Blaine has the good graces to soothe the waiter's embarrassment.

"What would you like to drink?" the waiter asks me.

"Iced tea."

Blaine says, "She'll have iced tea and I'll take whatever's on tap."

Our waiter leaves, and two young girls come to our table.

`"Can we have our picture made with you?"

"Do you mind?" he asks me.

"Not at all." Looking up from my menu, I watch his interaction with his fans and catch a glimpse of him as a person. He's at ease with himself and comfortable talking with the random people who stop him. He's not short or rude; he doesn't act like it's an inconvenience. And he's thoughtful enough to ask my permission for the interruption.

The waiter returns with our drinks and takes our orders. I order the East Coast Fish and Chips and Blaine orders the Sweet and Spicy Monkfish.

"Also can you bring the bread trio appetizer please?"

"Sure thing."

Adding the lemon to my tea, I look up to start a conversation and find Blaine staring at me.

"What?"

"You're not like most girls I meet."

"Really? How so?"

"Well…" He pauses. "You eat bread."

I laugh. "I eat a lot of things."

"Do you, now?"

"Do you always equivocate?"

"Apparently," he grins.

"I do eat bread. I like food. A lot. I am sure that is very different from the girls you meet."

"It's refreshing."

"It's going to add another workout is what it is." In my line of work, I have come across my fair share of hanger girls, who are a size two and eat a cube of cheese for lunch. I am not a hanger girl.

The waiter places a plate on our table. I move into telling Blaine what each appetizer is.

"This one is grilled artichoke and cloumage cheese, this one is crushed vine ripe tomatoes and sea salt, and lastly, sheep milk ricotta with roasted butternut squash, dates, and honey. I suggest you try them all," I say, handing him half of the one I bit off of.

Lunch flows like two people who have known each other for years, despite the fact that we just met. We swap stories and spend time talking about where he wants to take the next step in his music.

The waiter takes our plates and, before he can offer, I tell him that I would like to order dessert.

"Bananas for Bananas, please."

"Would you like anything?" he asks Blaine.

"No, thank you."

"Two spoons, please," I interject. "Do you like bananas?"

"I do."

"Then you'll love this. It's their twist on banana pudding. Its banana brioche pudding, salty peanut ice cream, peanut butter caramel, hot fudge, and whipped cream." I hold up a finger each time I announce an ingredient. "Now, tell me why you're resistant to being styled."

"How do you know I am?"

"I told you, nine-for-nine."

"I don't like pretending I'm something I'm not. It doesn't feel right." He's quiet for a minute. "I want to be seen as an artist, not a sex symbol."

"Everyone wants to be seen for who they are and not the label we put on them. I hope you'll trust me to not present you as something you're not. You can be more than one thing. You don't have to be known as the sexy artist, but there is nothing wrong with being the artist who is also sexy. Remember, you're my client. Not the label. I won't stray from that."

The waiter brings our pudding.

"Alright then. I'll take you at your word."

"Good, now dig in."

We finish dessert, and I pay despite his objections. We are making our way to the stairs leading to the bottom floor when I feel him before I hear him.

"Emelia." He's sitting at the table I am about pass.

I stop. He stands, buttoning his suit jacket, and nods a greeting to me.

"It's nice to see you," I say, not quite believing that I have run into him. His eyes lock on mine for what seems like a minute, but I'm sure it was just a beat.

"It's lovely to see you again. I see you arrived home safely." It's not meant to be a question. He pauses, and his eyes land on Blaine's hand resting on my exposed back. He gives nothing away to anyone else, but I notice the shutters that come down in his eyes.

"Blaine. This is…" I pause realizing I still don't know his name.

"Graham." *Graham. Finally a name.*

"Blaine Moore." Blaine's hand caresses my skin as he lowers it to the small of my back. Reaching around me he offers his hand in greeting.

"If you'll excuse us for a moment," Graham says, grabbing my forearm. My feet barely touch the stairs as he leads me down, nodding to the bartender before steering me into a small office off the restroom hallway.

"What the hell do you think you are doing?" My voice is louder than necessary. "I am with a client."

"A client? Really? You let all your clients rest their hands on your ass?" he asks, crossing his arms while he peruses my body.

"I write it into my contracts. Adds a little sweetener to the deal don't you think?" I respond flippantly, adding a shoulder shrug.

"You aren't dressed like someone meeting a client."

"I don't work in a business office, Graham. *My* clothing choice is appropriate." I lock my eyes on his, not backing down from his glower—one I get the feeling he is using to intimidate me into his way of thinking. He moves towards me, and I have to work to stand my ground when I realize I am backed into a corner. He's close enough I could run my tongue along his jaw line. The thought sends a shiver through me.

"So you think *this* is appropriate? *This* length?" He runs a finger along the inside of my thigh, tracing the hem of my jumpsuit before following with his thumb, the tip running along the crevice where my leg meets my hip. His touch sparks electricity in me. I know if he skims a little more to the right, he will find me wet for him. My breath catching is all the time he needs to turn me away from him, his thumb now traveling the crevice where my ass meets my thigh. His other hand is plotting a course down my back.

"You sent me an iPod." I go straight to the topic I want to touch on. Avoiding for now my confusion at being turned on instead of angry at his unearned familiarity. Where's the man who held my hand and why is my body equally attracted to this one?

"I did." His voice is heavy in my ear.

"Why?"

"Because I can."

"You shouldn't have."

"I believe the polite response is 'thank you'" he replies.

"Thank you?" I turn towards him. *I don't need a lesson in manners.*

"You're welcome." His reply is authoritative and sarcastic at once. Reading me correctly he adds, "I would think twice before opening that smart mouth Emelia."

"Emme." I cross my arms to put some distance between us. "If you could give me your work address, I'll have it couriered back to you."

"If I say you're keeping it, you're keeping it." The shutters open a little, and I see the smirk in his eyes, baiting me to put a voice to what he knows I am thinking: *Asshole!*

"Blaine's waiting for me." Thankfully, my legs cooperate, and I walk away from him.

ch♥pter
three

Despite Blaine's disbelief, he left with fifteen looks. I know he noticed that I was lost in my own head after running into Graham. It's unnerving, really, that someone would have such an effect on me with very little interaction. I'm surrounded by men. Jackson, the dwarfs, my clients. I've never had someone that affected me the way Graham has. Even as I tell myself to snap out of it, I know there is something there that I want to explore.

I'm reviewing my calendar for tomorrow when my phone beeps.

Jules: Dinner tonight?

I have to check my account balance before responding. I'm covering an extra shift at the bar tomorrow night, so I should be fine.

Me: Sure! Lmk when and where

Jules: Bubby's 8pm

I finalize the prep for tomorrow's clients. My team does personal shopping as well as imaging. I have several repeat clients, some weekly that come to me for both. I have earned a reputation for knowing just the right gift to give someone. Some of it is common sense, and some of it is the same rating system I use for imaging. The questions allow me to see the recipient of the gift through the eyes of my client. It offers me the unique ability to pick out the perfect gift for that person.

Grabbing some flats out of the closet, I leave work at 5:15, which gives me plenty of time to swing by the grocery on my way home to stock up for poker night tomorrow night. Over the last six weeks or so, it has become a new Thursday night tradition. The guys have been honing their games while teaching me to play before the annual casino charity event in the Hamptons over Labor Day weekend. I stop at Eataly for the essentials, and one subway ride later I'm home with enough time to put up groceries and freshen up for my date.

It's about five after eight when I arrive to find Jules has a booth already. Bubby's is a staple in Tribeca and for me and Jules. The menu reminds me of my grandmother's comfort food with a twist. We always order the same three starters as our meal: chicken meatballs, Shishito peppers, and mac n' cheese.

Jules and I met when I first moved to the city, but our friendship has really just blossomed over the last six months. We've fallen hard and fast into a best friendship. Jules is an up-and-coming clothing designer. She called me last February to give some insight into her new line. After a couple of meetings, we were hooked—on each other. Other than my sister, no one but Jules can finish my thoughts, or know them without me saying them. She challenges me when I need it. She doesn't push me for info I don't want to give. In fact, for the first few weeks of our friendship, we only discussed fashions and passions. Her dream of starting her clothing line and my vision for a mentoring program. It was May before I finally met her fiancé Adam. Even then it was only at Adam's insistence.

Adam comes from a gregarious family with heavy financial ties in the city. And even though Jules' family is wealthy enough that she has some concept of what an affluent life is like, I think a part of her struggled to make sure she didn't lose herself in Adam once they were engaged. She kept our friendship as something meant just for her for a while.

I got to really know Adam during my weekend trips to the Hamptons this summer. I met his family when I stayed at their house with Jules over the Fourth. Despite their obvious wealth, they are down to earth and accepting. There is a lot of laughter and love in his family, something I have missed for so long now. I am especially fond of his parents. It's like they were made for parenting. It was so different from the environment I grew up in.

My Mama was amazing and always did her best, but my stepfather was never on her side, or mine for that matter. I never knew if she wasn't strong enough to stand up to him, or if she simply didn't know how. He left when I was in the 8th grade. After that, Mama, Addie, and I were a trio, and so much happier. Still, spending the week with Adam's family admittedly touched a void within me that nothing since my grandparents has come close to doing.

"So," I reach for her sketch book, about to tell her about Graham.

She puts a hand on the book to keep it in place. "Not so fast. How was Memphis?"

"It was Memphis. I got in and got out. What's to tell? The flight home was especially inter—"

"There's a lot to tell, Mags. I think I have been pretty patient, giving you time to tell me on your own, but I can see that is not going to happen, so I'm hoping a direct question might start the process. You have no family to speak of and going back is painful, why do you keep making the trips?"

Only Jules and my sister call me "Mags", a shortened version of my middle name. It's such a casual, almost trivial usage, but it touches me deeply.

"Have I ever told you that other than Addie, you are the only person to call me Mags? Well, you and now Adam. I forget you have a way of rubbing off on him." I wink trying to lift the seriousness of the conversation.

She shakes her head, her eyes loving and soft. "Other than now, you've only talked about Addie once. You know you can trust me." She sounds almost hurt.

"It's not about my trust in you, it's just...I don't know..." I turn the Mason jar they use for drinks around and around in a circle. "Difficult? It's like there aren't words to describe what it felt like to lose her." I shrug one shoulder, as if the gesture itself adds some context.

How do you explain what it feels like to have your heart ripped from you? Realistically, I know that I am not the only person to experience deep loss, but I am the only person who knows what it feels like to lose Addie as a sister. To know that my heart will never be whole again. On good days, it's more than I can handle. On hard days it feels like someone has sucked all the oxygen out of the room, and I find I can barely breathe.

"Did you see your asshole step-father? You know if you needed it, Adam would step in and help in any way he could."

"There's nothing to help with. The man is deranged and has no bearing on my life other than to cause me grief. I hope you don't have Adam riled up about Tony. You know I don't like to talk about life before New York."

"I know, I know," she rolls her eyes. "You are a compartmentalizer. Everything has its place and they don't cross over."

"Yep."

"Isn't that hard though, Mags?"

"It's survival."

That is probably the most honest thing I've said to her. She nods her understanding and I see her love for me in her eyes.

"So," I reach for the book again. "I can't wait to see what changes you've made."

"I love you, Mags." She lets me pick up the book this time and drops the conversation, in one cohesive gesture that elicits an appreciative smile from me.

Our food comes, and we spend the next hour eating and talking about her sketches. Jules is a talented designer, and I know she is on the cusp of rocking the fashion industry. She is working on her designs for a show next spring during Fashion Week.

"This one is amazing!" I draw attention to a sketch I particularly love. It's a slim cut halter pantsuit with a sheer skirt overlay. There are slits on the sides to access the pockets in the pants. The volume of the skirt and the way its cut on the bias allows it to flow like a ball gown. It feels fresh, unique, and high fashion.

"I'm glad you like it. That's my favorite sketch right now. I plan to start the pattern pieces while we are in the Hamptons. I was hoping you would help me." She gives me a beseeching smile she knows I can't resist.

"Okay," I giggle. "Stop with the begging! I'll help."

"Thanks, Mags! What would I do without you? So…" she pauses and visibly relaxes, "usual Thursday tomorrow?"

I roll my eyes. "Yes." I say with forceful, frustrated contempt. "John Michaels is coming in tomorrow."

"Why do you keep him as a client? If you would tell Jackson how much he creeps you out, he would get rid of him."

"That's why I don't. Jackson can't make decisions based on who I do and don't like. It's not smart business. We all have those clients that we would rather not work with. He just happens to be mine."

After dinner, we make our way up Hudson, where we run into Blaine. In a city of eight-and-a-half million, it never ceases to amaze me how often I run into people.

"Emme, what a surprise." Blaine plants a kiss on my cheek. "The courier service just dropped off my packages. Do you live in Tribeca?"

"I'm glad they've delivered them already. I actually live in SoHo, but Jules lives in Tribeca. Jules Redden, Blaine Moore," I gesture from one to the other by way of introduction. "Blaine and I are working on a project together." I gesture back, "Jules is my best friend." It's important to me to set Jules apart from my other friends. When I introduce her to someone I want them to know that she has a place of honor in my life. She is not just a friend. She is my best friend.

"Nice to meet you. I'm a fan," Jules says, acknowledging his celebrity.

"Thanks. If you're Emme's best friend, then I'm a fan of yours as well."

I laugh, "How many women do you roll that one out for?"

"Only you, babe. Only you." His eyes return my laughter and obvious knowledge that I pegged him as a bullshitter.

"Are you coming or going?" His double entendre is meant to humor me. "Can I buy you ladies a drink?"

"Su—"

"I wish I could," I cut Jules' answer off for mine, "but I have plans already. Maybe some other time?"

He places his hand over his heart as if wounded. "Guess I'll have to settle for what I can get. Thanks again for lunch today." He bends and kisses me on the cheek with an evident linger.

"Nice meeting you Jules." He gives his dazzling smile to her, the one that I'm sure has his fans dropping their panties, and walks away in the opposite direction.

"When did that happen?" Jules looks at me like I've been holding out on her.

"Oh yeah, by the way, Blaine Moore is now my client."

"I love Adam, but man, he's hot. Sex on a stick, I'd lick that…"

"Don't even say it, Busta Rhymes," I laugh. "Better watch it or I'm telling Adam."

"He's used to me," she shrugs, unabashed. "Besides, I think the only person Blaine Moore wants near his manhood is you. He looked like he'd take you right here on the street if you gave him the slightest encouragement."

"He's just a flirt. Don't read more into it than there is."

"I know even you are not that blind, Mags. But whatever you want to tell yourself. Who am I to judge?"

"Exactly!" I add in agreement.

We've made it to the corner of Hudson and Beach. "I'm going to grab a cab. I'm meeting friends uptown," Jules announces. "Want to share? I can drop you on the way."

"No, thanks. I think I'll walk. See you tomorrow night?"

"I'll be there."

The air is hot and humid, but a nice breeze makes the walk home pleasant. My thoughts land on Graham again. Since my first attempt to tell Jules was thwarted, I decided to hold onto it for a little while longer. Another compartment, for now. When I arrive home, I find I actually have the apartment to myself. A phenomenal treat.

I turn on some music, change into shorts and a tank,

check the calendar, and make the dwarves meals for the next couple of days. The song shuffles from MisterWives' "Our Own House" to Snoop Dog's "Gin and Juice" as I start a load of laundry and move on to cleaning the kitchen, living room, and bathroom.

An hour later I finally sit down with some ice cream, when Kyle and Drew come in looking more exhausted than I know I feel.

"Hey, James." Kyle flops down on the couch next to me. "How was your day?"

"Good," I say, feeding him a bite of chocolate marshmallow. "Worked with a new client. How was it saving lives today?" Living with six people who perform miraculous lifesaving surgeries every day puts any craziness I have going on into perspective. It's hard to be too upset about most things when you realize there are people out there dying and losing their loved ones. Living with these guys has given me an appreciation for healthcare workers.

"Shitty," he exhales as he moves his head into my lap and unfolds his body down the remainder of the couch. I run my fingers through his hair, massaging his scalp. A minute later, I hear snoring. A minute after that Drew comes into the room and sits in one of the chairs, leaning his head back and stretching his legs out on the coffee table. "Any more ice cream?"

"Yep. Want me to fix you a bowl?"

"I'll get it. Moving might wake him up and he's had a tough day."

"Why? What happened?"

"He lost two patients. A 32-year-old who crashed on the table and an eighteen-year-old who died before making it to the OR. He had to tell the families. He's just exhausted." He moves to the freezer to get some ice cream for himself. "Apartment looks nice." He acknowledges that I cleaned as he reenters the living area with a Jethro-sized bowl.

"Thanks. There are some towels in the dryer if you need one. Will you take the others their food when you go in tomorrow please?"

"Sure thing." He bends over and kisses the top of my head and shovels a heaping spoonful of ice cream into his mouth.

He tilts his head back slightly so the ice cream won't run out with his open mouth. "By the way, how's your ass?"

"A little sore."

"Tomorrow, just a little soap and water. Don't leave it under the running water. Did you pick up the antibiotic Matt called in?"

"Not yet. But I will"

"Make sure you do. Those aren't the sutures that dissolve, so one of us will have to remove them. Should be fine to do them before you go to the Hamptons next week. Night."

"Good night."

I tap into my ninja skills to replace my leg with a pillow for Kyle's head, grab my laptop, and set up on the other couch. Its midnight and I have some work I want to do before going to bed.

Three hours later, the remaining dwarfs, minus one, return home tired and worn out. Kyle wakes long enough to move to his bed, never taking his scrubs off. I fold the towels and start a third load of laundry. I finally wrap up around four in the morning and opt for the couch. If I climb into a real bed, I won't get up to run, and I have to run tomorrow. I've taken the last two mornings off and am behind in my training schedule. If I don't get back on track, I won't be ready.

If I can stick to my training schedule, my goal is to run the New York Marathon in November. I was asked to do it to raise money for charity, which I will do regardless. The marathon was just the catalyst; the running part is really for me. I didn't think I would like it when I started training, but I have really fallen in love with the process, the time to myself, and the challenge.

Within minutes of my head hitting the pillow, my alarm goes off. One look at my watch tells me the minutes have actually been a full hour. I have a conversation with myself about do I or do I not get up. Apparently I'm a masochist, which explains how I find myself lacing up my running shoes. I do some stretches, grab an energy bar, my old iPod (I haven't decided what to do with my new one), and head out.

Most days I run a different path, just to change it up a little. Today I'm running west to the Hudson, down to Battery Park, over to City Hall, across and back over the Brooklyn Bridge, and home to Greene Street. A little more than six miles. I should be running seven, but I don't have the time nor the energy. In August if you don't get your run in early, you'll cook from the heat. Especially me. I'm not one of those runners who look like they run with so little effort, like they could go straight from running to work with no problems. I hate those bitches. They look like they're doing a light jog while cool air is blowing on them. I hope they slip on my sweat and fall.

Running gives my mind too much time to overthink Graham's intentions. How did he know my given name was Emelia? I try to think of ways to take back some of the control, but seeing as I only know his first name, it's difficult. He looked delicious yesterday at lunch. I should try Google Image to see if I could find some clues about who he is. Would it matter? Do I want to see him again? Even as I ask myself the question, I already know the answer is yes. Something about Graham has me off balance, like my equilibrium is off. It's unsettling. I can't get him to fit into a compartment.

Outside of our building, I grab a paper from the corner and head up to shower. I'm earlier than expected, making it a little too soon to start our morning routine. The guys are still asleep when I'm out of the shower and start breakfast. Slowly they begin to stir as the smell of bacon and French toast fills the air. I am loading the last of the bacon onto a plate when Matt announces, "You're on Page Six."

"Who is?" Kyle says grabbing the paper from his hands.

"James. She's on Page Six."

"I am?" my brain is addled.

"Yep." Kyle reads, "Page Six has confirmed a rumor that Blaine Moore and Jackson Hollingsworth's 'it' girl, Emme James, are a hot new item. Here's betting his song 'Sex with You' takes on a whole new meaning for her."

"Seriously, whatever happened to journalistic ethics?" I place meatballs I am rolling for tonight's dinner a little too forcefully into the slow cooker.

"You know that goes out the window, James, when it comes to celebrities." Kyle sets the paper on the counter as I pour the sauce in. There's a picture of Blaine and me sharing dessert at Bryant Park Grill. I'm saying something and he's laughing. He looks young and carefree. At least this picture will soften his image some.

"Great. Just what I need. I guess it's better than outing him as my client." The last thing the label is going to want is a leak that they are tweaking his image.

Tossing the paper to the side, I head to my alcove to dress for the day. I grab a new DVF wrap dress in one of her signature fun prints. They are a staple in my wardrobe and in the closet at work. Easy to wear, and they look great on someone with actual curves. You don't have to be a hanger girl to wear them. They show off just the right amount of cleavage and just a hint of leg. Professional but sexy.

I run my fingers through my air-dried hair and muss it up a little giving it a tossed about look. Throwing on some flats, I circle several bangle bracelets up my wrist, grab a Chanel shoulder bag and say my "love you" to the guys as I close the door.

I've barely entered the office door when Amanda tells me that Jackson wants me to stop by his office first.

"Great," I mumble under my breath.

Making my way to his door, I know he has seen Page Six and has a comment. I knock and enter all in one motion.

"Hey, babe. You looking for me?"

"I am. Sit for a minute. Want to go over some accounts with you. You look gorgeous as always."

"You're good for my confidence." I smile my innocent smile at him.

Laughing, "You know that smile always works on me."

"Yep. That's why I do it. Give the boss what he wants."

Jackson Hollingsworth is a self-made businessman. His mind for business is like unchartered waters. You don't know what all is there or what it holds, but its creations are nothing short of amazing. I'm such a fan of his and how he conducts his business. He's genuine, in a crowd that is not.

He's also loyal. To Patrick. To me. To his business. I think that is what draws me to him. He is twelve years my senior. He never talks down my ideas or dreams. He'll use his questions to guide my thoughts without me realizing it until I've moved my decision into the lane it really needs to be in. Much like family would. He and Patrick have been pillars in my decision making process since I started working for Jackson. I spend Christmas with them every year. They're solid ground for me.

"So, where are you on the mentor program?"

"I'm going up early to work on the grants."

"Great. I saw the list of CEOs Adam gave you. I think they have strong companies and are open to experimenting. I know he already arranged a meeting for you with Richard Raines of Raines Shipping. I emailed you his profile this morning. It should have all the background you need."

"Thanks. He'll be my first. So, we'll see how it goes."

"Speaking of firsts," he raises a brow. "Let's start with the next steps regarding Blaine Moore. You have his style working perfectly. I really love the direction you're taking him. It's an edge that people haven't seen out of him. I like that it looks easy, too. Like he's not trying too hard."

"Just him being him," I chime in.

"Exactly. Now the next item the label wants us to address is his personality. The ebb and flow of conversation when he is interviewed."

"Why? I think he's got a great personality."

"I know. I saw TMZ."

"You mean there's video?" I'm now exasperated. "Please tell me you don't believe that story. We had lunch. I take all my clients to lunch."

"I know that. Just make sure he does. I saw the way he watched you yesterday."

"You're incorrigible. As far as our job goes," I divert his attention back to the conversation I'm more comfortable with, "I think we should push the label to go with the real Blaine. He has all the goods. We just need to give them an outline of how best to promote him. They need to adapt. Not him. I've sexed his look up, so that should help." I glance at my watch "I have to go. I have a meeting."

"Ok. Who's on your calendar today?"

"I'm meeting with Baker. This afternoon is Michaels." I make a face on the last name.

"Your best and worst all in the same day. Too bad Baker isn't your afternoon appointment. At least you could end on a good note. I can always take Michaels, if you like. Just say the word."

"No. For the hundredth time, I'm fine. It's called a job. You have to deal with things or people you don't like. It's fine. I have it under control."

"Alright, message received." He holds his hands up in a relinquishing manner. "Patrick wanted me to double check that you don't want to stay with us in the Hamptons over Labor Day? He's got your room all ready."

"Thanks, but I'm staying with Adam's family. There's a group going. You can actually have a weekend to yourselves."

"We love our weekends with you, but I'll let him know." Looking up from his desk while he's grabbing some files, he adds, "Don't forget you're my date to the dinner and casino night. Patrick can't make it."

"Like I could forget," I smile. "I'll be the luckiest girl there."

"I think you have that backwards, sweetheart."

Blowing kisses, I head to my office to prep for my day.

"Your assistant emailed me your calendar of events for the next three months," I tell Baker an hour later in my office. "I've pulled together all the items you will need and have them already built into ensembles for you. As always, it's a no brainer. All you have to do is go through the portfolio I built you. I'd like to go through it together now, make sure you're ok with everything I've chosen, then I'll have Henry organize them into your closet tomorrow.

"There are a couple of things that are different this time that I want to draw your attention to. I know you are launching some new products to a younger audience, so I've hipped up a few outfits for when you have to make appearances for those products. I have them marked here." I point to the last pages of the book I have assembled for him.

"I know a couple of things might feel out of your wheel-house, but you'll have to trust that I won't make you look like your trying to be twenty-one again. I want you relevant and hip, but also age appropriate for the business mogul you are. I want you try on these looks in the office today for me to see and make sure you're comfortable with the outfits."

"Sounds good. You've thought of everything as always. I feel like every dad with a daughter that wants him to look cool." His eyes sparkle when he smiles.

"You *are* cool. This is just cherry stuff." I smile and he laughs. "Also, before I forget, I have birthday and anniversary gifts picked out. If you're pleased with them, Joy will wrap them up and have them delivered to your office. We'll do Christmas at your next appointment."

"Well then, let's get started, because I'm taking you to lunch after this."

At noon, we leave the office building and walk two blocks to a pizzeria. We share a large pizza and Caesar salad as he teaches me things about business.

After lunch I make my way back up to the office. John Michaels, my afternoon appointment, is a no show. I can't say

I'm disappointed. The guy creeps me out. There's just something about him that seems off, like he's always picturing me naked.

I use the extra time to catch up on some orders for other clients, and spend the afternoon on the phone with the Armani office in Italy. One hour and $150,000 later, I have suits ordered for one of my best clients.

"Do you mind if I head out, Emme? I want to run by Barney's on my way home and see what's new."

I look up to see Henry standing in my door.

"Sure." I look at my watch to see that it's three-thirty. "Joy is at Bergdorf's picking up some items for me now. Let's call it a day. See you tomorrow."

"Thanks! Don't stay too late."

I take some pictures to Amanda. "Can you catalog these for me please under the O'Keefe account? I don't need them until his next appointment in October."

"In that case," she looks at me hopefully, "if you don't have anything else, I wanted to also head out. It's my little sister's birthday, and I need to pick up a cake on my way. Need anything before I go?"

"Nope. Have a great time."

I'm almost around the corner when the door buzzes. It's John Michaels and his right hand man. My no-show has shown. Two hours late. Amanda buzzes him in.

"I'm sorry. I got hung up in a meeting and then traffic was a nightmare."

"Funny enough, they have these things called cellphones. You dial a few numbers and it will connect you to me, so you can let me know that you're delayed. I've already sent everyone home. We'll have to reschedule."

"Can you maybe show me the looks and I can leave with

one? I have a causal event tomorrow that's going to be in the papers and I need something to wear."

Amanda looks at me with a fake smile that tells me she is as frustrated with this fucker as I am.

"Fine. I have something for you that will work." John's guy takes a seat in the reception area. I nod to Amanda who is putting her purse back in her desk drawer. "Go ahead and go Amanda. I don't want you to miss the party. I'll lock up. "

"You sure? I don't mind staying. I'm scheduled until five, anyway."

"I'm sure. Have fun."

I turn the corner and John is standing there. He hasn't entered the office. It's like he was listening to our conversation. This should have been my first clue that something was off.

You know how you have that feeling in your gut that tells you not to go into the basement, but you do anyways. You're not quite sure why you shouldn't go into the basement, but you feel silly because you can't put your finger on it. So, you tell yourself you're overreacting. That's the feeling I have when John is here.

"Do you have any Scotch?"

"In the middle of the day? At the office? No. I don't," I respond, exasperated. I take in his movements. "Have you been drinking?"

He doesn't answer. Clue number two.

I take three of the looks we had ready for him and hang them in the dressing room. "Try them on in the order I have them. If the first one works, we won't have to try on the others."

He looks at me with a smile that doesn't go anywhere. "Want to help me? Remember, I dress to the left." Clue number three.

"Do I look like I do?" My question, like my look, minces no words. I move out of the doorway.

"You look like someone who does a lot of things." He steps in front of me, his six-three stature hovering over my five-seven frame. I've measured him enough to know that he's 210 pounds of solid muscle.

"You know what? You need to come back on a different day. I'll see you out." I move to step around him.

He grabs my upper arm, hard. "I think I'll stay and you can show me a few things."

I look him straight in the eyes, as if I can detour him. "Take your hand off me, now! You're leaving," I say in my most demanding voice. I remember being told that when you come across a bear, you're supposed to make yourself as big and fierce as you can. This will help scare the bear into backing down.

I jerk to move out of his hold, but he tightens his grip and pushes me against the wall, pressing his body against mine. His free hand wrapping around my other arm.

"I'll leave when I'm fucking ready. We're going to finish what you started. And don't fucking act like you don't know what I'm talking about. You made sure that we were the only ones in the office. You've wanted this from the beginning. Don't be shy now."

What I started?

"You're delusional, John. Get off me."

My fight or flight response has kicked in, and I know that to get out of here, I'm going to have to fight. He's had too much to drink to reason with. I try to free my arms. When that doesn't work. I start kicking at his legs, trying to catch his feet with mine. *Why didn't I wear heels today?*

I claw at him, but he uses his grip on my arms to slam

me into the wall. My head hits hard enough that I momentarily lose my bearings. That second is all he needs to turn me toward the wall with my hands behind my back. I think he's going to break my arm, and in this position, with his body pinning me to the wall again, I can't get leverage to fight back. It doesn't stop me from trying.

"Listen, you stupid cunt, I don't mind a little fight, but this is starting to irritate me, and you really don't want to see me irritated. Understand?"

He turns my head to the side and runs his tongue down the side of my face. I can finally smell how much he has had to drink.

I move my head back around and try to push off the wall with my shoulder and forehead, but I'm still not moving. He binds my wrists into one hand. Reaching the other around, he sticks his hand in my dress grabbing my breast. Hard. He makes a groaning noise, and I can feel his erection against my lower back. The more I try to move and fight back, the harder he restrains me.

"John. Stop this. This is not what I want. If you go any further, I will report you to the police. Do you understand? Stop this now!" *Where the fuck is his guy?*

His hand has found the slit in my wrap dress and he forces my underwear down. I hear a noise and realize it's me screaming. A deep, feral scream. He brings his hand to my mouth. "I like to hear you scream, but right now I want you quiet." As soon as his hand covers my mouth I clamp down with a vengeance, until I taste blood.

Cursing in pain, he is stunned enough to release his hold on me. I make my move to get around him, but he grabs my hair and pulls me back, letting me go in time to bring the back of his hand across my face with enough force to knock me across the worktable and on to the floor. I take some of the chairs with me.

"You stupid bitch! Who the fuck do you think you are." He lunges towards me, when his guy steps in between us, restraining him and talking him down in a hushed voice. He wipes the blood from his mouth and spits the rest on the floor.

"The slut's not worth it anyway." They turn and walk out.

I hear them leave and know they can't get back inside without being buzzed in. I lay entwined with fallen chairs. For how long, I don't know.

Taking my time, I finally make my way off the floor. I turn the chairs upright. I have a split lip in the left corner of my mouth, and my body is so tense it feels like I was hit by a truck. I'm able to keep my balance, but I'm in shock. Shaking, I pull up my underwear from around my ankles, straighten my hair, and grab my purse.

ch♥pter
four

I'm standing in my apartment. I'm not sure how I got home or how long I've been standing here. I go into my closet and change into leggings and a tank. Wrapping my grandfather's cardigan around me, I glance at the calendar to see which dwarf is out tonight and climb into his bed. Pulling the covers around me like a protective shield, I drift off into a restless sleep.

My mouth is dry and I hear voices. It takes me a moment to process that they are coming from the living room. Poker night is starting.

"I thought you were on a three-day?" I hear one of the dwarfs say, but I'm too groggy to discern which one.

"I got someone else to cover the last day for me," he says. "I came home and found Goldilocks in my bed."

"Mags is here? Is everything ok? How long has she been asleep? She never sleeps in the middle of the day." Jules' concerned voice fires off multiple questions.

"I've been here about two hours," one answers.

"Let her sleep. She was still up when I got home at three-thirty this morning, and Drew said she was already gone for a run when he was up at five-thirty. The crock-pot has meatballs in it, so I'm sure she'll be up soon."

"Ooo, I love her meatball subs," I hear Adam say.

I can hear them setting up for the card game. A glance at my watch tells me I've been asleep for about three hours. My body feels like I've been under for days.

Sitting up, I try to get my bearings in the dark room. I shove the mess with John Michaels into a compartment and shut it, all nice and neat until I'm ready to deal with it. I know if I don't get up and moving, Jules will be in to check on me. Plus, I need to get a few things done before my shift at the bar.

I grab the hair tie off my wrist and pull my long hair into a messy bun. Standing, I gather myself enough to act like everything is okay.

In the living room, I try to not meet anyone's eye as I make my way to the fridge to grab a Diet Coke. Jules is the first to speak.

"Hey. You okay?"

"I am." I pop the top and take a long sip, holding the cold can to my sore mouth, my back to the table.

"I'll have dinner ready in a few minutes," I announce before the door opens and Drew and Kyle come in.

"We made it! What smells so good?" Drew rounds the kitchen corner to greet me. "What the fuck happened to you?" His voice is loud and demanding.

I can feel that everyone's eyes have turned to see that he's talking about me. I should have looked in a mirror before I came out. In two steps he's towering above me, tilting my head back to look at my face in the light. Wincing from the pain, I pull my chin out of his hands.

"Language, please. I had a run in with the stairs at work. The stairs won."

"I'll say. You look like you were fucking dropped kicked."

He mutters while examining my arms for signs of more injuries.

"Let me see." Kyle steps around him and tilts my head back.

I swat his hands away. "Just wash up. Dinner's ready and I want to eat before I have to go to work." And that was the truth. I wanted a couple of hours of meaningless diversion. Fake it until I decide what I'm going to do. I turn around to start building the meatball subs when Jules is beside me looking at me like I've grown two heads.

In a low whisper meant only for me, she says, "What the hell, Mags? What's going on? You're a shit liar." She adds that part before I even say anything, knowing I'm not going to willingly share information.

"We'll talk later. Help me make the sandwiches."

We carry the subs and chips to our round dining room table that seats eight. We've had as many as twelve squeezed around it. I sit down next to Jules, close my eyes, take a deep breath and exhale. *Lock your shit down, James.*

I would usually start the passing of the food, but my hands are shaking and I haven't been able to make them stop.

"Adam, since I made your favorite, why don't you start?" With the strongest smile I can muster, I finally look up at the group. Adam is sitting to Jules' right.

Graham is to sitting to Adam's right.

What the...?

Adam introduces us. "Mags, this is my brother, Graham. Graham, this is Mags."

"You're Adam's brother?" I didn't think it was possible to be this shocked twice in one day.

"*Older* brother. Remember I told you I had a brother in Japan for the last few months? This is him." He passes the platter to Jules.

"We've met," we say in unison, drawing the attention of everyone around us.

"You're the guy from the airport," Drew states absently, finally placing him.

"I am," Graham replies his eyes locked on mine.

In a tailored suit, he is breathtaking. In jeans and a t-shirt, he's delicious.

"Mags is the girl on the plane?" I hear Adam asking him. Graham moves his eyes from me to his brother and without a word spoken, Adam drops the conversation.

"What are they talking about?" Jules asks me.

I feel like I've gone down the rabbit hole.

"I thought your brother wasn't expected home before Thanksgiving?"

"I finished early." His eyes are on me again.

"Are you here to practice poker?" I redirect the conversation, trying to gain my footing by acting like this shock isn't a shock, and to prove it I pretend I can carry on a normal conversation.

"I'm here to spend some time with my brother. He already had plans tonight, so I came with him. I'm glad I did," he adds taking a bite of his sandwich.

"Hope you like subs," I chirp. I'm not sure what he is thinking, but I see a humor in his eyes that moves out as quickly as it came in.

I almost drop the platter when it is handed to me.

"Shitake!" I catch a sandwich before it hits the table.

Adam laughs, "You know you have me saying that now instead of shit."

"James is too polite to cuss," Kyle says passing the potato chips. "It's the sweet Southern girl in her." He gives his best imitation of my accent, while winking at me.

"Are they serious?" Graham looks at me. I know he's referring to my colorful language on the plane.

"They are. My mama didn't like curse words. Taught me that a real lady never uses them." I raise a brow, daring him to rat me out. Cussing has been something that I only say to myself. Mama always said I needed to watch my language that it paints a picture of who I am. Her expectations trained me not to cuss in front of others. Already Graham knew something about me I never showed to the others.

"Wonder what your mother would say now?" he counters. He thinks he has the upper hand.

"Nothing. She's dead," I say, matter-of-factly. Some would say it was crass, but my mother would be the first one to say, "by all means necessary."

Two things happen. Everyone at the table looks at me like they aren't sure who I am. It's rare they hear me talk about my family. And then Graham looks at me like he knows exactly who I am and what I'm doing. It's a cocky gesture that throws me off my game.

"Did you say you were working tonight?" Kyle pulls my attention back to him. "You work too much. I wish you would quit."

"It's no biggie. I've only had to work two jobs since moving in here."

"No "biggie"? I'm not sure that's even a word."

There's a knock at the door, and Drew disappears to answer it. We've begun clearing the table to set it up for poker when he reenters carrying a large vase of dark red roses. There must be three, maybe four dozen. He opens the card.

"Do you have an admirer?" I smile at him.

"No, you do." He looks from the card to me.

"If they're for me, why are you reading the card?" I snatch it out of his hands, giving him my best mean face.

As soon as I see the card, I perform an Emmy-worthy act to keep my face from showing too much. My mouth didn't catch get the memo.

"How did who get your address?" Drew asks.

"What?" I look up at him like I'm just now realizing he's standing there. I lower my hand so he doesn't see it shake.

"You just said, 'How did he get my address?' Who are those from James?"

"No one." I pick them up and throw them in the trashcan.

"If it was no one, there would be no reason for them to sign the card 'I'm Sorry'. Plus, you love flowers. Why are you throwing them out?"

I grab the trash bag and take it into the hall and throw it down the trash shoot. *I can't believe that fucker sent me flowers. How does he know where I live?*

Entering the apartment, I'm relieved Drew has dropped the inquisition and they have the game ready to go. I grab another Diet Coke and take my seat. I pop the top on my drink.

Looking up to see who's placing the first bet, I catch Graham looking from me to the Diet Coke and back to me. There's a dare in his look, and I'm immediately reminded of our flight when he refused me my soda. I take a long drink and look at him, catching the tick in his jaw.

Don't fuck with me tonight buddy. I'm not in the mood.

"We're here!" We all turn to see Matt and Becca enter into the apartment.

"Just in time," someone responds.

Matt walks around the table and sets a Junior's cheesecake in front of me.

"What is this for?"

He plants a light kiss to the top of my head. "Happy Anniversary."

"Today?" I ask, looking from him to the cheesecake trying to remember.

"Yep. Three years ago today, you came into our life."

"And I don't know what we would do without you!" Becca throws her arms around me and kisses my cheek. "I know I wouldn't have made it without you, and I don't even live in the same city." She darts accusatory glances at the dwarfs. "Hello," she says to Graham, just now noticing someone in the room she hasn't met before. "I'm Becca, Matt's wife."

Graham introduces himself.

"There's food on the stove," I instruct.

"Great, I'm starved," Becca starts to the kitchen, halts, and comes over to me.

"I almost forgot. Let me see." She pulls on my arm to raise me from my chair causing me to flinch.

"I'm sorry, James. Did I pinch you?"

I shake my head, ignoring the stare coming from Graham.

"Well," she looks at me waiting. My look of confusion has her explaining.

"Your incision. Matt said he stitched you up. I want to see if he did as good of a job as I would have." Becca is not about to be outdone by a man.

"What happened?" The dwarfs who weren't here for the injury ask.

"Long story short, roach in shower."

"Ah," they say in unison, and though no other words are needed, Drew continues.

"It was deep enough that she needed sutures. Trauma-with-a-stint-in-Plastics over there thinks he's better than the rest of us.''

"I am," Matt interrupts.

I stand and lift my cardigan to the side, pulling down my leggings just enough to show Becca my incision.

"There's quite a bit of bruising, and it looks like it's been bleeding." She leans closer and looks up at Matt. "You didn't match the incision."

"What are you talking about?" He sets his plate down and walks over to look. "I went slow and made sure she wouldn't have any scarring." He pulls my leggings down so he can see. I cross my arms and roll my eyes.

"What happened?" he asks. "It looks like it was ripped open."

"Nothing happened." I swat him away and sit back down.

"Didn't you say you fell in the stairway?" Graham asks, regarding me. I move my eyes from him back to my cards without saying anything.

"So, he sutured her," Drew continues "Twelve stitches. Took him forever."

"I didn't want her to have a scar." Matt bites into his sub.

"It's on her ass. What's the big deal? I'll take two," Russ says throwing down two cards.

Graham's eyes are still on me.

"Well," Drew says, studying his cards, "if you had seen the ass we got to see yesterday, you would understand. Three please." He says to the dealer.

Becca walks by him and slaps him on the head.

"Damn! Why do people keep doing that?" He rubs his head.

"Because that's like talking about your sister. It's gross and inappropriate. And Emme is more than her ass!"

"Start the next one without me. I have to change for

work," I say grabbing my poker chips, having won that round.

"Why don't we all take a break," Drew suggests. "Anyone want cheesecake?"

"Save me a piece," I say over my shoulder moving to my alcove to get ready. I barely have the curtain closed before it's pulled open again. Jules steps in.

"Cut the shit, Mags!"

"What?"

"What's going on? You're sleeping when I get here. You're in a mood. You get flowers from someone with an 'I'm Sorry', and you'd think they were about to combust the way you had to get them out of here. What happened? Somebody did something wrong, and I want to know who and what."

"Stop being so dramatic."

"That's not an answer! The more you deflect, the more I know something isn't right!"

Adam opens the curtain. "Everything okay in here?"

"Fine," we answer simultaneously, not looking away from each other.

"What's going on, Mags?" Adam demands.

"Great, now you've got him started." I motion towards Adam.

"I was talking to you only. I didn't expect him to hear," Jules responds, but not apologetically.

"It's a curtain, Jules, not a cloak of invisibility. What did you think would happen?"

"Mags?" Adam crosses his arms, waiting for a response.

I look to Adam. "It's fine. It's nothing. Get Jules some cheesecake." I dismiss them both. Adam pulls a pissed off Jules out to the living room, and I close the curtain. Again.

Ten Thirty Eight is more of a bar than a club. It does have a small dance floor, but most people are just as happy to hang out in the places where you can sit and attempt to talk above the music, or shoot pool on the upper level. A lot of business people come in on their way home from Downtown. Tonight I'm working the bar, where I usually make the most in tips. Black ankle pants that are fitted to show every curve and a black corset top is the standard uniform. I'm covered, but that's about all I can say.

Sliding the pants on, I'm fastening the corset when the curtain pulls back and Graham steps in. Without a word he's behind me and our eyes hold each other's in the mirror as he moves my fingers and slowly connects each fasten. The tips of his fingers touching my skin along the way. His eyes move to the rise and fall of my chest, lifted by the boning of the corset, before landing back on mine in the mirror. Neither of us says anything.

"Who sent you the flowers?" He finally breaks the silence.

"No one of consequence. Why did you give me an iPod?"

"Because I can. What happened today?"

"I don't know what you're talking about," I say, casually, putting in my earrings. "You can do a lot of things, doesn't mean you should."

"Emelia." His tone implies a warning.

"Graham," I reply with a just a hint of mockery. His jaw ticks in response. "Why do you use my given name?"

"Because it's obvious that you're many things to many people, each with their own name for you, but under all that is Emelia. Who you really are."

What the hell does that mean? Who I really am? Like he would know. Like anyone would. I'm proficient at showing people what I want them to see. They know me, but there are still parts that I haven't shared with anyone. Not since Addie.

"How did you know that was my name?"

"I have my ways."

"So, you're an expert on me, even though we've only spent a little more than three hours together?" The sarcasm in my voice is not to be mistaken.

"Careful. Are you seeing Blaine Moore?"

"Only professionally."

"What about your roommates?"

"The dwarfs? No. They're like brothers to me. Like Adam."

"Including Drew?"

"Especially Drew." With exasperation, I pull my hair into a ponytail. "What is it you want, Graham?"

"Who sent the flowers?"

"An acquaintance." I move in front of the mirror to apply a little cover up to my lip and add a hint of pink lip gloss. I'm refreshing my mascara when he moves into the tight space and stands directly behind me.

"What happened to your arm?" I follow his gaze to my arm where there is definite bruising. *Shit.*

"I fell. Can you hand me that purse please?" I point to the Chanel I carried today that is sitting on the chair. His eye still on my arm, he studies it for a moment before wrapping his hand around it, matching his fingers and thumb to the bruises. I can see the pieces fitting together and the fire coming into his eyes.

"I don't tolerate dishonesty, Emelia"

"Just because I don't answer your questions doesn't mean I'm dishonest."

"Omission or diversion on purpose is dishonest."

I reach around him and pick up the purse.

"If you stopped buying Chanel, learn to live within your means, maybe you wouldn't have to keep two jobs." His judgment catches me off guard, and for a minute he looks regretful.

I hate that I care what he thinks. Anyone else and I wouldn't give a damn.

"Not that it's any of your business, but it's not my purse. When you work for Jackson, he expects you to present yourself in a certain way, so he gives me open access to the closet at work. In his line of work, image is everything." I start switching the items into a little clutch I picked up at H&M. I don't like to take things of value to the club.

"Did you take these?"

Above the chair hang three 11x20 antique metal frames with white matting, one above the other.

"I did." I am confused by the sudden change in conversation.

"Is this your mother?" He points to one. I stop what I'm doing and look up. Today of all days, I really could use my mom.

"It is. I took it just before she was diagnosed with Lymphoma." I absently stroke the frame.

"I'm sorry for your loss. She's beautiful. You look just alike." He studies the picture.

"She was."

"What's her name?"

"Laura James."

"What about the others?"

"Others?" His question pulls me out of my reverie.

"The other pictures?"

"Oh." I move a step closer. My body brushing his.

"Those are my grandparents," my voice softens.

"I love this one. This was on their farm. They didn't know I was outside, and I found them in this loving embrace, kissing. I love the lines in my grandfather's face." I point to him in the picture. "Like a map of who he was. Hard working. Honest. Reliable. Faithful. My grandmother's face soft and giving of herself. Pliant, even though she was so strong." Graham's eyes move from the picture to me.

"This one," I move on without prompting, "was my first and only car. It was my grandfather's. We inherited it when I was ten. A 1965 International Harvester Scout. I loved it. The paint job had seen better days, but I remember he said the color was Vegas Blue. Not sure why, but that has always stuck with me." I get lost in the pictures for a minute.

"I can't believe you're Adam's brother." I stare at him, for the moment having found the easiness we had on the plane. "I adore your family. I'm staying with your parents over the holiday. Maybe I'll see you there." I purposefully make it a statement and not a question.

Pulling the curtain back, we step back into the living area. Everyone has finished their cheesecake and are starting another round of poker. All eyes move from me to Graham.

"I'm off to work," I announce.

"I have to be at the hospital at three-thirty. Want to grab some food after you get off and before I go in?" Kyle asks.

"Sure. I'll text you when I'm leaving. We can meet at the all-night on 11th."

I lean over and kiss the top of Becca's head. "I'll call you about lunch tomorrow."

Moving around the circle kissing the temples of all the dwarfs and Adam. I get to Jules and we kiss each other's lips like we always do. I whisper "I love you" in her ear and squeeze her hand to soften our earlier disagreement. I have to get my thoughts together before I can share them.

"I get hard every time you two kiss like that," Drew says while rearranging the cards in his hand, warranting another slap across the head, this one from Matt.

"There is seriously something wrong with you," Matt says.

I pat the spot on his head as I walk out. It has to be getting sore by now.

I'm out the door with Graham on my heels. I'm almost to the stairs when he turns me towards him. With one hand at the nape of my neck and the other at the small of my back, he pulls me to him and kisses me. It's a kiss that is slow and learning. His lips, rough with just the right amount of softness, has my lips opening for him, giving his tongue access to mine. It lights a path deep in my belly and the small moan that escapes my throat has him deepening his kiss, adding strength to it. Both of his hands cup my face. My hands come to rest on his forearms. This man can kiss. I find myself wondering what sex with him would be like, when he pulls back and takes a breath like he's trying to gain control. His blue eyes give nothing away, but they are a shade darker than they were earlier.

"Good night, Emelia."

Before I can respond, he's back inside the apartment.

ch♥pter
five

My shift at the bar is uneventful, and I'm out of there with enough time to meet Kyle. I'm exhausted, but sometimes I have to find creative ways to spend time with my guys. Their shifts are long and erratic.

Kyle eats a full breakfast, while I snack on a strawberry and crème waffle. Conversation with him is always relaxed. He is my sweet guy, always considerate of others.

He can tell that I just need this time together to be easy, so he keeps our topics light and fun. It's a reprieve from the craziness of this week. Despite my protest, he takes care of the bill and we step outside to hail him a taxi.

"Inside," he motions with a bow of his head towards the backseat of the taxi door. "I'll drop you on my way."

"I'll walk. It's out of your way."

"It's not, and I'm not letting you walk home at three in the morning. Get in."

He instructs the driver that there'll be two stops and gives him our address for the first.

As the taxi makes its way into traffic, I look around at my surroundings. New York is always busy. Even at three in the morning.

"You know you can talk to me right?" Kyle says pulling me out of my thoughts.

"I'm sorry?"

"You can talk to me, if ever you want someone to talk to."

"I'm good. I promise. It's just been a crazy week, and I haven't had a lot of sleep. Next week will be better."

"You know I try to take it easy on you, and not push you into discussions you don't want to have. I just don't want you to mistake that for my not wanting to be here for you."

I rest my head on his shoulder. "I love you, Kyle. I know there isn't anything you wouldn't do for me. What I needed the most, you gave me. Time to just be me. Thank you." He allows my response and kisses the top of my head. We ride the remainder of the way home like this.

Kyle deposits me on the doorstep of our apartment and makes sure I am inside before he has the taxi pull off. Its nights like this I wish we had an elevator. I make my way up the five flights of stairs and enter the apartment as quietly as possible. There is no way I am getting up to go running. I'll have to make up the miles later.

I change into an oversized t-shirt and grab my pillow and blanket from the chest in the living room. Stretching out on the couch, my mind wanders to the events of yesterday. There's no way around it: I will have to let Jackson know that I am dropping John Michaels as a client. I need to decide if I am going to file a report. Normally, I wouldn't hesitate and would be furious with anyone in my position for not going to the police. But John has a great amount of influence, so I am not sure it would do any good. It's my word against his. I know his guy will protect him and contradict my story. And if it goes public, which I assume it would since it would be a part of public record, it could get nasty. I already have one legal battle on my hands. But what if he did this to someone else? I couldn't live with myself knowing that my decision to not report it might impact someone later.

I hear far away voices that are coming closer and closer.

"Sleeping Beauty." Drew is lightly shaking my shoulders. Reluctantly, I open my eyes, adjusting to the light.

"Good morning," he says.

I stretch and bend into a sitting position, trying to acclimate to my surroundings.

"What time is it?"

"Past eight," he reports. "Everyone's gone. I didn't know what time your first meeting was, so I was afraid not to wake you before I leave."

"Oh, I'm sorry. What did y'all do for breakfast? Do you have to leave now? I can make a lunch before you go."

"You know we love how you take care of us, but we can make it on our own, too. You needed the rest."

"I know y'all can." I'm standing now. "I just like knowing y'all are looked after."

"And you do a great job. I'm off." He blows a kiss and is out the door.

I fold up my bedding and send a text to Jackson letting him know that I'm running late. Thirty minutes later I'm on the subway headed to work. It's not as crowded as usual, I guess people are already leaving the city, which is common on summer weekends. Anything to get away from the heat. I love New York, but the subways in the summer leave a lot to be desired. The whole place smells like two sweaty truckers pig wrestling.

It's no time at all before I'm at the door for Amanda to buzz me in.

"Good Morning," I greet her.

"Good Morning, Emme. This is for you." She hands me a black box. "Came for you earlier." She's smiling like a kid on Christmas, waiting to see what's inside.

I open it to find a stunning Mikimoto Pearl Lariat necklace. Twenty-two inches in length with a white gold clasp. I bought one for a client last month. It runs a little over $4,700. "Who delivered this?"

"A courier service. There's a card on the back of the box." Amanda flips my hand over so I can see. I remove the card and open it.

"I'm sorry," it reads.

Enough with the "I'm sorry"! I exhale a frustrated breath.

"Can you have these couriered to John Michaels before noon today please? His office address is on file." I hand the box back to her.

She runs her fingers over the pearls. "But they're so beautiful? Are you sure?"

"Yep. Make sure they get there before noon."

I start around the corner when I think of Addie. Turning back to Amanda's desk, I instruct her, "If at any time John Michaels shows up and you are the only one in the office, you do not answer the door. Do you understand?"

"But he can see me sitting here." She crinkles her brow in confusion.

"I don't care. You tell him it's a new office policy."

She nods her understanding, but her guise tells me she thinks I've lost my mind. I continue to look at her letting her know that I want a verbal confirmation that she understands.

"Got it," she confirms.

I leave a confused Amanda, who has the good graces not to ask me any questions, in the reception area and head to Jackson's office.

I knock and enter all in one motion, taking my usual seat in a chair in front of his desk. He's wrapping up a call and motions that he'll just be a minute. I watch my friend as he commands the conversation. I have learned so much from him in my time here. I couldn't ask for a better mentor.

Jackson leans forward, lacing his hands together with his fingers. He's wearing slim cut jeans and a white dress shirt with the sleeves rolled up. A polka-dotted handkerchief peeks out of the pocket of his navy pinstriped vest. His aged brown leather belt gives the ensemble youth and edge.

"Good morning, beautiful. How are you?"

"Good thank you. Sorry I'm late. I overslept."

"The perfect opener for what I want to talk to you about. What do you think it says to others that my number one has to work a second job?"

"Oh, goodness. Not this same nut." I shake my head.

"I've been patient long enough, but now it's interfering with my business." He moves around and sits on the edge of his desk in front of me.

"Are you saying I'm not doing my job?" I bristle and sit up.

"No. You are excellent at your job. The best in the city."

"And you already pay me like I am. I'm already paid more than anyone else in my line of work. It's not your fault that I have debt to take care of."

"It's not yours either, so don't get me started."

"Who peed in your Cheerios this morning? My mom and Addie's bills are my responsibility. Is it ideal? No. Is it fair? Probably not. Is it a fact of life? Yes."

"Well, starting today, your salary is increased to cover what you make at the bar. I won't have you working all hours of the night and serving people who may be potential clients."

"Since when do you care what people think?"

"I could give a fuck, but we are in the business of imaging, and you know as well as I do that labels are hard to shake. Perception is reality."

"No one is going to label you cheap because I work a second job."

"It's done. Call the bar and tell them or I will." He moves back into a place of authority behind his desk.

"I'm so sick of men this week." I shake my head in frustration.

"I'm your boss and you are my employee. This has nothing to do with the fact you are female and I am male. If Henry were fighting me on a second job, I would be having this conversation with him."

"It feels like money I didn't earn," I try to explain.

"Those are your issues, Emme. Not mine. If you didn't earn the salary I'm going to pay you, you wouldn't be getting it. Your life feels like it's unraveling because it is. You won't let me help you pay those bills, fine. But this is my business, and I will run it as I see fit." And because he's Jackson and can't stand the thought of my being upset, he softens the conversation with "We've already agreed you would take a paid leave of absence to get the mentor program operational. If you really want it to succeed, you can't continue at this pace."

He circles his desk one more time and pulls me into an all-encompassing hug. He's done being my boss. He's being my friend right now, and I burrow into him.

"You would move mountains for me. Don't you understand what it means to me that you won't let me do the same for you? I love you, Emme, but it's hurtful and you have to own that. You have to learn to rely on people."

"Now," I say, pulling away and repositioning the conversation.

"Guess that ends bonding time," Jackson laughs as he moves back to his chair.

Ignoring his jab, I continue, "I'm dropping John Michaels as a client. Henry will be his stylist from now on."

His demeanor shifts to match mine, and his eyes probe me. "What brought this about?"

"It's just time. Henry is ready to go solo on some accounts, and Michaels is not really a big enough client for me anymore. Add to it that I have the mentor program starting. It's the right step."

He studies me for a long time. "That sounds reasonable. Care to tell me the real reason now?"

"I just did."

"Emme."

"I have a few calls to make before my lunch meeting," I effectively end the conversation. He reluctantly nods as I close the door behind me. I release a long breath and lean against the door. I know Jackson well enough to realize that I didn't exactly make it out of there unscathed. Pushing off the door, I head to my office.

The next three hours fly by. I work on the outline of how to best position Blaine in the market. Henry, Joy, and I work on pulls and the items I want them to pick up. We have designers who send us their inventory to use on celebrities, but we also shop clothes ourselves. Over the last year, I have passed a lot of the shopping to them, but I still do my fair share. It helps keep my relationship strong with the stores. I also do most of the vintage shopping, which is something I enjoy.

Taxis to meetings are a work expense, and I'm thankful I don't have to do another subway ride in these heels. Since it is a causal Friday meeting, I am in a white fitted shift dress with elbow length lace sleeves. The dress shows off my Khloe Kardashian ass. If I don't stick to running, it'll make its way to Kim status. On her, I think it's a fabulous ass. On me, it would look ridiculous. My jewelry is minimal. I have my hair pulled into a long ponytail.

Marty, the doorman at the St. Regis, greets me by name, and informs me that Ms. Cameron is already seated in the King Cole Bar. Thanking him, I make my way through the opulent lobby that always manages to take my breath away.

Entering the mahogany-paneled bar, I see Colleen Cameron seated at a table for two. She is facing the Old King Cole mural that sits above the bar. With a silly grin on his face, Old King Cole sits in the middle of the mural upon a throne while jesters sit at his feet. The mural extends across the bar with other medieval looking characters whose purpose is to entertain the king. It contains a secret that you can usually get a bartender to divulge after you've ordered a few drinks.

As I come up to the table, Colleen stands and greets me with a kiss to each cheek. She is a picture of beauty and elegance. She is in her late 40's. Her brown hair is pulled into a chignon. She is wearing a demure black dress with a slight flare to the skirt, the perfect backdrop to her signature pearl earrings and necklace that she has worn every time I have seen her.

"Emme, darling. It's so good to see you. I took the liberty of ordering you a Bloody Mary. I hope you don't mind." Her look is mischievous as she takes her seat. "You can't come here without having at least one."

"Is that so?" I know her game. "You know I don't hold

liquor, Colleen."

"King Cole Bar created the Bloody Mary. You simply have to have one. I will make sure you are seen home safely if need be." Her smile coaxes me, causing me to giggle as I take my first sip. It is delicious.

"See?"

"I know. I don't know why I question you, Colleen. You have never led me astray."

And it's true. Colleen has been my client since the first week I started working for Jackson. She has watched me grow into this role and has directed her fair share of clients my way. We have a non-disclosure agreement in place, not that it's needed. How Colleen conducts her business is not for me to say.

Colleen Cameron is the high-class madam of New York City. She has a variety of girls who work for her and cost a minimum of ten-thousand dollars a night. More than once she has tried to get me to work for her. First as one of her girls, then as a partner. She wanted to use my rating method to match the right John to the right girl. While I don't judge Colleen or her girls, it's just not the scene for me.

"You look tired dear." She assesses my appearance.

"I had a late shift last night."

"If you came to work for me, you would only have to work a couple of nights a month, and still have more money than you would need."

"You're sweet, Colleen, but I doubt you would make the money with me that you do with your other girls," I muse as I look over the menu. "I'm not the hanger-size girl most of your men would expect."

"Nonsense. I'd make more. I see the way men respond to you, like you're a package they want to unwrap. Trust me, I know my business."

I blush and attempt to divert the conversation to a new topic. "What are you having?"

"The tuna. And the fact that you are blushing is exactly what would have them coming in droves. My sweet Southern girl."

"I think I'll have the filet," I state, ignoring her comment.

We sip our drinks and talk business for a while. I style the closet Colleen provides for her girls. Mostly elegant and dressy clothes, but it also runs the gamut with casual looks, swim wear, and of course, lingerie. Once a quarter, I revamp their wardrobes, and what I purge Colleen puts on a website and sells. The money goes to a charity of her choice. Since I have worked for her, she has donated over a million dollars.

Talking with Colleen is like talking to the fun Aunt in your family that likes to spoil you and tell you how amazing you are. I admire what a strong business woman she is, and she's taught me a great deal. She doesn't take shit from anyone.

"I'd like your advice." I take a long sip of my drink to build up my courage. Colleen motions for the waiter to bring us two more.

"What's going on?"

I straighten my posture and begin, "I have a client who got a little out of hand yesterday." I pause while the waiter delivers our food and another round of drinks.

"Actually," placing my napkin in my lap, I look up at her. "He attacked me. I don't know why I'm softening it".

"Is that what happened to your lip?" Her look is cold.

"Yes."

"Did he…"

"No," I answer before she finishes her question. "He didn't rape me," I say quietly and glance around to make sure I am not overheard, even though we are in the corner and there is no one sitting next to us. The tables are close together, and I don't want to broadcast our conversation. "He just scared me. But I think he might have if his security guy hadn't stepped in."

"And the lip?"

"I bit him. Hard. He backhanded me across the face."

"I see." She's reticent. "What did Jackson have to say?"

"I haven't told him. Or anyone for that matter. You're the only person I've shared this with."

"Why haven't you reported him?" She has stopped eating and is giving me her full attention.

"Honestly, I don't know. If it had been anyone else, I would have had them at the police station already making sure that at the very least a complaint was put on record." I look in her eyes and I know she can see the shame in mine. "I know it is a he said/she said deal, and he has power. I don't know that I want it to get out, and it will. I don't know if I want to go through all that for nothing to happen to him. But I don't want him to do it to someone else either." I'm so conflicted for reasons I don't even understand.

"Who is it?" She asks, but doesn't demand. When I don't respond, she says, "You keep my secrets, Emme. You have never once strayed from that. You know I will keep yours."

She's right. I know that I could tell Colleen anything and she would take it to her grave.

"John Michaels."

"I see," is all she says, but I catch a glimpse of the woman that runs an empire, and it's clear she has had to deal with more than one John Michaels in her time.

"What do you think is the right thing to do?"

She picks up her fork and starts eating again. I can see the cogs turning in her head. "What I think is the right thing and what right thing is for you are two different things. I'm friends with the Commissioner. I'll have him send one of his detectives over after we are done with lunch, and he'll make sure it stays out of the public reports."

"What is the right thing for you?" I ask curiously.

"Nothing for you to be concerned about. I would handle it just like I would if you were one of my girls."

"No, Colleen." That has my attention. "You can't."

"Eat your lunch darling. It's getting cold." And that's that. She has officially ended the topic.

Apprehensively, I give in and start eating again. I'm left imagining John Michael's balls as trinkets hanging on Colleen's keychain.

She's right. The right option for me is to file the report. It's the only way I could live with myself if he tried to hurt someone else.

We finish our meal. Colleen declines dessert, but orders tea.

"You have an amazing body. Why don't you eat dessert?" I ask taking another sip of my drink.

"I can't eat like you and look like this, Emme." Our conversation moves onto easier topics, and I show her the slideshow of looks that I have pulled for the closet update. Colleen only rejects three looks, but other than that we are on target.

"So Emme, how are you spending Labor day weekend?"

"I'll be in the Hamptons. I'm going up early to work on the grants."

"That's wonderful! It's all coming together. Tell me, did you take my advice and go with all male mentees?" I'm about to answer when Colleen excuses herself for a moment, stands, and takes a couple of steps behind me.

"Colleen." The voice is cool and all business. "It's lovely to see you."

I know that voice. How is it that now that our paths have crossed, they continue to merge in all areas of my life? I don't make a move to turn around. In all honesty, I hope he doesn't notice me and keeps on moving.

"Why don't you have a seat and join us?" Colleen suggests, clearly moving to an introduction. "Graham, I'd like you to meet Emme James."

I expect to see the same "Can you believe we ran into each other again?" look on his face, but I'm met with a look of disbelief that flares into anger.

"Cut the shit, Colleen. What are you doing?" Graham doesn't verbally acknowledge my existence. He's looking directly at Colleen, the disdain dripping from his words.

Colleen shows me once again why I admire her so greatly. She doesn't back down. She doesn't even bat an eyelash. If anything, I would say she's standing a good two inches taller than she was a minute ago.

"Obviously, Graham, you have an issue. I would be happy to discuss anything that concerns you, other than that you know my business is off limits to anyone," she answers with direct eye contact.

"Get your purse," he says, finally acknowledging me. "We're going."

I turn, pretending to look around me. "I'm sorry. Who are you speaking to? Because I know it isn't me." I fold my arms across my chest and cross my legs giving him my best defiant glare. *Who the fuck does he think he is?*

"Don't start with me, Emelia." His tone is ice cold. He turns back to Colleen. "Off limits. Do you understand?"

Unexpectedly, a slow, genuine smile spreads across Colleen's face. She looks from me to Graham. "I do now. When did this happen?" she directs her question to Graham.

His suit coat is unbuttoned and he has both hands in his pockets. "Off limits," he says, raising a finger to point in her face for emphasis.

Colleen looks at me with true enjoyment. I am so confused.

"Emme, I was going to have Hector see you home, but now that Graham is here, he'll make sure you get home safely. I greatly enjoyed our lunch. I'll call you and set up our next meeting." She pulls on my shoulders coaxing me into a standing position and kisses me on each cheek, smiling at my perplexed glare. I feel a hand around my elbow, and I am being guided out of the hotel into a waiting black SUV.

Graham hoists me into the back seat then practically sits on top of me when I don't make a move to shift over.

Fine! I'll go out the other door.

I slide across and reach for the handle.

"Don't even think about it," Graham barks. "Drive, Smith." He says to the man in the front seat. I can't even look at him I am so furious.

"Who the fuck do you think you are?"

"Watch your damn language. 6th and 42nd Smith."

"Seriously, where do you think we're going?"

"I'm taking you back to your office. I assume you have work to do." He pulls his cell out of his pocket and punches a button.

"Call Lieberman and tell him I have to reschedule. Give him my apologies for leaving the bar." He disconnects the call.

I cross my arms, fuming. My head feels like it's about to explode from the emotional pressure.

"It's less than 10 blocks. I am fine to walk it," I assert.

"In those heels? I doubt it. Add to it the number of Bloody Mary's you had."

"How do you know I had something to drink?"

"What were you doing with Colleen Cameron?" Graham asks.

My eyes catch the driver's. Did he say his name was Smith? I think I catch a glance of sympathy in his eyes. Leaning forward I place my hand on his shoulder. "Emme James. Nice to meet you." I smile at him.

He nods and I assume is about to answer when Graham punches a button and a privacy shade slides into place.

"Emelia," he says with authority.

"Graham." I mock his tone, with a smile of defiance on my face happy to fuel his frustration. I notice he is running his thumb across the tips of his fingers, like he's itching to do something, but holding himself back.

"I've told you before, when I ask you a question, I expect an answer. What were you doing with Colleen Cameron?"

"Not that it would be any of your business, but I'm not at liberty to say."

"Meaning?"

"You know for a bright man," I say, trailing off sarcastically. "I'm not at liberty to discuss my nature of business with Ms. Cameron." I say this slowly and deliberately, as if he's having difficulty understanding.

"So, it was business." Irritation rises in his voice again. "And when you said that you were only seeing Blaine Moore professionally, is that what you meant? Are you one of Colleen's girls?"

It takes me a full minute to understand that he is serious, that he is actually insinuating that I am a prostitute. No offense to Colleen's girls. I mean no judgement and I'm sure they are peachy in their own rights, but they do have sex for money.

"Do you sleep with men for money? It would make sense. You make $150k working for Jackson, yet you still work a second job. You have $478 in your bank account. You have one savings account that has had menial deposits in it for the last few years and you bring in about $50k with your second job. You have perfect credit, no debt, and you withdraw, in cash, 85% of every check you earn. You're funneling money somewhere, and if the one-fifty Jackson pays you isn't enough, I'm guessing the extra you make at the bar isn't doing it either. Supplementing by working for Colleen would make perfect sense. What are you involved in?"

If a feather fell out of the sky and landed on me, I would have tipped over. I am stupefied that he just rattled off my financial statistics like he was my accountant. How did he get all that information?

Smith has pulled up to my office building, and I catch a glimpse of Graham looking at my legs. In my haste to move across the seat, my dress has pulled up under me and is maybe an inch from showing my panties.

"You've got to be kidding me?" My disgruntled voice pulls his eyes up. His anger breaks and his face splits into a grin like a school boy caught with his hand in the cookie jar. This only fuels my hate-fire.

I open the door and exit the car. Pulling my badge from my purse, I scan myself through security and call an elevator. At least I know I am safe here. Unless Graham gets someone to sign him in, and I'm sure as hell not going to, he can't get back to the elevators. The elevator arrives and I step in taking a deep breath, trying to calm the fury I am feeling. Pushing the button for the twenty-first floor, I lean against the cool metal wall and close my eyes as the door closes.

I am so sick of this week.

I hear the doors being halted and open my eyes to find Graham stepping in the elevator.

"How the hell?"

"I own this building, Emelia." He holds up a key card.

I really need to Google this asshole.

I go to step off the elevator, but he pulls me back in as the doors close. I look straight ahead. Like I am traveling up the floors with a perfect stranger.

He pulls the stop button. "I asked you a question. I want the answer."

It takes me a second to register the sound echoing in the elevator. The hand print reddening on his face is the clue I need to realize I have slapped him. His eyes turn a midnight blue, and just like that, he has me backed into the corner, his mouth crushing mine. His tongue is hot and invasive, moving strongly against mine. This is not like our kiss last night. This is a possession. His shadow of a beard scratches my face.

My body responds, and I'm giving as good as I'm getting. My hands find their way to his hair and I tug on it, giving my tongue better access to his. A deep groan escapes him, and he moves his hands roughly and quickly over my body, like we're on the clock. He lifts my dress up to my hips, pushes my panties to the side, and plunges two fingers deep inside of me. My sex pulses around him.

"Fuck, you're soaked." He moves his fingers in and out of me, his thumb finding rhythm on my clit. My body senses the same urgency, the same three-minute clock, and I am coming around his fingers in a matter of minutes. My orgasm is shooting stars behind my closed eyelids. Graham lifts me up, and I wrap my legs around him. I feel his erection between my thighs and start moving against him. His kiss is more aggressive and demanding, and he's frustrated that he can't get to my breasts through the high neck on my dress. He lowers my feet back to the floor, making sure I have my balance before he spins me around and starts to unzip my dress.

"No." I almost look around to see who said it, but I know it was me. Graham's hands stop immediately.

"No," I confirm, shaking my head for extra emphasis, before my body overrides my ethics. I lean my forehead against the elevator wall and try to catch my breath. Graham is leaning against me, his front to my back. I feel his erection pushing into my ass, and his breathing is as erratic as mine. I push off the wall and Graham gives me the space I'm looking for. Hitting the stop button, I put the elevator back into motion. My eyes never leaving his. The elevator opens on the twenty-first floor, and I step out.

"You don't get to call me a whore and then fuck me." My eyes blaze with the contempt that I struggled to display before he brought me to orgasm. My words are like a verbal wall that stops Graham mid-step to exit the elevator. My eyes never leave his as the doors close behind me.

ch♥pter
six

manda buzzes me into the office, smiling brightly when she sees me. "Were you mauled in the elevator?" she asks and hands me a mirror. I look at her knowing expression before straightening my hair and smoothing my dress. "Here," she hands me the black box with the necklace. "The courier said Mr. Michaels refused the delivery and paid him double to bring it back."

"Then I hope you like pearls." I shove them back to her.

"No, Emme, I can't. These are yours."

"I don't want them. Keep them. Sell them. Whatever you want. Just don't give them to me."

"Oh my god, Emme. This is four months' rent. Thank you so much!" She can tell from the look on my face that I'm doing the math. "I'm one of the few people left who have a rent controlled apartment," she clarifies, almost apologetically.

She removes the pearls and places them around her neck. The lariat falls between her breasts.

"They're beautiful. You should think about keeping them." It's not their fault they were gifted by a jackass.

Entering the work room, I make my way to my office when I receive a text from Colleen asking me to meet her out front in twenty minutes.

Henry comes in and hands me a Diet Coke from my favorite deli on the corner. They have crushed ice and just the right amount of carbonation.

"I could bear your children for this." I draw a long sip.

"Did I see you getting out of a Bentley Bentayga?"

"If that's the black SUV I was just in, then yes."

"Those aren't even being offered to the public yet. Do we have a new client?"

"No. Someone just gave me a ride after lunch so I wouldn't have to walk in heels."

"What was it like?"

"The car? I didn't even notice."

"I want your life, Emme, where I ride in a Bentayga and don't notice," he teases and heads back to his desk. Grabbing my laptop and everything I am going to need next week, I say my good-byes to my team and make my way down to meet Colleen. Climbing into the back of yet another car, she greets me with the same smile she left me with.

"So, you and Graham Taylor. You should have led with that today."

"Honestly there isn't anything to tell. We meet on a flight earlier this week. His brother is my best friend's fiancé."

"Graham Taylor flying commercial?"

"Does that surprise you?"

"The man owns an aviation fleet, so yes, it does."

"Seriously? What does he do?"

"You mean you don't know?" I shake my head. "Graham Taylor is the multi-billionaire that started and owns Taylor Organization. He's probably one of the top fifteen richest people in the world."

"He's so young. He can't be more than what, thirty-three?

Thirty-five?"

"He's thirty, to be exact. He just presents older because he's so serious all the time." She turns a little more towards me, her eyes filled with mirth. "He thinks you're one of my girls."

"Yes, he made that very clear once we were in the car."

"And did you correct him?"

"No. As a matter of fact, I didn't. You know I don't discuss my clients, and if he wants to think the worst of me, then let him. No offense. You know what I mean."

"I do dear," she pats my hand. "Just be careful. I'd hate to see a sweet girl like you get lost in Graham Taylor. He expects a certain behavior out of the girls he dates—well, screws, anyway. He's not really one to date. To him a girl is an ornament to be seen with. He expects them to toe the line. Come to heel, so to speak. That's why you never see him photographed with a woman standing next to him. They're to always remain a step behind, and you never see him show or acknowledge affection in public. We're here," she announces. I didn't even realize we were moving.

While I am frustrated with Graham for trying to take control, what Colleen says doesn't totally match up with my experience. My first interaction with Graham was intense, yes, but it was also kind and unselfish. When I was scared, he took care of it. He held my hand. He accepted and returned my embrace. Granted, the encounter in the elevator just now was pure, unabated sexual attraction, but his kiss the other night was giving. Caring.

"Where are we?" I ask with furrowed brows getting out of the car. We're in front of a brownstone with a red door that has no markings or signage.

Climbing the stairs in front of me, Colleen answers, "This is a private club."

"Ms. Cameron. Ms. James." A man in a crisp butler's tux greets us and shows us through the door. "You're in the Huntington Room. Right this way." He leads us in.

The Club is rich in design. We walk past a smoking room with deep red leather chairs and Old English hunting pictures above the fireplace. Entering what they call the Huntington room, we are greeted by three men. The most imposing one I recognize as Commissioner Ralston.

"Teddy," Colleen greets the Commissioner with a kiss to each cheek. He's an older man with a large presence, friendly eyes and a bushy mustache, that I imagine tickles his granddaughter's face. "I didn't expect you to be here. Thank you for taking time out of your day."

"My pleasure, Colleen" He holds her hand is his. "I wish it was under better circumstances. You must be Ms. James." He releases Colleen's hand and takes mine. "Colleen has filled me in. Thank you for coming forward and making a complaint. You would be surprised how many young women never do." He nods towards the two men standing behind him. "These detectives are part of my personal detail. They will be taking your statement today. I understand you would like to keep this out of the papers?"

"Please. I realize there is not a lot you will be able to do in regards to what happened with me, but I want to make sure there is a paper trail, in case he tries it again with someone else. They'll have the ability to make a stronger case."

"I'd like to focus on your case, actually." His voice is deep and scratchy. "We can have him picked up and charged. The DA will likely drop the charges because of lack of evidence, but anyone willing to do a search will find the charge on file. Your name will be protected and cannot be released to the papers. We can also put a protective order in place."

"Thank you. This is very kind of you." I relax for the first time since yesterday. Colleen is just what I needed to put this into perspective and take charge of what I want the next steps to be.

"Just doing our jobs." His demeanor is commanding and comforting all at once, characteristics I suppose you need if you're in charge of policing the city. "This is Detective Lang and Vincent. They'll take your statement and we'll go from there."

The detectives direct me to the four club chairs that sit facing each other in front of a grand mahogany mantel. We take our seats and I recount my story, while they ask questions throughout. I notice Colleen and the Commissioner talking off to the side. I ruminate on what a striking couple they would make. I notice the Commissioner doesn't wear a wedding band.

Detective Lang makes his way to a beautiful silver tray and pours water into a glass. He places one of the stark white napkins in the glass and squeezes the excess water from the cloth. "Would you mind removing the makeup on your lip so I can take a picture, please?"

"Is that necessary?"

"I'm afraid so, ma'am. It will give us the evidence to substantiate your claim."

Nodding, I wipe the wet napkin across my mouth removing the cover up I applied this morning. The cut and slight bruising more evident. I turn my head to the right based on his directions, and he snaps a few photos.

"Now if you wouldn't mind showing us your arms." Lifting my sleeves to my shoulders, he takes a round of each arm from a few different angles, then thanks me for my cooperation. The detectives finalize their report, and we are joined

again by Colleen and the Commissioner. I thank them all
for their kindness. I know they have made this experience as
painless as possible, and I have only experienced a sliver of
what girls who are attacked must endure.

"If you have any problems, you let us know. I can put a
protective detail on you if you feel you need one."

"Taylor has his security team on her already," Colleen ap-
prises the Commissioner.

"Graham Taylor?"

Colleen nods her answer.

"Well, then. Smith will make sure you're taken care of.
You have nothing to fret about," he offers reassuringly, mis-
reading my look of confusion for worry.

They see us to the door, and Colleen and I exit to her
waiting car.

"Thank you so much, Colleen. Without you I know this
would have gone so differently. You took all the pain out of
the process."

"You're welcome, dear. Teddy is a good man."

I ask what I really want to know, "What did you mean
when you said Graham had his security team on it already?"

"He has security following you. I noticed his men when
he dragged you out of King Cole today. I assumed you knew."

"Why? Did you tell him about this?"

"Of course not. My guess is you have made quite an impression on him, and Graham is protective of those around
him. His family has constant security."

Really? I never noticed Adam having any security around
him. Actually, I wouldn't have known that Adam is affiliated
with the wealth Colleen described. I mean I knew the Taylor's
parents were rich; his mother is a highly acclaimed OB-GYN
and his dad is an attorney by trade. I do recall Adam saying

he and his dad worked for his brother. I just had no idea. They never mentioned it. Jules has never mentioned it.

"The Commissioner mentioned Smith. Who is that?"

"Smith Allen. He's Graham's driver and head of security. He oversees the security of the Taylor family." I think back to the man in the car today and wonder what he has seen and heard while working for Graham.

"Am I being watched now?" The thought is unsettling.

"I'm sure you are. That's why I scheduled the meeting at the club. I got the impression you haven't told anyone else about what happened with John Michaels, and I wanted to protect your privacy." She looks out the window as we ride in a comfortable silence. My mind is still reeling from today.

Her driver pulls up to my building. I give Colleen a hug that she accepts uncomfortably. I know people have certain views on how she makes her living, but I have nothing but admiration for the strong woman in front of me.

The meeting with the detectives took a little over an hour. I have a just enough time to change before I have to be at the bar for my last shift. On Fridays I try to be there at five when the Wall Street guys show up. Once they get a few drinks in them, they really start to show off with the tips.

I redo my sleek ponytail into a high ponytail that looks a little wild like it has been windblown. Applying extra concealer and my usual lip gloss, my face is ready to go. I put large gold hoops in my ears and grab three gold thin bands, placing them one on the index, middle, and ring fingers of my left hand.

Grabbing a hot dog on the corner before catching the subway downtown, I look at the people around me to see if I recognize any of them. Is Graham really having me watched? Why would he? If you thought someone had sex for money, why would you care what they do? If he's trying to frustrate me, he's succeeding.

Maybe I should stay with Jackson next week? As I consider it, I know I don't want to. I want to be with Jules, Adam, and his family. I have been looking forward to spending time with them since we planned this weeks ago. Plus, I promised Jules we would work on her designs. Graham is just going to have to deal. The house is more than big enough for us not to have to be in the same room as each other. I can pretend, if he can.

The bar is busy and the night flies by, and I'm thankful for the distraction. Heading down the stairs to the subway, I realize that I haven't thought about anything other than serving drinks all night. The banter with the brokers kept me occupied, and I had a successful night in tips. My legs in shorts with the heels always helps. I won't miss the time commitment, but I will miss the people. I've always enjoyed listening to the stories customers tell and in truth I will miss serving. It's been a steady job that helped me when I needed it most.

Back up to the street level, I run into Drew and Kyle. We head a couple of blocks over for a slice of pizza before making our way up to the apartment, so it's two-thirty in the morning when I finally change into the large t-shirt I wore to bed last night. I grab my pillow and blanket and crash on the couch, grateful I don't have to work tomorrow. With plans to sleep as late as possible, I grab my phone to change it to vibrate. I have one missed call and a text.

"917-555-1073: What the hell Emelia! Do not take the subway alone again after 10pm. I mean it!"

I know it's Graham. I save his number to my contacts and go to sleep without responding.

Waking to the sun on my face and the smell of bacon, I lay there for a while, hoping I might be able to go back to sleep but it's a lost cause. My eyes open to see Becca sitting at the counter, holding a cup of coffee. Matt and Drew are in the kitchen cooking. One of them closes the oven door with more force than necessary, garnering a sharp comment from Becca that they are going to wake me.

"Are you serious? Nothing wakes James," Drew educates her. "She can sleep through anything."

Matt turns facing Becca, putting pancakes on a waiting plate. "Except her nightmares. Ouch!" He puts his finger into his mouth, having gotten it a little too close to the hot pan he's holding.

"Nightmares? How often does she have nightmares?"

"Depends," Drew says putting the syrup on the table. "I have noticed they're more frequent after she's been to Memphis."

"You talk about me while I'm the room?" I sit up and stretch.

"Good morning, Sleeping Beauty. Would you rather us talk about you behind your back?" Drew adds butter to the table.

"Snow White," I correct him.

"Breakfast is ready," Matt announces. Russ and Kyle join us, and we all sit around the table and begin passing plates of food.

"Your work here," Becca looks at me taking a bite of bacon, "has been nothing short of miraculous. Matt and Drew have cooked breakfast and actually cleaned the kitchen as they went. Without being told." She bugs her eyes in disbelief and tips her mug to me.

Laughing, I tip my Diet Coke to her. "The foundation was always there, it just needed a little tweaking."

"You talk about us while we're in the room?" Drew mimics my earlier comment.

It's rare that we all sit down to a breakfast on a Saturday, and I take a minute to enjoy my roommates. Each one is special to me.

"By the way, Bec, Adam invited us to his family's house in the Hamptons next weekend if you want to go," Matt informs her.

"Are you going to be there?" she asks me.

"Yep, so is Jules. I'm going up tomorrow to get some work done before everyone gets there. Jules, Adam, and his family are getting there Tuesday. You should come. It would be great for us girls to have some time together."

She looks to Matt for his thoughts. "It's a week in the Hamptons at the Taylor house. Doesn't get much better than that," he points out.

"Cool, we're in. I need to do some shopping." Her excitement starting to bubble.

"I have to go to the office to get some clothes for the trip. Why don't you go with me and I'll pick out a few things for you? Save you from having to buy anything."

Becca claps her hands. "Designer clothes and a week in the Hamptons. God I miss New York."

"I'll go with you," Matt invites himself and kisses Becca. I know he misses her.

At the office, I take Matt and Becca to the workroom to go through the closet. I grab the items I need and several for Becca. Becca is a sample size, so it's no problem fitting her. She loves and approves my choices for her. I lock the doors behind me as Matt pushes the elevator call button, carrying the garment bag for us. Jackson steps off as we move to step on.

"Matt. Becca," he nods in their direction. "Hello, Beautiful." He hugs me.

"Hello Beautiful."

"Did you get my message?" He twirls his keys.

"No…" I start to pull my phone out of my purse.

"I cancelled your Jitney reservation," he says, referring to the shuttle from the city to the Hamptons. "Patrick and I are going up tomorrow so you can just ride with us. We'll be by around noon."

"Oh, thanks! I would much rather ride with you two. I'll make sure I'm ready."

Matt and Becca talk while Jackson and I tick through a few items. Wrapping up, we step into the elevator and I halt the elevator doors as they're closing.

"I've decided it's time for us to drop John Michaels all together."

Jackson's hand freezes as he's about to enter his key into the door. He turns to me.

"We'll talk later," I wink at him and let the doors close.

Back in the apartment, I give Becca some accessories I think she can use. This day of nothing has been just what I needed. I change out another load of laundry and grab a Diet Coke. Pulling the curtain to my alcove closed, I start to read some of the book I started last week. I'm only a page in when my cell rings. It's Jules.

"Hey, babe," I answer.

"I'm out running some errands. Want to meet me for ice cream in the village? Say, thirty minutes?"

I glance at my watch. It's one-thirty. I'll run now and read later. "Sure. Big Gay, right?"

"You know it. See you then." She hangs up.

I change into my running gear, throw on a ball cap, and make my way to the Big Gay Ice Cream in the West Village. The shop sits on the corner across from me as I wait for the light on Seventh to change. Their windows are painted with a large rainbow-colored soft serve ice cream cone on one side and a large glittery unicorn licking an ice cream cone on the other. There's usually a line that moves quickly.

I cross the street just as Jules is getting out of a cab. Perfect timing. A picture of Bea Arthur greets us as we enter. There are so many great choices, but I always get the same thing. The Salty Pimp. They start with soft-serve vanilla ice cream on a cone, dip it in chocolate, shake sea salt on it before the chocolate hardens, and use a syringe to inject dulce de leche into several places around the cone. It is hands down my favorite flavor.

Jules always tries something new, but inevitably ends up stealing a bite of my Pimp, much to my chagrin. I try not to share, but Jules knows I would give her all of it if she really wanted it. We talk effortlessly about nothing. It's not long before we finish our ice cream, and I buy a bottle of water for my run before we step outside for Jules to catch another cab.

"How many miles are you running today?" she asks waiting for a cab with its light on.

"I should be doing twelve, but I'm saving my long runs for the beach. I'm only doing eight today." I stick my arm up, catching a taxi for her. I open the back door giving her a kiss goodbye as she slides in.

"So that's it? You're not going to tell me about the flowers or about Graham?"

I realize that we spent this whole time chatting, and she

never once asked me two things she must be dying to know—a true testament to her respect for my need to reveal it all to her at my own pace. "This week. We'll have plenty of time to talk. I'm still in…I don't know…" I gesture like I can't think of the words I'm looking for. I finally settle on, "thinking mode."

"You've never been one to overthink things, Mags. It's another reason I love you. You're decisive. What you're in is denial mode."

I ignore her look, close the door to the cab, and watch as she disappears around the corner.

I grab my water and start up Broadway. I used to feel accomplished when I walk to the corner and back. But I was asked to participate in a group that runs the NYC Marathon for charity, and I could hardly turn that down. That and I was to the point that if my ass and hips got any bigger, I'd have to buy new clothes, which I can't afford.

Running used to make me feel selfish, like I should be doing something for someone else instead of taking time for myself. As I trained and started running longer distances, I've landed on a place where I don't apologize for running. Admittedly, some days are harder than others, but for the most part, it's a breakthrough for me, making myself a priority. After Mama died and I lost Addie, I was no one's priority. Even with the family units I have built here in the city, I'm still not any one person's exclusive priority. So, I am making me my own.

What I have found is that running gives me whatever I need that day. If I need time to think, then I do that. If I need time to just listen to music and forget about things, then I do that. If I need time to do prep work, then I do that. I have styled whole closets in a run. It's become more than just training for a marathon, it's become therapeutic.

My phone buzzes as I am running past Grand Central

Station.

Blaine: I'm near Madison Sq Park. Shake Shack has opened back up. Care to join me?

Me: Sure. meet ya there in 20? I'm sweaty and stink from running - grab a table downwind :)

Blaine: It's a date.

Me: It's food.

Blaine: You're *coming* aren't you? Alright then.

I make it to the park entrance and stop to stretch for a minute. I always think of my mom here. She loved the Flatiron building. Always said it was her favorite place when she lived here. She used to talk about reading in the park and watching people bring their dogs to the dog run. Now there are food and outdoor shopping kiosks, and Eataly is across the street. This area has expanded into a great place to eat. As great as all the food options are, Shake Shack still rules for me.

"Emme!" Blaine walks towards me. He's wearing jean cutoffs that hang loosely from his hips showing his sculpted v-shaped lower torso when he raises his arms to hug me. His Ray-Ban aviators hang from his Memphis Grizzlies t-shirt collar. I take a step back halting him.

"I'm nasty."

"I'm a sure thing, babe. You don't have to talk dirty to me." He pulls me into a hug.

"You." I try to stop the smile coming to my lips. "You need professional help. Love your t-shirt." I tug on the hem.

"I've had Memphis on the mind the last few days," he says with a shy smile. "I got this when JT and I were collaborating on a song. He had just become an owner. Came into the studio giving everyone t-shirts."

"JT, as in Justin Timberlake? I am so not in your league," I laugh.

"Actually, you have that all wrong. It's me who's not in your league." His eyes are sincere. He takes a breath as if to lighten the topic, his charm is disarming.

"I'm glad you could meet me. I was nearby and wanted a burger, but no one to eat it with. Then I thought of my good *friend* Emme and how much you like to eat."

He has me there.

We walk through the park towards the shack.

"I wish I had grabbed a t-shirt." I motion to the running bra/capri set I'm wearing.

"Do you run often?"

"As of recently, yes. I'm training for the marathon in November. Do you run?"

"Only if I'm being chased. I was surprised you weren't busy." He looks at me as we make our way forward in the lengthy line to the window. The trees are providing a nice shade. It's a beautiful day.

"I actually had an entire day where I had nothing to do. I could just be where I wanted to be. It's been wonderful."

The girl in the window asks for our order. "Ladies first," he smirks and gestures me forward. I roll my eyes.

"I'd like the Smoke Shack burger with crinkle fries and a vanilla milkshake."

"Make that two," he says, "and one t-shirt." He hands her money and takes the pager and t-shirt she hands him.

"You didn't have to do that, but thank you. I love t-shirts." I pull it on and re-tighten my ball cap and ponytail.

He shrugs. "My manners win out over my wanting to watch you eat in that outfit." His look is sexy and inviting.

"What's your story? Don't you have a groupie you can sex

with?"

"Are you a groupie? You've said you like music."

"I'm a fan. There's a difference."

"Are you seeing someone?"

His question has me pausing. I'm not technically seeing anyone, but even as I think it, I know that I wish I was. What is that and where is it coming from? A week ago I would have been all over Blaine. On paper he's perfect for me: funny, loves music, easy going, uncomplicated. Not to mention sexy as hell. I mean, I'm just a regular girl from Memphis. The fact that I am sitting across from one of the hottest musicians in the industry is not lost on me.

But a lot can change in a week.

"It's complicated." I finally land on a response.

He nods and reluctantly moves on to casual dinner conversation.

His niece is the first topic of conversation, and it's obvious he adores her. We talk about Memphis and the places he got to see while he was there performing, the music that comes out of the city. We talk about my work and his next album. I tell him about the mentor program I want to start. It's easy, comfortable. Deep down inside, though, I know its only friendship. I don't get the same feeling in my stomach as I do just thinking about Graham.

We make our way to the entrance.

"Thanks for dinner. It was perfect." I lean into hug him, but instead he plants a panty-dropping, feel-it-in-your-sex kiss on me. It takes me a minute to realize that I'm kissing him back, and another minute to stop it.

"I'm sorry, Blaine. I shouldn't have done that. I don't want to lead you on. I don't want to make you think there's something here. I'm in the middle of something complicated with someone else," I tell him. His arms are still around me and his hand is resting on the curve of my ass.

"I don't mind waiting."

"No, that wouldn't be fair to you. Plus, you're my client. It's just bad timing for us." I finally push off him. "I'd like us to just be friends?"

"Just friends?" he echoes, as if he's testing the thought. I nod my head in response.

"Alright, friend." He puts his arm around my shoulder, and I loop mine around his waist. "I'll walk you home. That's what 'friends' do."

ch♥pter
seven

No matter what is scheduled for the day, Sundays always make me miss my family.

We had a very bourgeois, godly grandmother who expected us to go to church as a family. She was a hard-working, no-nonsense, Bible-Belt woman. Grandmother could drive a tractor, milk a cow, and then show up to have tea with the ladies at the local tea room in a hat crowned with flowers and feathers.

From as early as I can remember, we spent Saturday nights at their farm. We'd wake up on Sunday to a large family breakfast, chores that we were expected to do, church, then a big lunch of at least one fried dish and all of it from the garden. After, we would sing and play music. Sometimes I would play the cello, but mostly on Sundays, Grandmother liked the piano. Hymns as a rule, with a few old soulful songs mixed in.

My grandfather would sit on the bench with me and teach me new cords. He would tell me stories about courting my grandmother, how she made him work for her heart. "She didn't give it easily," he'd say. Then he'd slide off the piano bench and make her dance with him. My grandmother would blush and laugh about how her wiggle has turned into a jiggle, and make him crazy until he'd finally stop and start dancing with my mom. He was a wonderful grandfather, but I could see by the way my mom adored him that he was also an amazing father. Always on her side, always in her court. I would watch them and wonder what it would be like to have that. I never begrudged her relationship with her father. I was always happy for her. I felt like the one break Mama got in life was to be born to amazing parents.

My mom is who inspired my move to New York. She came to the city after she graduated college in Tennessee. Working in a bookstore, she met and fell in love with my father. He died shortly after. She later found out she was pregnant and moved back home. She always talked about him with only love, but there was a sadness to her eyes. I don't know that she was ever whole again after that.

I wanted more information. I'd ask her questions about him, what he was like, what his favorite color was, his favorite music—anything that popped into my head. But all she would tell me was that his name was Harry, and eventually I tired of asking the same questions to never get an answer. She always told me that I reminded her of him, that our spirits were the same.

That must have been why my step-father, Tony, hated me. He was a controlling, emotionally abusive fucker who made our lives hell until he finally left us when mama was diagnosed with cancer. Real gem, that one.

"What time are you leaving?" Becca's voice pulls me from my thoughts. I've been staring absently at the pictures of my family.

"Noon. I'm almost done packing." I should have finished last night, but I had finally decided to use the iPod Graham sent me. It took me the rest of the night to get my music organized and loaded after I finally admitted to myself that I truly loved the thoughtfulness behind the gift.

"I'm so excited! I've never spent a week in the Hamptons. We don't arrive until Tuesday, but I'm already packed." Becca points to her bags in the hall.

"I can't wait for you to be there." I return her excitement as I pack my grandfather's cardigan, when my phone dings. I have a text from Amanda that includes only a link.

It takes a minute to load. When it does, it leads to a web page that houses celebrity gossip, and there's a group of pictures of me and Blaine from yesterday in the park. Us hugging, him giving me the t-shirt, us eating and laughing, and then three different ones of us kissing at the park entrance. All with his hand visibly cupping my ass. At the time I knew it was there, but I didn't realize how low his hand had gotten. Addie always said my ass was like a shelf; it's just a natural resting place. This is going to be a thing. I already know it. Kill me. Kill me now.

I almost don't answer my phone when it rings a few minutes later, but it's Jules and I know she won't stop calling until I answer.

"Yes?" My greeting is short.

"Good morning to you, too, sunshine," she says with fake cheer. "Do you have time to come here before you leave today? I'm stuck on the outfit I want you to wear to casino night, and I need you to try it on." She clearly has not heard the latest celebrity gossip.

I check my watch. "Um, sure. I can do that. I'll just have Jackson pick me up there. Be there around eleven?"

"Perfect. Grab some donuts on your way." She makes a little begging sound, and I hear Adam laughing in the background.

I hang up with Jules and call Jackson. He's going to swing by, grab my bags, then pick me up in Tribeca.

I take a few minutes to spread my work things out on the table. I want to make sure I have everything I need since I'll be working from the Hamptons for the next several days. I load my laptop and files into a bag and throw in my camera. I'm distracted when the guys come in from their shift at the hospital. As always it's a whirlwind of conversation. I go over the food I precooked for them with strict instructions they aren't to eat junk the whole time I'm gone.

Colleen and I meet at Square Diner in Tribeca for breakfast to finalize a few items for her girls at Casino Night in the Hamptons. It's a causal meeting and I have no problems fitting in with my sundress and flip flops.

"So, how are you?" I ask Colleen who is taking a seat in her booth. Even on a Sunday, she is polished in white fitted jeans and a navy blue tank. She really is beautiful.

"I'm well, thank you. How are you?"

"Out of breath," I say on an exhale having had to jog most of the way to make it on time.

"Is that because of Blaine Moore? I saw you kissing in the paper," she teases me.

"You saw that?"

"I see everything."

"No. I know it doesn't look like it in that picture, but we're just friends."

"Trust me, I know. I saw how you looked at Graham. Although, I won't lie and say I wouldn't like to be a fly on the wall when Graham sees the picture."

"I doubt he will even see it." I look over the menu to see what I want to order.

"Like me, Graham sees everything."

"Not everything. He still thinks I work for you."

"And why is that?"

"Because I haven't told him otherwise. He's just so…"

"Dominating, sure of himself, bulldozing…"

"Yes, yes, and yes. He jumped to a conclusion based on nothing. Also, he has all this information on me, and he thinks he knows things when he doesn't."

"Graham is a business man who doesn't take no for an answer, Emme. He's used to getting his way. He's also very protective of his inner circle, which consists almost entirely of his family. So, you aren't telling him that you don't work for me, why? You think it gives you the upper hand?"

"I guess I want him to figure it out on his own. He can research all this information, but he doesn't sit me down and ask for it. He just demands it and then jumps to conclusions."

"Emme. You have been on your own for a long time. Some of this is Graham being Graham, but some of this is understanding what it is like to trust someone to take care of you. You'll know when it's the right time to set him straight. I think this could be a good thing for you. Trust your gut and trust Graham. Of course, one way to solve this would be to actually come work for me." She smiles into her orange juice.

"I love you, Colleen." I answer her mischief with a laugh.

"That's sweet, dear. Order your breakfast."

It's starting to sprinkle and I'm running behind, so I grab a cab to Jules's place. I thought breakfast with Colleen would settle my thoughts some. She was supposed to be a totally unbiased opinion. It befuddles me that she basically advocated for Graham.

I'm so caught up with overthinking all of this that I totally bail on bringing donuts, which leads to a very disgruntled-looking Jules in front of me now.

"Are you feeling okay?" She touches my forehead. "I have never known you to forget donuts."

"I wanted to have breakfast with Colleen before I left, and I was running late," I whine.

"Okay." She easily lets me off the hook. "I have the pants for you to try on. I want to see how they fit across your honey pot. Make sure I have all the lace in the right place."

Laughing at her words for my lady parts, I run my hands over the dress form in her work room. Jules and Adam live in an industrial loft in Tribeca that is connected to a large open space that Jules has turned into her design studio. It has great natural light and views of all the cool architecture people love about this area.

"Jules." I turn to look at her. My proud smile mimicking hers. "It's amazing. When did you design this? I thought you were working on a dress you wanted me to wear?"

"Well," she says as she pulls the pins out to take the pants off the dress form, "that was before you inspired me last week."

"I inspired you?"

"Yep. You did. I have seen more sides of you this week than I can remember. You've been in the papers twice, one of those times involved in a kiss that made women everywhere apply the lip gloss."

"You are so crass," I scold. "Where do you come up with these terms?"

"I'm in the know," she shrugs. "Now, try these on." She

hands me the pants.

I drape my sundress over her couch and pull on the pants, careful to make sure I don't stick myself with a pin. Jules walks around me and makes some adjustments. "Squat for me," she directs, and I do.

I stand back up, and she runs her hand over my backside placing a couple of pins under the bottom curve. "As I was saying," she says, removing a pin from between her teeth, "I've never seen you so affected by a man, like I have this week." She pauses looking me in the eye. Circling me again, she continues. "It inspired me to make you look as hot as you can for Casino Night. There will be lots of press. Now that you are being touted as Blaine's 'it girl', someone is bound to ask you who you are wearing, and I don't want it to be because of a dress that anyone could have made. I want it to be something that will have people talking the next day."

"Would you mind taking off your underwear and then putting the pants back on?"

Not sure if I'm confused by the actual question itself or the way she so nonchalantly asked it. "Are you serious? How is that me?"

"A week ago, it wasn't. Today, it is." She looks at me like I'm slow catching up. "You're different. Now trust me." She removes the pin that's holding the pants closed.

I slide the pants off, remove my underwear and slide them back on. She walks around me, marking a few places with a white fabric pencil.

"This is perfect. Just the way you should wear them that night." She guides me to the mirror. I'm standing there in my bra and the pants she has sewn for me. I have to give it to her. They are amazing. The base fabric is sheer with lace and beading placed strategically to cover all my girl bits.

"Jules. These are stunning! I'm not sure I'm the right person for them, though. They're very daring. Why don't you wear them?"

"Because I don't have your silhouette. That's what makes the pants." She turns me to the side. "Most people don't have the pronation here that you do." She points to the bottom curve of my behind. "Because yours is so pronounced, it makes the pants sexier than they would be on the average person. These are not made for 'hanger' girls as you call them. They're made for a thick girl like you."

"But they also need someone who has the attitude to pull this look off."

"That's totally you, Mags. Trust me." She exits for a minute. I turn from one side to the other. Maybe she's right. I would see these on a runway and wish I could wear them. They are hot without being vulgar. Tastefully sheer.

"Look, babe." Jules is back in the studio with Adam trailing behind her.

"Hey, Mags." Adam lifts his chin to me. "Nice bra."

I roll my eyes at him. "What do you think?" I ask him as I turn around. He has his hands in his front jean pockets and studies my look. He's used to seeing me half-dressed trying on clothes for Jules.

"Put these on." Jules kneels in front of me, tapping my foot. "Heels are going to lift your behind. I need to adjust for that." I am standing four inches taller now. Jules continues, "I think they would look better as a pencil tuxedo-cut pant. The top will be a sheer…t-shirt, if you will, with beading around the neck and wrist, and lace and beading that crosses over your breast and back down towards your stomach."

"Damn. Smoking hot! No one will be looking at anyone else. Good job, babe." He kisses Jules with a look of pride—

one that says even with an almost naked woman in the room she is the only one he could ever want.

"Thanks, sweetheart." Jules smiles back at him, giving me one more look over.

"I think a little more coverage here would be good," Adam points and Jules marks. They move around me. "Make sure you visit the salon that day."

Oh my God. It takes a lot for me to blush, but that did it. He throws his head back and laughs, and for the first time I see a resemblance between him and Graham.

I kick the shoes off as Adam goes back to whatever he was doing. Jules closes the door giving us some privacy.

"They'll be tasteful," Jules promises as I hand her the pants. I slide on my underwear and step back into my dress.

"I know they will be. This really is some of your best work. I'm excited to showcase it for you. You deserve the credit, Jules."

"You were my inspiration."

"There's nothing going on between Blaine and me. It was a kiss that I should have never let happen. I kissed him back 'cause he's a good kisser. Not because it meant anything."

"I'm not talking about Blaine."

She is waiting for me to be the first one to say it. I'm saved by a knock at the door.

ch♥pter
eight

Jackson hands me the keys to his Range Rover.

Jackson and Patrick had interrupted before Jules could coerce the Graham story out of me. Luckily, she was so distracted by Jackson's praise for her design that I didn't have to think of a way to describe what I am feeling when I'm not sure I even know. Finally ready to leave this week behind, I am relieved to be hitting the road with another one of my favorite couples.

"I know you have control issues, plus I have work I want to finish on the way so I won't have to do it when we get there. Patrick wants to read, so here. You drive."

"Cool!" I bounce into the driver seat and Jackson closes my door and climbs into the back. In the cup holder is a Diet Coke.

"You, sir, are my ace buddy."

I adjust the mirror and seat and we're off. In no time we are across the Brooklyn Bridge and headed to 495. Depending on traffic the drive can take anywhere from two-and-a-half to three hours. Patrick and I are singing about how we went from San Berdoo to Kalamazoo just to get away from you, courtesy of the Black Keys. Jackson is sound asleep in the back seat. So much for accomplishing work.

An hour into the drive, Patrick pulls out a magazine and turns down the music.

"What are you reading?" I glance at the cover.

"Cosmo."

It sounds funny even coming from Patrick.

"See," he points to an article about how to give the best blow job. "I want to make sure I'm always in the know on the latest techniques," he says like he's preparing for a business meeting. "I'll read aloud, so you will be too. After the pic in the park, I would say you might have an opportunity to try a few new ways to 'satisfy your man'" he teases, using air quotes.

"I told you. They aren't seeing each other," Jackson interjects from the backseat, changing positions but never opening his eyes.

"So, just sex then?" Patrick looks at me like a kid in a candy shop.

"Like you need advice." I change the subject. "You've got more experience than any woman writing that article. They would be smart to do an article that is from a gay man's point of view telling straight women how to give the best blow job."

"What a great idea. I'll have to pitch that idea to them."

After reading the entire article to us out load, he announces, "Hell. I will definitely have to call them. That article was lacking. It didn't mention anything new and it doesn't teach women what they really need to know." Patrick spends the next fifteen minutes going over what he thinks should be in the article.

The rest of the drive is easy. Spending time with Jackson and Patrick is always fun. They're so easy going and they really have it together. They love each other. All the other bullshit is just that. Bullshit. They're solid.

"I'm about twenty minutes out of your way. Want me to Uber it to the Taylor's?"

"Of course not," Jackson says, suddenly awake. "We'll drop you."

"I don't mind," I say looking at him in the rearview. His look tells me I might as well drop it.

Patrick and I dream about the amazing houses we start to pass. These are the ones that you can see. There are so many that are obstructed by hedges and gates, leaving the house to your imagination. I can't comprehend the need for a twenty-thousand square-foot house. Who would want to live in something that big? I would love a cozy one bedroom with a big porch. That would be the perfect size for me.

The Taylor's house is smaller compared to some we are passing, but no less incredible. It has seven bedrooms and nine baths. It's huge by my standards. By Hampton's standards, it could be considered modest. The last time I was here, Mrs. Taylor, Ruth, told me they own the largest private beach front in East Hampton. The property is extensive. Her great-grandfather bought it before East Hampton exploded with high-end real estate.

I pull up to the gate, where I'm greeted by a security guard. He gives me entrance, and I wind my way up the path to the house, about three miles from the gate.

The house itself is what you would expect to see in an East Coast beach house. With cedar shingles, large windows, and a lot of beautiful molding. It's grand but not pretentious. It feels like home.

I park in the circular drive. The air here is much cooler than it was in New York. It feels like it might rain.

"You guys want to come in?"

"Thanks, but I think we'll head out and get some groceries on our way. You going to be okay here by yourself?" Jackson hands me my computer bag and camera but carries my suitcase up the six cobble steps, leaving it inside the large door.

"I'll be just fine," I assure him with a round of hugs and kisses before they head out. "Thanks for the ride."

I enter the house and set my items on the round table next to an expansive staircase in the front foyer. The first thing I notice is the view. This house was built with the ocean in mind.

I stand in the living room and take it all in. The entire back of the house is made up of two-story floor-to-ceiling windows and doors with a large expansive deck off the main level. To the left is a large kitchen and a dining room that seats twenty. To the right is the Taylor's master wing. There is a basement area below that is only visible from the beach. You can access the pool on that level. There are two bedrooms down there and a game room.

Making my way to the kitchen, I see a note from Rosa, the Taylor's housekeeper. She has left a stocked kitchen for me. Opening the refrigerator, I see that she means business. It's like a farmer's market in here: a bounty of fruits and vegetables—plenty of things to choose from. Seeing all the beautiful colors makes me hungry.

I grab my suitcase and climb the stairs. From the upstairs landing, there is a wing on the left that has two rooms and an office, and a wing on the right that has two rooms and a library. The wings are offset to each side so as to not disrupt the large bay of windows rising from the family room below. I take a left and head to the room I stayed in the last time I was here. Like the rest of the house, it's impeccably decorated. The highest level of comfort. I can't keep the smile away at the blissful thought that I have a whole room to myself. Just like downstairs, it has a full wall of windows and a door to a private balcony accessible only by the three rooms on this side of the house.

I have had dreams about being in this bed again. It's like being wrapped in a cloud. I slide off my dress and climb into the silky cotton sheets. The sky is turning gray from a storm moving in. Pulling the covers up to my neck, it's not long before I drift into a peaceful sleep.

Thunder wakes me to a dark night. The clock on the night-stand reads seven-thirty. I've slept two hours. There's usually a little sun left at this time of day, but I guess the darkness rolled in early with the storm.

Climbing out of bed, I pull the suitcase into the large walk-in closet and open it to unpack. Nothing looks familiar. I dig through it and realize these are all Becca's clothes. Jackson must have seen it in the hallway and grabbed it instead of mine. Great. There is no way her clothes are going to fit me. Not to mention she's a good three inches shorter than me. I text her to let her know about the mix up and to make sure they please bring my suitcase with them.

There's no way I am going through Ruth's closet, and I know their sister Lucy's clothes will not fit me. Jules doesn't have any clothes here, either.

I try the door to the other room on my end. I'm guessing it's Graham's since no one was staying in it last time I was here. I locate the closet to grab a few things to get me through until Tuesday when my clothes arrive. He doesn't picture me as someone who shares, but he can get over it. He's had his tongue down my throat and thinks I'm a whore. He can lend me some sweats.

Not surprisingly, his closet is pristine and organized. He even keeps suits here. I shuffle to the causal side and grab a couple of white t-shirts and a pair of jeans with a rip in the knee. I pull out an oversized sweater for cool nights on the beach. I look around at my other options and grab two white button-up Oxford shirts and a pair of slippers. This should do me. Something to bum around in, and something warm to go to the market in.

Back in my room, I put away my make-do wardrobe, slip off my bra, and put on the white Oxford. I roll up the sleeves to a manageable level, pulling the collar to my nose to inhale his scent. Combing my fingers through my hair, I slide my feet into the slippers and make my way downstairs. I open the door off the kitchen that leads onto the deck, but it's gotten cooler since I arrived and I end up closing it, opting to eat inside. I am in love with this house and looking forward to a few days to myself.

It takes me a minute to figure out how to use the sound system in the kitchen. Once I have some music to cook to, I turn it up and shop the fridge.

Rosa has left a jar of homemade peach salsa, which inspires my fish tacos with fresh guacamole and salsa. This kitchen is a dream to cook in, and Rosa has anticipated anything someone might need or want. The only thing I can't find are soft tortillas for the tacos. I know she has to have some in here. I search the cabinets while Stevie Wonder sings to me that I shouldn't worry about a thing. I assure him I'm not worried, I just need some damn tortillas.

It occurs to me that some people keep them in the fridge. Sure enough, on the back of the bottom shelf is a bag of what looks to be homemade soft tortillas. I'm shifting everything around to reach them when I hear, "Ahem…"

I freeze. I'm waist deep in an oversized fridge, and my ass, sporting a pair of black lace boy-shorts underwear cut high across each cheek, is in the air. I grab the tortillas, climb out of the fridge, and peek around the door. Graham is propped up against the door frame to the kitchen with his arms folded across his chest and one ankle crossed over the other. He's wearing a Yankees t-shirt and a pair of sweats that drape off his hips in the sexiest way.

"You're in my kitchen."

"Actually I'm in your parent's kitchen," I retort. "When did you get here?" I feign nonchalance, not wanting to give him the upper hand.

"I came up two days ago. When did you get here?"

"A few hours ago. Adam didn't tell me you were going to be here. Did he tell you I was coming early?" *I'm going to kill him. He knew Graham was here already.*

"No, he didn't." He seems irritated with his brother.

"Hungry?" I opt for polite conversation to distract from the fact my ass was in the air. Plus, we have to be in the same house this week, we might as well figure out how to have a civil conversation.

"I am. What are you making?"

"Fish tacos with chips, salsa, and I just made guacamole," I say dipping a chip into it and taking a bite. He walks towards me. He's so close that I have to look up to see him. He swipes his thumb across the corner of my mouth, removing the remnants of guacamole. He puts his thumb in his mouth and sucks the dip off it, never taking his eyes off mine.

"Sounds delicious." He takes a step around me and gets two glasses out of the cabinet.

What the hell was I thinking? There's no way I'll make it here with him. The way he said those two words alone about got me off. *Lock it down, James.*

I concentrate on my breathing and begin the prep work for the fish. I realize we are working in a comfortable silence. Me cooking and snacking, Graham setting the table and snacking.

He starts chopping the cilantro I set out, then moves to cutting up the limes and lemons. I finish the sauce just as the fish is ready.

Graham hands me a platter and I quickly assemble six fish tacos. Bringing the platter to the rectangular eat in kitchen table, I sit at one of the spots Graham has readied. He picks up my Diet Coke and replaces it with a glass of Dos Equis, then takes his seat across from me. We haven't said a word since "sounds delicious".

He takes a drink of his beer. "You have beautiful hair. I've never seen you with it down before." Then as he continues to assess me, he cocks his head to the side and says, "Are you wearing my shirt?"

"Yep." I mean there's nothing else I can say. Clearly I am.

"Jackson accidentally grabbed Becca's suitcase, so my clothes won't arrive until Tuesday. Seeing as how my ass is bigger than hers I didn't have anything to wear." I bite into a taco, making a light moaning sound. Rosa's homemade tortillas are so good--I'm going be doing a lot of running this week. He watches me eat before taking a bite of his taco.

"So, why is it your closest friends have never heard you cuss before, but every time we're together you have no hesitation in using explicit language?"

There's no way I'm going to tell him it's because I don't care if he sees the real me. I want to fuck him and only him. I believe that if you're going to get to that level with someone, it only works if they know the real you.

"I guess you pull it out in me," I shrug and take a sip of my beer, committing to nothing. He looks at me for a long minute, trying to turn another puzzle piece to see if he can get it to fit.

We eat the rest of our meal without another word spoken. Just looking at each other like two stubborn goats about to ram each other. I finish the last of my tacos and stand to clear my plate.

"Finished?" I break the silence reaching for his plate. He nods his answer and I carry our plates to the sink. He stands and helps me clear the table.

"Wash or dry?" I ask him from the sink holding a cloth for each.

"I'll dry," he says taking the towel from my hand. A few minutes later, the kitchen is clean.

"Well," I look him directly in the eye. "I have some work to do. Thanks for the dinner company." I grab a Diet Coke out of the fridge and make my way out of the kitchen.

"I think it's customary to ask permission before you take someone's things. I don't take kindly to people taking what belongs to me." His eyes are dark blue again. He has one hand on the kitchen island, leaning against it with his other hand in his pocket. What is it about a man with his hand in his pocket that drives me wild?

"I've met your mother. I know she taught you to play well with others and share," I challenge back, like I understand this game, when I really don't.

He pushes off the island, moving until he is in front of me again. I lean my head back and my eyes land on his Adam's apple. I wonder what it would taste like to take a bite of it. My nipples harden and my breath catches as I move my eyes up to his. His lips are formed into a tight line.

"This isn't a sandbox and I am not four. Now, are you going to ask permission, or am I going to have to take back what rightfully belongs to me?" He takes a step closer, causing my nipples to brush against his chest. Though he is wearing the same clothes, his entire look has changed from mellow to maestro. I imagine this is the look he gets in acquisitions right before he goes in for the kill. He's dominating. He knows it. I know it. This is CEO Graham. On a level I don't want to explore, it calls to me and has me wet between my legs.

"I expect an answer," he prompts. When I still don't answer, his tone grows more demanding. "Emelia."

"May I..." I pause.

"Good girl," he says, his eyes softening in victory.

"...get you to hold this?" I ask in my sweetest southern voice as I place my Diet Coke in his hand. Then without taking my eyes off his. I slowly unbutton his shirt and slide it off my shoulders dropping it to the ground, leaving it where it falls. His eyes slowly leave mine and electrify when they land on my breasts. My nipples harden immediately in response. I take back my drink, turn, and walk back upstairs. Two can play this game, asshole. Mentally, I put a tick mark in the win column for me, grinning because I already have another one of his shirts in my room.

Buttoning the other shirt, I'm not sure if I'm surprised or disappointed that he didn't follow me. I know I have just poked the hornet's nest.

Already tired of this game, I set my laptop on my desk and grab my folders. I have a lot of work to do in the next couple of days, which is why I came up early. Snagging glasses out of my purse, I put on some music and get started. It's dark out, but the lightning from the approaching storm highlights the balcony outside the windows. I can hear the ocean from here. Between that, Van Morrison and Mumford and Sons, I relax and start plowing through the grant. I'm just about to submit it when the power kicks out. It's pitch back. Unsettling. I'm feeling around for my phone when a familiar feeling hits me. He's here.

"The generator will kick on in just a minute." His voice is coming from the vicinity of the bedroom door.

"Thank you," I say, grateful. I don't love the dark.

As predicted, a minute later the generator kicks on. It takes a second for my eyes to adjust to the light

"Oh, no. Whew. Okay, thank goodness." I go from frustration to elation aloud. "I thought I had lost all the work I just did," I follow with an explanation. Taking my glasses off while standing to stretch, I catch the approbation in his eyes when he sees I am wearing another of his shirts. A smile that he doesn't try to hide shows his approval, and I flower a little under his respect.

Returning his smile with my best and brightest, he laughs and shakes his head conceding I won that round. "Want a snack?" I ask him making my way to the door.

"You're hungry? Again?"

"I'm always hungry. I saw some apple pie in the fridge earlier. I'll cut you a slice."

We make our way back to the kitchen. I grab the pie dish and cut two large slices. While they are heating I grab the heavy cream, powdered sugar, and vanilla to whip up some homemade whipped cream. I spoon a large dollop of cream on both slices, sprinkle with cinnamon, and done. We sit on stools at the kitchen island and dig in.

"Mmm." I close my eyes and take another bite. I lean

across the island and grab another spoonful of whipped cream. I hold one up in offering to Graham but he just shakes his head.

"Watching you eat is one of the sexiest things I've ever seen. The sounds you make and the enjoyment that shows on your face."

"I've always figured you for a 'hanger girl' kind of guy," I probe, running the back of my spoon across my tongue.

"Hanger girl?"

"You know the girls that look like they could model. They're a size zero, *maybe* a two. Everything hangs perfect on them, they never have to try it on beforehand. Hanger girl," I shrug. His silence tells me I am spot on.

"So, what are you working on?" he asks.

"A corporate mentor program." I finish the pie and snack on the rest of the cream in the mixing bowl.

"Tell me about it."

"I want to start a mentor program for graduates who are smart, but high risk. Either they don't go to college or drop out of college—because of the environment they come from, or in many cases, because they can't afford higher education."

"How would it work?"

"Well," I take a breath, "I have an interview process that I do when I image a client. I'll take that same process and shift the questions to match the right candidate to the right corporation. That corporation would commit to mentoring the young man for one year. At the end of that year, they could choose to hire him and pay his way through college while he continues to work, or release him. I'm betting we'll have a 100% retention rate at the end of the year."

"And you're predicting that based on what?"

"My matching abilities. I'm very good at what I do," I say

without arrogance.

"The grants are for…?"

"The corporation will be expected to pay them five-hundred dollars a week, but I'm working on several grants that will cover everything from the mentee's room and board to a wardrobe suitable for the office, and any supplies they might need."

"What does the corporation get out of it?"

"Well for a start, publicity for participating. They would also have loyal, dedicated hard-working employees they can train from the ground up with little to no expense to the company. These guys are hungry for opportunity. Of all the interns they hire, my guys will excel to number one. No question," I say unequivocally. "Most of all the companies will know they are doing some good."

"Only guys?"

"For now."

"Why?"

"Because I don't trust executives to keep their dicks in their pants." My bluntness seems to throw him off a little. He pauses for a beat.

"How are you going to get companies to participate?"

"Actually, your brother is helping me. Adam's matching me with CEO's he thinks would be interested in the program. The rest is on me to convince them. Between his connections and mine, I should be able to convince six companies to take the risk."

"What companies?"

I list off the companies Adam has suggested.

"Taylor Organization is the parent company of two of those. I'll have to ask him who he planned on you meeting with."

"I had a meeting with Richard Raines on Friday, but he had to cancel. I have two meetings next week with CEO's I help image."

I can see his wheels turning as he takes in the information I'm giving him. Watching his mind at work is kind of fascinating.

"Where do you get the mentees from?"

"For the first year, they will all come from my old neighborhood in the Bronx. There's a group of guys I used to tutor who all graduated last spring, but don't have the money to go to college. It's either try and make a way for them or watch them get pulled into gangs."

"You lived in the Bronx?"

I stand and put the pie back in the fridge. As I load our dishes into the dishwasher, I explain, "For four years. It was all I could afford when I left Julliard." I drape the towel I was using to wipe down the counter over the sink. Leaning against the island and placing a hand on my hip, I decide to jump into it.

"Why do you have security following me?"

"Because you refuse to be honest with me." Just like that, the air has changed and he's primed and ready.

"I have been honest with you," I counter.

"I told you, Emelia. Omission or diversion on purpose is dishonest"

"And I told you, Graham. Just because I don't tell you everything doesn't mean I'm lying to you. Trust is earned."

"It's also a two-way street." Frustrated, he starts a list to prove his point. "Who sent you the flowers?" He continues when I don't respond, "Where did you get the bruises on your arm? On your face?" Another pause. "You said two days ago you weren't seeing Blaine Moore, yet your photograph is all over the place with his tongue down your throat and his hand taking up residence on your ass." Another pause. "You refuse to tell me about your professional relationship with Colleen Cameron. Shall I go on?"

"So, has your security detail given you those answers? How's that working for you?"

"Careful." It's a warning. "It's not," he concedes. "That's not the intention. They are there to ensure your safety until I have a better understanding of what I'm dealing with."

"What does that mean?"

He's in front of me now. "It means, Emelia, that I want you in my bed. I want to fuck you. More than I've ever wanted to fuck someone." He presses his body into mine. "I need control. I insist on it. I can't have control if I don't know what I'm getting into. So, do you have any answers to my questions?"

"No."

"Then security stays."

His look and tone tells me he is not to be brokered with. Then, suddenly, something shifts. He leans down and kisses me hard. His hands cup the bottom of my ass, and he lifts me onto the island, his lips and tongue never breaking contact. His hands move up my thighs, and he runs his thumbs over my panties, up the middle of my sex. He's teasing me. The moan that escapes me and the smile I feel on his lips tells me he knows exactly the effect he's having on me.

Continuing their path, his hands slide under his shirt and map their way to my breasts, pulling and tweaking my nipples then moving to caress my whole breasts, only to come back and pinch my nipples. He repeats the pattern.

I wrap my legs around his waist and try to get some relief by rubbing my sex against him. He pulls his hips back, denying me. I voice my displeasure in a frustrated growl.

"Frustrating isn't it?" His kisses are coming in staccato between his words. "To be denied something you want, something you need so desperately." His hands never stop the repeating pattern on my breasts.

"Graham."

"Yes?" His kisses are lighter, now, teasing.

"Please."

"Please what? You're very responsive. Do you want me to let you come like this?" *God yes.* I want nothing more right now. I'd hump his leg if he'd hold it in place for me.

"Answer me," he demands sharply.

His authoritative manner bristles me and I don't reply. I am not going to beg. *At least not a second time.* His response is to slow his movements almost to a stop.

"You will beg, Emelia." He reads my defiance, driving me crazy with his slow movements. His lips leave mine and he trails his kisses down my neck. He unbuttons the shirt down to my navel. Pulling it to the side to expose my left breast, he twirls his tongue over my peak then applies a deep suction. My hands move to either side of his face, trailing my thumbs up his cheeks and into his hair, giving it a tight tug. He bites my nipple in retribution, then softens it with a lick of his tongue. Pushing aside the rest of my shirt, he moves to my right breast and starts again. I am so close. Sensing this, he kisses back up my neck and dives his tongue back into my mouth, his kisses coming faster, but still controlled.

"Please, Graham." I don't care anymore. I just need to come.

"Yes, Emelia?"

The bastard is going to make me say it. Out loud.

"Please don't stop. Make me come."

"Good girl" escapes the smile on his lips and he quickens

his ministrations. I try again to push into him. He moves his hand to my hips to stop me from coming closer but slides his thumb down the front of my panties and applies the slightest amount of pressure. This sends me into an orgasm that leaves me shaking as he wraps his arms around my waist and holds me close to him. I rest against him for several minutes as my body climbs down.

"It's like my body was designed to respond to you," I muse softly. Docile, I nuzzle my head into his neck. My admission wins me a passionate kiss and he lifts me off the island, wraps my legs around him, and carries me to the foyer, starting up the stairs. The movement has me bouncing on his erection and I push my weight down on it. He groans and stops half way up the stairs.

"I have to taste you. Now." His words are forceful while setting me down and leaning me back against the steps. Reaching up, I caress him through the sweatpants that are working hard to contain him. He takes my hands off him and moves them to the step above me.

"Don't move them. Understand?"

"Yes."

"Good." He rips open the last two buttons on his shirt I'm wearing and run his hands from my shoulders down my breast and over my stomach.

"God you're beautiful." His eyes follow his hands.

"The curve of your hips…" He leans down and works over my hip bones with little licks and kisses. I move my hands into his hair urging him further. He drifts over me and pulls my hands back over my head to grab the step again.

"I don't need your help. Move them again and I'll punish you, got it?"

Uh, not really. Punish me? I start to remind him for the

second time that I'm grown and he is not the boss of me, but
he preempts my response.

"I'm in control, Emelia. Not you. You submit to me. I *will*
punish you. Do not move your hands again."

"I'm..."

"Emelia," he admonishes. "Got it?"

It's a battle of the wills, but my necessity to have him inside me diminishes my will to be in control and I submit with
the nod of my head.

"Tell me."

"I got it," I say like a spoiled child.

He shakes his head like he understands exactly how hard
it was for me to say it.

Pressing his hands over mine one more time, emphasiz-
ing his directive to hold the step, he moves back down kissing
the side of my waist and working his way down to the middle
of my thigh. He works his way back up, running his tongue
over my underwear, against the folds of my sex down my other thigh and back again. This time while he kisses the spot
where my leg and hips come together he tugs on my underwear ripping the lace from my body. The sound is so erotic, I
almost come on the spot. He presses his tongue to my clit, and
I'm wound so tight it sends me straight into another orgasm,
lifting me off the stairs. I'm vaguely aware that I'm still holding
onto the step. His tongue continues to weave its way through
my folds, licking and sucking every part of me. Drinking me
in. He begins to fuck me with his tongue, moving it in and
curving it up on its way out.

"Graham," I'm breathy and barely able to get his name
out.

Pulling his tongue out of me, he submerges two fingers
into me while placing his other hand under my buttocks po-

sitioning me against his hand, slightly off the step. "You are so tight." He moves his fingers in and out until his tongue takes over again. With his mouth now wrapped around my clit, I feel his wetted finger move to my backside. He creates a suction with his mouth, pulling on the bud of my sex, and then he plunges the tip of his finger into my ass. The hybrid of sensations spirals me off the edge into an orgasm so intense my body convulses. Graham catches me as my hands release and I begin to slide down the stairs, unable to control my own body.

He holds me, absorbing my tremors, soothing me after the magnitude of what I just experienced. He runs his fingers through my hair as my breathing slows to normal.

"I love to listen to you, to hear what I do to you. How I make you feel."

I blush at his praise.

"Only you, baby," I whisper.

I had no idea I had even made a sound, I was so lost in the experience. I initiate the kiss this time, injecting it with every ounce of thankfulness I can show. I dance my tongue across his, tasting myself on him. Making sure I'm secure on the step, he stands in front of me and offers me his hand. I reach up, but move my hand to the waistband of his sweats instead, pulling his hips closer to me. Standing on a step a few down, he's at the perfect level. I slowly slide his waistband down, exposing his happy trail and more of the v-cut of his abdomen. His body is god-like, toned to perfection.

"What are you doing?" His voice is an amalgamation of teasing, daring, and need.

Displaying all the sincerity I feel, and with as innocent a look I can muster, I say, "I want to suck your dick."

I know exactly what I am doing. I feel raw after that experience, and I need to regain some control if I'm going to keep a grip on whatever is happening between us.

"Fuck me," he breathes, caressing the side of my face. "Those words in that sweet voice." It's all he needs to say for me to understand the effect I'm having on him, too.

His erection springs free, and I move his sweats down just below his buttocks. I'm usually the first to admit that penises are not beautiful to look at. Until now. Graham's is perfect in girth and length, and is encased in a velvety smoothness. I grab the base of it with one hand and the tip with another moving my hands until they meet in the middle and back again. He has one hand on the banister and one on the railing. His lips part and his breathing quickens. His response encourages and entices me. Leaning in, I place the head into my mouth and run my tongue through his slit, causing a little tremor to run through his body. He groans and moves his hands into my hair. Gentle, not trying to control the pace.

I get the feel for him and think about all the tips Patrick was talking about in the car. Who knew it would come in handy this week.

Suckling the head of his cock, I lick the skin just below the rim all the way around before taking him back into my mouth, deeper this time, stroking him with my mouth as I bob back and forth. Coming to the tip again, I run my tongue through the slit, suckle the skin around the head and take him deeper. I repeat the pattern each time. When he responds more intensely to my strokes, I pull back and tease a little, placing light open mouth kisses down his shaft. Exhaling, I concentrate on breathing through my nose and pull him to the back of my throat. Turned on by how deep I've been able to take him, I hum, feeling the vibration move up his shaft.

"Fuck me," he whispers. Looking up at him through my eyelashes, I see a look of pure bliss on his sculpted face, as I slide my mouth back down him. His hands move and just like that he has taken back control. His hands dictating the pace as he fucks my mouth. My hand cups his sack and I run my finger across the smooth skin right behind it. Another shiver ripples through him. I make a mental note of his response. The next trip I take to the tip of his head, I run my tongue on the underside of his cock, humming my way. I feel his control snap, and he starts to really move his hips, but never at the detriment of harming me. He's close, I can feel it. Releasing one more breath I take him all the way in so that my lips brush against his pelvis, while I rub his sensitive spot.

"If you don't want me to come in your mouth, you need to stop now." His knee comes on to the step near my head and he leans me back where his body is hovered over mine. I like this angle. My lips touch his pelvis again, and he pulls back slightly coming on my tongue and down the back of my throat. My excitement to undo him outweighs the taste and I continue to milk him to the last drop. His knees give out and he slides down, laying over me. Pressing me into the stairs.

"Fuck," he says again. "That was…I've never had…I'm not sure I can find words to do it justice." His breath is coming in gasps.

I love the feel of his weight on my body. I could use a softer spot than the stairs, but I'll take what I can get. I hold him and caress his scalp as he continues to settle down. Eventually he lifts his head and places a tender kiss on my lips.

Standing he slides his sweats back up and lifts me into a standing position. I arch my back to stretch it. He moves his shirt I'm wearing to the side, taking in the full view of my ass as he turns me, walking behind me the rest of the way up the stairs. We make it to the landing. He turns me again, this time leaning me against the railing that overlooks the family room below. My nails dig into him and I squirm in his arms.

"What's wrong?"

"I don't like heights," I look over my shoulder and grasp him harder.

Moving me to the opposite wall, he bends slightly to kiss me.

"I would never let you fall. I promise you."

There's a truth to his promise that comforts and surprises me.

"I can't get enough of you. I have thought of you constantly since our flight. Who you are. What you taste like. What you kiss like. How you would feel under my hand. How your mouth would feel around my cock. What it would feel like to be inside of you. The noises you make when you come. How your eyes would look when I'm making you come." He leans forward and kisses the whimper off my lips, trailing his kisses down my throat.

"I want you only, Emelia, but I won't share. I already texted Colleen and told her I would pay double your rates. I want exclusive access to you."

I'm so sexed up it takes a minute for his words to sink in.

"Excuse me?" I say, dumbfounded.

"I'll pay double what you make if that is how I have to have you."

Pushing him off me, I wrap his shirt around me. "Fuck you, Graham."

ch♥pter
nine

I can feel the tears prick the back of my eyes, which I'm not about to let happen. Locking my shit down, I pull back the covers, take his shirt off and climb into bed. Sending the room into darkness when I hit the button to turn the lights off.

I can't believe we're back here. Tonight was different. I know he was with only me, saw only me tonight. But he still thinks I have sex for money. I shouldn't have to tell him he's misunderstanding. He should be able to figure it out.

The lightening backlights the storm clouds that are billowing in. They're dark and ominous, mimicking my mood. I listen to the wave's crash onto the shore. I replay the night, trying to figure out where it went off the rails until I finally give into exhaustion. My nights of little rest over the last week set in, but my sleep is restless. I bounce from one tumultuous dream to the next, stuck in that sleep state where I'm aware that I'm dreaming, but can't make myself wake up. There's a loud boom of thunder that finally jolts me awake. My breathing is erratic.

"It's just a storm. You're okay." Graham's is sitting on the bed.

"What are you doing in here?" I grumble.

"Watching you sleep."

"Why?"

"I wanted to make sure you were okay." He rubs his hand over my exposed back. His tone regretful. I pull the sheet over the front of me even though it's too dark to see anything.

"I'm always okay, Graham. There's nothing to worry about."

"Save that bullshit for all the people who think they know you."

"And you think you know me better than they do when we've spent less than a day together? You think I'm for sale. I guarantee you, they don't think that."

"I may not know your stories or preferences, but yes, I think I know the real you better than they do," he says. "And if you think I want to buy you, you haven't been paying attention. But I won't share you."

I'm so frustrated with him, because he's right. That's what's had me so off balance this last week. I can't reconcile the feeling that he really sees who I am at my core, but also believes I'm a whore. I realize it is because of my association with Colleen, and if he had never seen me with her this would not be an issue. He jumped to a conclusion that I have given him no answers to. Maybe I'm being too hard on him. Thinking I am a high-priced call girl easily filled in missing pieces to his puzzle, but instead of working it out or asking me first he went straight to hooker—he accepted an easy answer. We're both at fault. Him mostly, but I suppose I could have settled this already.

"You're so arrogant."

"Don't mistake certainty for arrogance, Emelia." Lightening fills the sky and I jump when a deafening clap of thunder immediately follows. He lays down beside me and pulls me into the nook of his arm. I hesitate.

"Emelia," he says in a tone that is both scolding and patient.

Relinquishing, because this really is where I want to be, I place my head on his shoulder. He drapes his arm around me, resting his hand on the curve of my hip. He's such a contradiction, that I feel like I'm all over the place. He rubs his hand up and down my back to soothe me.

I'm too tired to argue with him anymore, and frankly I like him being here. I knew he thought I was "for hire" before I let tonight happen. In some ways, he has said things that shows he truly does know me better than most, but there are a few things where he is so far off the mark. I can't figure out if it's just the way circumstances have fallen to lead him in that direction, or if he really thinks that about me. The thought is unsettling.

"I can hear the wheels turning in your head Emelia. Want to tell me about it?"

"Nope."

"Then go to sleep."

I didn't close the drapes last night, so the light of morning wakes me. It takes a moment to remember that Graham was here when I went to sleep last night. He's left a glass of sparkling cranberry juice beside the bed and a single rose in a bud vase.

I force myself out of bed, wrapping Graham's shirt around me, and open the French doors. They're unlocked, which explains how he got in last night. This room shares a balcony with Graham's.

I step outside and breathe in the salt air. From this vantage point you can see the pool, parts of the property, the beach, and the ocean. The sky is an assortment of grays, matching the water. The waves are still going strong—good surfing conditions.

The storm has brought in cooler air. I go back inside to find the sweater I took from Graham's closet. He ripped the only pair of underwear I have at the moment, so I dig through Becca's bag to see if she has any that have some stretch to them. I find a black pair and a matching tank top. These should work. The underwear that is meant to give full coverage, barely covers me, and the tank stops about four inches from its mark. Luckily, the sweater falls mid-thigh. I bury my nose into it for his smell.

I turn on the news while I brush my teeth and check some emails. There's a tropical storm off the coast that is accounting for all the rain and the strong currents. They have red-flagged the entire coast line. More rain and cold today, but tomorrow should warm up and make for a nice week on the beach.

I grab my camera. I want to take some pictures of the waves in this lighting before the rain comes. Getting my toes in the sand, even if it is cold, is just what I need.

The stairs are a visual reminder of what happened last night, of how things went from amazing to nothing in no time. Still processing my thoughts, I put the mostly full glass of juice Graham left me on the counter and grab a Diet Coke. It's a short walk to the beach from the house. I leave my can on the railing of the wooden steps between the house and the beach and head toward the water.

The ocean has always been a love of my family. We used to go to Seagrove Beach in Florida every summer. Play, get a tan, and just have fun. There were never any worries that followed us to the beach. Even dark waters like today's have a way of calming me with their music. A peaceful wind chime, if you will.

Adjusting the aperture on my camera I begin taking shots of the beach and the water. Several times I have to turn and face the wind to keep my hair from tangling around my face. I'm grateful for Graham's thick sweater. Moving to the water's edge, I turn to take pictures of the house from the shoreline. The water around my ankles is cold and the waves are really picking up.

Walking north, I explore the beach, taking pictures from different vantage points. I adjust my camera settings again and look out over the ocean to take consecutive pictures of the waves coming in, catching them as they break.

Skimming the view screen, I run through the pictures to make sure the lighting is right in the pictures I'm taking, when I notice something in one of the pictures. I look out over the ocean and jog down a little ways, searching. Then I see it. A person in the waves. It takes me a second to realize they are struggling to stay afloat. Dropping my camera, I sprint towards the water, throwing off my sweater. I look back to the beach to line myself up with a landmark for reference and dive in.

The Atlantic water is freezing. I'm able to get under the first waves and make my way out. I turn to get my bearings searching for the landmark where I last saw him. Before I can get under it, I am pounded by a wave that crashes over me pushing me under and holding me down. Determining which way is up, I kick to the surface ready for air. Turning to face the shore again, I see the post that I associated with my last sighting. Based on the strength of the current, I start swimming to the area he should be, getting under as many waves as I can. I pull up and tread water for a minute to look for him. I know he's out here. I didn't imagine him. Just then I catch a glimpse of his arm coming out of the water. Lowering my head, I power swim towards him, my fingertips brushing his arm. He's exhausted from trying to escape from a rip current.

I grab him, but he slides underwater. I lose him when a swell of water comes through. Taking a deep breath, I dive to the ocean floor and back up in a deliberate pattern to find him. The water is dark with little to no visibility. Down, feel my way around, up again. I've been at it for several minutes now.

My lungs are on fire and I'm pretty far out. It's fifty, maybe sixty yards to the shore. I take a deep breath and start the down/ups again. On the second one down, I feel him. Latching on, I start pulling him up. He's holding on to me and just like that, he let's go. I kick back down, grabbing him again this time tightening my hold. I pull his deadweight to the surface panting for air. He's bigger than I am, and in the waves it takes me a minute to get him into rescue position. I swim parallel to the shore until I feel the pull of the rip current finally give way, and then I start making my way to shore.

We're about three-quarters of the way in when were pummeled by a wave, pushing us under. The water is shallower here and I get slammed into the ocean floor. If he wasn't wearing a wet suit that I was able to grip onto, I would have lost him again. Surfacing, I gasp for air, coughing out water. Pulling him into the rescue position again, I eventually get us to shore.

I've been in the cold water with no protection for at least twenty minutes and I'm having a hard time getting him and me out of the water. White foam wafts around us, and I get him far enough onto the sand that I know the current won't take him back out while I try to find the strength to pull him further onto the shore. He shifts from under me, and I realize he's being moved. Looking up, I see Graham getting him safely onto the beach. He comes back to help me out of the water.

"Call 911," I tell him dropping to my knees next to the unconscious body.

"They're already on their way."

He can't be more than twenty years old. I position his head, clear some seaweed from his airway, and start compressions. Thirty compressions, two breaths. I'm on my fourth round when he starts coughing up water.

"Help me get him on his side."

Graham and I turn him as large amounts of seawater pour from his mouth. He gasps for air. The paramedics arrive and begin stabilizing him.

"Does he have any health conditions we should know about?"

"I don't know him." My teeth are chattering so much I can barely get the words out.

"You're going with," the paramedic says, looking me over, while his partner works to stabilize the victim.

"I'm f-f-fine. I j-j-just n-n-need to g-get warm."

"Emelia," Graham bellows.

The paramedic checks my body temperature and vitals and listens to my lungs. "Okay," he looks at Graham, "but warm her up slowly. Torso before extremities and stay with her for the next twenty-four hours. Make sure she doesn't dry drown or have problems breathing. Any issues and you call 911. Understand?"

"I understand she's going," Graham says again.

"Just g-g-get me warm," I tell him trying to comfort him

by placing my hand on his arm. I can't afford a hospital bill.

"We got this. Go!" The paramedic waves us off.

Graham lifts me into his arms and swiftly takes me into the house. My body is shivering uncontrollably now. I'm freezing, and all I can think about as he carries me up the stairs is what happened on them last night.

He takes me to his room, into his bathroom, closing the door behind us. Making sure I have my balance he sets me on my feet in the shower, holding me up while he turns on the water. It's hot almost instantly. I cry out in pain as the water hits my cold skin feeling like knives are going through me.

"Stupid dick," he chastises himself as he lifts me into his arms wrapping my legs around his waist, adjusting the temperature. He moves us out of the water letting my body adjust to the hot steam. Slowly he acclimates me to the warm water. Starting with my back, he moves me in slow circles, taking time to warm my arms and legs.

"Set me down. Quick!" is all I'm able to get out before my feet hit the floor, but not in time to turn away. I throw up down the front of him, my stomach convulsing, pulling up strands of brown seaweed. He holds me in place keeping my hair pulled back.

"Finished?" he asks.

I nod and hold onto him while I regain my balance.

Once he knows I'm stable, he removes my tank and helps me step out of my underwear. Shedding his clothes, he moves us both under the water, pulling me into his arms, holding me while the water rolls over us, slowly adjusting the temperature warmer until the chattering and shivers cease. He grabs the shampoo on the shelf behind me. He lathers my hair and massages my scalp, then quickly washes his. Rinsing us both, he repeats the process, this time leaving the conditioner in my hair while he washes over each inch of my body. Standing me under the water to stay warm, he quickly washes then rinses his body and his hair. Working the conditioner out of my hair he gently squeezes the excess water out of it and turns the shower off. Wrapping a towel around me and then his waist, he leads me to the sink pulling out the vanity stool.

"Sit," he directs, leaving the bathroom and returning with a blanket.

I comply and close my eyes as he wraps me up. He dries my hair, brushing it out as he goes. He disappears into his closet and comes out with a t-shirt.

"Arms up."

I comply, grimacing at the soreness I feel as he pulls it over me.

"Bed," he directs again.

I'm too exhausted to argue. He pulls back the covers and I climb in.

"I'll be right back."

"Emelia." He shakes me gently. "Wake up."

He sets a tray on the bed. I must have nodded off.

"Can you sit up, baby?"

"Of course," I answer, trying to hide the fact that it is easier said than done. "I'm ok Graham," I reassure him as he moves the tray over my lap and takes a seat next to me.

"You made me lunch?" The gesture touches me deeply.

"You need to eat." His gaze is tender.

"No Diet Coke?" I look from the tray to him.

"Hot tea," he answers with a smile and chuckles at the disgruntled expression on my face.

"You look like a little girl when you pout."

Sitting cross-legged on the bed, he picks up one of the bowls of chicken noodle soup on the tray.

"It has a little sugar in it. You'll be fine," he says, referencing the hot tea as he eats a spoonful of noodles. I eat all of my soup, drinking the broth. It was delicious. And I will never admit it to him, but the tea hit the spot as well.

"What's this?" I look at a bandage wrapped over my finger.

"Something one of my companies is trying out. They sent me a prototype so I used it on you. It's a Bluetooth pulse oximeter." He pulls his iPhone out of his pocket. "It sets off an alarm on my phone if you stop breathing. We're working on a smaller bandage and a different placement on the body. Parents will be able to put them on their babies and an alarm will sound if their breathing drops. A way to combat SIDS."

Setting the tray on an ottoman, he adjusts my pillows and pulls the covers up to my chin. He kisses me lightly on the lips and runs the tip of his finger over my nose.

"More sleep."

He hits the button on the night stand that closes all of the shades. Thunder is the last thing I remember as the rain lulls me to sleep.

My body is moving with the waves. It's dark and I can't see anything, but I can tell I'm being pulled away from the shore. I call out, but no one answers. Panic and fear grip me and I am frozen, bobbing in the waves like a buoy. Something grabs a hold of me and tries to hang on. It's a person. It's Addie. I'm her lifeline. But like a buoy, my sides are slick and she can't get enough leverage to hold herself out of the water. She clings to me for as long as she can, eventually letting go and sinking away. I cry out for her, but my arms won't move to reach for her. I watch her slip under the water knowing I will never see her again. Sobbing, drinking in the water around me. Someone tries again to grab hold of me. He's pulling me under. He's going to drown me! He slips away, but this time my arms can move and I reach for him, but to no avail. I try to find him. I swim for hours. Crying. Calling for Addie. Calling for him. The sea turns stormy and the waves are crashing into me over and over. I feel his wetsuit. He's here. I try to save him, but the waves are brutal. He's crying for me to rescue him. I see his face. He's a young boy. I don't know who he is. His hand clasps mine as another wave hits and he's pulled away from me. I yell out to him, kicking and fighting to get over to him. The wave is stories high now and curls over us. The noise is deafening, like a jet engine. It breaks and begins to crash over me...

I spring up into a sitting position gasping for air. My face is pouring sweat, and my hands move across the bed trying to find him.

"You're okay, baby. You're safe. It's alright," Graham coddles softly. His arms cocoon around me, while he whispers his assurances.

"I lost them. I couldn't get to them. I couldn't save them." My breathing is erratic. My heart races and the panic evident in my voice.

"Shh," he says. "There was only one, and he's at the hospital. I called to check on him a couple of hours ago. He's okay. You saved him."

"He's okay? You're sure?"

"I'm sure."

My body eases against him, my breathing slowly returning to normal.

"It's okay, Emelia. Everyone's okay. You can rest." His intentional words are like taking a sledgehammer to my perfectly compartmentalized life. For the first time since the safety of my grandparent's I find myself feeling like control is not a necessity. *Everyone's okay. You can rest.* I let him hold me and comfort me. "Want to tell me about it?"

"It was just a bad dream. You're positive he's okay?"

"Yes, Emelia. I'm positive."

"What time is it?" I sit back up, Graham reluctantly letting me.

"Six o'clock. You've been asleep almost seven hours."

"I'm going to the hospital."

"You need a doctor?"

"No. I want to check on him."

"You can tomorrow. You need rest today."

"I've been resting for seven hours." I move out of the bed.

"Emelia," he warns.

"Graham," I counter as usual.

"God, you're a smart ass. And thick headed," he adds for good measure.

"I'm fine. Really." I try to divert his concern with a sweetness that has no fight in it.

He ponders for a minute. "Fine. But I'm going with you."

"Whatever, Trevor," I say over my shoulder as I walk out of his room to get dressed.

ch♥pter
ten

"Can I drive?" He has opened the passenger door to one of the four cars lined up in the garage.

"It's a manual," he says like there's no way I would know how to drive one. Like girls can't.

"I know how to drive a stick," I bristle.

"Get in the car, Emelia."

"So that's a no?" I ask for clarification.

"Do you know how to get to the hospital?"

"No."

"Then. Get. In. The. Car." He points to the seat of the passenger door he is still holding open.

"You. Don't. Have. To. Speak. To. Me. Like. I. Am. A. Child." I give it back to him. "It was just a question."

I slide into the seat. He closes my door, mumbling, "I swear if you didn't look so damn hot in my clothes..." and climbs in beside me. I am wearing the jeans I snagged from his closet the day before. I had to cuff the pant legs, they were so long. I've tucked in the front of the t-shirt he put me in the night before. His belts were too big for me, so I had to grab a tie and pull it through the belt loops knotting it to make sure my pants don't fall down. My hair falls over to one side, curling over his cardigan.

The seat of the car encases me with luxurious leather. He pushes a button on the dash that opens the garage door and starts the car. The sound of the engine is impressive. This is not a car to be messed with. Another button raises the convertible top. Putting the car in gear we glide forward, making our way off the property.

"This car is amazing. What is it?" I run my fingers over the leather dashboard.

"An Aston Martin V12 Roadster"

"Of course it is," I shake my head in response. It takes me a minute to figure out the sound system, but eventually I do and chose a station. I want to listen to whatever is on the radio. I'm too tired to choose a playlist.

When we get to the hospital, Graham parks and we walk into the main entrance. Either he's familiar with this hospital or he knows the room number already, because he doesn't stop at the information desk.

We make our way past a nurse's station to a door with the number eighteen on the wall. He's about to knock on the door when we hear his name called. We turn to see an older couple walking towards us. Graham shakes hands with the man, and his height changes by a good inch or two. This is CEO Graham. Dressed in jeans and a sweater.

"Richard, Jean," he addresses them. "I'd like you to meet Emme James." He introduces me, and I'm aware that they are, at the very least, acquaintances.

I'm engulfed into a Richard and Jean sandwich. Tears of gratitude flow as they thank me for saving their son. Uncomfortable with the attention, I console them and put a little space between us.

"Emme, Richard and Jean Raines." Graham looks at me

to confirm I've made the connection. This is the man I was supposed to have met with last week.

"Ms. James…" Richard starts.

"Emme, please" I interject.

"Emme. We cannot begin to thank you for saving our son."

"Please, no thanks necessary," I say with sincerity. "How is he?"

"Sore. Tired. Cranky. They cleared him a few hours ago. He was extremely lucky. He wore a heavier suit than the one the water temperature called for. He's under observation, but unless something unexpected happens, he should go home in a day or two."

"That's wonderful."

"If you hadn't been there and risked your own life, I would have lost a son today." Richard says with a graveness only a parent could feel. "He's had such a difficult year. He's struggled to find his path and he's been…" he pauses, searching for the right word, "angry. We told him not to go into the water today. He promised. What good that did him, or us."

"I'm glad I was there. Honestly, I didn't even see him in the water. I was looking through the photos I had taken and happened to catch sight of him being tossed in a wave. He's very lucky. Blessed, actually. He was caught in a rip current." I pause. "May I see him?"

"Please," they motion to the door.

"What's his name?"

"Holt," they say in unison.

I knock on the door but enter before I am given permission. Holt is propped up watching a muted TV mounted high on the wall in front of him. He sees me and turns it off. He's younger than I thought.

"Angel."

"Emme."

"I thought you were an angel. Right before I passed out, I was under the water and you were suddenly there with all this bright hair flowing around you. I thought I had died."

"You almost did." I tap his legs and he moves them to the side. I sit opposite him and I rest my feet near his shoulders. I grab a single-serve tub of Jell-O from his hospital tray and starting eating it.

"Do make yourself at home," he chuckles.

"Want to tell me what happened?"

"I was kayaking and flipped. I guess I was caught in a rip-tide. It was like I was swimming but not going anywhere." His answer sounds rehearsed.

"I don't mean how you got into the water to begin with, I mean why you gave up. What happened?"

His eyes never leave mine. I wait him out.

"I didn't give up," he tries again.

"Don't."

"Don't what?" He seems surprised by my reaction.

"Don't play me. I was out there with you. I had your hand. You knew I was pulling you up and you let go. It felt deliber-ate."

He moves his eyes off me. His hands move over his thighs in a manner that tells me he's struggling with how to answer.

"I don't know. It's just hard sometimes, you know. And right then, letting go and resting seemed...easier."

"What's hard?" I ease up on him a bit, hoping he'll open up a bit more to me.

"All of it. I'd been in the water a while and was exhausted."

I take a minute to assess him. "You're acting like a punk."

"Excuse me?"

"You heard me. You're acting like a punk. You broke your promise and went into the water, risking your life—and mine, for that matter. How old are you?"

"Seventeen."

"Where do you go to school?"

"St. Andrews."

"Are you depressed?"

"No."

"Would you know it if you were?"

"Yes."

"Your parents seem nice. Do they abuse you?"

"No." He seems amused.

"Is someone abusing you?"

"No." He looks at me like I've lost my mind.

"Are you being bullied?"

"No, Jesus. Enough with the theatrics. I just didn't feel like it anymore."

"Language," I chastise. "Are you trying to be someone you're not?"

"I'm not gay, if that's what you mean."

"Well, it wasn't what I was asking, but it would be ok if you were. I was really more trying to get to the reason you're tired. I don't know what your story is, and I won't pretend to be a counselor, but I do believe you've lost your way. We all do at some point or another. I don't think you were trying to hurt yourself, but I do think you are struggling with something."

We sit in comfortable silence for a few minutes.

"Ever wonder what you're meant to do and if you are really making a difference?" he asks.

"Sure. But that's on me. If I can't list a way I am making a difference, then I know I need to make a change. Not give up. It's not on anyone else to give me purpose. I have to seek it out.

I have to know what that is for me."

"What if you don't know? What if you can't figure it out?"

"Then you trust the ones around you, who love you, to help guide you until you know for yourself. You talk to a professional, you don't give up. Especially someone as blessed as you. I'm not going to pretend your life is all rainbows and unicorns. I can tell you that, for me, when I can't answer that question, it's usually because I am too wrapped up in myself. I'm being selfish. You're important. Here for a reason."

"Who are you?" he asks with a smile. He's a cute boy.

"Just a girl who's known what it feels like to lose her way." *And who lost someone who lost hers.* "Everyone does." Leaning over him, I kiss his forehead. "Take care of yourself, Holt." I turn and start to the door, surprised to find his parents and Graham are standing there. I hadn't realized they were listening.

I face Graham with a look that lets him know that I'm ready to go. He takes my hand and squeezes it, tugging a line straight to my heart.

We leave the room. Once were in the hall way, Richard envelopes me into another hug. Graham doesn't release my hand.

"Emme, we are indebted to you. While you were talking to Holt, I was trying to place where I know your name from, and I remembered. Adam set up a meeting for us. I had to cancel because we decided to leave earlier to come here. Can you meet this week?"

"Mr. Raines..."

"Richard," Jean corrects.

Smiling at her, "Richard, these two things are not connected. You don't owe me anything, not even a meeting. When you had to cancel, I emailed a proposal to you for your consideration. Read it at your convenience. If it interests you, we can meet then. If it's not for you, then no worries. This is strictly business. Deal?"

"Deal," he smiles. "I think you have me as smitten as my son." He looks from Graham to me. "I'm not sure I remember the last time someone did something for us without an ulterior motive."

"Then you need to expand your circle. Y'all are too sweet for that to be your story." I smile and hug them both once more. It dawns on me that most of my clients who have the status the Raines' have, probably feel the same way. What must it feel like to not know what people's intentions are?

We say our good-byes and Graham and I walk hand-in-hand to the car. I think back to the things Colleen mentioned after we left the Huntington Room, about how Graham is with his women. Is it because he doesn't trust them? He thinks they only want him for his money or status? I'm about to broach the subject when Graham tugs on my arm spinning me around to face him, pushing me up against the car. Before I can say a word, his mouth has covered mine. His hands moving to the sides of my face. I twine my fingers into his belt loops, pulling his hips to rest against me and return his kiss with as much passion as he's giving. It's more than a long moment. He finally breaks the kiss, needing a breath. He rests his forehead against mine, and I can feel his hardness against my stomach.

"Who *are* you?"

"Just a girl who likes a boy." I lay my cards on the table. He pushes back and stares at me. His hands not leaving my face. I lean forward and give him a quick peck on the lips, letting him know that the moment has passed.

"Would you like to drive?" he asks with a smirk, opening the driver's side door.

I can't help but grin at his concession. "Thanks, but think I'll ride."

His look of complete confusion tickles me, and I giggle my way to the passenger's side. He catches up as I reach for the handle and opens my door for me.

"You could feed me though. I'm starving"

"Have a taste for something in particular?"

"Anywhere I can go in looking like this," I say, reminding him that I'm wearing his clothes.

After Graham's order of melt-off-the-bone good ribs with fries and coleslaw at the East Hampton Grill, I, of course, order dessert. Between the excitement of the morning and my full belly, I'm exhausted. The soreness I felt before the shower has amplified, and I'm starting to realize what a beating I took today. When Graham asks what I'd like to do after dinner, I opt for home.

"Emme, baby." His voice is as tender as he shakes me. "We're here."

I open my eyes to see we're parked in the garage of his parents' house. "Just let me sleep here."

"Need me to carry you?"

"No, I just need to stop being a baby and suck it up," I say climbing out of the car and yawning my way through the house and up the stairs. I run my hand over the railing, remembering.

I turn to my room, but Graham stops me and pulls me into his. Standing me by the bed, he undresses me, slowly and methodically. I get goose pimples as he pulls his clothes off me, piece by piece.

"Clever," he says, untying his tie around my waist. He pulls his jeans down my hips and over my ass without unbuttoning them. He runs his fingers lightly over the outside of my

sex and pulls the jeans all the way off. I know he means only to
tease, not to start anything. I'm in only his t-shirt.

"Get in," he orders, pulling back the covers.

"I have to pee first," I say, turning to the bathroom. I sit
down and he walks in, leans against the vanity, and looks at
me.

"Can I help you?" I ask.

"You're not very modest are you?"

"I share one bathroom with six guys. I don't have room
for modesty."

"A yes or no would have sufficed. I don't like thinking that
you are this open with someone else."

"I'm not. There's a difference between peeing in front of
you, and peeing in a bathroom where someone is behind a
shower curtain. But no, I'm not super modest. Does it bother
you that I would pee in front of you?" I ask.

"Nope. It's just different. That's all"

I reach around him to wash my hands then make my
way to the bed. Undressing, Graham climbs in behind me,
his front to my back, rubbing his hand over my ass, eventually
draping his arm around me to hold my hand.

"I almost died when I realized you were in the water." He
says this like he's been holding it in all day.

"How did you know where I was?"

"I saw you from the balcony. You were taking pictures. I
came down to walk with you and you were gone. All I found
was your camera..."

"Oh no! My camera!"

"I got it while you were sleeping earlier."

"Oh? Thank you. I'm sorry, I know that wasn't the point
to your story."

"All I found," he moves back into his thought, "was your

camera and my sweater. I finally deducted you were in the water, but I didn't know where. When I saw you coming to shore, I was so relieved. That's when I ran up."

"Thank you. Honestly, I don't know if I would have been able to pull him up. I was so exhausted."

"You could have. It took all I had to pull him out first. You know, on the one hand, I want to beat your delectable ass for going into the water like that, but on the other, I'm learning that is who you are to your core. Your impulse is to help someone when they need it. You confound me, Emelia. I've never met anyone as forthright as you. It unsettles me. I don't know what to do with these feelings."

His honesty surprises me. It conflicts with the mogul people have told me about. I realize maybe he's not the only one passing judgement based on misguided assumptions. Turning to face him, I push my leg between his.

"Why do you have to do something with them? Just take it one day at a time. We'll figure it out together. No one has ever had this effect on me either. I'm working without a guide, too. I promise to forgive you your mistakes, if you promise to forgive me mine."

We lay there for a while. I don't want to end this connection between us, but I am exhausted.

"Thank you," I run my hand across his chest, draping it over his waist.

"For what?"

"Being there today. Taking care of me. Mostly, thank you for holding my hand. It's my most favorite," I admit, snuggling my face into his chest. He wraps his arms around me tighter.

"You're very kind," I say with my eyes closed.

"That's twice now you've called me 'kind'. It's not a word most people would use to describe me."

Without opening my eyes, I reach my hand to his face, resting it against his cheek. "I'm sure it's an oversight on their part."

I can feel him leaning into my touch. Despite my own pleas to lock my shit down I know the damage is done. I have fallen hard for Graham Taylor.

ch♥pter
eleven

I wake the next morning surrounded by Graham. He's either trying to climb inside me or mount me, given the way he is draped over me. Actually, both of those things sound just fine to me. I run my hand over his happy trail and wrap my fingers around him, when he stirs and opens his eyes.

"Can I help you?" He raises an inquisitive eye-brow.

"No, but I think I can hel—is that bacon?"

"Yes."

"Breakfast. I'm starved!" I move to get out of the bed, but my body protests the loss of Graham's warmth.

"You're kidding me, right?" he's says nonplussed. "Talk about leaving someone hanging."

Stretching and happy to find I feel like my normal self, I pull off the covers. "Get dressed. Someone's cooking and it smells delicious." I glance at my watch. It's ten-thirty. I can't believe we slept so late.

I open the balcony door to test the air. The storms have moved out. It's sunny and warmer. I find a pair of pajama bottoms in Graham's closet and slide them on, pulling the drawstring tight and folding them down over my hips before adding his cardigan. He follows me down the stairs in sweats and a t-shirt.

"Mags! Graham!" Everyone greets us as we enter into the kitchen. Everyone is here: his parents, Ben and Ruth, his sister Lucy, Adam and Jules, Matt and Becca. Lucy bounds over to me and gives me a hug. We spent time hanging out together the last time I was here, and I helped her organize her closet into some new looks.

I hear him coming before I see him. I turn just as Bruiser slides across the floor right into me, almost knocking me off my feet.

"Bruiser," Graham admonishes as I drop to my hunches to love on him and get slobbery kisses. He is the Taylor's guard dog. He's a big baby, but I know he would tear someone apart if he had to. Bruiser and I ran a lot the last time I stayed here. He slept most nights with me, too. Graham bends to pet him.

"Even my dog is smitten. Bruiser doesn't like anyone, do you boy?" Graham says the last part in a low voice that humans use for only two things: to talk to babies or to pets. He's a beautiful Shepherd-Pit mix. Eighty pounds of solid muscle.

Graham makes his way to his parents, kissing his mom and shaking his dad's hand.

"I brought your suitcase," Becca tells me.

"Ah, I was wondering about your choice of outfits," Jules comments.

"I was stuck. I'm not a hanger girl like you guys. No way is my rear fitting in a two."

"I have some fours in the closet."

"And I'm a size six, sometimes an eight." I make a face at her.

"You could have raided my closet dear, I'm an eight." Ruth greets me with a kiss to the cheek.

"It was no big deal. I hung here most of the time."

Everyone's already started setting the table on the deck for brunch. The French doors across from the kitchen are open to the outside. I take the plates out to the table and start setting spots for everyone. Their deck, like the balcony that covers it above, overlooks the pool and the ocean. The breeze coming off the water is perfect. I bring out the flowers from the table in the kitchen and place them on the blue paisley table cloth.

Once all the food has found a home on the table, we all take a seat and start the passing of plates. There's spinach quiche, bacon, biscuits, fresh fruit, cheese and an assortment of homemade jams. This all must have taken so much prep work, I can't help but wonder how long everyone must have been here before we heard them. It reminds me so much of our Sunday breakfasts with my Grandmother. My distant thoughts have me pausing with one of the plates in mid-pass, prompting an elbow to my side from Adam, who is sitting next to me.

"Earth to Mags...Where'd ya go?"

"Oh, um, sorry," I say softly. "I was just remembering Sunday breakfasts when I was growing up." I say passing the fruit to Ruth sitting at the head of the table to my right.

"Do you miss home dear?" Ruth asks from across the table. She passes the fruit to Graham on her right. She has to tap him on the shoulder to get his attention. He's reading something on his phone.

"I don't miss home, but I miss my family." Knowing that I have lost everyone in my family, she reaches over and squeezes my hand. It's a motherly gesture.

The table bustles with conversation. This is the first time that Ben and Ruth have met Matt and Becca.

"Emme, did you get along with Graham okay the last couple of days? I should have called to tell you he would be here. The last time you visited he was still in Japan working."

"We got along fine, Ruth. There were no problems at all," I answer, trying desperately to make sure my face doesn't reveal more.

"Well, we're so glad you're home dear," she says to Graham, who still has his head in his phone. I kick his leg with my foot to get his attention. As if she doesn't notice, or as if she's used to him multi-tasking, she continues with her thought.

"Are you done sweetheart or will you have to go back?"

Crickets. Bueller?

I reach across the table and grab the phone from his hands and put in on my lap. He looks at me like I have lost my mind. Leaning slightly up, he reaches for it just as I slide it between my legs.

"I'll go in there," he threatens.

"Not if you expect to leave with all your digits attached. Your mother is talking to you. She deserves your attention." *Put that in your pipe and smoke it, Taylor.*

"I'm glad to be home, Mom. If I have to go back, it will be a regular trip. I won't have to stay as long as I did the last time." After he responds to her, he looks at me with a glare that tells me he indeed can multitask.

I realize everyone is watching us. It must be the first time they've ever seen him challenged, and they're curious to see how he handles me taking his phone.

I look to Jules to ask her a question when I catch his hand reaching for my Diet Coke out of my peripheral vision. I slap his hand just before he picks it up.

"Leave my drink alone." My tone is sharp. "I don't drink coffee. This is my start-off drink." I look at him like he has eight heads and is trying to maim a small child all at the same time. It's a battle of the wills and I don't intend to lose.

"Did I miss something," Ruth asks.

"Mags is the girl I told you Graham met on the plane," Adam answers with a piece of pineapple in his mouth. Something flitters in Ruth's eyes and she smiles and nods, like the recognition just set in.

"You're going to have two-headed babies drinking that much soda," Graham announces like he's the six-o'clock world newscaster.

"Actually, she's good. James can't have kids," Becca explains. I know she thinks she is taking up for me, but she realizes that she might have shared too much. "I'm sorry, James," she says embarrassed.

"No worries. It's not a secret. It's not like it's something I have any control over. Plus, Ruth is my OB-GYN," I say nodding to my right.

Everyone carries on, and I catch Graham looking at me. He's so hard to read. I can't tell what he is thinking.

"Oh my God, Mags, I can't believe I didn't ask first thing! Tell us what happened?" Jules says from the end of the table.

"Happened with...?" I say asking for a clue.

"The rescue. It was in the paper. You rescued Richard Raines' son."

"How was that in the paper?"

"A billionaire's son is rescued, it's going to make the paper," she says like I'm dim.

"Richard Raines is a billionaire?" Okay, so the looks I'm getting now tell me I am, in fact, a bit dim. I had no idea. I mean, I figured he was wealthy, but never a billionaire.

"There's nothing to tell. He was in distress and I helped him. He's recovering at the hospital and doing well. No big deal."

"Three people died in the currents yesterday, Mags. I

would say it was a pretty big deal," Adam informs me.

"My sister was an ocean life guard for a summer. She trained me to handle rip currents."

"When did you live by the ocean?" Becca asks.

"The year she and Addie lived in their car. They moved to the beach for the summer," Matt answers for me, digging at the food on his plate.

"Who's Addie?" Lucy asks.

"My sister."

"You were homeless?" she asks.

"We had a home. It just had four wheels." I focus on eating.

"Why?"

"Lucy," Adam admonishes.

"What?"

"It's okay," I tell Adam. I know it is hard for her to understand. She has had a privileged life and I am sure has never known someone who lived in their car. Her intentions aren't hurtful.

"After our Mama died, we didn't have a home to live in." Graham catches my eye.

"You didn't have any other family?" Lucy's thrown and genuinely perplexed.

"My grandparents were killed in a small plane crash when I was ten. They had a farm and a little money they left us, but Tony, our step-dad, took everything and left the day we found out Mama had lymphoma."

"What did you do without any money?"

I don't want to be questioned, but I'm patient with her.

"I was fifteen. I found a job that week, and Mama started chemo. For a year it was the three of us. Mama, me, and Addie. I stayed in school but I also worked full time to compensate what her disability didn't cover. We moved to a small one-bedroom apartment, and Addie took care of her while I was at work. I'd relieve her when I came home, and she would study while I took care of Mama. Some days were harder than others, but we still had laughter and each other. Mama made every day as special as she could." I say all of this as matter-of-factly as I can, thanking God I made it through it without a breakdown.

"I'm so sorry, Emme," Lucy says sincerely. "How long 'til she died?

"She died May the next year." I add before she can press for more, "Mama had a small insurance policy that she had cashed out, and it was just enough for a private burial with just me and Addie.

"So that's why you lived out of your car?" Becca joins the questions.

I shrug. "We called Tony. Mama had arranged for him to stay our legal guardian, but he wanted nothing to do with us. We had no family other than his. We didn't know any of his people. They never cared about us. Never met us. So," I exhale, "we told our friends and their parents we were living with Tony, that he had moved back, and we made it on our own. We stayed in our apartment until we couldn't afford it anymore. After that we lived in our car, my grandpa's Scout we inherited when they died. Addie worked the desk at a local gym on weekends, so we had open access to showers. We would go each morning, work out for thirty minutes or so and then shower and head to school. All a normal-looking routine to the average observer. We made it to graduation with only a couple of close friends knowing that we lived out of our car for a year."

Addie and I were a team. We had been through the unthinkable and survived it. Together.

I pass a plate of fruit to Adam, he leans down and kisses my temple. I'm suddenly aware of the eyes on me.

"Don't," I say to Jules when I see a tear fall down her cheek.

"Shut it. I'm allowed." She's softly defiant.

"I don't need you to."

"I'm sorry if I upset you," Lucy says as I rise and start clearing the plates.

"You didn't, baby. I promise. Ask Jules and Matt. If I didn't want to answer, I wouldn't have."

Changing the subject, I announce that I'm going running. "It's rained so much here the last couple of days, I'm behind in my training schedule. How is yours going, Ben?" He is training for the marathon, too.

"I'm a day or so behind myself."

"Want to go with me?"

"I would love to, but we have our annual softball game. There's a track there if you want to go there to run?"

"Really?" He has my attention now. "I'd rather play. Can I?"

"Sure," Ben says.

"No," Graham says at the same time. "It's a league of grown men. She could get hurt," he clarifies for everyone looking at him.

"Oh my goodness! You make me want to lay square eggs. I played in high school," I tell him still holding the two plates I picked up.

"Nonsense, son. It's just a yearly pick-up game. You can play on my team, Emme." I knew I liked Ben. I can see similarities in all the Taylor men. They are all very good-looking, starting with their dad. "I have an extra glove you can use."

"Alright then. Cheering section it is for Becca and me,"

Jules says rising to pick up more plates.

With everyone pitching in, it only takes about fifteen minutes to clean the kitchen. Matt carries my suitcase upstairs and grabs Becca's to take to their room on the first floor. He stops, enveloping me in a hug that is comforting.

"I love you," he says with no explanation needed. I know it is because I opened up at breakfast.

"I love you, too."

A throat clearing brings our eyes up. Graham is in the door way. Not bothered by Graham in the least, Matt kisses my forehead before grabbing the suitcase and heading downstairs.

I sit to put on my tennis shoes. I think he wants to say something, but he either thinks better of it or he's working through my friendship with Matt.

"I'm serious," he starts. "This is an annual game, and these guys play hard. I don't want you playing."

I move into the bathroom and start French-braiding my hair into two long pigtails, the way my mom always did before my softball game. I put on a t-shirt and a pair of tight black running pants that fall just below the knee. I continue to ignore Graham and head downstairs. Everyone is ready to go. I just now notice that Matt, Adam, and Graham are all wearing the same blue shirt. Ben's is yellow. Different teams. *Great*.

"Are we playing you guys?" I ask.

"Yep," Graham says like he is trying to finish his point from upstairs. "And we haven't lost a game in ten years."

"Well that was before they had me. *I'm* their secret weapon."

Once we've made it to the ballpark, Ben and I go into one dug out and the boys go into another. Ben introduces me to the other men on our team. Two of them are my clients, but I don't tell anyone, of course. I also learn that teams are divided by age groups and these men have been a team together for almost twenty years. They're all fit and healthy-looking men in their forties and fifties.

It's slow pitch softball. I prefer fast, but I'm just happy to get to play. You can steal bases after the ball leaves the pitcher's hand, other than that, the rules are pretty standard. The lineup has me batting last, which I don't mind since I know that I won't be able to hit it as far as these guys do. I'm also catching. I'm younger, I have better knees, they say. We all get our hands into the circle and I smile through their little pre-game chant. Once both teams circle around home plate to meet the umpires, the trash talk begins.

Both sides are dishing it out pretty good, but I'm just minding my own business when one of the guys starts really giving it to me. I saw him earlier with a girl who eye fucked Graham and Adam. Jules noticed it, too. She wasn't as nice about it as I was.

After a few warm-up insults, the guy finally says, "I knew you guys were desperate, but desperate enough to take on a girl?"

My team looks to me to see how I am going to handle it. I see my boys about to say something to him, when I hold up my hand to stop them. Ben just stands there with the confidence that I will address this asswipe.

In my sweetest southern teaching voice, "See, y'all," I say to the men on my team, "you can have a little penis and still be a dick."

Matt and Adam fall over themselves laughing. I'm going to have to pick my team up out of the dirt they are laughing so hard. The umpire just shakes his head. Then I catch a smirk and slight nod from Graham. He knows I won that one, and he's proud. Something about knowing that swells my heart a little.

We're visitors, so we bat first. We have a productive first few innings, but we are tied two-two in the bottom of the fourth. Small-penis guy gets a hit and makes it to first base. I've been watching him, so I know he is going to steal second base. Ben is playing short stop. I call his name and make eye contact so he knows what my plans are. As soon as the ball leaves the pitcher's hand, he takes off for second base. I catch the strike then come up on a throw to second base. The throw couldn't be more perfect. Ben tags penis guy out by a mile. Whew, is he pissed. At the top of the fifth, Graham's team moves in close when I step up to bat, like I can't hit far enough for them to stand in their usual places. They're trying to intimidate me, but my strike zone is much smaller and I get walked.

We make it to the bottom of the ninth. We are up by two. There's a runner on second and small-penis is on first. We have two outs. Graham comes up to bat. I let the team know we only need one out then I quietly cheer Graham on, even though he is on the other team.

He takes the first pitch, and I come up throwing to third, pushing Graham out of my way, but I'm a tad behind the runner. He's safe.

"You pop up too soon. You're going to get hit with the bat." He's still mad that I'm playing.

"You didn't even swing." I'm equally short. Graham's foot placement tells me he is going to hit to center field. I yell our centerfielder's name to let him know it's coming his way. The next pitch Graham gets what he wants and hits it straight to where I predicted.

It lands at the fence, the centerfielder just missing it. He throws to the cutoff, who gets the ball to me just as small penis, the tying run, rounds third. He gets the signal to hold from the third-base coach, but ignores him. He barrels towards me. I brace myself. If he would just slide, I could tag him out, but I know he is going to run over me in hopes I'll drop the ball.

I thought I was prepared, but he lowers his shoulder like he's busting through a door to get out of a fire. Right before he makes contact I jump out of his path, tagging him with the ball in my gloved hand. The lack of expected body contact has him tripping and rolling ten to fifteen feet with a loud thump. A hush falls over the crowd not believing what just happened.

The umpire looks at me and I open my gloved hand to show him the ball. He calls small-penis out with what looks like pure enjoyment. Our team wins by 1.

Before I have time to respond, Matt has firmly planted his fist into small penis's face, shouts a few expletives at him, and walks away. *What the hell?*

Once everyone is settled, we make our way back to the car, all squeezing in. Everyone is talking about the game. I'm in the middle row and Matt is in the back seat. I turn towards him.

"What were you thinking?" I'm indignant. "You could have hurt your million dollar hands. Don't ever do that again! Not to mention that it makes me look like I need my big brother to fight my battles for me. And I don't!"

"Don't start, James. I'm allowed to care about you. You didn't need me to fight your battle today, but I won't apologize for it. If the tables were turned, we would have had to pull you off that guy. All I did was give him a little love pat to let him know his attempt to ram into you wasn't appreciated."

"That's right, baby," Becca kisses him. Proud of her man.

"Also," he adds, "that's the first time I've ever heard you say a curse word."

Despite the fact I know what he says is true, I'm still steaming and everyone knows it. We ride in an uncomfortable silence until Lucy can't take it anymore.

"'Dick' is a curse word?"

There's a second of silence before a burst of laughter. Graham pulls Lucy into a hug and just like that my ire is forgotten.

ch♥pter twelve

I have to get some running in today or I am going to be an entire week behind schedule. Grabbing a leash for Bruiser, I pull up the playlist I run to and we head to the beach. The weather is perfect for running. Despite my mind going in several directions, I'm finally able to set a pace. I let Bruiser off his leash. He enjoys running into the water and chasing birds as they flit across the sand.

I received a text from Colleen earlier telling me that Graham had contacted her about my services. She didn't correct him or accept his offer. She wanted to go in the direction I sent her. I know that I need to correct him, but it ruffles my feathers that I even have to. On the one hand, Graham already feels comfortable to me. Familiar. On the other, he still thinks I sleep around for money. Guess we still have some things to learn about each other.

One thing I know is that he's a contradiction. He's soft and tender with me one minute and dominating and harsh the next. If I'm being honest, I must say I like both sides. Who would have thought? I'm usually so strong minded and self-sufficient, but I do like giving over some control to him. But I am certainly not telling him that.

Bruiser and I hit mile six. I take a minute to give him some water from my bottle and a chance to cool off. We turn and head back to the house. We're only a couple of miles away when we see Graham coming our way.

"You getting a run in?" I ask, breathlessly pulling out my earbuds and taking a swig of water, pouring a little more for Bruiser. "Good boy," I praise him. Standing I look at Graham for his answer. He's wearing gym shorts and no shirt. I could work out for hours each day and still not look like he does. The definition in his muscles is remarkable.

"Thought I would see if you want some company," he laughs. He's caught me checking him out.

His laugh is attached directly to my sex. It must be because it shows a side that so few get to see. He seems reserved and guarded except for times like this spent with his family. There's a part of me that loves the fact he shows this side of himself to me. I wonder what he has been like with his previous girlfriends.

"Bruiser is keeping me company, but I would love some more. I was headed back towards the house. Is that okay or do you want to run some more?"

"I'm good. Let's head back." We start the last few miles back to the house at a leisurely pace, neither speaking for several minutes. He rubs his hand over my ass. "I don't think I'll ever have my fill of you." He gives it a slap and then grabs my hand, slowing us to a walk.

"Well, you're gonna. Because I'm not having sex with you on the beach," I announce like that is his intention. "Do you know how many girls think sex on the beach is sexy, only to leave with a horrible infection because they got sand in their honey pot?" I pause. "As Jules calls it," I add for clarification.

"So," I continue, testing the waters, "how many times

have you said that to someone and how long did it take you to get your fill?" I pull on his hand leading us to the water's edge.

"I've never said that to a girl, Emelia. Then again, I've never dated anyone like you before. Actually, date isn't a very accurate word. I don't date."

"Colleen said your girls never walk next to you in public, why is that?"

He doesn't answer at first. We walk a bit more. "What is it you're looking for Emelia?"

"I have no expectations, Graham. I'm not looking for anything, but I do need a level of honesty and respect, and you are sending an awful lot of mixed signals. If you want something akin to a one-night stand, I'd like to know up front."

"I don't date or do relationships. I fuck. The girls I'm with understand the rules and what is expected of them. I don't want there to be any confusion of what this is." He struggles to put a term to it. "Call it more of an affair than dating. Affairs run a course. They don't walk next to me in public because I don't want them to. They are submitting to me and part of that is to be only available to me. Not to anyone else."

"So, you're into being a dominant?"

"No, Emelia. I'm not. I am in charge when we are in the bedroom and I enjoy toys and games, but I'm not into play-rooms, canes, and crosses that everyone enjoys reading about these days."

"Seen, not heard, then?" I interject.

"On some levels, yes," he answers unapologetically. "No hassles. Their role in the affair is to please me, and in doing so I bring pleasure to them." As if to add more insight, he continues. "My life is hectic enough. I don't need the complications a relationship brings. I want someone who understands that. They understand what I want them to bring to the table, full control of them, and they understand what I bring to the table."

"That being?"

"Money. Connections. Status. Whatever they might need at the time to further them into their next step."

"How do you ever know someone's true intentions?"

"Because I am very forthcoming about my expectations and what I want. I know going into any affair what it is they expect in return. And if they please me, I will please them in return. Whatever that might be. I also don't get involved with someone without an extensive background check." *That explains all the info he had on me.*

I nod but I don't say anything. I'm still absorbing this. It's at odds with the man I have come to know in a short amount of time.

"I want that with you, Emelia."

"That doesn't work for me, Graham." I might as well be honest from the beginning. "I don't want to mislead you." I stop and look him in the eye. "I will never be okay being behind you. Not because I want to be in front of you. I want to be beside you for every step. That's the only relationship I'm looking for. I don't think I'm the girl for you." I squeeze his hand and start up the five steps from the beach to the house. I whistle for Bruiser to follow me to the house.

We make our way into the kitchen. There's a note letting us know that everyone ran to the market to get supplies for grilling out and movie night. I grab a Diet Coke and make my way to my room when Graham's arm comes around me from behind. His lips pull on my ear and he kisses down my neck. His other hand finds my breast as he begins to knead it, causing my nipples to pucker.

"You're exactly the girl for me," he whispers. It hits me that he's attracted to me even though he thinks I'm a high priced hooker. Is it because I would be a professional? He would definitely have no hassles from me. I'm ending this back and forth over my being for sale once and for all.

He moves my jogging bra up releasing my breasts. His hand moves from one to the other, testing their weight in his hand. He pulls on my nipples, ending with a pinch, then starts the process again. Just like when we were on the stairs.

I set my drink down and raise one of my hands to rest behind his head. Running my fingers through his hair as his tongue continues to taste the salt from my body. I move my other hand behind me and run it up and down his now hardened shaft. He moans against my throat. I turn facing him and initiate a kiss that lets him know that I want him. Now!

I lift myself into his arms and wrap my legs around him. I remove my top, arching my back to give his lips unconstrained access to my breasts. He carries me to the stairs. We're half way up them when he stops. *Are we ever going to make it to the bedroom?*

"Bedroom," I instruct.

He smiles. "We're going to finish what we started." He sets me down on the step never breaking his impassioned kiss. "I've wanted inside you since the first night I met you on the plane," he says kissing down my body, removing my running shorts as he goes. He deposits them in his back pocket, and stands there, drinking me in. After several long breaths, I grow wetter between my legs as his eyes feast over me. When they meet mine, they are a midnight blue. He's taller. Despotic. This is dominant Graham.

"Turn around." It's a command. One I know he intends for me to follow.

Slowly, I turn my back to him. He's two steps below me.

Making me a good inch taller than him. I can feel his eyes on me. He reaches out and runs his hand from the top of my spine to the top of my bottom. He takes his time rubbing his hand over each buttock to the arch of my ass, testing its weight like he did my breast. His soft touch stimulates a moan from me.

"Spread your legs."

Without hesitation, I do. His hands continue their journey, pausing to run over the outside of my sex, teasing me. He inserts his finger, pad up, at the top of my folds and slowly moves it back until he finds my entrance, sliding it in and out.

"God, you're so wet. That pleases me, Emelia."

It delights me that he is pleased—and that shocks me. Right then, I know that I am in over my head. He takes a step up. Standing one step below me, he's just a couple inches taller than me now. I can feel him down the back side of me. He pulls his finger out of me and runs it over my lips, placing it on my tongue, "Suck".

I move my hands to wrap around his and slowly move his finger in and out of my mouth. I bite the end, warranting me a light slap on the ass.

"Let go," he trains.

Pulling me tighter against him, he moves one hand across my chest and the other to my sex. Kissing the back of my neck, his fingers enter me from the front this time. I copy his stance and move my arm over his across my chest, my fingers lacing with his, both of us kneading my breast. My other hand moves slowly from his elbow and down his arm. My fingers lightly skip across his. I entwine mine with his, both of us pleasuring me. A deep moan falls off my lips, and I deliberately slide a finger inside me along with his.

"God, Emelia. I have to have you. Right now," he says, as

if all control has broken.

Pushing on the small of my back he bends me over, so my knees go down to the step. He places my hands on the stairs above me. From this position I can see him below me. He pulls something from his pocket before pulling his shorts down and runs his hands up and down his imposing length. He rolls on a condom. Positioning himself over me he runs his dick back and forth over my sex. I lift my ass higher in the air, trying to entice him to take me.

"Graham, please," I beg. He is driving me crazy. I can hear his light chuckle.

"So impatient," he torments. Finally, just when I think he isn't going to give me what I want, he slams inside of me. I let out a cry of surprise and discomfort. My breath catches.

"Emelia?"

He doesn't move. His breathing is labored. I groan. It feels so deep and so amazing. It takes me a minute to acclimate to the intrusion.

"Emelia," he says, stronger this time.

"Just fuck me, Graham. Please."

"Emelia, when's the last time…"

I cut off his question. "You're my first."

I pull off his length a bit and slam back on him. My movements mobilize him, and he begins an arduous pace. From this angle, I can see him moving in and out of me. It's mesmerizing to watch and it turns me on. I'm giving as good as I'm getting, and I know I won't last long. I continue to push back against him. He pops my ass, and I tighten around him.

"Control, Emelia."

But I don't have any experience at controlling it. I want him too badly, and I quicken my pace. His hand slides around me and applies pressure to my clit sending me off into an orgasm that causes my arms to buckle. I would have hit my head if Graham hadn't caught me. Three more hard thrusts and he's coming. He continues to move in and out of me, riding his orgasm out. Eventually he collapses over me. Both of us are trying to catch our breath. We stay like this for several minutes.

Pulling out of me, he stands, removing his condom. Knotting it, he pulls his shorts up and lifts me into his arms. Climbing the rest of the steps up, he maneuvers us to his bedroom, kicking the door closed. He lowers me onto his bed pulling the sheet and comforter back. He pulls his shorts off and climbs over me.

"Why didn't you tell me?"

"You didn't ask."

"Emelia, you let me think…"

"I didn't let you think anything. You came to your own conclusions that you seemed bent on believing, and I chose not to correct you."

"That's semantics and you know it. I never would have… I can't believe you let me take you on the stairs like that."

"Graham." I say his name to get his attention placing my hands on each side of his face. Pulling his face to mine, I implore him, "make love to me."

I kiss him with every ounce of feeling and forgiveness that I have. Just when I think he isn't going to respond, he pulls me into his arms and returns my kiss with a slow possession.

Laying me back down on the bed, he says my name in supplication. Skillfully, his hands chart my body, learning each crevice. The slow trails he makes drive me crazy. I move my body under him, showing my impatience. He smiles and continues taking his time.

"So impatient." He runs his fingers through my trimmed

pubic hair and teases the outside of my sex. I am so amped up by his touch that it's enough to have me curving off the bed.

"Please, Graham," I plead.

I can't take much more of this, when finally his hand lifts my breast to his mouth. His other hand lays a trail from the middle of my breast to my stomach, across the outside of my sex, and finds a home inside of me. It's still not what I want. He concedes a little and adds another finger to allow me some of the fullness I crave. I voice my appreciation. I can feel his approval. Sensing my body responding to his ministrations and feeling how close I am, he pulls his fingers out, licking two of them clean and putting the third one in my mouth.

"See how good you taste, Emelia."

I nod. An aroused moan escapes my lips.

"That is for me. Me only. Do you understand?"

I nod again.

"Answer me." He stops all movements and his eyes lock with mine. He's stern, unyielding. When I don't answer right away, he grabs my hands holding them above my head and positions himself between my legs.

"I promise you I've been checked and I'm clean. I want to be inside you with nothing between us. Is that okay? It's okay to say no."

"Yes. I trust you Graham."

"What about birth control?" he asks.

"I'm good, remember?" He acknowledges the previous comment made at breakfast, and I can tell he has questions, but this isn't the time for them and he moves on.

"Can I show you what your first time should have been like Emelia?" In response to my nod, he slowly and gently enters me, filling me with the fullness I crave. I lift off the bed, my pleasure vocal. He begins to move slowly and precisely as my hips raise to meet his. Gently and with care, he makes love to me.

I am just reaching climax when he slows his movements and stills.

"Only mine. Do you understand?" He comes back to his unanswered question.

When I don't answer again, he rotates his hips to hit a sweet spot inside me that has me clawing his hands. He trails kisses down my neck and back up again. Rotating his hips one more time, I catch on. He's not going to let me come unless I agree. His tongue moves up the base of my throat, his lips finding mine. His kiss is searing and forceful. Possessive. He bites my lip hard. The combination of the softness and hardness of his kisses pushes me over the edge, and I finally answer him.

"Yes."

"Yes what Emelia?"

"Yes. Only you."

"Because?"

Because? What does he mean because?

"Graham," I say hoping it will satisfy him.

"Why only me, Emelia? Who do you belong to?"

"I'm no one's." I try to return his kiss.

"Wrong. You belong to me. Me only. No one else has been where I have been. You are mine." He punctuates the last three words with the rotation of his hips, hitting my sweet spot again and again. His possession confuses me. If I wasn't a virgin, would he have felt this way? I'm building again, and this time he lets me. He glides in and out of me, picking up his momentum. Despite my confusion, there is a connection between us that I can't deny.

"Look at me," he insists.

His orgasm is set off by mine. I can feel him coming inside me. The sensation is like no other. My sex pulses around him in response, causing him to jump inside me. We lay there, trying to catch our breaths. I think he is as shocked by the connection as I am.

Our breathing finally slows. Graham kisses me lovingly and pulls out of me. I wince. Without a word he stands, pulling me up with him. We make our way into his shower, turn on the water, and settle in. He runs his hand across a panel and it opens, revealing a sound system. After he hits a few buttons, "You Got What I Need" starts to play through the speakers. He places soft kisses on my body while he washes me. We're a few words into the next song when I reciprocate, washing him with the same care he's shown me. He leans his head down for me to rinse out the conditioner. I kiss his chest and playfully suck his nipple. He likes this.

Our hands explore each other, and he drops to his knees in front of me. He moves his lips up my thigh, using his chin to push against my legs, indicating he wants me to open for him. I comply. He buries his nose in the apex of my thighs, and his tongue begins to work its magic on me. It takes little time before my legs are giving way to another explosive orgasm. Who knew it could be like this?

Holding me up, he makes his way up my body, pushing his against mine, and sinks into me. My body easily accepts his even though soreness has set in. I wrap my legs around him, the water running over us, and his body moves to the beat of the music.

"Not yet," he says in my ear, anticipating how close I am to climaxing. "Control."

They are the only three words that he has spoken since we got into the shower. He wants this to last. I watch him. It's hypnotizing to see him lose himself in me. Graham, the CEO. The man who needs control like I do.

I don't break the silence, but my body obeys his commands. He continues to move inside me. In this position, the stimulation is more acute and I'm having a hard time delaying my orgasm. Graham finally has mercy on me.

"Now, Emelia. You can come now."

And just like that I break into pieces around him, finally getting the release I crave, proving that he is in control of my body. I am his. No matter how much I resist telling him.

His forehead rests against mine, and as if he thinks I need one last reminder, he tells me again: "Mine."

My legs feel like rubber. I'm sore. We finish our shower. He dries me with a towel and brushes my hair. I dry my hair and move into my room to get dressed. I'm sliding on a short sundress that falls a couple of inches down my thighs when Jules comes in.

"Hey, babe," I greet her.

"I think you may have *dropped* this downstairs." She twirls my running bra around in a circle, laying it down on the bed. My cheeks blush, but I don't say anything. She stands and looks at me. "When you're ready," she states and heads toward the door. "Everyone's back. We're starting dinner in about a couple of hours."

"Okay. I'll be down shortly."

I'm finishing a couple of things, when Lucy comes in.

"Do you have anything I can wear tonight, Emme?" she asks, sitting down on my bed.

"To dinner? I thought we were hanging out here?"

"You guys are, but I'm going out with Brody tonight." She has a dreamy look in her eyes, and I can tell she is having a hard time keeping a silly smile off her face.

"Who's Brody?"

"A boy from my school. He's been here all summer, and we've gone out a few times."

"Is it serious?"

"I think so," she says with a shrug.

"Anything I have is going to be big on you. Let me look." I come back out of the closet with a white loose fitted jumpsuit that I brought in hopes I could squeeze into it. It has a low v-neck in the front and back held up by spaghetti straps. The shorts fall a couple of inches above mid-thigh. It's a romper that can be made sexy or bohemian—which would be more age appropriate for Lucy—depending on the accessories and how its worn. "I have a great long necklace that you can wear with it. I would pair it with sandals. Wearing it with heels will look like you're trying too hard. Wear it with a pretty bra since it will show a little. What do you think?" I hold it up for her. She bounces over to it.

"I love it! Thank you, Mags!" She kisses me and heads out the door.

I slowly make my way downstairs into the kitchen. I had no idea sex would make you this sore. The French doors all along the back of the house are open. There's a great breeze coming in.

"We're all headed to the beach for a little while before we start dinner. Would you like to come?" Ruth asks me.

"Thank you, but I think I'll stay here and read." I move into the pantry to grab a twelve pack of Diet Cokes to restock the one in the kitchen. I notice a calendar on the wall. It can't be. I look again. Putting my finger on the date just to make sure I'm seeing right. A lump forms in my throat. I move to the fridge in the kitchen loading my drinks.

"What's wrong?" Jules question brings my eyes up.

"Nothing," I give my best smile and start breaking down the now empty soda box. She stands there waiting for my answer.

"I just didn't realize today is the first. I thought it was tomorrow. Today was my grandmother's birthday. It's the first time since she passed I didn't wake up thinking about it."

Jules runs her hand up and down my arm before she leans in and gives me a loud kiss on my lips. "Want me to hang out with you?"

"Don't be silly. Y'all go to the beach. I'm going to read a bit."

Drinking my Diet Coke, I'm amazed by how much I'm changing, just in the span of a week. There is a part of me that has always dreaded and celebrated the birthdays of my family. There is such a void in my heart that was occupied with such life when they were living. The idea that I didn't even realize today was my grandmother's birthday until now—it's surprising, actually. Unfamiliar.

Pushing off the counter, I enter the great room. It's a beautiful room with a large fireplace in the corner. There is no overhang of balcony here, so the view is unobstructed. There are two overstuffed couches that sit perpendicular to each other. One longer than the other. On the other side of the room are two oversized chairs in a subtle pattern of blues. Between the sitting area and the kitchen is a grand piano, an August Forster.

I run my fingers over the top of the piano. I haven't played piano since…in a long time. I take a seat on the shiny brown stool and stare at the keys for a while. Lifting my right hand, I lightly push down on a key. The tone reverberates through the great room. I push on another and another. After a few keys, I play a chord. It's like riding a bike. I add my left hand. It doesn't take long and the keys are making music.

My fingers know what they want to play today. In honor of my grandmother's birthday, I play her favorite hymn "How Great Thou Art." As the sounds start to come back to me, I accelerate to the third and final verse when the music crescendos at the chorus.

I lose myself in the memories the song rains down, pounding away at the keys, playing for my Grandmother.

I finish the hymn and move straight into her favorite piece of music. *Nuvole bainche* composed by Ludovico Einaudi. She would have me play it over and over for her. She had read an article about the composer where he talked about how happy the song made him. Einaudi thought it sounded like white fluffy clouds in the sky, or something like that. I think that's why she loved it so much. I am sad and disappointed in myself that I have not honored her by playing this song again until now.

I finish the last chord to a soft applause. I'm a little mortified to see that everyone has gathered into the living room to hear me play.

"I'm sorry, sweetheart," Ruth offers when she sees my expression. "I hope we didn't intrude, but we heard you playing and came to listen. It was a joy. I see why you were accepted to Julliard." She gives me a motherly kiss on my forehead.

"Actually, I would have never made it in on my piano skills. I was admitted for cello," I share with her.

The room empties out as everyone prepares for dinner. Graham comes to sit by me on the bench.

"You really played beautifully."

"I think you're biased when it comes to me." I nudge him, hoping to change the topic to something I am more comfortable with.

"I would say I am completely biased." He leans down and kisses me gently. "Dinner then movie."

ch♥pter
thirteen

Preparing dinner is loud and enjoyable. There's music and wine and stories. Ruth and Ben are making lamb kabobs with the items they picked up at the market today, and I am whipping up a peach pie to put in the oven while we sit to eat. I don't know how they ever leave to go back to the city. This place is like living in a storybook. It makes it easy to put what's happening between me and Graham to the side and simply enjoy the here and now. The vibrant family that surrounds me at the table.

What I am learning is a customary family ritual, clean-up duties are assigned. Becca and I were relieved of dish duty and placed on snack preparation, so that by the time everything is cleaned we are ready to sit down for the movie.

Jules has picked, so it's an old black and white. Everyone is situated around the flat TV that comes up from a console. The long couch is vacant, so I spread out with a bowl of popcorn and a Diet Coke. The French doors are still open and a chill fills the air. Ruth passes out blankets as she claims her spot next to Ben.

I have stretched out on one of the loveseats, when Graham casually sits down next to me, lifts the pillow my head is laying on, and positions it on his lap. I stare straight ahead at the TV, but I can feel all the eyes in the room on us. Just as I become uncomfortably self-conscious, someone outside honks a car horn. Lucy bounds down the stairs yelling good-bye to us.

"Wait!" I yell, trying to hold my dress down while climbing over the back of the couch, making sure she doesn't get outside before I get to her, letting out a high pitched yelp when I fall off the back onto the floor with a loud thud.

"I'm alright," I assure everyone. I see Graham peering over the back of the couch with an amused question on his brow as I stand.

"Don't you dare go out there!" I tell Lucy.

"You're not wearing that," Graham follows.

"Shush!" I say to Graham. "She looks great."

"That outfit is not appropriate." He stops and looks at me. "I'm sorry did you shush me?"

The horn honks again.

"The outfit is mine. I lent it to her. Ruth approved it. She looks great. Now, leave her alone!"

I redirect my attention to Lucy. The movie has been paused and Ben and Ruth are watching our exchange. "You do not go outside for a honk. This boy can come to the door to call on you. You are not a honk-and-go girl. Do you understand?"

"That's right!" Becca and Jules chime in from their spots on the chairs.

"But it's not our first date…"

"But nothing!" I interrupt her. "If you don't demand respect, he will think it's okay to not give it to you. Understand?"

She tentatively nods her response as the doorbell rings. I answer it.

"Is Lucy ready?" he asks. He seems like a polite enough young man.

"She is, but she is not a girl that you honk for. If you want to take her out, then we expect you to have the courtesy to come to the door to get her. Do we understand each other?"

"Yes, ma'am" he responds, nervously looking over my shoulder. Graham and Adam have entered the foyer and are standing behind me. Neither offer a greeting.

"Great. Wait here and I'll get her." I walk around the corner and whisper to her to wait a minute before going to the door. I can see her counting down the time, like she has butterflies in her stomach. She takes a step and I stop her, whispering to her that she needs to make sure he opens doors for her.

"Demand respect," I tell her, embellishing it with a corny little fist pump. I place a kiss on her forehead.

After they leave, I take my spot back on the couch as Jules starts the movie again. Graham idly plays with my hair as he watches. He's perplexing. He says he wants an affair with me, but he shows public affection when he's with me, something he admitted he was not into.

I struggle to stay awake through the movie, so I turn over, facing the back of the couch, and curl up for a nap. Graham cups the back of my neck with his hand, his thumb rubs a light path back and forth my jawline. The gesture so tender I open my eyes to look up at him. He's watching me, but his expression gives me no clue what he is thinking. Gently, he runs his thumb over my eye, gesturing to close them.

Just as I'm about to drift off, my eyes pop open to his light touch between my legs. He's looking straight ahead at the movie, but his fingers continue their exploration. He is pleased to find I'm not wearing anything under my dress.

I shift the blanket to make sure I am covered. It doesn't take long before his fingers are moving in and out of me in a frustratingly slow but arousing rhythm. He already knows how to read my body, and he adds a third finger knowing I crave the fullness. I shift slightly to better accommodate him. I cannot believe he is doing this here, in front of everyone. In front of his family. I feel like a 16-year-old getting away with something.

I wrap my fingers around his arm and run my thumb across the soft part of skin just inside the elbow. He increases the pace of his fingers moving in and out. He moves his thumb back and forth over my clit. The movie comes to an intense scene and the building of the music only adds to the building of my orgasm. Graham increases the speed and pressure. My climax cresting with the movie's. Before I can catch myself, I look up at Graham. He gives the slightest movement of a permissive nod, and I close my eyes as my orgasm explodes within me. My nails dig into his arm. It takes everything I have not to utter a single moan or move my body. Knowing how loud and vocal I have been with him each time, I'm surprised he trusted me to stay quiet. He pushes his palm against me, prolonging the beat between my legs. My breathing slows and I let out one long breath.

A slow, sexy smile spreads across Graham's face as he withdrawals his hand and cups my head as he did earlier, only this time he's running his thumb over my lips. I skate my tongue across it and taste myself, slowly pulling it into my mouth. Shifting slightly, I place my hand under my pillow and rest it between his thighs on his hard cock and give a slight squeeze before running my thumb up and down his length while I continue to suck on his thumb. His eyes close for a minute, letting me know he is affected.

When the movie ends, Jules slaps me playfully on the rear, exclaiming, "Let's fix the pie." As I stand, I make sure everything is covered, leaving my pillow on his lap to hide his excitement.

We dip out ice cream and slice the pies while the guys talk about Hitchcock movies in the other room. Without a word, Ruth kisses my cheek and picks up some plates to start serving.

It's almost 10:00 when we finish dessert. I'm ready to call it a night when Jules suggests we all go out for a drink while the guys turn on a Yankees game to watch with Ben. She looks at me with her puppy dog eyes that she knows I can't resist. Shit, this means I'm going to have to get dressed.

I can tell by the look on Graham's face that he'd rather I stay. We had an amazing connection today, but there is a side of me that wants to remind him that I make my own decisions, that I am self-sufficient. Have been for years now. After I reflexively asked his permission for an orgasm not an hour ago, this gesture feels especially crucial. I give him a casual shoulder-shrug and head upstairs to change.

I change into a pair of black leather shorts with a jean top and a pair of heels. Casual but current. My hair is in a ponytail, and I have on only mascara and lip gloss. I grab the keys to the Mercedes and we make our way to the garage. Before we can even get on our seatbelts, Graham and Adam stop us.

"I don't think so," Adam says.

Jules rolls her eyes and tells me to start the car.

"Not without security," Adam clarifies with a stronger voice.

Fuck that!

"Drive, Mags," Jules instructs.

I put the car in reverse and start us on our way. I halfway

expect the guard at the gate to stop us, or for Adam and Graham to come after us, but they don't.

There's a late night festival going on in town, and the local chamber has run lights from one building to another in a zigzag pattern across the street, creating a canopy of lights. Several of the bars and restaurants are serving outside, and a band is playing on a stage at the end of the street. Making our way through the crowd, Becca and Jules each grab a drink. I grab a bottled water. I don't drink when we go out. I can't be in control if I am drunk.

I've forgotten how much fun it is to be out with them. We're dancing and having a great time when a bell goes off and everyone around me cheers. I let out a yelp with the others and look at Jules confused. She laughs and points behind me. Some people come through the crowd with trays of shots. She and Becca each throw a couple back and start dancing again. I glance at my watch and notice it's almost one in the morning. Gathering my girls up, Becca stumbles a little and laughs. I put her arm to go over my shoulder and hold her by the waist. At least this way I have a little control over guiding her—not an easy feat in these heels.

Jules is still grooving to the music, but following me as we make our way through the crowd. I stop when I notice a white jumpsuit in my peripheral vision. *Surely not?*

I look over to see Lucy dancing in the middle of several guys, but her face seems altered. I nod my head in her direction for Jules and Becca to see, before I make my way to her.

"Mags!" She throws her arms around me, kissing me on the cheek. "I love you so much." She is definitely altered. I look around for Brody. He's nowhere to be found.

What a little fucker!

The guys she is dancing with circle us and keep dancing. I grab Lucy and try to make our way out.

"What's your hurry, mama?" says one of the guys blocking my path. I side-step them and start in a different direction. They move with us, blocking me again.

"Look, guys," I say over the music. "We don't want any trouble. Just let us by," I try again to get past them.

"Let me help you." One of them begins to lift Lucy out of my arms.

"Thanks," I say, tightening my grip, "but I'm making it just fine."

I take a few more steps, but he's more aggressive this time. I maneuver her to my other side, effectively placing myself between her and the guy. I have Jules' attention now, and she is coming up the other side of Lucy. Becca catches the eye of a policeman and gives a slight wave so he knows we need his assistance. I make a rookie mistake and take my eyes off the guys for just a second while pointing Jules to an opening in the crowd.

A couple of his friends join in and close our exit. One puts his hands on Lucy, pulling her towards him, informing me he is going to finish his dance with her. I try to position her out of his reach. I use my free hand and nails to unwrap his hands from her wrist. He swears and yanks on her, causing her to fall backwards.

Just as I catch her, Jules firmly brings the bottom of her palm into contact with his nose. He releases Lucy and I turn to move us out of there, when he grabs my ponytail, pulling me back and down in one motion, taking Lucy with me. I try to drive my heel into his foot hoping he'll release me, but before I know what is happening, Jules punches the guy across the jaw.

The policeman finally makes his way to us, so he hasn't

seen what happened before Jules throws the punch. He only knows that the guy is yelling about his broken nose. Jules and I tell Becca to call a cab and take Lucy home. Ten minutes later, we're in the back of a police car being charged with assault. *You've got to be kidding me. I never touched the guy.*

We try to explain to the officer on the way to I don't know where. I guess East Hampton has a police precinct. I think we would have had a little more leverage with him had we not been laughing about the whole thing, making fun of the guy getting beat up by Jules.

We are fingerprinted and placed in a cell that reminds me of something out of Mayberry. We're the only two in there. A man comes to our cell and introduces himself as Sheriff Baker, asking for our side of the story and reminding us that we get one phone call.

There is no way I'm calling Graham. I would rather stay the 24 hours to be released. I know he is going to be pissed. Instead, Jules calls Adam

Jules lays on the bench and puts her head in my lap. She's out in no time. The girl can sleep anywhere.

I'm playing with her hair when I notice a shadow fall across the floor. I look up to see Graham standing on the other side of the bars with his hands in his pockets. As I suspected, he does not look happy. I gently wake Jules when Ben and Sheriff Baker join Graham at the cell door. It's obvious that Ben and Sherriff Baker know each other.

"Three of the guys at the scene corroborated your story. We aren't filing the assault charges," Sheriff Baker says.

"I always knew you would be beside me if I ever got arrested," Jules winks at me sitting up, and I giggle. The guys are not amused by us at all.

"Thank you," I say to the Sheriff as I exit the cell.

"Miss James. I do have some business to discuss with you before you go." The look of confusion on my face has to tell him that I have no idea what that business would be.

"Do you have a dollar in your purse?" he says handing us our stuff. I nod my head. "Give it to Ben there." I do as I'm told. "Good. You now have legal representation. I'd like to see you and your lawyer in my office please."

Jules and I look at each other before I follow him to his office.

"You can't come son. Lawyers only," Baker says to Graham. I didn't even realize he was behind me. He wasn't happy before, now he's simmering.

"Take Jules home, son. Emme and I will be right behind you," Ben tells Graham. I can tell he is not pleased with this directive, but he knows better than to say so.

"Call me as soon as you leave," Graham says to me.

It's an order, not a suggestion. He puts his arms around Jules and heads out.

Sheriff Baker's office is standard, nothing fancy. There are drawings from his grandchildren on the bulletin board. Ben points to a seat in front of the desk. I sit and he takes the one next to it.

"What's going on, Ray," he asks. This is Lawyer Ben. His demeanor has changed and he's all business.

"I never touched the guy. I promise."

"Miss James has a warrant in the city," Baker says, addressing Ben.

"For what?" I ask. "There has to be a mistake."

"You've been charged with assault."

"Assault?" I say in disbelief. Ben raises his hand to silence me.

"What are the exact charges?" he asks.

"A one, Mr..." he puts his glasses on to read the paper he's holding, "John Michaels, has filed a suit alleging you attacked him."

"You've got..." Ben raises his hand to stop me from saying anything further.

"Is your purpose to detain her?"

"No. I talked to a sergeant, a friend of mine in the city, and he changed it to a desk ticket. When she gets back to New York, she will need to go to her local station and turn herself in. I suggest you take Ben with you, young lady. Stay out of trouble until then. You understand?"

Ben stands.

"Yes, sir," I nod.

"I knew we would get the other guys to confirm your statement. I just needed some time to get the story out of them. I'm sorry my officers didn't get to you before you were put in a situation where you had to defend yourselves."

He has an officer take us back to the Mercedes. Ben opens my door for me and I climb in. He slides in the driver's side with an easy grace that reminds me of Graham. Without a word, he starts the car and we head home.

We pull into the garage and he turns the car off. He stops me as I go to open the car door.

"I want to thank you girls for protecting Lucy. She ditched her security about an hour before you found her. The boys and I were out looking for her when Becca called. That said, I know you are tired. It's," he looks at his watch, "almost five in the morning. Why don't you go to bed, and we'll talk about the rest of this after you've had some sleep? Okay, sweetheart?"

"Thank you." I hug him.

"Until you and I talk, you say nothing to no one. Understand? By law, they have to repeat anything you say if asked. Until I have all the information, not a word."

"Got it," I say climbing out of the car.

When I walk into the kitchen, Ruth greets me with a hug. "Can I get you anything dear?"

"No, thanks. I think I'll get some sleep." My eyes lock with Graham's and he starts to say something.

"She can only tell you what happened with Lucy tonight," Ben cuts in. "I have instructed her not to say anything other than that. That includes to you, son." He looks at Graham. "Not a word." Graham opens his mouth to say something. "Son," Ben says, meaning business. Either out of respect or fear of his Dad—my guess is the first—he keeps his mouth shut.

"How's Lucy?" I ask Ruth.

"She's sleeping. Honestly, I'm not sure she is aware of what happened."

"She will be when I finish with her tomorrow," Graham says. He can't focus his anger on me, so poor Lucy will catch it all.

"We're her parents. We'll take care of it," Ruth says in a tone not to be messed with.

"Mom, it's inexcusable that she ditched her…"

Ruth cuts off Adam's rant. "I said we will handle it. Can you tell us what happened, Emme? Becca didn't have all the details, and Jules was asleep by the time Graham got her home."

I recap the story for them. Graham and Adam are fit to be tied when I'm finished. Mad about Lucy, mad about me and Jules. Ruth and Ben are seasoned veterans and are handling this better.

"I told you that outfit was…" Graham starts.

"Lay off the outfit. This had nothing to do with her outfit. She's a teenager. She's testing her boundaries. Your parents will deal with it and her. It will be fine," I say, exasperated and exhausted.

"Emelia…"

"Graham," I cut him off again. "Enough!"

I can see the vein in his neck popping and his thumb moving across his fingers like he's itching to touch me but doesn't. Adam throws his head back in laughter and slaps Graham on the back, like he's been let in on a secret. He says his good nights.

"You're doing just fine dear," Ruth says, squeezing my hand.

"Yes she is," Ben chuckles and kisses me on the forehead. They walk out of the kitchen. "Not a word, son." He says loudly from the other room.

Graham and I stand there staring at each other. I blink first and head upstairs. I'm too tired to argue. We check on Lucy. She's asleep. I'm headed into my room, when Graham pulls me into his without a word, closing the door. He heads into his closet and I undress where I'm standing. He comes out in his pajama bottoms and pulls one of his t-shirts over me, and we climb into his bed. He hits the button lowering the room-darkening shades and pulls me into his chest. He kisses the side of my head.

"Sleep," he orders. And I do.

ch♥pter
fourteen

The room is dark and cool when I wake. The darkening shades must be down still. I'm alone. "No sex for me I guess," I mutter to myself.

I'm quite sore. Stretching my arms, I head to my room and throw on a yoga outfit. It's eleven. I've only slept a few hours, but I feel rested enough.

Making my way to the stairs, I hear Graham talking. I'm about to walk to Adam's room to say good morning, when Graham's frustrated tone stops me.

"Stay out of my business, Adam."

"Look man, I want this to work. I think Mags is the best thing that could happen to you. Last night in the kitchen, when she was giving it right back to you, it reminded me of me and Jules, and I want that for you more than anything. All I'm saying is that Mags is not like the other girls you date. She's different. I don't want her to get hurt."

"That we can agree on. Now stay the fuck out of it."

"We're good then, bro. Mags is not a fuck-her-and-leave-her kind of girl. Got it?"

"You don't know shit, Adam."

"I know spending three days with her doesn't make you

an expert."

"Well, your time spent with her doesn't make you one either. I know Emelia."

Slowly, I back away from the door and start down the stairs. *This is why you shouldn't eavesdrop*, I remind myself. I understand Adam's need to be protective, but honestly, I can handle myself. I wish people would let me. I'm sick of being handled.

Entering the kitchen, I grab a Diet Coke and put a bagel in the toaster. When it dings, I slather it with cream cheese.

"A little bagel with your cream cheese?" Matt swipes across my bagel, sucking the cream cheese off his finger. I was so caught up in being annoyed with Adam, that I didn't realize there were people in here.

I laugh when I see Jules and Becca sitting at the kitchen table donning dark sunglasses. Too much to drink and too little sleep. They are each nursing a coffee, and both have serious bedhead.

Lucy, sitting with them, isn't looking much better. I know she has been in trouble with her parents. I will have to make sure to pull her to the side and spend some time with her, give her a chance to talk. Ruth and Ben are on the opposite side of the table from the girls, hiding their smirk behind their coffee cups.

"Good morning," Adam sings. Graham follows him into the kitchen.

"For the love of all things holy, please don't talk so loud." Jules puts her hands to her temples.

I laugh where I can be heard this time. Grabbing my breakfast, I move to the table and pull out a seat at the end. I'm only one bite in when Graham kisses me on the top of my head and whispers "good morning" in my ear. I catch Ruth and Ben's glance. It's a sweet, tender moment that is shot to hell when he reaches for my Diet Coke to replace it with a cranberry juice. He's in mid-motion when my hand finds his, halting him.

"I would think long and hard before you take my Diet Coke," I warn him, catching the smile appearing on Ruth's face. I give her a "this is not cute" look.

"Emelia."

"Graham. I refuse to have this argument with you every day. I don't drink coffee. Diet Coke is my wake-up drink." I take a big bite of my bagel.

"That would be fine, if you drank something else the rest of the day, but you don't. All you ever drink is Diet Coke."

"You are not the boss of me!" *Better comebacks, James. You have to work on better comebacks.*

"That's a completely different topic," he says in a tone only I pick up on. "I bet you can't go a week—scratch that, you can't go three days without having Diet Coke withdrawals."

"And if I can?"

"Then I'll lay off. If you can't, you agree to give up all except one a day at a time of your choosing."

I think on it for a minute. "Deal."

I shake his hand. He lifts my Diet Coke off the table and I slap his hand. "Can't touch this!" I am getting my one a day.

"Actually, MC Hammer, I can. The one a day doesn't start until *after* you have gone three days with none."

I think back over our conversation and make a face when I realize he's right. *Dammit.*

"Won that one, son" Ben pats him on the back. "Emme, let's talk in my office."

I shake my head in annoyance that this is even an issue, a movement intended only for me, but I catch Matt's eyes and I know he saw me. Becca puts her hand in his and gives a slight shake of her head, letting him know this is not the time to ask questions.

I follow Ben to his office, sitting as he closes his door behind me. "Now, Emme, I am legally bound to not share anything you tell me. Do you understand?"

"I do."

"Good. I don't want you to withhold anything because you think I will tell Graham." He visually confirms I'm with him. "Now, tell me about the alleged incident John Michaels is charging you with. Don't leave anything out, no matter how small a detail."

I go over everything that happened that day, including the flowers and necklace afterwards. I include the information about Colleen and how she introduced me to the Commissioner who helped me report the attack. I leave out no details.

"I've never liked John Michaels." Ben moves from leaning against his desk to sitting behind it. "He's always been a sleazy son of a bitch," he says with some venom. "I'm friends with Commissioner Ralston. I'll see if we can't handle this through some back channels, keep it out of the news. I should be able to arrange the desk ticket to be withdrawn. Have you have told anyone besides Colleen?"

I shake my head.

"Well, it's your decision to tell anyone or not. You won't be jeopardizing your case at this point. I honestly don't think he will want this in the press, and I don't see any way for him to spin this in his favor. I don't know how he wins this, so I don't know why he is trying. I don't trust him though. I would like you to have some protection until this is resolved. Will you let me arrange that for you?"

"Graham is already having me followed," I say somewhat

embarrassed.

"I see. Well good for him. My son is nothing if not thorough. Do you plan on telling him?"

"No, sir. Not at this time I don't."

He doesn't say anything for a beat.

"Alright then. I'll call the Commissioner now, and we'll handle the rest when we get back to the city next week." He stands and moves towards the door. As I make my way out, I stop to give him a hug. He wraps his arms around me and kisses the top of my head to let me know everything will be okay.

Graham clears his throat. He seems puzzled by the scene. I give Ben one last squeeze and make my way out the door.

"I'll give you two a minute," I say.

"Emelia?"

I squeeze Graham's hand as I walk by.

The girls are still in nursing hangovers when I re-enter the kitchen.

"I really like your yoga outfit, James. I need you to shop for me," Becca whispers.

"I can. All you have to do is ask and give me a budget. I style anyone. Let's go, ladies. Yoga on the deck. It will do us some good."

"I don't think so," they say in unison.

"Come on. You'll feel better I promise." I give my best puppy-dog look, but to no avail.

"Fine. Lucy?"

"Thanks, but I'll sit this one out."

"Ok. I'm going riding later. Want to go?"

"Sure." She looks a little brighter. I can tell she is still down about what happened last night. I don't have all the details, but I know it has been a long morning for her.

I reach for a Diet Coke, but remember the bet I made with Graham. I grab a bottle of water and head up to my room to do yoga on my balcony.

It's so pretty up here. The ocean looks like it's never ending. I try to clear my mind and get into the groove of my yoga. It feels good to stretch my body. Remove some of the soreness.

I've moved from a warrior pose to a downward dog. My hands and feet are flat on the ground. This is one of my favorite poses - it stretches everything.

Graham walks out and stands behind me, rubbing his hands over my ass. I'm noticing a pattern with him. Without a word spoken, he slides my pants over my hips and down my legs. He moves to his knees and puts his mouth on me from behind. With his hands on my hips, he continues to make a meal of me, fucking me with his tongue. I'm beginning to see that Graham likes to take me in unexpected places. I lift my head, but the balcony is solid and private. We can't be seen from here. He pulls his tongue out of me and runs it up and down my sex.

"Don't move," he commands, and leaves. In a minute he's back with something in his hand. "I'm going to put this in your ass."

Uh, I don't know about that, I think to myself.

"It's small, it will feel foreign at first, but you'll adjust to it. When I say so, I want you to shift your weight into it, understand?"

"Yes."

"Yes what?"

"Yes, okay?"

"Who's in charge, Emelia?"

"We both are."

SLAP!

"Emelia," he warns with a whisper. He inserts his fingers in my sex, extorting a moan from me.

"You, Graham. You're in charge," I concede in a whisper.

"And how do you address someone who's in charge?"

When I don't answer, he slowly rolls his tongue around the bud of my sex and back down my folds. He repeats the pattern, but this time he bites the little bud, then soothes it with his tongue. Then he stops and waits for my answer. I try to hold out, I really do, but he has me so amped up that all I want is for him to bring me to climax.

"Yes, sir," I acquiesce.

"Good girl. Now, be quiet. The others are on the deck below."

What the fuck? Then why is he doing this now?

His tongue moves down between my cheeks before entering me again. This time he uses his tongue to fuck me as slowly as he can. From his vantage point behind me, he's able to get deeper. His tongue should be illegal. Biting my lip, I keep my moans to a whimper. He stops and pushes a cold object into my sex moving it back and forth. It takes me a minute to realize he's lubing the object with my own wetness. Pulling the object out, he wets his fingers in my sex and runs them up my ass spreading the moisture over me. Placing one hand on my ass cheek, he positions the object against the pucker of skin and slowly pushes it in.

"Push into it, Emelia."

I push back slowly giving my body time to adjust. It only takes a second before it slides into place.

Graham rubs my ass affectionately, fucking me again

with his tongue. I'm in sensory overload. Between the fullness in my ass, the job his tongue is doing on me, and the shaking from holding this position so long, I can barely contain the noises I am making.

Graham continues a repetitive movement that has me detonating around him. He continues to drink me in, unfazed, until my arms give way. He catches me and slowly eases me to the floor of the deck. I'm on all fours now.

"That was…"

"Shh," he cuts me off. "Quiet baby." He reminds me, as he slowly enters me from behind, that knows what he's doing. He already knows my body and the fullness I crave. I need him inside of me as much as he needs to be. He sets his rhythm, intermittently turning the object in my ass while his other hand pulls on my hair. I can feel myself climbing again.

"Control," he grits.

I'm still learning, and my body is not my own. I am learning that I like to be taken from behind. I like watching him glide in and out of me.

His hand cups over my mouth silencing me as he turns the object again, this time removing it just as the most explosive orgasm rips through my body. Once he knows I'm not going to scream, he puts his hand back on my hip and continues to pound into me until he meets his own orgasm. His body drapes over mine, shaking with orgasmic convulsions.

"What are you doing to me, Emelia?"

"I could ask the same of you," I reply as we continue to catch our breath. Thank God the girls didn't want to do yoga.

Finding his own balance, Graham raises off me, adjusting himself back into his shorts and returns my pants to their former placement. Without another word he kisses me, but the kiss seems off. I can't put my finger on it, but it feels almost like a goodbye kiss.

"Graham?"

I know he feels it, too, but he doesn't respond to me. He caresses my face, his eyes empty. Just like that, without a word, he's gone.

I can't shake the feeling that something has changed. Did Ben tell him about John Michaels? Does he not want me anymore? What was that thing he used on me? I have so many questions.

After a quick shower, I head downstairs. Ruth is in the kitchen, preparing food for the day's meals.

"Where is everyone?" I ask, grabbing a sparkling water from the fridge.

"Not sure where they were all going, but it's just me and Lucy."

"I'm meeting some friends to go riding. I was wondering if you have some riding clothes I may borrow."

"I do. I even have an old pair of six's. I'll get them for you. Would you mind taking Lucy with you? She loves to ride."

"I remember. We rode together last time I stayed. I was hoping she would want to go. By chance," I bite the bullet and ask, "did Graham say where he was going?"

She stops dicing, giving me her attention.

"No, dear. I'm sorry he didn't." She goes back to chopping a pepper. "I like you two together. You're good for him. Graham has always put everything else first. He always says he wants no-hassle dating. You are a hassle. Ben and I like that about you." She winks at me, wiping her hands on a dishtowel. "Now, let's get you those riding clothes."

Ruth's closet is smart and functional, while maintaining style. She has some pieces that are to die for. I run my hand over a long multi-chained vintage Chanel necklace.

"Jules showed me her design for you to wear to Casino Night. It's beautiful. I was thinking that I have the perfect earrings you could wear with it, if you would like." She hands me a pair of riding pants. "Try these on and see how they fit. They are too small for me. I have another pair if these don't work."

I take off my shorts and put the pants on. They fit like a glove. They have leather at the knees and leather across the top of the hips which gives the illusion that my already ample backside is rounder and perkier. I look at myself in the full length mirror.

Ruth laughs, "I don't think anyone will be looking at the horse." This makes me blush.

"These are the earrings that I was thinking would be perfect for you to wear." She takes out a red leather Cartier box, opening it to reveal a beautiful pair of diamond earrings with a dropped sapphire.

"Ruth, these are so beautiful, but I could never wear these. I would be terrified of losing them." I close the box and hand them back to her. "It was so sweet of you to think of me."

"Nonsense. That's what insurance is for. If you lose them, I'll replace them."

I know she is being cavalier about it, but there is no way she could replace these. They are definitely vintage.

"Just think about it, dear. What size shoe do you wear?"

"Eight and a half."

"Perfect. These will fit you." She hands me a pair of black leather riding boots. I take them and give her a kiss on the cheek. I think she knows I am thanking her for more than just the boots.

I French braid my hair into a side braid and tuck in the thin, white t-shirt that I am wearing. I look at my watch and yell for Lucy. It's almost one, and I promised Colleen I would be there at 1:30.

Ruth gives us a ride to the stables, since everyone absconded with all but one of the vehicles. We pull up at exactly 1:30 to find Colleen waiting for us. Exchanging cheek kisses, I introduce her to Lucy.

"Where are the girls?" I look around for Colleen's nieces.

"Lessons." she informs me. "But you'll get to see them soon. They can't wait to ride with you. Until then, why don't you and Lucy go for a ride without them tagging along? I have a horse for you to ride, Emme." She walks me to a large stall. The name plaque beside it says Scout. "Like your first car, and the character from your favorite book," Colleen points out.

He's a milk chocolate stallion with a black mane and black tail. I look over the stall door and see he has black on all four legs from the knees down. He has a white marking at the top of his head in the shape of a diamond.

"He's perfect."

I gently test his demeanor to see if he will let me pet him. He does. I run my hand from his forehead to his muzzle. He lets me kiss him and I coo into his dark, soulful eyes.

"Jackson says you grew up riding. I would have chosen a mare, but he believes you can handle a stallion, so I trust him."

"I'd be happy to ride whatever horse is available," I tell her. Scout pushes at my hand for me to pet him again.

"Well," Colleen says, uncharacteristically beaming, "Scout will always be available for you to ride." She pulls down a sheet of paper that was covering part of the plaque.

I look from the plaque to Colleen and to the plaque again. It reads, "Scout. Owner, Emelia James."

"You didn't." I say in disbelief.

"Happy Birthday, Emme."

"But my birthday isn't until the end of the month."

"I know, but I wanted you to have him this week so you could enjoy riding him."

"Colleen, this is too much. Get me some perfume, or a great book. You don't buy me a horse. I can't accept this."

"Why not? You know you are special to me. I've given my nieces horses for their birthdays. So, you get a horse."

For some reason the only image that is in my mind is Oprah pointing to everyone saying "You get a horse and you get a horse! Everyone gets a horse!" The image and the absurdity of it makes me giggle.

"He'll stay here with our horses. They groom him, feed him, and keep him trained."

"There aren't words…" I trail off. I'm overwhelmed. I had an issue with a $350 iPod. This is more. So much more.

A stable hand opens the stall and guides him out. He's huge, a stellar horse. I can tell just by looking at him. He's been prepped for riding already.

"Colleen, I can't."

"You can and you will."

The stable hand gives me a hand as I mount and then brings Lucy's horse, Sky, around. She's named for her blue eyes.

"Here you go." Colleen hands me a riding helmet. "I got your measurements from Jackson."

The stable hand leads me to a training pen, where I can ride him in a confined area to get a feel for him. I easily get into a groove with Scout. He's a dream to ride. He's responsive, easy tempered and sure-footed. He's a strong horse and has a will of his own, but he doesn't hinder my movements or directions.

Lucy has started ahead of me, and I ride him out of the arena to meet her. Colleen comes up beside me to hand me a crop in case I need it.

I think about how different my life would have been if I hadn't met Jackson. His faith in me opened me up to a world I never imagined. I never pretend that I belong in this class of people, but I also have no ideas that I am inferior because they have money and I don't. I find they are like everyone else. They want to be loved for who they are and not what they have. Granted, there are plenty of people with money who are absolutely horrible, but I've been able to steer clear of them for the most part.

Lucy and I slow our horses to a walk and she gives me the story of what happened last night. I talk to her about the dangers of not being in control of your surroundings. I can't prove it, but I swear I think Brody had put something in her drink.

I follow her into the stables. Colleen has already left. Lucy takes Sky to her stall while a stable hand helps me dismount and takes the reigns.

"Hi, beautiful." I turn to the voice I am so familiar with.

"Jackson, what are you doing here?"

"Polo match. Patrick is home."

"I didn't know you were playing today. I would have come. Colleen gave me a horse." My thoughts are tripping over themselves. I feel like there's so much to tell him—and so much I can't.

"I know, sweetheart. Don't overthink it. She's been wanting to since the last time you rode together."

I put my arm around his waist, and we walk for several minutes.

"Out with it." He stops and looks at me.

"Out with what?"

"Whatever's on your mind?"

"I may or may not be seeing Graham Taylor." I just blurt

it out. I exhale a deep breath that I feel like I've been holding for days.

"You're still in the decision making process?"

"He is."

He considers this for a moment and then says, "You're aware he has a reputation about the girls he dates."

"I do. That is not how this would play out," I assure him.

"But you're interested."

"I am." I pause. "What do you think about him? Do you know him?"

"On a business level. Its Graham's building we work in."

"Is he a suggestion for my mentor program?"

"Yes."

"Because…"

"Because I think he's a good guy. He's smart, extremely talented. He's a phenomenal business man. He treats his employees well. His is the top corporation in America to work for. He's a good man, Emme."

"But…"

"But, you're like a sister to me. Who I trust my business to isn't the same as who I trust my sister to. That said, I could see that you would be a good match for each other. Not sure why it never occurred to me before, actually. Why do you think he's still deciding?"

"I just do. I can't put my finger on it yet, but I just do."

"Well, I can't blame him for wanting to be careful where you're concerned. Just take it one step at a time." He hugs me. "Can I give you and Lucy a ride home?"

"Thanks, but Ruth is coming for us. Besides it's out of your way. We'll be fine."

"Oh, Richard Raines called me. He wants to meet. Maybe we can later this week or next week. I almost had a coronary when I read what happened in the paper." He looks a little miffed that he didn't hear it from me.

"I'm sorry. I should have called you. It never occurred to me you would be worried."

"I'm always concerned about you."

We say our goodbyes, and I walk over to Scout's stall to brush him down.

"Holy fuck."

I turn to find Blaine smiling at me. I don't hide my surprise at seeing him.

"What are you doing here? You know they have group meetings for stalkers." I can't help but smile back at him.

"I've had some crazy stalkers. You ought not to joke. My parents own these stables, so maybe it's you who's stalking me."

I roll my eyes, and he continues, "I grew up working here. Can I just take a moment to worship your body in those riding pants?" His eyes wander to my ass, which, I can't deny, do look good in these pants.

"Smoke and mirrors, my friend." I put extra emphasis on friend. "The way the leather is cut." I run my finger across the seam.

"Not possible. I've seen it before today, you know."

He picks up a dandy brush, combing behind my rubber curry. We make our way around the horse, each changing to a body brush, Blaine on one side, me on the other.

"Where did you learn to care for a horse?" Blaine asks. "Most people who keep their horses here don't know the difference in the brushes, much less how to use them."

"My grandpapa had horses. He taught me to ride and to care for them."

I take a comb to Scout's mane. Blaine moves to his legs and hooves. We work in comfortable silence.

"He's good," Blaine says, dusting off his hands. "The stable hands will finish the rest. Why don't we go to the café and grab a bite?"

I look at my watch. "I have dinner shortly, but a snack sounds perfect."

"I remember," he nudges me laughing. "A girl who likes to eat."

I close the stall behind me and run my fingers over the owner's plaque. I grab my phone out of my boot and text a picture of the plaque and the horse to Jules. Lucy comes around the corner. The sight of Blaine stops her in her tracks. I can see in her eyes that she's a fan.

"Lucy Taylor, I would like you to meet Blaine Moore."

She's speechless—something Blaine seems to be used to. He speaks first, offering his hand to her.

"How do you know each other?"

I wait for Lucy to answer, but she's a little awed.

"Lucy is my best friend's fiancés sister. Say that three times fast," I laugh. He makes small talk with her, winning her over even more with his charm.

"I was just coming to get you. Want to get a snack?" I ask her.

"Sure, if you don't mind."

"Of course not," I answer. "Lead the way," I say to Blaine.

We make our way to the café they have on the property. Blaine introduces us to his mother, and I can't help but wonder if she saw the pictures of me kissing her son. She is a strong, feisty woman, and I like that about her. She reminds me of my grandmother, just years younger. She gives us tea and cookies, which makes me like her even more.

"So, I'm almost out of clothes," Blaine says to me.

"I'm not sure that's as big of a problem as you might think

it would be," I quip.

Lucy chokes on her tea, and I pat her on the back. Blaine laughs at the two of us. He has a wonderful laugh that I like very much, but it doesn't rumble the place deep in my belly like Graham's does.

It's easy to see that Blaine is used to being around all types of people. He has no problem engaging Lucy in conversation so she doesn't feel excluded. I take a pic of them for Lucy.

We make our way back towards the stables in time to see Ruth's car pulling up. Lucy reluctantly says her goodbyes, but gives me a cheeky wink before giving Blaine and I a moment alone.

"I'll be back in the city next week. Call me and I'll schedule some time to work up some new looks for you. Make sure to thank your mom again for me."

"Are you going to Casino Night?"

"I am. It's a working night for me and Jackson."

"If something changes let me know. I would love to take you." He's hopeful.

"As friends?" I playfully remind him. "That's sweet of you, but it's already finalized. I'm sure you have someone else you would love to take."

"That's just it. I'm beginning to think there isn't."

He pulls me into a hug, his hand moving to my lower back. I break the contact before he kisses me.

"Take care of Scout. I'll be back later this week to check in on him," I say casually patting Blaine on the chest, trying to defuse the one-sided sexual tension. Blaine reluctantly lets go of my waist and I turn on my heels to head to the car. But not before running straight into Graham's chest.

ch♥pter
fifteen

"Graham?"

"Emelia, wait in the car," he says without taking his eyes off of Blaine.

"I don't think so. Let's go, Graham."

"He needs a reminder of the definition of friends," he growls, finally looking at me.

I say good-bye once again to Blaine and stomp my way toward the car, leaving Graham behind. *What the hell? He's the one who left me today!* I'm just about to open the driver's door when Graham locks the door from behind me.

"What the hell, Graham! Unlock the door!"

"Emelia!"

"Graham!"

"You're not driving!" Without another word he picks me up at the waist, walks around to the passenger side, unlocks the door, drops me in the seat, fastens my seatbelt, slams the door, and hits the door lock again. He makes it to his side of the car before I have a chance to get out.

Like most sixteen-year-olds, Lucy is completely oblivious to what is actually going on between us. She gushes about how sexy Blaine is and that she just cannot believe I know him.

When she tells us that Blaine is on her "list", I actually think Graham might run into a tree.

I talk with Lucy like everything is normal, which pisses Graham off even more than he already is. He pulls into the garage, and I'm out of the car before it's in park. Lucy is right behind me. We clear the mudroom and enter the kitchen. Half the crew is around the island cooking, and the other half is around the table. The Eagles are playing in the background, the doors are open, it's another storybook night.

I open the fridge and start to grab a Diet Coke. *Dammit! I can't. I'll lose the bet.* As if she anticipated it, Ruth hands me a glass of wine, winking at me as Graham storms into the kitchen. The entire mood in the room changes from the tension radiating off him.

"Son?" Ben says with a furrowed brow, taking a sip of his beer.

"What's going on?" Jules says to me.

"He's an angry elf," I say bulging my eyes and adding a smart ass look. They try to keep their laughter in so that they don't stoke the fires, but to no avail. Everyone cracks up.

"Emelia!" he bellows again.

"Graham!" I bellow back. "I do not like to be handled!"

This draws Matt's attention. "Word to the wise man: don't try to handle James."

"Did you know that Mags knows Blaine Moore? He's so hot for her," Lucy says popping a strawberry in her mouth, oblivious still or just tired of this show.

"Emelia. Now," Graham says.

There's a vain in Graham's neck that does a little dance when he's angry. It's unnoticed by most, but I have charted that neck with my tongue, and I know it wasn't there earlier. We stare at each other like fools. I'm the first to dismiss him. I turn to the table and start a conversation.

"Fine. Have it your way," Graham says before throwing me over his shoulder, carrying me upside down out of the kitchen.

"Graham!"

"Dinner in twenty minutes," Ruth yells to us, like this is an everyday occurrence.

I'm relieved when he doesn't stop on the stairs. In his room, Graham tosses me on his bed and kicks the door close.

"Emelia," he says through gritted teeth.

"Graham, I *do not* like to be handled."

"Well, you're going to be, so move past it. Work through it. Whatever you have to do. I don't want to have this argument with you again. Do you understand me?" He's towering over me.

"I don't like to be handled."

"Emelia!"

"What even gives you the right? You left me today, Graham. And don't tell me I don't know what I'm talking about. I know you."

He doesn't deny it, but he doesn't say anything. His breathing is still erratic.

"Fuck this," I say, raising on my toes to kiss him. He doesn't kiss me back.

"I'm not the right person for you, Emelia. It would be selfish of me to keep this going knowing you want more than I'm able to give."

"Able to or willing to? Because there is a difference, Graham."

He doesn't answer.

"So let me get this straight. You don't want me, but you don't want anyone else to have me either. How does this work,

Graham?"

When he still doesn't answer me, I move around him, opening the door and leave.

Dinner is light and fun despite Graham sulking like a school-boy. We decide to build a bonfire on the beach and roast marshmallows and make s'mores for dessert. We're pulling the items we need, adding some beers to the basket, when the phone rings from the security gate and I hear Ben tell them to bring it up.

"Package for you," Ben tells me.

"From who?" I ask.

"Whom," he corrects, "and I didn't ask."

I sign for the delivery and bring the box into the kitchen. Jules and Becca have gathered around me—signs that they are both nosy. It's from B&H photo in the city. The note inside reads: "Because nothing will ever be enough to repay you. The Raines."

I remove the packing paper and pull out a camera bag. It's a Hasselblad, a ten-thousand dollar camera. There are also two Sony lenses and an assortment of other things that only a professional photographer might need.

I stand in stunned silence. Jules is the first to break it.

"How awesome! Weren't you just saying that your old one stopped working from all the sand that got in it?" She says this with the kind of nonchalance of someone who grew up with affluence.

"I don't need a camera like this. It's too expensive. A cheaper one would have done just fine."

"He called me today," Graham says behind me. "He wants

you to have this. It would mean a lot to him if you would accept it."

"But…"

"I know," he cuts me off. "But sometimes a gift is more for the person giving it than it is for the person receiving it."

This camera costs more than my first car. I'm used to getting gifts from clients after a large project or as a tip for Christmas, but I usually return them and send the money to Memphis to cover my responsibilities. I start to explain it to Graham, but stop when I remember I'm mad at him.

"It's very kind of them," I say, setting it back in the bag.

"Ready?" I give my best smile to everyone in an attempt to shift the focus back to our outing, but I know Graham noticed the subtle change in my demeanor. He nods and picks up the basket to carry to the beach. I grab some blankets.

The weather couldn't be more suitable for a fire on the beach. Adam has a great one going, and I curl up on a blanket with Lucy. Between the songs, the s'mores, and the cheesy ghost stories, it should have been a great night, but I'm having a little trouble shaking my melancholy mood. I don't know if it's Graham, but I know it's guilt. I feel guilty for the gifts I have received today. I mean, who gets to live a life like this? It's not every day you get a horse or a ten-thousand-dollar camera, much less both in the same day. Why me? There's nothing more special about me than someone else. I'm not more deserving than the next guy. It's overwhelming.

It's past eleven. Adam kicks sand on the fire, ensuring its out before we head back to the house.

As everyone heads back to the house, I pull Ben to the side and ask, "Would you mind if I use one of the cars?"

"Of course not, sweetheart," Ben says. "It's late though. Do you want to wait until morning?"

"Thanks, but I'll be fine."

I grab the keys to one of the Mercedes and hit the road. With the windows down and the music up, I drive. I remember I didn't tell Jules I was leaving. Knowing she'd be worried, I pull out my cell to text her. I have two missed calls and a text from Graham. I hesitate to text him back. He doesn't want a relationship with me, so what do I owe him. But, I realize, not answering would create needless worry—it would be petty. I don't want to be petty. I finally text him back.

Staying at Jackson's 2nite. Plz tell Jules. Back in morning.

I put my phone away, turn up Gomez's "Little Pieces" and drive.

The words to the song strike a chord with me. Without realizing it, I chose a song that parallels what's happening between Graham and me. We both have pieces that we aren't sharing. Really, how is he supposed to decide if he wants a relationship when I don't give him the information he needs to make an informed decision? Games. Drama. I've never been a girl for either.

The sound of seashells underneath the tires is the telltale sign that I have made it to Jackson and Patrick's house. Some of the tension I've been feeling over the last few hours dissipates. Their place is cozy and welcoming—it feels like I'm home.

Jackson opens the door before I get out of the car. "Jules called and said you were on your way. I'm supposed to call her if you don't make it."

He hugs me and hands me a glass of Diet Coke. "Hi, beautiful," he adds, kissing the top of my head.

"Patrick already went to bed." He answers my question

before I ask it, directing me to the sofa. We sit on opposite ends.

"So…" he says.

"I have no idea," I sigh and wave my hands in a gesture of resignation. "I just felt like I was losing touch and needed to get a way for a minute." He listens patiently and attentively as I fill him in on the events of the day—the horse, the camera.

"You know how much I love Colleen, and the Raines' are such nice people, but it just was overwhelming. I mean who gives gifts like that?"

"The people we work for. You know, Emme, accepting those gifts doesn't make you a bad person. You work hard. You give back. You carry more than your fair share of the responsibilities in Memphis. Until this week you've worked multiple jobs. I could go on and on. These are blessings, and therein lies your problem. You don't understand why some people have more blessings than others."

"I feel inadequate," I confess.

"That surprises me. I've never known you to be self-deprecating. You're the most self-assured person I know."

"I would have to go into so much to explain it and right now, I just want to curl up and forget about it."

"I have your room all ready. You get one night and then no more running."

I smile at these words only a true friend could get away with saying.

"Thank you." I give him a kiss and pat the top of his chest. "I can't have this." I hold up my drink. "I have a bet going that I can go three days without. I'm twelve hours in."

"Then you only get one night here for sure," he shivers in jest.

I don't know if it is all gay men, or just Jackson and Patrick, but they know how to prep a guest room. The room is quaint but subtly luxurious. The sheets feel like I am sliding between silk. I usually sleep so well when I'm here, but tonight I'm uncharacteristically restless. I can't take my mind off Graham. Sometime after three, sleep finally claims me.

"Good morning, sunshine…Good *morning*, sunshine!"

I open one eye to see Patrick lying next to me. I close it back and bury my head into the pillow.

"Jules texted and said you are to get up. Now. You are meeting them for breakfast at nine."

I mumble something unintelligible. The covers come off, and he drags my feet to the floor.

"It's a good thing I wasn't sleeping naked."

"It wouldn't have mattered. Strictly dickly, remember? Now, get dressed."

The guys are sitting at the table reading the paper and drinking coffee when I come downstairs.

"You two look like you should be in *Better Homes and Gardens*." I go to the fridge to look for something to drink that might get me moving.

"You've had an eventful week, darling," Patrick says. "I've been following you."

"What is the sudden curiosity with my life? I mean how hard up do you have to be for news?" I spot some sparkling water and mix it with cranberry juice. A little fizz goes a long way when I'm looking for a pick-me-up.

"How was Blaine yesterday?" he asks me, smiling overtop of his paper.

"Leave her alone," Jackson says taking a bite of his fruit.

"Shush, I'm talking to your 'it girl.'"

"You know you're my only 'it girl,'" Jackson deadpans.

"Don't you forget it, honey. Seriously, Ems. You said nothing was going on, but I hear you spent the day riding together. Even shared a meal."

"Please tell me that is not in the paper," I cringe.

"Page Six, honey."

I roll my eyes and stand. "I have to jet. We're having breakfast at Sunny Side Up. Want to come with?"

"Thanks, but I have a long list of things to get done around the house today." Jackson stands with me, walking me to the door. Patrick follows. Jackson turns my back to him, and in less than a minute I leave with a braid cool enough for a photo shoot. I admire his handy work. I wish I had someone to do my hair every day. I thank him and Patrick and then head out the door to the restaurant.

It's packed for a Thursday, and there's quite a long line out the door.

"I was just texting you, Mags," Jules says as I walk up. "I think we are going to go somewhere else. We're starving and it's a two-hour wait."

"Give me a minute."

I walk to Maria at the hostess stand and give her a hug. In the style of vets of the restaurant business, we catch up in record time as she shuffles menus, lists, and hungry patrons. "I can't believe how slammed you guys are," I say.

"It's the holiday, and this place is pretty hot. But you know that," she winks. "You're lucky you have friends in high places. I'll pull a table together for you. Just, for the sake of our survival, pretend you called ahead. Grab your group and it'll be ready before you guys can make your way through this place." Maria motions to the packed restaurant and greets another family walking up.

I motion for my group to come up.

"I texted last night and asked her to hold a table for us," I say, keeping Maria's shady little secret. "It's ready."

The restaurant has been featured in several magazines, not just for its food, but for the architecture and design of the restaurant. Its white shiplap walls and barn-red vaulted ceiling evoke the style of an old family farm, but there are also classic diner pieces and current, high-end chic pieces mixed in. All of the mismatched tableware and some of the design pieces were picked up at garage and estate sales over the course of about a month out by the owner and me, which is how I got to know Maria and the rest of the staff. There's a wraparound bar that seats twenty, decorated with the daily offerings of breads and muffins. Each table has fresh fruit in the middle for people to eat while they wait for their food. The air smells like sugar and blueberries.

We take our seats and talk about what we want to order. The waitress, who I remember from my styling days with the owner, brings two carafes of Orange Juice and Milk.

"Sorry, sweetie," she apologizes, giving me a pitiful look. "You know we don't serve sodas."

I catch Graham's smirk, but I ignore it.

"You all take a minute to look at the menu and I'll be back," she says, hugging me before leaving us to our menus.

I can tell she and the other wait staff are overwhelmed, so I get the orders from my crew and refill our carafes in an attempt to help her out. I've eaten at this restaurant many times over my weekends here with Jackson. There's something settling about this place—the hustle and bustle of all the tables, families coming together over breakfast, the sound of heavy plates clinking together. The familiarity comforts me. It reminds me so much of home—Memphis.

"Emme!" Colleen's nieces shout and try to jump into my arms all at once, drawing the attention of almost everyone in the restaurant. I let them lead me to their table where they are having breakfast with their parents. I say hello to some other regulars I remember from my waiting days on my way to the restroom.

"I'd like a word with you," someone hisses as I exit the restroom. It's John Michaels.

Why does everyone in the city have to go to the Hamptons?

"I'm busy. Plus, you're not my client anymore. You need to talk to Jackson." I walk away from him without looking back.

His hand tightens around my arm in the same place he left the bruises last time, and he attempts to move me backwards.

"Now," he says in a low whisper.

"Michaels." I look to my side, grateful to see Ben standing there. To the normal observer, Ben looks like an old friend catching up, but I can tell he is struggling to keep his demeanor calm. He looks from the hand John has around my arm to John himself.

In a low voice meant for the three of us only, Ben says, "Remove your hand this second, or I'll break every last finger."

John slowly lowers his hand.

"I'm representing Miss James and I will be reporting this as a violation to the restraining order in place. If you have any issues, you have your attorney call me. Otherwise, we will see you in court."

Court? Is this really going to court?

"Pops," Adam says, patting Ben on the shoulder as he and Graham walk up. "Why don't you introduce us?" I'm positive they didn't hear the exchange, but they know their dad and they know his feathers are miffed.

"Another time, son. He was just leaving." Ben nods curtly at John.

I keep my eyes on Ben, hoping to divert any questions the guys might have. Ben doesn't move. He watches as John walk away without a word. As I make my way to the table, I hear Ben tell Graham, "I want to talk with Smith when we leave here."

We make a solemn return back to the table, but the merriment of the rest of the breakfast helps us put the matter to bed. After breakfast, the Taylors leave in their car as I say my good-byes to the owners. I make my way to the Mercedes that I've parked in one of the back overflow parking lots. I'm rather distracted by my cell phone when I hear a voice in front of me.

"We need to talk."

His voice draws my eyes up. Will I ever tire of looking at this man? His faded jeans skim his body, and my sex quivers just looking at him.

"I didn't realize there was more to say."

"Emelia."

"Graham." Just saying his name back to him encompasses so much conversation that I don't even have to put words to.

He opens the driver's-side door for me. He's letting me drive? I swear he does it just to make me crazy. He's trying to throw me off my game. I slide in and he shuts my door. He climbs into the passenger-side seat.

"How long have you been waiting?"

"Longer than I've ever waited for someone before."

His honesty surprises me. "Where to?" I ask him.

"Back to the house. I want to show you something." Graham hits a button to lower the top and hands me a pair of Ray Ban aviators. Picking up his phone, he connects the Bluetooth and pulls up his music. I pull off the main street and head to the coast, to take the long way home. I cut my eyes over to him and issue an imperceptible grin when Nina Simone starts to sing, "I Want a Little Sugar in My Bowl".

I turn onto the property. After the guard opens the gate for us, Graham has me take a sharp right past the guard stand onto a dirt road. Following it around for about four miles, we come to a house. Actually, the word "house" doesn't do it justice. It's a work of art that seems to double as a house. Graham gets out when I park the car and comes around to open my door.

"Where are we?"

"My beach house." He takes my hand and leads me to the beautifully carved door. The front entry walls are a bluish gray slate. He places his hand on what looks like part of the slate. It lights up from underneath, and I hear a clicking noise. Graham opens the heavy door and pulls me in behind him. The space is large and modern, but it's oddly open, airy, and homey. Whoever designed this room did a great job of making what could otherwise be a very cold, stoic room into a welcome and comfortable one.

"Graham, I'm in awe." I run my hand over some of the wood work.

"You're the first person to see it finished. This room, anyway. They still have a few bathrooms to finish, and then it'll be completely done. I meet with designers next week to decide on furniture, art, and finishing touches."

He shows me the kitchen. It would be any chef's dream. He could easily host a party for a couple hundred people out of this kitchen. There's an eight-car garage off the butler's entrance. The wall in the kitchen mimics his parents in that it's all doors, but these are iron framed doors instead of French, which fits the style of the house much better.

We head back into the living space. Graham hits a button on his phone and the back wall begins to fold into itself like an accordion; they come to rest seamlessly into the walls. The large outdoor space could house a small army. It's been beautifully decorated. There is an outdoor kitchen near the back of the space that puts to shame most people's main kitchen.

He leads me to a set of stairs off the living space. They open into a master suite made for a king. The walls are a soft light blue that complements the colors of the ocean view. The en suite bathroom is the size of the apartment I share with the dwarfs. The shower has a panel in the top that looks like it would rain down over the entire space. There are jets in the walls that come from all angles and a beautiful mosaic tiled bench on the end. There's a solid-pane window that provides an ocean view from the shower. On the other side of the bedroom is one huge closet that would easily suffice for two people. There are stairs leading to an outdoor area only accessible to this room and out of view of the rest of the house and property.

Graham places his hand on a pad built into the wall and a door opens to two personal offices and a smaller exercise room. In this hallway, he puts his hand on another pad and a door opens leading to the remainder of the house. This provides access to the other rooms without having to go back downstairs and up the other set. The doorways are built in, and unless shown, you would never know they are there.

There are three bedrooms on the other side of the house, each with their own bath, all have great ocean views. There is a library on this level. On the third level there is a large media room and three more bedrooms each with their own bath.

"Graham, it's incredible that you can build this home for

yourself. You deserve it."

"So, I deserve this house, but you don't deserve a camera?"

"It's not the same and you know it."

"You're right. It's not the same. I don't deserve this house more than someone else, but I can afford it. The camera was a gift that you were given. You saved their son's life. They wanted to show you their appreciation by replacing something you lost in the process." He pauses as if charting his next thought. "If you had saved the son of someone who had no money, but they picked you some flowers from their garden and gave them to you, there would be no difference. The spirit of the gift is the true gift. I know you're familiar with the parable. Don't look so shocked, Emelia. I grew up going to church, too."

He watches me for a moment before he continues. "It occurs to me that I never apologized to you for thinking you were a high priced escort."

I think he is expecting a response, but I don't give one.

"When I saw you with Colleen that day, I had just read your background report and I drew the wrong conclusion. I talked to Colleen again today. She told me that you style the closets she keeps for her girls, so you don't need to guard that she is your client."

"Are you and Colleen close?"

"I would say we're friends. I have used her services before. It's a hassle-free affair. The girls get paid and I get a professional with no strings attached. It's been a win-win for us in the past."

I'm not sure why this information surprises me. It makes sense, but, well, I admit I'm a little taken aback.

"I know it's hard to understand, especially considering your lack of experience, which I have come to value," he adds quickly when I make a face at his reference to my lack of experience. "I don't know relationships. I have never met someone I would want one with."

"Then why all the 'his and hers'?" I say.

He looks confused.

"His-and-her sinks, his-and-her studies," I clarify. "Why build a house for a 'her' if you never met someone to have a relationship with?"

"I see what my parents have, and I hope one day I will want that too."

"But not today?"

"No. Not today. Or anytime in the near future."

I nod. "And if I say I want a relationship?"

"Then you should have one. You deserve it."

"And if I agree to an affair?"

"Then we'll take it as far as we take it. When it's done, it's done."

"What's the longest affair you've ever had?"

"Three weeks."

"Three weeks? We're already a week in. So, two more weeks?"

He moves towards me, and I have to tilt my head to see his face.

"You're different, Emelia. I don't think I'll have my fill of you in two weeks. I would like to propose six."

"Six weeks?"

He nods, never taking his eyes off mine.

"Your rules?" I ask

"My rules."

"I'm not going to walk behind you, Graham."

"That rule, among others, is moot at this point. I've already conceded things to you that I never have to anyone else."

"What won't you concede? I'd like to come to an agreement on those terms, so I know what I am truly considering."

"I won't concede on honesty."

"Not a problem. That goes both ways."

"I won't concede where your safety is a concern."

"What if…"

"No concessions, Emelia," he cuts me off. "I also won't concede control. I won't abuse it, and I'll give you a chance to plead your case, but in the end, I'm in control."

"In the areas you listed, you're in control or have complete say-so? You can't choose my clothes, or what I eat, or who I'm friends with. You can't interfere with my job. I would have to trust you not to abuse the control if I trust you enough to give it to you."

"As long as you are honest about those things you listed and they don't put you at risk, then we won't have any issues."

"Will our relationship be public?"

"I often draw a certain amount of attention when I'm out, Emelia, not unlike you as of late." His tone derisive, and I know he's referring to the gossip about me and Blaine. "I am sure there will be speculation. I would trust you to neither confirm nor deny. It's no one's business but ours."

I don't respond. Instead, I make my way through the rooms.

"What are you thinking?"

"That your mercurialness is confusing. You don't want me, but you don't want anyone else to have me. I need time to think about it."

"I would expect you would."

I'm halfway down the stairs when he stops me.

"Make no mistake, Emelia. I want you. Maybe I should afford you a preview."

He moves his lips down my neck, running his hand down to cup my sex. "Plus, these stairs need to be christened."

ch♥pter
sixteen

It's official, I have no self-control, I think to myself in the shower as Tegan and Sara wonder where the good goes.

I went to Jackson's last night to get a little distance, but Graham blew it all to hell when we did the bunny dance on his stairs. I guess I should be happy that he wants an affair twice as long with me than he had with others, but he didn't know them. He basically used them for sex. Wait, is it "using" if both parties are in agreement?

I'm also confused that he's ready to walk away if I say no, but he gets all caveman when I'm with Blaine. There's no way this ends well for me. I'm already attached. There has to be more behind the reason he's like this. Did someone break his heart? I wonder if Jules knows. It's about time I came clean on all of this anyway.

I dry off and throw on my running clothes. I know I did it backwards, but I wanted to wash sex off me before going on a run. I don't want to run tomorrow, so I have a long one to do today. Sixteen miles. I'm sore and tired just thinking about it.

I head to the first floor where Jules is working. She is on a push to finish both of our designs before tomorrow night.

"Hey, babe," I greet her, opening the door to her makeshift workroom.

She waves me in, trying to get all the pins out of her mouth.

"I didn't know you were back," she says with her attention still on the dress form in front of her.

"Jules," I rub my hand down the dress. "Is this what you are wearing tomorrow night?"

"Yep. If I get it done."

"This could walk the runway in Paris tomorrow." I take a picture of it and text it to Jackson.

"I'm glad you're here, Mags. I could use a break." She stretches and we sit. I know what's coming and for once I don't dread talking about it. I need some unbiased clarity on what is happening between me and Graham. It doesn't surprise me to learn she and Adam are already familiar with Graham's dating predilections.

"Maybe Graham just says he wants an affair as a starting point to see what it is you really want?"

"No," I shake my head. "You weren't there. He's serious, this is all he wants. But it's so contradictory to how he acts when it's the two of us. He constantly wants me to show him more of who I am, but it's a struggle to give that to someone who admits they will only be around for a limited amount of time."

"So, which way are you leaning? For what it's worth, Adam and I love the idea of you two together. I know their parents do too. I heard them talking about it. They said you're the first person they have ever seen give it right back to him. Even with his family, he always tries to take the lead."

"I heard Adam trying to warn him off the other day."

"He just wants to make sure that Graham is aware that you aren't like the other girls. He's going to have to work for you, talk to you. Not just fuck you and leave you. Adam wanted Graham to understand if all he's looking for is to get laid, then you aren't the girl for him. If he wants to give it a go, then we think it's a great idea."

"I'm worried I'm going to get hurt."

Her eyes and voice soften, "You run that risk in any relationship, Mags. If he says he wants to give it a chance, don't let fear hold you back."

"I want more than an affair," I finally admit as much to myself as to Jules.

"So, what are you going to do about it?"

"Actually, I've been thinking about winning him over by showing him what he will miss about me if I'm not around. We have a lot of fun together and even though my experience is limited only to Graham, the sex is phenomenal. You know the adage, 'kill him with kindness'? Well I'm planning on killing him with a lot of Emme. Make our times together so great, that he'll miss being with me when I'm not around. Since sex is always a good place to start, I've decided to dance for him." I bite my lip with an apprehensive smile waiting for her response.

"You?" She says not unkindly, but knowing this is way out of my comfort zone.

"Yep. Maybe showing vulnerability, and believe me, me giving a lap dance will be making myself sexually vulnerable, it will chip away at his resolve."

"That would definitely crack Adam's wide open. Might want to let me know when you plan on doing it. I want to make sure you make it out alive," she adds, "You might need crutches to walk the next day." She giggles

"Well, there is one part you can help me with. I need to practice the dance. I've never done a lap dance for someone, and I don't want to look stupid. Can I dance for you?"

"Hell yeah. Bring it!" She bounces over to a chair and sits in it.

"There is seriously something wrong with you," I laugh.

"Now, I watched a couple of videos to get some ideas. The part I need to try out on you is called the basic chair invert."

"The dances have names?"

"They do. I'm a very educated lap dancer. Now, sit with your back straight against the back of the chair. Hands to your side."

"Are you going to walk him through all this? Because this is kind of un-sexy."

"No!" I say, exasperated already. "I'll direct him, just like I will you once I start the dance, but before then I need to practice this move. I put my hands on her knees and spread them a little, lower my head so the back of my neck is braced against the front of the seat between her knees. Using my feet to push off, I brace myself with her knees while lifting myself up and slowly curve my body against her chest where my crotch is right at her mouth. I attempt to spread my legs out, but decide at the last minute to add my own spin on the move. I try converting into another move, losing my balance. We tip over, landing in a pile on the floor, her head between my legs.

"Call me Winnie the Pooh," she quips. "'Cause my head's all up in your honey pot."

We crack up like idiots, her head still between my legs when everyone walks in.

"I don't even want to know," Adam says.

"I do!" Lucy counters.

"I live with her. I'm used to this," Matt says. Becca breaks out in the giggles.

"We're going into town to shop. Do you girls want to

come?" Ruth asks, ignoring the scene in front of her.

We stand and try to straighten our clothes. "No, thanks. I have to finish sewing," Jules answers.

"I think I'll skip, too. Thanks for asking."

As soon as they close the door, I put my hand over my face and shake my head. "I can't even…"

Jules is still cracking up. "That couldn't have been planned any better."

When I finally get her to stop laughing, I start the music again, and we manage to get through the whole dance, this time.

"Oh my God, Mags! That was hot! If that doesn't do it, then, yes, you will know for sure all he wants is an affair. *I* wanted to fuck you by the time that was over. Where the hell is Adam?" She leaves without another word.

I grab a bottle of water from the fridge, explaining to Bruiser this run will be too long for him to go with me. His sad doggy face pulls me in, so I sit on the floor and rub his belly. Ben comes around the corner and smiles at the scene.

"Good boy!" he says, leaning down to rub Bruiser's belly. Ben looks from Bruiser to me with a sudden seriousness. "Can I see you for a minute, Emme?"

"Sure," I answer more as a question than an affirmation. I follow him into his office and take a seat. He closes the door and sits next to me.

"Have you told Graham, yet?"

"About?"

"About John Michaels?" He rolls his eyes.

"No, sir. I haven't decided if I'm going to."

"What's your hesitation?" he asks.

"I'm just not sure it's something that needs to be on his radar."

"I know for a fact it is something he would want to know. He's already asked me about it a hundred times since we left brunch. I'm sorry that I drew attention to him today, but I don't want him getting that close to you again, and I don't want him to ever lay a hand on you. I've done some checking on him. He has a history of doing this to girls. All of them drop the charges later. My guess is that he coerces them." He hesitates like he's not sure he wants to tell me something. "He's been accused of rape."

He can tell I'm shocked, so he gives me a minute to process. I'm thinking of all the things that could have happened that day…

"There are three things I want to discuss with you. The first is I talked with his lawyer today, and they claim he has a witness that confirms you attacked him."

"What? They're lying!" I say a little louder than I intended to. Ben raises his hands to stop me.

"I have no doubt of that. It's his hired man that goes everywhere with him. This is becoming a he-said-she-said situation and, unfortunately, these don't get very far." Another hand comes up to stop my interjection.

"The second thing you need to know is that I met with Smith today, and I have increased your security. He covers Graham, but he handles all the security for our family. Wait," he sighs and holds up a hand again. "Might as well let me get it all out, then you can have at it. I think you need to re-consider telling Graham. He is going to find out. He knows that I met with Smith, and even if you or I don't tell him, he has his ways. My son is very adept at getting information when he wants it. Plus, Smith works for him, not me."

"This is why women don't file charges," I say defeated. "Because of instances like this. No one wins in a he-said-she-said. Now he's out there, angrier that I've pursued charges. Most women don't have the money for security. Why should I be any different? I really appreciate all you have done. I can't begin to express my gratitude, but I'm not yours or Graham's problem to fix. That's why I haven't told him. I don't want the extra security." I stand. "As for telling Graham, do what you think is best. I would never ask you to lie for me."

"You're a client. It's not a lie. If Graham finds out, it will be because you told him, not me. I hate to tell you, Emme, but in the short time we've known you, you have contributed to this family as much as anyone. You are mine to worry about. Security stays. *It stays!*" He raises his voice for a fight when I start to protest.

"You're as frustrating as your son."

"Who you don't want to find out is Ruth. She's the true gangster in the family."

That makes me smile. "Gangsta," I correct him. "Like the cool kids." I wink at him and leave.

I wasn't looking forward to running today, but after all this, I just want to get away. I grab my iPod and hit the beach. Running in the sand will slow me down, but it'll make my legs work harder.

I realize about an hour into the run that I left my phone. I have no idea how far I have run. I usually do about an eight-minute mile but considering I'm running in sand, it's probably closer to a ten-minute mile. I start another playlist and keep running. When I stop to rest and finish off my bottle of water, I can tell by the houses in front of me that I'm pretty far from the house and I've probably been running for about an hour and a half. The sun is setting as I start the run back.

When I make it back onto the private beach, my side is starting to protest. There's no way I can run the rest of the way, so I start cooling down with a walk. I think it's been about three and a half hours since I left for my run. If I'm right, this is going to put me running about twenty miles today. There's no way! I smile and silently congratulate myself on my progress, when I hear something that sounds like an ATV. Two ATVs, actually. A minute later, Graham and Smith come to a stop in front of me.

"Hey," I greet them. "Y'all getting a ride in before the tide comes in?"

"I got it from here, Smith," Graham says, his eyes dark. Smith nods and turns back to the house.

"Get on," Graham demands, his voice low.

What is his problem?

"Can I drive?"

His jaw ticks and he looks like he is restraining himself.

"Emelia."

"Graham." I sing his name a little being a smartass and trying to inject a little humor into his lackluster mood.

"Sorry," I draw out, climbing onto the back of the ATV.

"Put this on." He hands me a helmet,

"You're not wearing one."

"Dammit, Emelia," he booms.

"Fine. Don't get your panties in a wad." I snap my helmet into place.

"Arms."

I wrap my arms around him and he starts back towards the house. We used to ride these on the farm. I've forgotten how fun they are. I lean into Graham and tighten my grip around him. He eventually thaws and takes his hand off the handle long enough to squeeze my hand.

The lights to Graham's house are on, making it visible from the beach. He continues towards his parents, riding up a sandy road and into a garage.

Graham turns the ATV off, but doesn't move. I slide off the ATV, removing my helmet.

He turns and watches me for a minute, his eyes narrow. His lip twitches. He's in his workout clothes, his chiseled arms exposed.

"Strip."

What?

When I don't comply, he takes his hands off the handles and places them on top of his thighs.

"Emelia, strip. I won't say it again."

I'm surprised how turned on I am just from a simple word.

I look around. It's obvious an ATV is still missing, which means Smith is not back. What if he comes in? Graham can read my hesitation.

"Did we or did we not talk about rules today?"

"We did." I don't move or say anything else.

"Do you think I would put you in a position for someone to walk in on you?"

"No." I know he wouldn't. I trust him.

He looks at me expectantly. "Emelia."

I slide off my running shoes and slowly pull my running bra over my head. My breasts fall heavy back to my chest. Without taking my eyes off him, I hook my fingers into the elastic of my shorts and slide them down, revealing myself to him.

I stand there naked, waiting for him to tell me what he wants. He waits. His eyes darken and I can see the testing in them. I know he can see the challenge in mine. He slides back towards the seat I was riding on.

"Sit." He points to the seat he was just vacated. "There's no sand," he says anticipating my objection.

I straddle the seat in front of him.

"You like to be in the driver's seat, Miss James. Now, I think we need to revisit the rules we discussed earlier. Uh uh uh, don't even think of opening your smart mouth right now." He runs his hand over my back and down my arms. My nipples harden and I can feel my sex begin to pulse just from his touch.

Will it always be like this?

He moves his body up against mine, wrapping his arms around me. He runs his hands over my breast and works his way down my torso, over my hips to my sex. Gently with one hand, he leans me back a little. He runs his fingers to the middle of my sex and over my clit. He uses his fingers to separate me. With his other hand, he leans me back into the sitting position while he holds me open. He removes his fingers once I'm in position, my sex directly on the seat.

His hands move to my hair, freeing it from the ponytail holder I had containing it. It skims my lower back, and he runs his fingers through it before sliding it to one side, giving him access to my ear and neck.

Slowly and deliberately he begins to trail nibbles, bites, and licks from my ear to my shoulder. His hands move in his signature pattern over my breast. He continues his stroke down my stomach and the length of my thighs. From this angle, he has to lean into me some to reach my knees, causing me to lean forward slightly, putting pressure on my sex. I draw in a quick breath. He reverses the path of his hand, his thumb grazing a line along the inside of my legs before reaching the apex and brushing my clit gently on the way back.

"I wonder if you'd come from this alone?" he asks, mostly to himself, starting the pattern again. "No one makes me harder than you, Emelia. From the first time I saw you, to when I finally got to taste you." His hands keep up their pace. "You had on a blue cardigan when I met you. I had no idea this was underneath it. If I had, I would have fucked you on the plane." His hands circle the globes of my ass.

"I was on a conference call today, discussing a merger and I started thinking about your tight pussy and how it feels to be inside of you. Do you know how hard it is to conduct a meeting with a raging hard-on? You do that to me, Emelia." His hands keep their pace. My breathing is labored and my breasts feel heavy with arousal. He runs his hands down my stomach and lightly touches my clit, causing me to cry out.

"That's right, baby. You know I like to hear you. Only my name on your lips. Your lips around my cock. Do you understand?"

"Graham," I moan. My orgasm is building.

Graham pinches my nipples causing me to cry out again.

"Do you understand?"

"Yes."

"Yes, what?"

"Yes, sir."

"Good girl. See how good you submit, Emelia. Almost as good as how you fit my hand. Your body was made for me. You can move."

I didn't realize I wasn't moving until he said it. He's right. My body belongs to him. It knew he wouldn't want me moving or gaining pleasure until he was ready for me to.

I begin to rock my hips, the seat giving me the friction and pressure I've been craving. My fingers dig into his thighs letting him know I'm ready.

"Go ahead, Emelia. I want you to come. I want to know every time I ride this that you've been here."

It only takes a couple more movements and Graham catches me as I fall towards the handle bars, my orgasm exploding from me. I barely have time to catch my breath before Graham issues more instructions.

"Lift your ass."

I comply. His arm snakes around me, and he slowly lowers me onto him. He holds me in place for a minute.

"Oh my God," I whisper.

"I know, baby. It's deep this way. I want you to feel every inch of me."

I raise up slowly and slide back down his hard cock. This time it's Graham who moans.

"Move, baby," he commands. And I do. I set a grueling pace, riding him hard and fast. His hand rubs over my lower back down to my ass.

"Watching your ass grind over me…" he trails off, his words labored.

"God you're tight," he says as his hands move to my arms, holding them at my elbows causing my back to arch as he pulls them behind me and towards the middle of my back. He's using them as a rein to guide me and take control of the pace.

His breathing quickens and I know he's close.

"Come, Graham," I command as I raise up on him and slam back down. He shouts my name as he explodes inside me, setting off another intense orgasm within me. My sex continues to pulsate around him, drawing his out longer. His dick is still jumping and setting off little tremors in me minutes later.

Neither of us say anything for a long time. We try to catch our breath and ride out the last of our orgasms.

"Is it like this for everyone?" I say with altered breath, leaning against him.

"Not in my experience, no." His admission surprises me. "I don't think I'll ever have my fill of you, Emelia."

"Don't worry. You will in six weeks," I say sarcastically.

"You never stop, do you?" He says kissing my neck. I can feel his smile.

He leans into me and begins to massage my legs helping me stretch them. When he's sure I can stand, he lifts me off him. His body wet with the evidence of our sex.

I slide off the ATV, pulling on my running clothes. Graham slides his gym shorts back into place.

Once he's standing he cups my face and pulls me roughly to him, his mouth interrogating mine. He stops to squeeze air into his lungs, resting his forehead against mine.

"What are you doing to me?"

I realize now that he's really been asking himself that question, not me. It's like he's fighting a battle that I'm not privy to. He grabs my hand and leads me back to the house.

ch♥pter
seventeen

"**S**he's here!" I hear someone yell as I enter into the Taylor's kitchen for a water. It doesn't take long before the kitchen is filled with yelling and angry faces. Ruth raises her hand to stop everyone.

"Are you okay, dear?"

"I'm fine. I did my long run today," I explain.

"Hate to break it to you, sport, but if it takes you that long to run the marathon, you'll get swept," Ben says.

"I lost track of time." I take another sip of water. "How long have I been gone?"

"Five hours. Where did you run to?" Jules asks a little miffed.

"I'm not sure. I left my phone downstairs, so I didn't have a way to measure the distance. Graham picked me up on the three wheeler." I shrug my shoulders at the probing faces. "I'm going to get a shower."

"I would take a swim first. It'll help with the soreness in the morning," Ben says.

"Great idea. I'll eat after. I'm starved," I add as I leave the room. My legs are a little wobbly on the stairs, but I make it. I'm tying the string on my bathing suit bottoms when Graham enters my room. He stares at me with heat in his eyes. This man is insatiable.

"Can I help you?" I ask him, picking up my bikini top.

"I want to finish our conversation about expectations, and you meeting mine."

I stop and my face falls. "Am I not?"

"I mean in regards to rules, Emelia," he explains. "Why were you running without your phone?"

"I told you, I left it downstairs."

"And do you or do you not think it's smart to go running, by yourself, in an area you know nothing about, with no phone and no one with you. Not even Bruiser?"

Why must he talk to me like I'm a three-year-old?

He waits for my answer, his blue eyes narrowing when he sees my chin set in characteristic defiance.

"What exactly are you expecting?" I put my hands on my hips, my breasts still on display.

"You tell me, Emelia. It shouldn't be a surprise to you." He's cold and all business. Gone is the Graham from the garage.

"Graham."

"Emelia."

"I am not going to ask you for permission to run."

"You're going to and you will."

"You might as well ride out on the same crazy horse you rode in on, because that is not happening."

"Careful!"

"Fuck 'careful'! You can't continue to tell me you only want me for six weeks then go control freak on me because you were worried about me."

"I worried about the girls I've had an affair with. They all had security. It's not just you."

Ouch. I have to admit that stung.

"I'm a high profile guy with a lot of enemies, Emelia. Deal with it." He leaves the room. Just like that, this conversation is over.

I am so fucking pissed right now. I am going to show him once and for all that he is a walking mixed signal. He's too used to getting his own way and not being challenged.

Ask his permission. Fuck that.

I huff my way to the kitchen and pour a large glass of wine since I refuse to lose our Diet Coke bet, even though I would sell my soul to have one right now.

"What took you so long, Mags?" Jules and Becca are already in the hot tub.

"I was arguing with a mule." I climb in across from them. I wince as I sit down.

"Sore from all the running?" Becca asks.

I nod my head and take a deep breath. "This is just what I need."

Jules smiles and shakes her head. "I know that sigh. You forget I'm engaged to a Taylor man. They can frustrate the hell out of you."

"I don't want to talk about it. It will spoil my girl time." I say taking a long sip of wine.

"When are you going to dance for him?"

"Dance? Does this have to do with your face being in her crotch earlier?" Becca looks from me to Jules for an answer. I fill her in on the comings and goings she missed this afternoon.

"I would never have the guts. Matt would cream himself if I danced for him." She throws her head back and laughs. "Please tell me you will secretly record this so we can watch later."

"You're more twisted than you let on." Jules raises a glass to Becca.

"Don't let her fool you," I say to Jules. "Becca's a freaky freak of the week."

"Really?" Jules is surprised. I nod my answer.

"So," I say to Becca, "are you ready to be an actual married couple again in a few months?"

"I am. I miss Matt all the time. It's been hard. At the same time, it will be an adjustment again. Plus, we won't have you James. I know that is weird to most people, but you made this transition so much easier for us both. It will be a little odd only having two people in our marriage," she laughs. "That third person has really balanced us."

"It's the time apart that balances you," I correct her. "There's no reason to fight over the little things when you only have an allotted amount of time together."

"True. But Matt cares for you and that has made him a better man for me. He listens to you. All the dwarfs do. I don't know how you did it James, but you did. You have tamed the untamable. Here's hoping you do it one more time." She lifts her glass to me.

"Now, if I can just get them to replace the toilet paper roll," I quip.

"Can I join you guys?" Lucy takes her cover-up off. She may be seventeen, but she has the body of a grown woman. No wonder Ben and the boys keep such a tight leash on her.

"Did you get grounded?" I ask her.

"Yes," she pouts. "I can't go out for two weeks, and I'm not allowed to go out with Brody without my parents talking with him and his parents first."

"I'm on their side," I tell her.

"Traitor!" She playfully splashes water over me. "Truth

be told, I'm not that upset about it. Brody was a douche for leaving me."

"That's right. He's lucky I don't cut his little pecker off."

"Jules," I admonish.

"Cut the crap, Mags. You'd use his pecker for a pen. And that guy was lucky we got to him before security did. The only reason they didn't jump him was because they thought he was a minor and they didn't want the hassle."

"All I'm saying is....Wait? Security was there?"

Lucy and Jules roll their eyes at each other.

"There is always security there, Emme," Lucy educates me. "I won't let them walk with me, so they stay out of sight but close enough. I'd ditched my security but you all had yours. There's no way I was going home with those guys."

"Same for me, but sometimes I let them walk with me. It's just easier," Jules says.

"I've never noticed security with you?"

"I just don't make a deal of it. It's easier than arguing with Adam all the time. I was only arguing with him because he was sick of arguing with Graham about it."

"You're the one we feel sorry for," Lucy says, catching my mind drifting into thought. "Graham is the reason we all have security to begin with. He has no tolerance for anyone pushing back. If it weren't for mom and dad stepping in, I would have four men flanking me at all times. Try getting a date like that."

So he's this way with all his girls, not just me. Maybe he really does know what he wants. Six weeks and that's it. It just contradicts his actions. Despite having only known each other for a week, I *see* Graham. He tries to warn me off like I don't, but I know I do. I know it scares him to have a relationship other than the kind he's used to.

"Well, I have some hemming left to do," Jules says, climbing out of the hot tub.

"I think I'll go in, too. Take advantage of Matt while I have him," Becca winks. Lucy laughs, excited, I think, to be one of the girls.

"Graham is different with you." Lucy's playfulness gives way to seriousness when Becca and Jules leave.

"I wouldn't have anything to compare it to. I only met him last week," I tell her. I don't want to get her hopes up.

"He never brings his other girls home."

"He didn't bring me home, Lucy. Adam and Jules brought me."

"Maybe. But he doesn't hide his feelings for you. He holds your hand. He wants your input on things. He kissed the top of your head the other day." She's got a little laundry list going.

"I think we are both just taking it one day at a time, and I'm not convinced it will end up being much."

"I realize I'm young, but I know my brother. I know people say he's ruthless in business, but he has a good heart and I want to see him happy."

"That's all I want," I assure her.

"Well, goodnight." She bounces out of the hot tub and into the house. I soak for a few minutes and then dive into the pool to swim a few light laps before heading to my room.

"This is really good," Graham says when I walk in on him looking at something on my laptop.

"You startled me. What are you looking at?" I close the door and walk to the desk. He's reading the grants I have been working on.

"You write better grant proposals than my team does."

"Thanks. I believe there is a formula for most everything. If you can figure it out for whatever task you're working on, then you've found the sweet spot. The sweet spots for grants is to show what they get in return for their money and to accurately send the information they requested."

"How long have you been working on this?"

"I started it when Reggie was a sophomore. He graduated this year, so what, three years? That's from conception to now." I remove my suit and stand naked in front of him.

"You're sexy as fuck."

"Graham."

"Emelia."

We stand there like two stubborn mules, Graham wearing a goofy grin.

"Ride 'em and fuck 'em puts you in a playful mood." I raise my brow at him.

He moves to standing so close in front of me that my nipples almost brush his chest. I take a step back just as he reaches up to touch me. I leave to take my shower. He doesn't follow.

I sleep by myself. It's the first night we haven't shared a bed, other than when I stayed at Jackson's. I think he's trying to distance himself. I can't stand how all over the place I am. It unnerves me. I'm used to having everything planned— thought out. I'm used to being in control.

I can't sleep so I get up to work. It's almost four in the morning when I make my way down to the kitchen for a snack. My stomach is happy to find left over pasta. I fix a place at the island and dig in.

"Care if I join you dear?" Ruth grabs a glass from the cabinet, filling it with water. "Trouble sleeping?"

"It's so common place now, I don't know that I would call it trouble. I usually don't get more than four hours a night. My body has been catching up while I'm here." I offer her some pasta, but she declines.

"I just came for a glass of water. I woke up thirsty. You know, Emme, when Jules and Adam brought you here in July, I told Ben you would be a good match for Graham."

Her observation makes me blush. "Ruth..."

She pats my hand to let me know she isn't finished. "Graham can be his own worst enemy when it comes to relationships. He doesn't think he deserves someone like you. He's always treated his relationships like business deals. No one knows better than I how stubborn and controlling he can be. Don't give up on him. Most of all don't stop giving it back to him. It's a joy to watch. Reminds me of when I was dating Ben." She winks and slides off her stool. "Good night dear." She exits with another pat to my hand.

Bruiser and I finish my pasta, and I opt for the couch instead of going back to my room. I wish I had a barometer when it comes to Graham. I hear what Lucy and Ruth have said, but it contradicts what Graham himself has told me. Like tonight, we clearly had a bond and then he didn't sleep with me. Why?

I finally figure out what button to push to slide the TV up. Sleep finally claims me somewhere in the beginning of McClintock. I love this movie. Addie and I used to watch it with Grandpapa. He loved John Wayne. I hear voices in the distance. It takes me a minute to realize they aren't on the TV and they aren't at a distance.

"This is one of my favorite movies. My dad and I used to watch it growing up," Matt says.

"Me too," Ben chimes in.

"Breakfast is ready." Jules enters the room, placing a soft hand on my hip.

"Let her sleep. She doesn't get enough as it is," Matt argues. "I doubt there are nights that she gets three hours. I don't

know how she keeps the schedule she does. Her sleeping habits are the worst of all of us, and we're surgical residents."

"Ruth said she was eating pasta at four, so I doubt she's
hungry," Ben says.

I turn to face them. "*She* is awake. And *she* can always
eat."

With a roll of his eyes, Ben laughs and cuts off the TV.
"Then get shakin' bacon."

"Clever, dad," Graham placates, entering just as I stand
to stretch.

At the outdoor dining table, Graham sets a cranberry
sparkling water in front of me.

"How much longer?" I make a whining noise.

"Good morning to you too, sunshine."

"Don't poke the bear, Graham," Matt advises with a shake
of his head.

Graham gives him a look that says "I think I can handle
her."

Matt laughs. "I would like it to be noted that he has been
warned."

"Maybe if you got some decent sleep you wouldn't be so
grumpy."

"I'm not grumpy, you pompous blowhole. I just want my
Diet Coke!" Ruth walks by me, and I grab her arm looking up
at her with my best puppy dog eyes. "Please make him leave
me alone. I beg of you." Fat lot of good it did. All I got from
her was a wink and a loving pat on the cheek.

They made my favorite. Waffles. I cover mine with straw-
berries and whipped cream. It's just what I need to get moving.

"What's on everyone's agenda for today?" Ben asks passing a plate of bacon.

"Yum! Bay-con," Adam says in a really bad French accent. "I have some errands to run while Jules does the finishing touches on her and Mags' outfits for tonight."

"I have work to take care of," Graham adds.

"Becca and I are hanging at the beach today and having a picnic before she has to leave tomorrow," Matt chimes in.

"I have nothing to do," I say, crunching on a piece of bacon.

"Yes you do," Jules says.

"I do?"

"Yes, you do" she says, giving me a funny look.

"What?"

"You know."

"Clearly I don't."

"Yes, you do," she says more forcefully.

"No matter what kind of bow you put on this, I have no idea what you are talking about."

"I made an appointment for you…" she sings.

"I still have no idea what you are talking about," I sing back to her.

"Jesus, Mags! You have to get your honey pot tended to before wearing my design tonight."

"Please don't put 'Jesus' in the same sentence as my 'honey pot', and you could have just told me that in private."

"I tried to tell you privately."

"Looking at me with big eyes in a cryptic manner doesn't tell me anything. I need a manual for that look."

"Glad to know it's not just me you're in a bad mood with," Graham smirks from across the table. I'd love to slap it off his chiseled, good-looking face.

"I'm not in a bad mood! I don't get in bad moods!"

"Can I go with you, Mags? I've never done my honey pot before," Lucy says.

All I hear next is a chorus of silverware hitting plates.

"Not cool," Adam says.

"I'm going to be sick," Graham adds.

"Dear, you know you can't talk about your honey pot in front of your brothers," Ruth says, not missing a beat. "They prefer you didn't have one."

"I'm seventeen, and I'm not a nun. They can get over it," she announces defiantly.

"Here, here," I applaud her. "Yes, Lucy, you can go with me." I glare at Graham.

"As long as you take security," he returns my glare.

"One o'clock." Jules distracts me from staring at Graham.

"Right. One o'clock." I stand and clear my plate. "I'll wash. Graham, you can dry."

"I have…"

"You can dry. This isn't a hotel," I say firmly.

"Graham is drying," Ruth confirms with a smile.

"Something wrong with your hand son?" Ben asks.

"What, dad?" Graham asks.

"You were flexing in open and closed. I thought maybe it was bothering you."

"I wasn't aware I was doing it," he says as he follows me into the kitchen.

"Adam, you clear," Ruth adds.

Graham deftly dries the last pan as I empty the dishwater and wipe around the sink.

"When were you planning on asking permission?"

"Hmmm?" I ask folding the towel and draping it over the sink.

"Were you planning on asking my permission?" His midnight eyes focused on my reaction.

"For what?" I really am clueless.

"Getting waxed." I half laugh thinking he's bombing a joke, when I realize he's completely serious.

"Graham," he cuts me off when I start to really tell him what I think.

"This time, I'll let it slide since I know it's for Jules' design, but just a friendly reminder," he leans into me and runs his thumb over my nipple then pinches it before whispering in my ear. "Mine." And with that, he turns and leaves me panting in the kitchen.

I share my shower with Florence and the Machine, and try to calm my frustration that Graham is so mercurial. He doesn't want to share. Tells me I am his. "Mine." And then puts a cap on our time together. I'm frustrated.

Stepping out of the shower, I decide I am going to dance for Graham now. Try to move us towards a resolution in terms. It takes about forty minutes to get ready—thirty minutes longer than usual.

I opt for a white lace bustier that stops just above my hips. Its corset design bubbles my breasts up, with my nipples peeking through the fabric. I add a soft pink lace boy short that cuts high across my cheeks. I pull on a pair of silk thigh-highs that Jules lent me and grab a pair of six-inch heels that almost kill me. Jackson calls them my "fuck me" heels.

I lower the shades in my room so that it is pitch black, with the only light coming from the soft-lit lamp in the corner. I spent some time last night mixing a song together for my performance and I load it up so that it's ready to go. I place a scarf on each side of the chair and grab my phone while I head into the closet.

I text Graham, "Can you help me with my zipper?"

"Only if I'm helping it down," he replies

"Have a seat. I'll be right out."

I hear the door open and close.

"Emelia?"

"Have a seat, Graham," I say from the closet. I can see him, but it's too dark for him to see me. Once he takes his seat, I come up behind him, resting my breasts against his neck, kissing his temple.

"Don't turn around," I instruct, slowly running my hands down his arms. "Feet on the floor."

He complies. I pick up the scarf and gently tie his hand to the back leg of the chair. "No touching," I say softly in his ear, giving it a light lick before I move to his other side and repeat.

"Emelia." His voice deep and sexy.

"Graham." I whisper in his ear, ending with a soft bite to his ear lobe. Hitting a button on my laptop, Beyoncé starts an acapella

"Let me sit this ass..."

I move into a sitting position on Graham's lap. My back to his front, my ass on his dick.

"...on you, show you how I feel."

I dance slowly around him, running my hands over his body and mine. His breathing is shallow and his chest is wide. CEO Graham is getting a lap dance. Perfect. He's just the person I wanted to show up.

I keep the time I practiced. I sit on his lap, facing him, grinding my sex against him. My hair is loose and falls around us.

I echo the words to the song into his ear, *"hold me 'til I scream for air to breathe."*

I lightly kiss his lips, pulling away as he tries to deepen

the kiss. I can feel his erection. The song segues into Rhianna's "Skin."

I moan in time with the beginning lyrics, coming to the position I practiced with Jules. I move his knees apart slightly, and I slowly sway my hips down and then roll my body up his torso his so that my sex is within a half an inch from his face. The back of my head is between his knees.

I'm close enough that when he nods his head, his chin rubs down my sex, igniting a flame in me. I bounce my ass and then slowly bring my legs out straight and down, turning me back into the sitting position.

I mount his lap as I run my hands over my breast, pulling on my nipples through the lace. In a move I had not planned on, I slowly run my tongue over the swell of my breast never taking my eyes off his. I feel his breathing alter. I begin to grind against his erection, kissing him and letting him kiss me back, but at the pace I control. I pull back when he tries to take charge. Tutting and shaking my head at him. My hands find a home in his hair on each side of his face. I tug as I continue to skate my tongue over his. It's a false sense of control, but one I need. I intended for my vulnerability to be erotic, but my earlier frustrations come flooding back and I realize I can't continue this back and forth. This is more to me than an affair. I begin to deepen the kiss and quicken the pace of the movement.

Craving more pressure, I move my wet sex against him, my body shaking as I start to climax touching him, letting him hear my orgasm, letting him feel my shudders. As soon as I reach the deepest point of my climax, I pull myself closer to him, his face against my neck. And before my mind catches up with me, I moan deeply and whisper in his ear, "Oh, Blaine."

ch♥pter
eighteen

I would have had a better chance of survival if I had lit a fuse to a stick of dynamite.

As soon as Blaine rolled off my lips and Graham registered what I said, his hands were loose and I was propelled through the air onto the bed. Graham pounced on me like a lion out for the kill.

"What the fuck!" This is angry Graham. And he has shown up with a vengeance. Within what seems like a second or two at the most, Graham has ripped my bustier and underwear from me, slamming into me with a force I was waiting for.

"Graham." I say his name softly to soothe his anger.

"Don't start with the cautious tone! If I wasn't afraid I'd hurt you, I'd fuck your mouth till my name was the only one you *could* say."

He moves in and out of me, his pace relentless and rough. I'm surprised by my body's response time. I can feel myself climbing already. I am just about to orgasm when Graham pulls out.

"Don't even think about it, Emelia." He turns me over and pops my ass hard before he sinks into me from behind. "You played this game because you wanted to see me without control. Well, you've got it."

As he says it, I know without a doubt that he is in complete control. He would never hurt me or go to a place where he didn't stop the second I said to.

His dick is long and hard pulling out of me to the tip and slamming back into me. "I'm the only man that's been inside of you, and it will stay that way. Do you understand me?" he demands through gritted teeth.

I moan. Pop!

"Answer me, dammit!"

I don't answer.

"Fine. We'll play it your way, Emelia." I continue towards my orgasm almost falling over the cliff just as he pulls out and walks to the bathroom. My breathing is erratic, struggling to even out. *I survived it. It's done.* I start to lower myself to the bed when he re-enters the room.

"Don't fucking move."

He's behind me again. He rubs his cock over the folds of my sex. It takes me a minute once he's pushed into me again to realize he's applied a lubricant. *Why?* He begins to move. My nerve endings are on fire, my body craving release.

"Graham," I beg, my arms shaking.

He pulls out of me and rubs his hand up and down his length. I realize I'm licking my lips. His eyes heat up as he watches my reaction. At least I know he isn't unfazed by all this. I feel warm liquid against my sex. It moves up to the crack of my ass.

"You started this, Emelia. I will finish it. I'm claiming the last part of you. I promise you my name will be the only one on your lips before I'm done. Do you understand me? *Emelia?*"

"Yes."

"Yes what?" he sinks his finger in me, adding another after I've had a minute to acclimate. The foreign sensation feels amazing after I become accustomed to it. I do my best to form an answer over my moan. He slaps my ass hard again.

"Yes. I understand." My chest rises and falls in deep heaves.

"Do you want me to stop?" he rubs my lower back and even in his anger, his touch has gentled and the sincerity in his words are evident.

"No. I don't."

Removing his finger, he pushes the tip of his cock into my ass, stopping just inside to give me time to acclimate. My breathing is erratic.

"Steady you're breathing, baby." He gives me a minute to do this.

"Now, push out as I push into you. Make sure you go slowly."

I nod my understanding and slowly push back on him. The feeling is different. Not good, but not bad either. The fullness is painful at first, but it's gone quickly.

He patiently sinks deeper into me in intervals. A couple of minutes later he begins to glide in and out of me, his pace tender. As I become more accustomed to him, he finds his stride and begins to really move. I feel his pelvis hitting against my ass. I never thought this would be something I enjoyed or would even try, but with Graham it, I don't know, it just seems right for him to have every part of me.

I can tell by his breathing that he's as close as I am. Reaching around me, he lightly flicks my clitoris sending me into a wrenching orgasm, my body finally finding the release its craved.

"Graham!" As promised, it's his name on my lips.

"Emelia!"

He collapses on top of me as my limbs give way and we fall to the bed.

We lay there for long a while, neither of us speaking. This was intense. This was not just casual fucking between two people who are having an affair. It was a fusing.

"What are you doing to me, Emelia?" Graham's question echoes one he has previously asked. This time I answer.

"Calling bullshit."

He gently pulls out of me. I wince a little with his withdrawal. He picks me up and carries me into the shower, turning on the water to run over us. He washes my body and then my hair. He then hands me the body soap. His stance tells me he's waiting for me to bathe him. I do. When I finish rinsing his hair, he moves me under the water, titling my head back so the water runs through my locks. Slowly he runs his hands through, easing out the conditioner. He never takes his eyes off mine.

"Why?" he asks me. It needs no explanation. I understand him completely.

"I don't know." I answer quietly. "You send so many mixed signals that I don't know if I'm coming or going with you, Graham. I think you know this is more than an affair, but you refuse to acknowledge it. One minute you want me to tell you I belong only to you, and the next you are putting a six-week cap on this. Then you give me an ultimatum. It's an affair or nothing. I know I'm inexperienced, but I just don't think it's like this with just anyone. This connection. This fusion. It was stupid but in that moment, I needed you to understand what it would feel like to have another man's name on my lips when I came. That is what your ultimatum of nothing would be like." My lip quivers, but I lock it down before it goes any further. "I was hurt that you appear to be able to dismiss me so flippantly."

"I'm not looking for a marriage proposal, and I don't have a crystal ball. We might wake up tomorrow and decide this isn't for either of us, but I can't move forward with you if you won't admit what is really going on."

There. I've made my decision and I've said it. I release a breath I realize I have been holding in for the last twenty-four hours.

He runs his hands over my arms and pulls me to his lips.

"I'm sorry," he says sincerely. I'm aware it's a word he doesn't use often.

"I'm sorry, too." I hug him. He wraps his arms around me, the water cleansing us both.

"Why are you sorry?"

"For pushing your limit of control."

"How did you wait until you were twenty-five to have sex for the first time? I have seen so many men hit on you, want you. It boggles me. No, it really does." He adds when I roll my eyes. "I've never met someone so in touch with her own sexuality but who doesn't realize how sexy she is. Someone who believes in her own beauty but is unaware of how beautiful she is. How it affects others."

I shrug my shoulders and try to put an explanation together that he'll understand. "I never seriously dated anyone in high school. I was working and taking care of my family. Then once I got to a certain age, I realized I was glad that I hadn't. It should mean more than losing it in the back of a car with a boy who has no idea what he's doing. I wanted it to be with someone special. Someone who meant something to me. Once I got into the city, I met people, but I never had the connection I wanted. I knew from the first time you held my hand that I had that connection with you."

"Do you have feelings for Blaine?"

"No," I answer unequivocally.

"I don't want you spending time with him."

"He's my client, Graham. I have to spend time with him. Besides, I've already told him about us and that you are who I want to be with." This is exactly why I shouldn't let my emotions drive my actions.

He appears to be contemplating saying something, but just as quickly I see the shutters lower and he smiles a wicked smile, moving his body to press against mine. "Incidentally, I loved the dance."

We stand there for a few more minutes. "You're getting wrinkled." He kisses the ends of my fingers and turns the water off. He dries me off first, then himself. He does have a romantic side.

"You're very caring," I tell him as he finishes my feet.

"Another word that is not used to describe me," he says.

I wince a little as I sit in the seat he has moved me to.

"Gently," he reminds me.

"Normally I would have taken a little more time prepping you, but I couldn't wait any longer. I had to have you."

"What do you mean prepping me?"

"I mean using more plugs on you before I laid claim on your ass."

"Is that what you used the other day?"

He nods.

"It's not necessary to do it in steps, but I think it makes it easier for you. I would never..." he says almost ruefully.

"I know, Graham," I reassure him. "If I didn't want it to happen, it wouldn't have happened. And I have no doubt you would have stopped immediately." I study him. "Are you regretting it?"

"No. But it's hard to think around you. You beguile me on every level. I've never experienced anything like it before."

"Is that a good thing or a bad thing?"

He ponders. "Good," he finally admits to himself. "It's a good thing."

He dries my hair, brushing it as he goes. "I love your hair."

I put my watch on. "I need to get going. I have a one o'clock appointment."

"I'll take you." He's finishes drying off and I throw on a sundress with no undergarments.

Throwing my hair up in a clip, I say, "I can take us. It's no big deal."

"I'd like to go. Spend time with both of you. I'll hang out while you are getting…tended to. We can grab a late lunch. Plus, I know you aren't wearing anything beneath that dress."

I smile at him. "Okay."

I grab a couple of things and head out of the bedroom, calling Lucy's name down the hallway. Graham and I head down to the kitchen to wait for her.

"Are you still going with Jackson tonight?"

"I am. It will be a working night for us."

"I had plans to take someone already. Would you like me to cancel?"

"Do you plan on fucking her afterwards?"

He smiles and leans close to my ear. I love it when he whispers in my ear. Some of the sexiest moments to me start with a whisper.

"I love how you only curse with me. The only person I plan on fucking tonight is you." He ends his whisper with a kiss and a light lick of my ear. My nipples harden, and he chuckles when I moan.

"I'm ready," Lucy says. "Yeah. I'm in the room," she announces, rolling her eyes at our less than G-rated display of affection.

Graham opens the sunroof of the SUV, and we head into town. I can feel Lucy tapping on a screen behind my head pulling up some music. Graham lifts my hand to his lips, placing a soft kiss on my palm.

I'm aware that I should be paying better attention to what is really happening between me and Graham, but we finally had a breakthrough today. I really don't want to focus on anything else.

I watch Graham's interaction with Lucy. He's a great big brother, and I can tell he gets pleasure from agitating her. There are times where he is in charge because it's for her own good, and there are times when it's simply for his enjoyment. Lucy is not phased. She gives it right back to him. I admire that about her.

We pull up to the place where Jules made my appointment and head in while Graham waits in the car.

"So, what are you having done?" Lucy asks me while she looks over the list of services.

"I'm taking it all off. You'll understand why when you see my outfit tonight. Is this your first time?"

I can tell before she nods that it is.

"Why are you having this done?" I'm curious.

"I don't know," she shrugs. "I hear my friends talk about it and figure I might as well try it."

"Are you expecting anyone to see it?" I ask, already knowing I'm going to put my hands on someone if she says yes.

"Not *per se*. But I'll know."

"That's as good of reason as any. It will hurt at first, but only for a minute."

They call her name.

"Go to it." I pop her rear and send her on her way.

It doesn't take long before we are climbing back into the SUV.

"Everything good?" Graham says starting the engine. "Never mind. Don't answer that. I don't want to know." He looks like he ate something sour, and Lucy and I chuckle at his discomfort. I nudge Lucy to talk extensively about her first waxing experience, so she can keep the upper hand while it lasts.

Graham takes us to a place with outdoor seating that serves great burgers and fries. We talk about Lucy starting her senior year and the colleges she would like to look at. She queries us on our college decision processes. I learn that Graham and Adam were both Navy pilots for two years after college, following in Ben's footsteps. *That explains his comfort level with turbulence.*

"So, you went to college for four years and served for two. When did you have time to build your company?" I ask, stealing some of his fries. He gives me the rest of them.

"I started it my freshman year at Princeton. By the time I was deployed, I had people in place to continue the work, with my dad and Adam overseeing the final decisions."

"I want to be a female Navy pilot," Lucy interjects.

"No."

"Girls can be..." He cuts her off.

"Are more than capable," he agrees. "But I never want you to have to see that."

"See what?" she asks.

"War. Up close."

Something in the way he says it, a little haunted, stops her from arguing with him. She just nods and squeezes his hand.

We head back to the house. It's only four o'clock; I don't have to be ready for Jackson to pick me up until seven. We're having dinner at Michel's, the hottest restaurant in town. Anyone who's anyone will be dining there before Casino Night gets underway.

"Do you want to take a walk with me?" I ask Graham.

He looks at me a little puzzled, but replies, "I would love to."

We make our way to the beach, leaving our shoes on the bottom step, and head north. I ran south yesterday, so I've seen what's down there—I want to see something new.

We're walking in comfortable silence when I place my hand in Graham's. He stops to look at it, and the water swells around our ankles. He rubs his thumb over my knuckles. He looks like he's struggling. He drops my hand, wraps his around my cheeks, and kisses me deeper than he ever has. His motion is slow and tender but not without passion.

"I was lying to myself that I could let you be with another man or that I would have my fill of you in six weeks."

"Then why do you insist…"

"It's what I know, Emelia. It's how I control things."

"Things or people?"

"Both."

Neither of us says anything else for a while. I wrap my arms around him and pull him to me, hoping my love flows through me to him.

"This is what I mean," he says, pulling back to look at me. "You just give affection lovingly and freely. You have no expectation of anything in return. It's very natural to you. I don't know that I've ever met anyone like that before. And it rubs off on the people around you. Richard Raines will barely shake hands with someone, and your affection touched him deeply. I could see it."

"And you?"

He begins walking again, pulling on my hand to follow. The water rolls ups in waves. We each pick up seashells along the way, not releasing our joined hands.

"I'm unsettled by it," he admits. "Not because I don't like it, but because I do."

We walk a little further before he adds, "If I agree not to put a time frame on it, will you agree to having an affair with me?"

I know he wants to push me when I don't answer right away, but he's patient.

"Do we have to call it an affair?"

"Don't get sidetracked in the semantics of it, Emelia. Look at it for what it is. Do you want this?"

More than anything, but...

"What's your hesitation?" he stops us again.

"Fear."

"Of?"

"Getting hurt."

"That's there in anything new you try."

I turn and start walking, but he holds me back.

"If you aren't honest with me, then this will never work. What are you really afraid of?"

"Graham." I try to deflect.

"Emelia."

"I've lost everyone that has meant anything to me. My mom, my grandparents, Addie. I just don't think I have the capacity to keep losing people."

"You have Jules and Jackson."

"They aren't mine to lose. I love Jules and Jackson. To my

bones, I have a love for them, but their hearts truly belong to someone else. I know it doesn't make sense, but loss changes you. I really don't know how else to explain it. I don't know if I have the capacity to keep adjusting to the changes. Some days I'm barely holding on." I realize I've never actually admitted that to anyone.

"Emelia, even in this short time, I've come to know you. I have witnessed times you were barely holding on. When you were exhausted but kept going. When you deflected so the person you were talking to wouldn't open a wound. When you don't tell me the whole story because you feel the need to protect yourself. When you were reluctant to trust or give over control. I see you, Emelia. If you give me control, you wouldn't have to worry about anything."

"Really?" I say. "That's how this works?"

"Careful." Controlling Graham is never far behind.

"No, really. How does it work? Do you have them agree to terms? Do they sign something? How does it work with the women you fuck?"

"Language." He's displeased.

"We come to an agreement of terms. The only thing I have them sign is a legal agreement that they cannot discuss our relationship or anything related to me or my business with anyone."

"Is that necessary?"

"In my world, yes. You wear rose-colored glasses, Emelia. I truly believe you would never tell anyone anything about me, but that is rare. Everyone wants something, and they will use whatever means necessary to get it."

It sounds so cynical, but I know it's true. I've been in the business of smoke and mirrors long enough to have seen it. People will sell out their best friends if it elevates them in any way. It gives me some insight into why Graham is cautious.

"What are your terms?" I ask.

"*The* terms," he starts, and I stop him.

"Hang on. You have terms, but so do I. Deal with it, or we can call time of death now."

He smiles and I'm frustrated that I love it so much. It's obvious that he was expecting my little rage racket, causing me to confirm "You're an ass," I say with a grin.

He pulls me to him.

"Say yes, Emelia. You won't regret it."

I realize that if I don't say yes to this, I'm letting my past win—I'm letting it control me.

"Pending an agreement on the terms, yes."

"I promise you won't regret it."

"Don't make promises you can't keep, Graham."

He begins to say something but I cut him off, initiating a kiss so deep it can only lead to one thing. I run my hands the length of him. Kneading and caressing his body. His hand moves under my dress and my breath catches when I feel his fingers skim over my smooth sex. He kisses me back, his lips wrapping around my lower one, tugging on it. He follows it with a light bite.

He raises an eyebrow pulling something out of his back pocket. It's a handkerchief.

"I need to see this."

He pulls my arms behind my back and ties the fabric around them, binding my wrists together.

"Graham?"

"Don't move."

Dropping to his knees, he lifts the front of my dress, inspecting the change. I feel his tongue running over the crevice where my leg and hip meet. *Fuck me.* The sensation. He kisses his way across my now bare sex to the other side and repeats before his tongue runs up the middle. He stands and runs his tongue between my lips while his fingers enter me and begin a taunting, steady movement.

I lean into him for support as his fingers move in and out of me. He spreads his pinky and thumb letting me know that he wants me to open my legs a little more. When I comply, he enters a third finger and adds a swirling movement. I know I should be worried about someone seeing us, but I trust him not to let that happen, and I can't stop the building of my orgasm. My breathing picks up and my moans are carried off by the winds and the waves. He pushes his thumb to my clit, and it elevates me. Right before he lets me come, he whispers in my ear, "You are a promise of what can be. That's a promise I intend to keep."

As if to prove it, he propels me off the cliff I was teetering on, my orgasm exploding around him. He holds his fingers inside me prolonging my vibrations, letting me come down at my own pace. Removing his fingers he wraps his mouth around each one individually, sucking them clean. So simple, but erotic, I'm wet again just watching him.

ch♥pter
nineteen

"Need any help, babe?" I ask Jules.

"Perfect timing! I just finished." She takes her dress off the dress form.

"Jules… I am in awe!" I exclaim, evaluating her work.

"You are biased. Which I love," she adds. "This is yours." She hands me two hangers.

"Do you want me to do your hair?"

"I think I'm wearing it straight, so I should be good."

"Okay. If you need me, I'll be in my room."

The ensemble is exquisite. Jules pushed the envelope just right. Any more and it would be overworked. Since the outfit is enough on its own, I keep it simple: a smoky eye, a simple lip, and my hair pulled into a sleek ponytail to emphasize what I'm wearing.

Pulling on one of Graham's shirts until time to get dressed, I sit at my laptop to review some of the pictures I took with the new camera. One of Ruth and Ben catches my eye. They weren't aware I was taking pictures, so I captured them in an intimate moment. Ruth is laughing about something, and Ben is looking at her with profound love. I place an order for it to be printed at a local store.

"You. In those glasses."

I don't look up, but my smile tells him I approve of his affection.

"Come here." The command in his voice draws my eyes up. He's in a tux with the top two buttons of his shirt open and his tie hanging loose.

"You. In that suit." I walk up to him and place my hand to his cheek. "You're beautiful." He leans into my touch. "I've never seen anything as beautiful as you. I have something for you."

"You do? Is it a kiss?"

He leans down, wrapping his lips around my top lip. His tongue skates over mine, and he ends with a nibble on my bottom lip. I'm wet in no time. He unbuttons his shirt I'm wearing and plays with my nipples. One hand slides down my torso, and he moves a couple of fingers in and out of me, breaking his movements on my first moan.

"I'm going to put this inside you." He holds up a silver metal object in the shape of a bullet, it has a small string attached. "Bend over."

"Emelia," he says when I hesitate.

"Remember, no hesitation. I'm in charge."

"We haven't agreed to any terms yet."

"First term. I'm in charge. Bend over."

I know I will regret the precedence that I'm setting, but I'm too curious not to obey. I slowly bend over.

"Normally, I would add special underwear to go with these, but since I hear you aren't wearing any with the outfit Jules' made you…" He doesn't seem comfortable with the idea, but he doesn't protest.

When my ass is in the air, he slides in the metal tube into my sex.

"Touch yourself."

I do as I'm told and feel the small string that is attached.

"This is safe," he tells me. "You won't lose it inside of you, understand?"

I nod.

He pulls me back into a standing position, buttoning my shirt back up.

"Will this just have me sexed up all night?

"Something like that." He kisses me lightly and runs his index finger down my nose, his eyes on mine. "I had this made for you."

He hands me a thin, black leather box the size of an envelope. I look from him to the box and back to him. Opening it, I find another black leather box that opens down the middle. I pull back each side and there is a simple but elegant necklace attached to the binder. It's a ruby in the shape of a heart, encased in nothing but a simple platinum chain coming out of each side of it, giving the ruby the appearance that it is floating free over the chain. It has to be five, maybe six carats.

"Graham."

"Emelia."

My eyes meet his. "I can't…"

"You can and you will. Second term. You do what pleases me. I'd like for you to wear it while we are together. I want you to have it and to think of me while you wear it."

I stop his hands from placing it on my neck.

"Graham, I don't need a necklace to think of you. You are infused in my thoughts."

He doesn't say anything. I close the case and hand it to him.

"Not until we have all terms negotiated. You can't dictate them as you go. That is not how this works. I'm not in this for what you can buy me or do for me. Just be with me. That's all the gift I need." I grab each side of his tie and pull him to me for a kiss.

"Emelia," he says with more force.

"Graham," I counter with the same amount of force.

"You will…"

I cut him off. "Don't ruin the moment with your control freakiness."

We stand there looking at each other. I'm not budging. I gave into his silver bullet that is squarely inside of me. I'm not giving into to the second term until we have some other things worked out.

"You're not dressed?" Jules enters the room. Stopping for a moment when she feels the vibe we are sending off. I have never been so grateful for her interruption because, let's be honest, I would have ended up wearing the necklace.

"I will now. Jules," I pause to admire her. "You're stunning." I twirl her around and take in her creation.

Graham reluctantly takes his eyes off me and our disagreement is tabled.

"Jules, your talent and beauty are a true match." He kisses her hand.

"Thank you, Graham. Now out, while Mags finishes getting dressed." She sends him on his way.

"I'll see you there." He sets the necklace on the desk. "You know what I expect." He bends down to kiss me.

"Did your trip today fix the problem?" Adam says entering the room.

"What issue?"

"Your honey pot issue," he smiles like a schoolboy.

"You are the only one that will be looking close enough to know," I chastise him. Graham punches him in the arm.

"Ow! Dude!" Adam says, rubbing his arm.

"Are you going or staying?" I ask, starting to unbutton my shirt.

"Staying. OW!" Adam says louder, giving Graham a nasty look. "Dude, I've seen Mags without clothes on before. It's not that big of a deal, but I'll go," he concedes when Graham starts to punch him again.

When the guys leave the room, Jules helps me into my outfit.

I turn to see myself in the mirror.

"Is it what you were hoping for?" I ask Jules.

"Better. Thank you so much for wearing this for me. I know it's asking a lot. It's revealing, and you can't Spanx or lift anything. It's all you, and you look fabulous!" Her smile is contagious.

"Spanx are overrated. They limit how much I can eat."

I am putting on a to-die-for pair of Louboutin's, when Ruth enters.

"You both look gorgeous," she says. "My sons are very lucky." She hands us each a box. "Ben's mother gave these to me and I would like for you to wear them tonight. Emme, I decided these suited your design better."

I open the box to see a pair of jaw-dropping earrings. They are three tiers of opened diamond squares that hang from a single solitaire. Each solitaire is at least three carats. All-in-all there must be around ten carats of diamonds to the pair. They are modern and simple in style, with a bit of edge to them. Just like Jules' design.

"Ruth…" I look from the earrings to her. I'm speechless.

"You will be fine. They're insured. Jewelry is meant to be loved and worn."

"Beautiful," she says to Jules who has hers on already.

They are chandelier earrings with a mix of white and black diamonds.

"Thank you," Jules starts to cry. "They are both perfect. Exactly what I would have chosen." She hugs her.

"Don't ruin your makeup, dear," Ruth says, patting her on the back.

"Ruth, I am so touched. Thank you. You have come to mean so much to me."

When I go to hug her, she kisses my cheek and whispers, "Your mom would have loved to see you tonight."

Watching us, Jules laughs and dabs her eyes. "This one," she points to me, "never cries."

I roll my eyes at her sappiness and inspect her eye make-up.

"You're good," I announce.

We make our way down the stairs where Adam is waiting for us.

"Baby, your designs are stunning. He turns me around, running his hand over the curve of my ass—not in a sexual way, but in admiration of Jules design.

"This is perfect. You need to be ready. Tomorrow is going to be about you." His pride is evident. He notices her earrings and looks to his mom, showing his appreciation that Ruth shared them.

"Where's Graham?" Ruth asks.

"He had to leave to pick up his date," I say moving things into my clutch. It takes me a minute to register the disapproving look on her face.

"I didn't feel it was right to change plans on someone the week of, especially something as big as this. Plus, I am going with my boss. It will be a networking night for us." My look assures her that I'm fine with the arrangement, and she reluctantly lets up.

Ben answers a knock at the door and ushers Jackson into the living room. I make the introductions. Jackson stops me, his eyes landing on every part of my body, evaluating Jules design.

"Vogue will want to know about this design," he says proudly to Jules. "Amazing work. Your ability to keep it sheer and work the lace and beading into the fit of a pencil pant. And it is fitted to perfection. Magnificent. Really, Jules." He moves to the dress she is wearing and gives it the same attention and praise.

"Would you like to ride with me and Emme?" he offers.

"Thanks," Adam says, "But Smith has arranged a car for us."

"Then we shall see you at the restaurant." We say our goodbyes and make our way to the car. He pulls me to a stop.

"Hello, beautiful." He kisses my cheek.

"Hello, beautiful."

He looks delicious in his navy blue Tom Ford tux. I need to remind Patrick how lucky he is. Jackson opens the door for me, helping me lower myself into the car before moving to his side. He has his usual driver in from the city to drive us to the event.

"I want you to enjoy tonight." He kisses my hand. "We can network if you want, or we can relax and just be together. Whatever you feel like. So, how are things with Graham?"

I fill Jackson in as much as I can without giving too much away about our arrangement. I want to be honest with my friend, but I also want to keep Graham's confidence. I'm finding out it's a tough balancing act, and I'm almost relieved when we pull into the circular drive of the restaurant.

"Have you ever eaten at a Chef Michel restaurant?"

"No. I am so excited to get to. Did you know he has a Michelin star?"

"Two, in fact," he corrects me. "You're in for a treat. I met him in Paris once. He's as an amazing chef as well as a flirt."

We exit the car to several flashes. The bulk of the press will be at the charity event, but there are several pulling double duty here. Jackson leaves me for a moment to speak with the hostess. When he comes back, he has an odd look on his face.

"It appears Graham and Adam have requested we join their table. Is that okay with you, or would you prefer we keep our table for two?"

"Whatever you like is fine with me."

"Let's go for the group. I can watch the show," he smirks.

"There will be no show."

He shrugs me off like he's not convinced and lets the hostess know we will sit with the group. She shows us to the table. We shake hands with several people along the way, clients or other business people Jackson knows. I've already heard several comments about what I am wearing.

The guys stand when Jackson and I walk up. Graham, Adam, and Matt are all seated next to their dates. There is also a couple that I have never met before.

Graham looks delicious and it's obvious he is thinking the same of me. I can feel his eyes undressing me.

"Graham Taylor, Jackson Hollingsworth," I gesture between the two.

"Mr. Hollingsworth. I'm a fan," Graham says with a firm shake. CEO Graham is in the house tonight.

"Jackson, please. It's nice meeting you."

"I'm sorry, we haven't met. I'm Emme James." I reach across and offer my hand with a smile to Graham's date. She looks at me with boredom.

"Andrea Lucas," she answers after a beat.

Okay then. If that's how you want to play this. I look at the other guy standing that I don't know.

"Emme James," I introduce myself.

He grabs my hand and lightly touches my fingers while kissing the back of it. "Sloan Abbott. It's lovely to meet you. I adore your accent."

I wait a minute for him to introduce me to his date. When he doesn't, I take matters into my own hands. She also has no use for me. Seems to be a pattern tonight.

I move on to reacquaint Jackson with the others. We are just about to take our seats when a client and his wife stop us. Making our apologies, we turn our back to the table for a minute and greet them. Jackson's hand falls to a rest on my hip. It's a common stance for us, but I can feel eyes from behind me. When I turn around, Graham, Sloan, and their dates are all staring at us. I wonder if it's too late to request a table for two.

We finally take our seats. The hostess comments on what I am wearing, and I pass the accolades and attention over to Jules. It hits me out of nowhere while they are talking that we didn't flashbulb test it. *Shit!* The last thing I want is pictures of me in the paper tomorrow looking more exposed than I am.

"What's wrong?" Jackson leans in, asking me quietly. I turn my head up to him to whisper in his ear. In his usual manner, he leans down so I can reach it. He shakes his head and makes a face letting me know that he doesn't think I have anything to worry about. When I look up, Graham is staring daggers at me. His eyes hold mine for a moment and he goes back to his menu. I notice he's flexing his hand. I take a long sip of water.

The waiter comes to the table to introduce the menu and

the options available tonight. Graham orders two bottles of wine to start us off.

"Do you offer a bread basket by chance?" I ask the waiter before he leaves. I'm starving. He smiles a large smile that I don't quite understand.

"We do."

"Thank you. May we also have some for the table?"

"Of course, Miss James." He leaves towards the kitchen. I give an odd look to Jules and she raises her shoulder like she has no idea either why he finds this so amusing.

"I'm sorry," Andrea says. "I sent the bread basket back. I didn't realize…"

"Didn't realize?" I ask with a forced sweet smile.

"I just didn't realize we would have such a *confident* eater here tonight."

Becca pats Matt on the back as he coughs into his water.

"No worries," I smile, unruffled. "They don't mind bringing more."

The waiter brings the wine and places bread on the table.

"I took the liberty of bringing you a special butter we offer. One is a sweet butter and one is a spice. I suggest the sweet for you," he winks as he places the butters in front of me.

I smile my thanks at him. "I'll start with the sweet then."

He begins taking orders with Becca and works his way around. I already know Jackson is going to get a steak. He loves them. He doesn't sway from them.

"Can I have a bite of your steak?"

"As expected." He drapes his arm over my chair.

Becca and Jules are boring, ordering a lighter portioned meal. The other two hanger girls order salads. The guys all order steaks.

"Y'all do know who the chef is?" I ask them like they've

lost their minds. They issue confused nods.

I turn to the waiter and call him by name. "Bring me whatever the chef wants to make."

"I'm sorry?" he responds.

"Please tell the chef to prepare a meal of his choosing. Whatever he is in the mood to prepare."

"Yes ma'am. Any substitutions?"

"None. Thank you."

He smiles and winks at me.

Jackson, ignoring my dig, orders steak.

Meaningless conversation begins to flow, and I catch Jules eye.

"We didn't flash test," I mouth to her. She cringes a little. I can see her mind turning.

"It should be okay," she affirms.

"So, y'all aren't going to Casino Night?" I ask Becca and Matt while buttering a piece of bread.

"No, I fly out in a few hours," Becca reminds me.

"Matt, you can come and hang with me if you like."

"I tried to tell him I could take a cab to the airport, but he wants to go. You should go after you drop me off," she looks at him.

"I'll see what I feel like. I'm heading back in the morning. I have a shift starting at six pm. The holiday is always a busy time."

"What is your shift?" I ask taking a bite of the bread, stopping to have a moment over the deliciousness of something as simple as bread.

"You have to taste this," I raise it to Jackson's mouth for him to take a bite. Watching to see if he has the same response I do. I'm delighted when he does. I pass it to Matt for him to take some. The bread on the other side of the table remains untouched, even by the guys.

"By the way, I'm on until Tuesday. I have to reciprocate for the guys that covered for me this week. I don't know what time you're getting back, but wanted to let you know so you could crash in my bed."

This is normal conversation for me and my dwarfs, but I forget there are others at the table who don't know us.

"You're okay with her sleeping in his bed?" Sloan's date derides.

"Not that it concerns you—and it certainly doesn't call for your dramatic tone--but yes. Matt and Emme could *share* a bed and I would be okay with it. I trust them both."

I don't hide my smile at her response.

"If you all are not going to eat your bread may I have it? I would like to try the other butter," I ask the other side of the table.

Placing an empty wine glass in front of me, the waiter tells me what he is pouring. Jackson chuckles to my right. He knows I have no idea about wine, nor do I have any idea what the waiter just told me. I smile and nod, winking at Jackson.

"To have with your amuse bouche," the waiter smiles. He leaves for a moment, returning with a small plate.

"Light Scallop Veloute with galangal and vegetables."

It's a piece of art on its own. It's too lovely not to share, but it's a bite-sized portion—not enough to go around.

"I don't remember seeing that on the menu?" Sloan says.

"It isn't," the waiter confirms. "Chef Michel has made it special to accompany the dinner he has chosen for Miss James."

"Really?" I ask surprised.

"Really." He seems to be enjoying this.

I cut the scallop in half and take a bite. I close my eyes

and savor it as it melts in my mouth. It is so good that it sends vibrations down to my sex. I'm having a food orgasm. Suddenly, my eyes pop open directly to his. My sex is vibrating! He doesn't give anything away, but I notice his hand is in his pocket. I realize now that he must be manipulating the bullet by remote. Our eyes lock for a long moment. Andrea draws his attention back to her while I close my eyes for a minute, relishing in the vibration and the knowledge that no one knows but us.

The conversation is flowing easily, and several people stop by to speak to either Graham or Jackson. The waiter brings a different wine for me to have with the starter. It has a long name that I can't pronounce, but it's delicious. He follows it with another decorative display of food, terrine made of cheese and vegetables followed by a wine with each course, the middle course, main course, pre-dessert, and dessert.

I'm in the middle of my dessert when Graham's sporadic concerto of vibrations finally brings me to a quiet climax that only he is aware of. I slightly arch my back, pushing down with my pelvis, applying the pressure I crave. I take a sip of water trying to calm my breathing. I hold back on the wine throughout the meal, trying to keep it to a half glass of each. I'm not use to this much alcohol, and as a rule I don't usually drink when I'm out.

"Slow down on the wine. You're flushed," Jackson leans in to tell me.

I don't correct him.

"As always, Miss James, you have them eating out of your hand."

I know the voice before I look up.

"Michaels," Jackson says, standing and pulling me up with him as per usual.

"Jackson. Emme," he nods to us both. "It's nice to see you," he says to Jackson.

Without realizing it, I take a step back and position myself behind Jackson. It's a move so slight that most people wouldn't notice, but without question Jackson does. His arm hooks around me, shielding me in a cocoon, his hand coming to rest on the back of my hip.

"Emme, may I have a word with you?" Michaels says.

When I don't respond, Jackson takes command of the conversation. "Why don't I catch up with you after dinner? I'd hate for Emme to keep our guests waiting."

"Of course," Michaels says through tight lips. "Some other time."

I take my seat and don't look up. I concentrate on taking another bite of my desert, when Jackson slides my chair slightly closer to him, putting his hand on my knee.

"What the fuck is going on, Emme?" he asks sternly, but softly so as to not be overheard.

When I don't answer, he leans in disguising his whisper with a kiss to my temple. "I know this has to do with why you turned him over as a client."

Graham clears his throat to get my attention. Anger is radiating off him. I stand to excuse myself to the ladies' room when a short, older gentleman wearing a chef's jacket approaches me.

"Miss James," he says with a French accent.

"Chef Michel?"

"Miss James, I had to come tell you what a delight it was to prepare a meal for you. You had no prejudices towards food or expectations of what you wanted from me. You let me be an artist for your palate. I thank you. You have an obvious love of food." He pats my hands while he talks.

"Was it her ass or hips that gave it away?" I hear Sloan's girl say behind the glass she has raised to her mouth. Andrea snickers. Chef Michel looks disapprovingly at her.

"Careful," Jackson reproaches them.

"Don't mind them. They're what I call hanger girls," I smile at Chef Michel. "Salads. No bread. No dessert. My dinner was amazing. A once in a lifetime experience. My sincere gratitude for the love and care you put into my meal. I'd like to introduce you to my date, Jackson Hollingsworth."

Jackson stands and shakes his hand.

"They may be hanger girls as you call them, but you have command of this room. All eyes on you, no? The food. It works to your advantage." He kisses my hand. "This not a one-time experience for you. You are welcome in my restaurant anytime. Whatever the city." He leans in and kisses me on each check. "Your dinner, my treat." And just like that he's gone.

I've had so much wine I'm about to pee in my pants. Plus, I want to take out this bullet. It has me too sensitized. Just as I enter the bathroom, a hard chest is at my back pushing me inside. He closes it and locks it. He notices the relief on my face immediately.

"Who did you think it was?"

"No one. You just startled me." I take a deep breath trying to relax.

"Bullshit, Emelia."

I hold up my hand. "You have to wait to argue with me. I'm about to pee all over myself."

I go into a stall and sit down. It's a $300 a plate restaurant; the seats are probably cleaner than my apartment.

"What's going on with you and that Michaels guy?"

"Are you going to stand in front of me while I pee?"

"Emelia."

"Nothing. He was my client and I had Jackson drop him. It wasn't his preference." I pull out the bullet, wrap it in tissue and hand it to Graham, then finish in the bathroom. I move to the sink to wash my hands, watching him behind me in the mirror.

"And Jackson?"

"You know he's engaged, right?" I ask him. "To Patrick."

He elicits the same amount of surprise that most people do when they find out Jackson is gay.

"Why not tell me that to begin with?" He turns me towards him. "I think you like me jealous."

"I think you have lost your mind," I chastise him.

"Every man in this place wants to fuck you. Remind me to be mad at Jules."

His eyes rake me in before he rests his head into the curve of my neck, nibbling his way around.

"They all want what's mine." He stops. "Why aren't you wearing your necklace?"

"Your mom gave me the earrings to wear tonight, and I didn't want the necklace to compete with them. And I'm not sure I'm accepting it."

"You will."

"You can't just tell me I will, Graham. That's not how this works. If you had any brains about you, you would know this is not the time to force your hand. You will lose."

He moves me to a wall. His hands wrap around my upper arms as he bends to kiss my neck and every open area he can get to.

"You are mine. Emelia. The sooner you realize and submit to me, the sooner your life gets easier."

"Let's finish this conversation at home." I return his kiss.

"We could skip Casino Night and go now."

"What about Andrea? She's special, that one."

"Dinner was the only thing I committed to. I've more than lost my patience with her. She can navigate Casino Night on her own."

"That's not very gentlemanly of you."

"I want to fuck you 'til my name is the only name you know. Is that gentleman enough for you, Emelia? When we get home, I'm going to make you strip for me. Then I'm going to fuck you from behind against the mirror in the closet."

He turns me, my front towards the wall.

"Your hands above you."

He moves my hands to mimic his words.

"My hands will find yours to hold on to."

He kisses my ear and moves to my neck.

"Because you like it when I hold your hands, and I like how you squeeze mine when I'm buried deep inside you. I'll let you turn your head so you can watch me move in and out of you in the mirror."

He pushes his erection against my ass.

"I know it turns you on to watch my dick sliding in and out of you. Wet with your juices. Claiming you. Making you mine. I'll smack your ass when you get greedy and try to take back control. This will only make you want it more. You like having your ass popped as much as you like to watch. I won't stop until you tighten around my cock. There's nothing I love more than to watch your face while you come for me. Expect your lips around my cock as I fuck your mouth."

He moans as he pulls one of my hands from above me and motions it into my pants.

"Touch yourself," he commands.

His words send me off into a spiraling climax the second my finger pushes against my clit. He pushes more of his weight against me, holding me as my fingers work to extend my orgasm and my breathing comes back down.

Fuck! All he did was talk.

He pulls my hand out of my pants and puts it to his mouth sucking on it.

My hands move to his waist and I begin to undo his belt. I want to wrap my mouth around him.

"No, baby. Not now," he stops me. "If you take me in here, every man out there will know."

"No they won't." I know he can hear the disappointment in my voice.

"Trust me, baby. They will. Your swollen lips, hoarse throat, and redness of your face will be like an announcement. And while I want each of them to know that you are mine, I don't want them looking at you in that way. Tonight," he promises in a gentle dismissal.

"Good girl," he praises when I follow his command.

ch♥pter twenty

Jackson and I wait at the valet stand for our driver to pull around. I'm exhausted and we haven't even made it to Casino Night. I lay my head on his shoulder and rest my eyes for a moment. Jackson folds me into his arms, letting my head rest against the nook of his neck.

"We can skip Casino Night, if you want."

"I'm ok. I don't know why I am so tired. I'll get a second wind," I say with a confidence I'm not feeling myself and nuzzle into his chest. I hear the click of a couple of cameras. Graham and Andrea come to a stop beside us.

"Guess I would be considered my boss' 'it girl' too, if I was fucking him," Andrea says.

I'm too over it to say anything. Jackson, on the other hand, is primed and ready.

"I know you, your boss, and the group you affiliate with. Say another word and I'll make it so difficult for you to work in the city you'll have to transfer to LA. I've had enough of your rudeness and jealousy." He moves me to his other side, positioning himself once again between me and what he assesses as a threat. "It's beyond me why I have to be the one to say something. I'm beginning to re-think entrusting her to you."

It takes me a minute to realize he is directing his ire to Graham now.

"Jackson," I say in a tone that lets him know he should tread carefully.

"Don't protect him. He should be protecting you. And it should be his first priority."

I chance a glance at Graham and his jaw is set in a hard line. Our driver pulls up and Jackson quickly deposits me in the car. Closing his door a little harder than necessary, he says nothing as we ride several minutes.

"Jackson..."

"Don't start with me, Emme, unless you are truly ready to have this conversation."

I take a minute to consider his words. I don't really know if I am, but I know it's going to hang over us all night if I don't.

"What conversation do you think we need to have?"

"My expectation of how Graham should be treating you. And don't act like I don't have a say so. There have been plenty of times you have called me or Patrick on the carpet for our lack of care with each other."

"Exactly. We don't all get it right all of the time. Graham is trying to make it through this night with someone that means nothing to him. He's doing the best he can. Already he's made progress. Just give him some time."

"He doesn't have time where your protection is concerned. A man like Graham has more enemies than he does friends. Once they realize Superman now has a kryptonite, they will come at him. And you. If he can't control a bitchy little girl, how is he going to protect you from everyone else? I won't let you be put at risk."

"You do know I have the final decision," I say a little

miffed.

It has dawned on me that Graham and Jackson are very similar.

"I know he can control that girl. My concern is why he didn't do so sooner. I don't care if he did fuck you in the bathroom."

"Language. That didn't happen. He's very quick to protect me. I'm sure he knows I don't need him to jump to my defense whenever the school-yard bully tries to upset me. I can handle myself."

"Did you with Michaels?"

It's a low blow, and he gets the reaction from me he is looking for.

"Shit. I'm sorry sweetheart." He pulls me into his side. "I just don't want anything to happen to you. You're my girl. I won't hand you over to someone who doesn't cherish you the way you should be."

I don't respond. I know his heart is in the right place, but I don't know that I have an answer for the cherish part. Does Graham cherish me? Am I expecting him to? What is it that I want from this relationship? Despite Jackson's observation, Graham has a deep need to protect me. That I know for sure.

"I don't know if I'm expecting him to cherish me," I admit out loud, surprising Jackson. "I might just want carefree and fun."

"If that's true—and I don't believe it is—you should be with Blaine. Graham is too intense for carefree and fun. You know how this works. If you don't set the expectation of how you want to be treated, then how is he supposed to know?"

His words echo ones I said to Lucy just the other day.

We pull onto the estate grounds. They are magnificent. The estate is on the bay, not the ocean, but it's no less amazing.

It takes several minutes to make our way up the drive, with each car stopping to let people out. Jackson lifts my hand to his lips and kisses it.

"I don't want to ruin your night." He gives me a once over while I apply more lipstick. "You look incredible."

We pull up to the door, and Jackson buttons his jacket as he exits the car, then opens the door for me. A red carpet adorns the fifteen to twenty steps up to the large doors of the mansion that is being used for the benefit. The organizers choose from mansions that are not being lived in and rent them out for the evening, empty them, change them into a high-end casino, and then put everything back once it's over. A lot of work. They must raise a lot of money.

We are directed to stop at the bottom of the steps for pictures. Jackson wraps his arm around me as we pose for the line of paparazzi. He is a seasoned veteran at walking the carpet. He moves us to the next landing where we pause for more photos, then again at the top landing, the last before we enter. A young blond girl addresses Jackson and asks him for a moment of his time.

"Will you be okay?"

"Sure. I'll meet you inside."

He kisses me on the cheek as several flashes go off. I turn to enter when an arm snakes around me, surprising me. I laugh at myself for being so jumpy.

"Are you going inside?" Blaine asks.

"I am."

"You know my motto: ladies first."

He laughs when I roll my eyes. I'm blinded by the flashes going off around us. I literally need sunglasses on to be able to see who is around me and where I am walking. Blaine tightens his grip and pulls me into him.

"Just hold on to me," he says in my ear and moves us inside the mansion.

"I don't know how you do it all the time. I'm still seeing spots."

"I'd like to tell you that you get used to it, but you don't. At least I don't," he adds. "I was hoping to see you tonight. I had no idea I would get to see *this* much of you. You look fantastic."

"My best friend designed it."

"Jules. I remember. Remind me to thank her when I see her. Are you here with Jackson?"

"I am. It's a networking night. Graham is not far behind."

"Ah. The boyfriend."

I don't respond to that because I am not really sure how to. Is Graham my boyfriend? Would he say he is? This evening is supposed to be fun and carefree and all I'm getting is pushback to define my relationship—scratch that, my affair with Graham. We come to another red carpet lined with cameras, microphones, and reporters. I look around for Jackson, but don't see him anywhere.

"Do you want to wait for Jackson?"

"You go ahead. I'll follow."

"Screw that. We're friends and I'm not ashamed of it."

He grabs my hand and starts me down the aisle. I remove my hand from his. It doesn't feel right to have him hold my hand. He puts his hand to the small of my back.

"Are you here together?" the reporter from Entertainment Tonight asks Blaine.

"No. We actually just saw each other outside and decided to walk in together."

We spend a few minutes talking about who we are wearing. I get some great plugs in for Jules. We move through several more reporters, all addressing the speculation surrounding our rumored affair. We, of course, confirm that we are only friends. Jason Kennedy from E! is the last reporter. Blaine spends more time with him than the others, talking about the same thing as everyone else, but Jason adds some questions in there about Blaine's album. *Sex with You* is still at number one after nine weeks.

"What direction do you see your next album going?" Jason asks him.

Blaine looks at me. We are both thinking about our previous conversation about determining who he wants to be as an artist.

"My next album will stay true to the music I write, but there will be unexpected moments you didn't see as much in the first one."

"Those moments being?"

"I can't give it all away, Jason. You'll have to wait." He gives a dazzling smile for the camera.

"Is it possible some of those unexpected moments are coming from your *friendship* with Miss James?"

"Anything's possible."

His answer draws my eyes to his, and he pulls me into his side. He's looking at me with heat and passion so hot I blush. *Shit. This is going to be a thing.*

"'Sex with You' was written before you were friends. We can't wait to see what comes now that you are. When does your tour start?"

After Blaine answers the rest of Jason's questions, we are relieved to exit reporters' row.

"Can I get you a drink?"

"I thought we understood each other?" I pull to a stop to make eye contact. "This is a friendship only."

"We understand each other, Emme. I understand you want only a friendship."

"I don't want to be unfair to you, Blaine. If I have led you to believe otherwise, please forgive me."

"You haven't. Now dance with me."

He pulls me to the dance floor while Frank Sinatra coons in the background. I assume the DJ spots us on the dance floor, because Blaine's "Sex with You" starts to thump through the speakers. He moves like his songs feel: like sex. The guy can dance. He looks down into my face and starts to sing his lyrics to me. More flashes and a camera crew insert themselves on the side of the dance floor.

"If you'll excuse me, I think I'll dance with my date," Jackson taps in.

"By all means." Blaine hands me off with a dramatic bow.

"Sorry, I was detained by Heather. A PR crisis."

"Do you need me to do anything?"

"Just dance with me. And forgive me," he says with that signature sexy smile that has all the girls and boys swooning.

He turns serious. "I'm sorry I pushed you so hard in the car. It wasn't fair of me."

"You're forgiven. I can't stay mad at you."

"Gonna roll back a little with this one," the DJ announces as Next's "Too Close" begins.

He sings the guy's part, and I chime in on the girl's part. It's clear to everyone that we are enjoying each other. Jackson performs a few old-school moves that have me laughing and trying some of my own. Movement comes naturally to Jackson, which makes him an expert dancer. He has removed his suit jacket and is in his vest with his sleeves rolled up. His fitted pants showcase his strong body. If someone didn't know him, they would think he has sex like he dances, charming with a bit of down-and-dirty mixed in.

When the song is over, Jackson moves toward the bar.

"Grab me a Diet Coke. I'm gonna stay and dance."

I move into the crowd and start moving my hips with the beat. I'm a couple of songs in when a hand runs over my back side, making me smile and my heart race. Graham pulls me into his arms, and we move like two people who know each other intimately.

"I ought to punish that sweet behind," he says seductively in my ear. "I should've known you were causing the stares. Out here in these pants, shaking that ass, all by yourself."

"If you play your cards right, you might get lucky."

I lightly grind against him. His eyes are a dark blue when I turn to face him, his hand rests on me in a way that tells others I am his. He runs a finger down my cheek and turns me again, my back to him. I raise my arm behind his head, he lightly runs his finger down the inside of my arm curled around his neck. His hand splays out on my stomach pulling me to him as I move against him. I'm completely unaware that there are people around us. I begin to dance around him and from behind I echo the words of the song in his ear. When the song wraps, he looks at me like he wants to fuck me on the floor. Suddenly, I can see the shutters come back down and he pulls me off the dance floor. Why?

We move to the bar and Jackson hands me my Diet Coke, I ignore Graham's disapproving look.

"You want to dance or hit the tables?" I ask Jackson.

"Patrick just called. He's back early. I'm going to walk out and meet him then hit some tables." He turns to address Graham, "If you don't mind looking out for her?"

The question holds much more meaning than the eight words convey. I know its Jackson's way of trying to make amends. Otherwise he wouldn't be leaving me for Patrick.

"No. I'll take it from here."

Graham still looks like he thinks of Jackson as an adversary. I am sure he's not used to being called on his shit. Despite that, he offers a conciliatory handshake to Jackson. Jackson kisses me on the cheek and leaves us at the bar.

"Water and a scotch please," Graham orders from the bar.

"I see you made an entrance with Mr. Moore," he says, displeased.

"We walked the carpet together. It wasn't planned. It just happened."

"He wants to fuck you."

The bartender brings his drinks. Graham takes the Diet Coke from my hand and replaces it with water. For some reason, I get the feeling he is daring me to say something, clearly not in the mood to be pushed. Is he mad? He didn't seem that way on the dance floor.

"I have some business to attend to. Will you be okay for a few minutes?"

"Of course. I'm going to find Jules and Adam, see how they are doing."

"They're in the casino. At the craps table." He holds his look at me, like he has something else to say.

"Yes?"

"Behave." It's a command and a warning rolled into one. No humor injected.

"Don't I always?"

"Emelia."

"Graham," I say as sweetly southern as I possibly can.

His hand flexes, and I arch a brow at him. Lightly kissing my forehead, he places a chip in my hand.

"No back talk. It's for charity, and I plan on donating

whether you play or not, so you might as well try your hand."

He leaves me with twenty-five thousand dollars. What the hell? Do they not have any hundred-dollar chips? I go in search of the craps table. It doesn't escape me that it's mostly men playing and women standing behind them.

"So, you're the new Carrie?" a tall brunette says to me. She's beautiful. She has bright blue eyes. Her dress fits her like a glove, despite the fact she's too thin for me. But something in her eyes has me on alert.

"I'm sorry, we're you speaking to me?" I ask politely.

"I saw you with Graham Taylor. He gets a new flavor every few weeks. You must be this week's special." She pauses and sizes me up. "I see he's going through a heavy-cream phase."

"I think you've had one too many. It's time for you to move on," Adam says, moving in between me and the woman. He's tall enough that I can't see around him.

"You boys sure are trading down these days."

She looks from Jules to me, and I swear I see Adam's stance gain inches right in front of me. He leans his head down and says something to her. I can't make out the words, but I can hear the venom in his tone. Her eyes widen as she grows angry and leaves in the other direction.

"You look incredible," Jules says to me in an attempt to right the wrong.

"You know I don't care what she or anyone thinks. I love my body. I don't need her approval. Where are you guys headed?"

Adam is still pissed and quiet.

"Don't worry about it," I place my hand on his arm. "I don't have some naïve notion that I'm the first person Graham has been with. Don't let it steal any of your night. It's not worth it."

He relaxes a little. "We're going to the poker tables. Want to come?"

"No, thanks. I'm headed to blackjack. Matt should be here soon. If you see him or Graham, let them know where I'm headed."

There's a seat at a blackjack table. The minimum bid is a thousand dollars. I place my chip on the table and ask for change. If I win, I don't plan on keeping it. It doesn't seem right to win from a charity, but it will be fun to play.

I win the first two hands, when a man sits next to me. He looks to be in his early thirties. I notice he isn't wearing a ring. He's handsome in a Chanel tux. He has dark hair with some silver sprinkled throughout, adding to his good looks. I can't quite place his heritage.

"Is this seat taken?"

"No," I smirk at him. He's already seated. Does it really matter now?

"Alex Russo."

"Emme James." I extend my hand to shake his. He kisses it instead.

"Miss James." He lays several ten-thousand-dollar chips down. He glances at my chips. "Are you enjoying yourself? You seem to be having some luck?"

"I'm only on my third hand. I'm really just here for fun."

He tilts his head to the side. "Where are you from?"

"I live in New York."

"And before that."

"Memphis."

Like always, a light turns on, indicating people have placed the accent. He's Italian, he should understand. I roll my eyes and glance at my cards. I stay at twenty.

It moves to him; he splits and stays one at eighteen and

one at seventeen. The dealer finishes with everyone and then starts turning his cards. He has to take one, he busts and everyone cheers. Alex makes a quick profit.

We play several more hands, drawing a bit of a crowd. There are five of us playing. Alex orders drinks for the table. We are on a roll. No one is losing. I bet a few more hands. I've grown my chips close to 45,000. I decide to go all in. I get a queen of hearts and a six of spades. This is the most difficult hand in blackjack to play. I try to remember what cards I have seen over the last several hands. I know the odds of it being a low card are in my favor. The dealer patiently waits for me to decide.

"Hit me," I tell him.

"Are you sure?" Alex asks with a combination of intrigue and disbelief.

"Yes, sir, I am."

I notice his breath catches and he looks at the dealer. He turns my card over and it's a five of diamonds. Twenty-one. The table around me lights up with excitement. We continue around and the dealer is out with nineteen.

I hand the dealer a five-hundred-dollar chip, the smallest I have. Pushing the rest of my winnings to him, I ask, "Can you make sure this is donated to tonight's charity please?"

"Certainly, ma'am," he nods his appreciation to me.

"It was nice meeting you," I direct to Alex as I slide off my stool and make my way to the restroom.

"May I buy you a drink?" Alex halts me as I make my way across the room.

"Thank you, but I'm in need of the ladies' room," I smile politely at him.

"I could come with you."

"I'm sorry?" I ask as my smile fades.

He moves closer into me. I take a step back, and a sphinx-like smile draws across his face.

"Don't be coy, Miss James. I've watched you tonight. You've given attention to three separate men since you've been here, one of which is Graham Taylor. I noticed he doesn't have a collar on you, so that means you're available. I can care for your needs and make it financially worth your efforts." He steps closer to me and runs a long finger down my jawline, looking at me with anticipation. "Why don't you let me show you a preview?" He leans in and places a soft kiss in front of my ear.

I'm shocked into place. My brain has frozen and it's lacking the ability to tell my body to move. He mistakes this for acquiescing, and places his hand softly around my arm to move me in the direction of his choosing, pausing when my feet don't move.

"You're mistaken, Alex. She doesn't belong to me."

My mind finally kicks into gear, and I turn to see Colleen standing there, looking like the business mogul she is. She easily reads the confusion on my face.

"Now, if you'd kindly remove your hands from her. I'd like to remind you of your contractual agreement. You do not proposition my girls individually. You want something specific, you go through me. Do we have an understanding?"

This is CEO Colleen. It's intriguing to watch her in action.

"Of course." He looks put out. Angry. "My sincere apologies, Miss James. Since you were with Mr. Taylor, I misunderstood."

"I don't expect this to be an issue again," she reprimands, holding his gaze.

"No, of course not, Colleen." He bows his head to her and leaves.

She motions with her finger, and out of nowhere there is a man wearing an ear-piece standing next to her. She turns her head slightly and speaks low enough that I can't hear what she is saying. The man nods and heads off in the same direction as Mr. Russo.

"I'm sorry, Emme." Her eyes inspect me to make sure I am okay.

"Colleen. So nice to see you." I start to hug her, but like I said, this is CEO Colleen, so I offer a kiss to each cheek, which she accepts.

"How are you getting along? I saw you dancing with Graham. I take it you have moved past all the confusion around your availability?" she smiles knowingly.

"We did," I say too quietly, drawing concern on her face.

What did Alex mean Graham hasn't collared me? I might not have a lot of experience, by choice, but it doesn't mean I've been living under a rock.

"Do your girls wear collars?" I ask Colleen.

"That's a question you need to ask Graham. Where is he?" she looks around. "He knows better than to leave you vulnerable. What was he thinking?"

She's unhappy. I realize then that, on a certain level, I am one of Colleen's girls. She has the same protective instincts for me that she does with her own. I just don't work for her.

My mood plummets and exhaustion has set back in. "If you see him, would you let him know I left."

She raises an eye-brow at me. "This will be interesting. I do enjoy what you bring to the table, Emme. Lunch next week? We need to finalize the fall closet."

"Please. Thank you, Colleen." I squeeze her hand despite her need to keep people at a distance. She softens after a moment and returns the affection.

I make my way to the exit, stepping outside onto the red carpet that still blankets the stairs. It's cool now that the sun has gone down and most of the reporters have left. The only remaining photographers are paparazzi. I take a deep breath and start down, hoping to see one of the drivers I know. They can have me home and be back before they are needed. I make it down to the first landing, but I don't locate anyone.

"Come on. I'll drive you home." Blaine wraps his arm around me.

"Blaine."

"Friends can drive each other home."

"Okay," I give in. I'm too tired to argue but am aware this is iffy ground. I want Graham to trust me, but I know Blaine is a sore spot for him.

We walk to a black Porsche and he opens the door for me, helping me climb in. This car is low considering I am wearing almost five inch heels. I give him the address and we ride in silence for several minutes. I text Jules, Jackson, and Graham that I have left and will see them at the house. Blaine's listening to the radio. The Stones are playing.

"Do you mind if I roll down the window?"

"You aren't afraid of messing up your hair?"

"You must date some really high-maintenance girls," I observe.

"No, I don't mind. I could use some air." He hits a button on the console that lowers my window. I can feel him watching me.

"You need to watch where you're going."

"I'd rather watch you."

"Take a right here," I direct, ignoring the comment.

He pulls into the driveway, slowing to a stop.

"Why didn't you have Graham bring you home?"

"He was seeing to some business, and Jackson's fiancé was able to make it. I hated to ask either of them to leave this early. I was just going to have one of the drivers take me home."

"So, to confirm, you are seeing Graham Taylor? I've been hearing mixed stories."

"Don't believe everything you hear," I say softly.

"So, you're exclusive?"

"I am."

"Does that mean Graham isn't?"

"I'm not saying that." I pause trying to define something for someone that I don't yet know what it is.

"We are still in the definition stages. Until we come to some more definitive terms, for me, yes, it is exclusive. Plus, you're my client."

"Screw that. If that is playing any reason into this, I'll fire your ass today."

I laugh. "It wouldn't change anything right now."

"Ok. I just don't want to have any regrets that maybe if I had asked the right questions, one of them would have produced the answer I wanted. Just covering all my bases."

"You're sweet. See you next week in the city?"

"Yep. We have an appointment."

"I enjoyed meeting your mom this week. How's Scout? I'll be over to see him before I go back."

"My mom loved meeting you. She had seen some of the pictures in the paper, so she was curious. She likes that you are a southern girl who knows horses. Scout is great, incidentally."

"Your mom is fun. Maybe I'll have time to see her when I swing by."

He starts back up the drive and stops at the security house. Smith is standing there with the guard. His feet shoulder width apart, his hands in front of him.

"Miss James. Mr. Moore." He's all business. "I'll escort you the remainder of the way. The grounds are closed to visitors tonight."

I roll my eyes and say my good night to Blaine. Smith offers me a hand out of the car and steers me into the back of the SUV.

"I don't need driven. I can ride in the front."

"Miss James," he starts to protest when I settle into the front seat. I think he wants to say something, but he wisely holds his tongue.

"Was that really necessary? He was just going to drop me at the door."

"I'm afraid so." He's adamant and offers no apologies, but smirks at me when I give him my best irritated look.

"I'm tired, so you can have this match. Next time, I win."

"Of course, Miss James," he nods with a smirk.

He pulls up in front of the house and opens my door. I take my heels off and we head in. The lamps are on, but I don't hear anyone. "Are Ruth and Ben here?"

"No ma'am."

"Emme. I'm not a ma'am. At least not yours. So, just Emme."

"Yes ma'am. Is that all?"

"Yes, sir. It is."

He nods, same smirk.

I loved wearing Jules' design, but right now I just want to change into something really comfortable. I slide into a pair of Graham's sweats and one of his t-shirts, grab a blanket, and head outside to enjoy some ocean air. I spot the hammock. Therein lies my destination. I maneuver myself onto it, so as to not go rolling right off the other side. It's an all cloth, navy blue hammock that curls almost completely around me, imitating a cocoon. Add to it the ocean breeze and the music of the waves and it's very soothing.

I lay thinking about how much has changed in my life over the last two weeks. Graham collars his girls? That would explain his wanting to have complete control, and these rules he keeps talking about. Why didn't he just tell me? How do I really feel about that? I mean, I haven't just unloaded everything about me on him either, it has only been a short time. I know the time frame has no bearing. It may only be two weeks of a calendar year, but in terms of growth, it has been like an invested relationship. I just don't know if Graham feels the same.

I listen to the waves coming in. My eyelids struggle as the wind does its best to rock me to sleep.

I have the sensation of being lifted into the air. It's Graham. His scent fills me. It smells like home. I nuzzle into his chest, and he places a soft kiss on my eyelid.

"I was worried. I couldn't find you anywhere."

Why worry? He had to have known I was here?

I garble some sort of response that I am sure is as unintelligible to him as it is to me.

"Sleep, sweet girl." He lowers me into a bed, removes my sweatpants and climbs in behind me. I turn, nestling my face into his chest, push my leg between his and sleep.

ch♥pter
twenty-one

My body feels heavy, like I can't move. The panic of feeling trapped sets in enough to make my eyes flutter open. The morning is just peeking into the windows. Graham is draped over me, almost completely on top of me. I turn us so I am on top, then I give him a few minutes to fall back to sleep before I slide out of bed. My best ninja moves payoff and he stays asleep.

I change into some running clothes and head to the kitchen. Ben is reading the paper, looking up when I enter.

"Good Morning," I greet him.

"Good Morning, Emme. How far are you running today?"

"Just ten miles."

I grab a bagel and pop it into the toaster. Who would have thought that the words "just ten miles" would ever leave my mouth in reference to running? There was a time not too long ago that I could barely make a mile.

"Mind if I join you?"

"Not at all. Do you want to run the beach or the property?"

"Seeing as we only have a couple more days to enjoy it,

let's do the beach. I'll get changed."

He folds his paper and heads in the direction of their wing. I layer some cream cheese on my bagel and nurse a Diet Coke.

"So the bet is over?" Ben eyes my drink when he re-enters the kitchen.

"Yes. And I won." I do a little victory dance.

"I had no doubts," he smiles knowingly and starts to stretch.

Bruiser follows us to the beach and runs the first couple of miles with us, when Ben orders him back to the house. Without hesitation he turns and heads back.

"John Michaels approached me at dinner last night."

Ben stumbles slightly, but regains his footing. I can tell he's angry.

"You need to tell Graham. Where was your security?"

"I have yet to see any security other than Smith."

"It doesn't mean they aren't there. Smith should have been made aware as soon as they realized you were in the same restaurant. I'll have to address this. I don't know what's going on."

"I haven't told Graham because I know he will try to fix it. I don't need him fixing things for me."

"It's what he's good at," Ben says, unapologetically.

"It's what I'm good at, too. Once you start accepting help, you become dependent on that help. And what happens when they aren't there? Then you're really screwed," I say, more than a little surprised by my honesty with him.

We run another half mile before Ben responds.

"I give you that Graham has a love-'em-and-leave-'em track record. His mother and I are not blind to his dating habits. But you're different, Emme. He's different with you. Don't give up on him. On the other side of the coin, I think you could use someone to rely on. Sounds like it's been a long time since you've been able to. You and Graham would be good for each other if you can both just get out of your own stubborn ways and give it a try."

Well I guess I don't have to wonder how Ben and Ruth feel.

We run the rest of the way home in silence.

Ben stays outside with Bruiser, and I head up to take a shower.

Graham is dressed in jeans and a white linen shirt and working at my laptop.

"Don't you have a laptop of your own?"

"You should have security on yours. I was learning more about your program. Richard Raines called. Wants to meet today to discuss the program. He read your email and is interested in hearing more."

"Today? I don't know that I'm ready," I say timidly.

"You are. I've read your business plan and looked at your slides. Seriously, you should come work for me." He stands and walks around the desk. "You can do this."

I nod and smile with gratitude at his faith in me.

"What time will he be here?"

"Thirty minutes. Get dressed. It's casual."

Casual. Smart, but casual. I think about what to wear while I shower. I decide on a flowy sleeveless black top that crisscrosses in the back and a pair of straight, melon-red pants, my father's watch, my rings, and I'm ready.

We're meeting at Graham's house. He pulls to the side. There is a separate entrance that leads to an office with two smaller work spaces and a conference room. Everything is state-of-the-art. One of the smaller work spaces is filled by a young guy. He looks to be close to my age.

"George, please set up Miss James' laptop with the projector system. We have a meeting in five minutes."

"I'm Emme," I introduce myself. Graham has already moved into CEO mode and is walking into his office.

"Nice to meet you. I'm George." There's something about him that I like instantly.

"Mr. Manners," I nod towards Graham, indicating he should have introduced us.

"Emelia," he says from his office. It's a warning. I giggle and wink at George who returns my smile.

I enter his office. Wow. I could work here every day. Two walls are solid windows with a view of the ocean. There is a private balcony off the office.

"Don't discuss me with my staff."

"I didn't," I bristle.

He looks at me like he knows exactly what I did. He probably has a camera out there.

I make my way to the conference room that also has a wall of windows overlooking the ocean.

"How is anyone supposed to work with that view?" I say to George.

"I know right? It can be a challenge some days." He shows me how to use the video display.

"Hi, sweetheart."

I turn toward Adam's familiar voice.

"Adam!" I hug him.

He chuckles and hugs me back.

"Ready?"

"As much as I can be with thirty minutes' notice."

George answers a phone and announces that Richard is on his way up. Adam and I meet him at the top of the stairs. Holt is with him, bringing a smile to my face.

"Holt. What a great surprise!" I acknowledge him first, folding him into a hug. He soaks up the attention.

"Richard." I offer a hand to him. I don't want him to interpret this as something other than business. He steps past my hand and kisses my cheeks.

We move into the conference room, where George offers refreshments. Graham enters, all business. It occurs to me that I will also be making a formal pitch to Graham.

We take our seats, me at the head of the table, Graham to my right, Adam to his. Holt is on my left, his dad next to him.

"So, you've read the business plan?" I direct to Richard.

"I did."

"Thank you. What about the program drew your interest?"

He watches me for a minute.

"I'm curious why you're starting your pitch with that question?"

"Because it gives me some foundation on how to best fit my program to you. The program is unique in that the companies don't mold around this program, this program is molded for each company. So, yes, there is an overarching measure of success for the program and mission statement if you will, but what the actual program achieves will vary based on the business and its owner." I pause, making sure I choose my words carefully. "You and I are in a different predicament than I will be with the other companies."

"Why is that?"

"You feel beholden to me. Based on your company's history, business practices, and acquisitions, I know what kind of business man you are. I have studied you. I've studied your reputation, your company's P&L. I've surveyed your teams. I know how engaged your employees are. I know what your customers like most and least about your business, and I know what areas you're strongest in. I could give you five areas you could make changes in and see immediate improvement, and one arena that you should tap into. What I don't know is, are you making this decision because you are beholden to me? What I also don't know, yet, is can we make it work despite your apprehensions about the program?"

"Who says I have apprehensions?"

"You. Your answer to my question tells me you do."

"But I didn't answer your question."

"I know. You deflected and chose to test my response. I presented this to Adam and he knew two ways he wanted the program to impact his team. Baker had three." I pause. "Business is instinctual. It should not be emotional. You don't need me to tell you that. If you were making this decision based on your instinct, you would have been able to answer my question."

Now he's studying me. He looks to Adam, a smile on his face.

"You weren't kidding."

"I warned you," Adam says.

I allow a moment for the exchange, but I also know I need to move forward. "Let's talk about the program. We can salvage this. Based on Adam and Jackson's perspective on you as a business man and the feedback I received from your employees, I feel this program can be a good fit for you. I think you are hesitant because this is the first business decision in a long time, possibly ever, that you know you're going with your emotions and not your instinct. It's unsettling."

"You're right on all accounts, except the first time. This would be the second. The first is when I chose to marry Jean."

"And how's that working for you?" I smile.

His laughter lets me know it was received in the spirit intended.

"So, what is the program you see for my company?"

I go through the slide presentation, hitting all the marks I think he needs to feel like he is making a solid decision.

"Impressive. I must admit."

"Overall, what is your inclination?" Inside, I'm nervous. This is my first real push. Outside, my shell is hard. I look cool and collected.

"I would like to pilot a group."

"Okay. I can work with that," I say coolly. Inside, I'm twerking and giving myself a chest bump.

"Now that I know you are making the decision for your company and not based on our first meeting, I would like to propose a separate agreement with you."

"Do tell?"

"I would like to enroll Holt in the program."

Holt looks at me, confused. "But I'm not poor or from the Bronx?"

"That's just finances and geography. In the end, you are trying to find your way just like they are. I would like for you to work after school and some weekends, if needed. You won't be assigned to a company. You will be assigned to the program. Working directly for me. There are certain privilege gaps between you and the young men who will be interning, but you will learn from them and they will learn from you. I see a leader in you. I think you will be good at this. What do you say?"

"Do I get paid?"

"No."

"Do I get my own office?"

"Nope."

"Will I get to work with you?"

"Yes."

"Will you have the same expectations for me that you do for the others?"

"More. 'To whom much is given…'"

"It's a deal," he smiles widely. My heart warms from it.

"Richard?"

"Holt can make his own choices. If he wants to do this, I won't stop it."

"Cool. Thanks, dad. I'm going to go call Mom while you all finish up." He leaves the conference room.

"You knew all along you wanted Holt," Richard says.

"Since the minute I walked into the hospital room."

"And if I hadn't agreed to this meeting?"

"I would have figured out another way. I don't take easily to the word 'no' when I know it should be a 'yes.'"

"No. I'm sure you don't," he laughs.

"You're laughing at me? You find me funny?"

"Yes, I find you funny, but I'm not laughing at you. I'm laughing at Graham."

Graham and I look curiously at him.

"She's exactly what you deserve. Someone who doesn't like the word 'no.'"

Graham's lip twitches, and Adam joins Richard in laughter.

"He's still new to this. Don't make it easy for him. Let him figure some of it out on his own," he says, slapping Graham on the back. It's evident Graham is not used to being the butt of the joke.

We wrap up a few logistics. My takeaway is to send him the profiles of the guys I will be placing on his teams and how to best utilize them.

"You still going to ride this afternoon?" Adam asks after Richard and Holt leave.

"I am. I'm planning on going now. What about you? You up for a ride?"

"I would love to, but Jules has a list for me today. You did great." He peppers my forehead with a kiss.

"I know." I'm doing a little happy dance. George comes into the room, and I grab his hands forcing him to dance with me.

"Why am I dancing?" he asks Graham.

"Happy dance," Graham smirks.

George looks from Graham to me and shrugs, warily adding a little shake to his move. I'm getting the impression he doesn't see the casual side of Graham often.

"Okay. I'm done." George nods and excuses himself.

"I'll walk out with you, Adam. I'll see you when I get back?" I ask Graham.

"You're going riding by yourself?"

"Yep. Unless you want to come with?"

"I have work that can't wait. Will Blaine be there?" His question direct, leaving no need for interpretation.

"I'll let you two chat," Adam says with an odd smile. "Great job today, sweetheart. I'm very proud of you."

"Thank you," I smile.

"I'm proud of you, too," Graham says once Adam has left. Something about those words coming from him swells my heart.

I pounce before he knows it's happening, pushing my tongue deep into his mouth.

"Fuck me," I beg him.

Graham hits a button under the table and I hear a click. The windows frost. Very 007. He pulls off my pants. His mouth finds mine again as he lifts me onto his conference room table laying me back. My hair fans out around me. He stops for a minute looking at me.

"You're beautiful"

"Thank you."

"I mean it, Emme. You're really stunning." I see his resolve snap. He undoes the fly of his jeans and without removing them, he slams into me on the conference room table. My back arches at the impact. Graham grabs my forearms and pulls me to him, like he's trying to climb his entire body inside of me. His stride is relentless as we both begin to climb.

"Quiet," he reprimands gently, reminding me George is near. He knows that's hard for me. I bite my lip to hold it in.

"Get there, Emelia." He pumps into me several more times and orchestrates us going over the cliff together. I find my orgasm as he pours himself into me. I tug on my arms for him to release them, wrapping them around him when he does. Our breathing comes in waves. Slowly, he pulls out of me, cleans himself then me before dressing us both. He pulls me into a deep intimate kiss.

"I'll see you at the house for dinner."

He's dismissing me? He leaves the conference room for his office. *Well alright then.* I tell George good-bye. Smith takes me to the house. I'm not sure where everyone is, but all the cars are gone. I guess I won't go riding. I explore the grounds and decide on a swim.

Their pool is perfect. It's heated so the water temperature is just right. The shape and size lends itself to swimming laps. The same sound system works at the pool, sending music over the speakers. I dive in and start a leisurely pace of swimming laps.

I'm on my sixth or seventh lap when someone dives in

beside me. It's Graham. Neither of us stops or say anything, we just continue to swim. As we round another lap, I'm aware that I have picked up my pace and am no longer swimming for leisure. This is competition. Graham senses it, too. His body is at ease in the water. His strokes long, hard, and graceful. I begin using my legs to push off each time, trying to gain some leverage. I see his smile when he turns his face for air. I'm keeping pace with him and even inch forward a little. I've just moved ahead when he grabs my ankles and pulls me back to him, lifting me partly out of the water.

"Hey, I was winning."

"You were, baby," he placates me, his hands coming around my breast, his erection at my hip. "Thought you might want your prize."

"Always, baby. I always want you. Only you. Fuck only you."

I hear a growl as he turns me to him, his mouth once again claiming mine. I knew what my words would do to him.

"Yo, bud." Adam's words stop our exploration. "Use your room," he says to Graham.

I laugh climbing out of the pool to dry off.

"You coming?" I ask as sweet as I can, laughing at the face Graham gives me. I know it will be a few minutes before he is able to get out of the water.

Grabbing a Diet Coke out of the fridge I head up to my room to shower the chlorine out of my hair. I'm not sure how long I have been in there, but the shower door opening behind me pulls my eyes up. Graham gets into the shower, his eyes distant. He pulls me to him and thrusts his tongue into my mouth. I draw him in like air. He pushes my back against the wall and his tongue starts the dance again.

We really need to talk, but I can't make myself stop. His

mouth works its way down my body in a pattern of kisses and love nips, his tongue darting out to soothe the bite. He takes his time with each of my breasts, sucking and rubbing my nipples while his hand massages the other one. I could orgasm by this action alone. Just when I think that is his intention, he drops to his knees. My hands fist his hair as his mouth works its way across my stomach and down my hips. He spends time on each thigh, finally making his way back to my sex. It's more sensitive than usual after waxing and he moans his approval when his tongue maps across it. My legs shake, his hands coming to my hips to support me. He runs his nose up and down my "v", taking his time. I'm impatient and try to urge him along.

He shakes his head chastising me.

"I want to memorize your smell." He sticks his nose between my legs and inhales deeply. It feels vulnerable, but also cared for at the same time.

Lifting one leg over his shoulder he drinks me in. My hands fist in his hair. He likes it when I tug. His name on my lips makes him smile as he continues pulling back each time I'm about to come. Its heaven and torture mixed into one.

"Graham," I beg, and he has mercy on me, catching my body as fireworks shoot off behind my eyelids. He continues to devour all my body will give him.

Once he knows I won't fall, he slowly moves up my body, his weight helping me stay in place. Our breathing is labored and we stand there, just being with each other. My body finally surfaces back to this planet. I turn his back to the wall. His lips roll into a knowing smile as my hand begins to move up and down his imposing length. His breathing quickens, an exhale whistling through his teeth. It's intoxicating to know I have this effect on him. I can't help but wonder who else has had this effect on him. For the first time, I realize I do actually have a jealous streak. I push that out of my mind and continue working his cock.

My eyes meet his and I see the challenge in them. I drop to my knees eager to taste him. I realize once I have him there, that I maybe should have spent a little more time working my way down, but I'm still learning and my greed overcame the best of me. The rise and fall in his chest tells me he doesn't mind, and his hands find my hair.

I run my tongue under his length and suckle just below the head, circling to the tip and working my way back down to his sac. I lightly apply suction with my mouth while gently massaging him with my hand. My tongue darts over the small landing just behind his testicles. He tugs my hair letting me know that he likes it. I start the whole process again, this time moving him to the back of my throat and out again. I push him to the back of my throat again and hum. His knees shake and I know he is close. I pull my mouth all the way off him, kissing and licking his darkened tip.

I take both of my hands and gently roll him back and forth. I give a slight tug as my hands slide to the end. I look up at him through my eyelashes and ever so slowly, I put his cock in my mouth to the back of my throat again, concentrating on breathing through my nose. I succeed and am able to hold it there a few seconds longer than usual. Not moving my eyes of his, I put my hands behind my back and hold my mouth in place, submitting. Being vulnerable. Giving him charge over the pace. Letting him fuck my mouth.

"Emelia."

The reverence in his voice reaches my heart. His eyes turn a midnight blue as he places his hands on the side of my face and begins setting a pace. Fucking my mouth. I can tell he's about to come and I increase the suction, giving him the permission to come in my mouth. He pushes to the back of my throat two more times before he stops. His come shoots onto my tongue and down my throat. He continues fucking my mouth, milking himself through his orgasm until he has nothing else to give.

His legs tremble. I move up his body, supporting him with mine. We stay there with the water running over us. Neither of us say a word. Once he has his breathing under control, he cups my jaw and kisses me.

What was that? That was not fucking. It was passionate. It was intimate. It was knowing.

Graham looks as bewildered by the experience as I do. It's time to lay our cards on the table. We're naked in the shower. We can't hide.

"We need to talk," I begin.

"Yes, we do. You left last night without telling me."

"I told you. I sent you a text. I think the words you are looking for is that I left last night without your permission."

I let my comment sink in for a minute. He doesn't respond.

"Are you a dominant?"

"I told you already. No. Yes, I have rules that I want the women I'm with to follow. No, I don't do contracts. I do use toys to heighten your experience, and I do want to punish you when you break the rules, but only to pink your bottom, never to mark you. Remind you who's in charge."

I look at him, pretending I need clarification about who he means.

"That would be me, Emelia. *I* am in charge," he clarifies, challenging me not to inject a smart comment here.

"I'm this way whether you choose to attach a title to it. If that makes me a dominant in your eyes, then so be it."

I purse my lips in thought. "Do you want me to be your submissive?" I ask.

"I want you, period."

"As an affair? For six weeks."

"I don't know that I will ever have my fill of you, Emelia. Every time I think I can make myself walk away, something pulls me back for more."

"Did you see Colleen last night?"

"Yes. She told me you left before I saw your text." He looks perplexed.

"Did she tell you who I met last night?"

He shakes his head, wondering where this is going.

"Alex Russo." I study his response, but he gives nothing away. "He propositioned me with money for sex. He said you wouldn't mind. If you did, you would have a collar on me."

I see the clouds brewing in his eyes. I don't say anything else. I wait him out, which doesn't take long.

"Emelia." I hear the uneasiness in his tone.

"Graham. Did you give me the necklace because you wanted me to have a beautiful necklace, or was it a temporary collar like you give your other girls?

His not answering is my answer.

I turn off the water and step out of the shower, toweling myself off. I don't say anything. I pull on his sweats and a black tank top. His eyes follow me.

I sit and braid my hair in pigtails and move to my room. He walks in soon after in shorts and a Giants t-shirt. He sits on the bed and watches me with unease as I tie a ribbon around the package I wrapped earlier. There's a knock at the door.

"Dinner is ready," Lucy announces.

"What good is giving me a collar to show ownership if I

don't know it? I want to belong to you, Graham. I am certain of it. But I don't want to be owned. And I can't be what you need. Add the time-frame restrictions and my own shit that I bring to the table, and I think we need to call this exactly what it is. You have been right from the beginning. You knew it. I just didn't want to admit it. This is and was an affair."

I move around the desk and stand in front of him, leaning down to press a light kiss to his cheek. He still hasn't said a word, and his expression is giving nothing away. I can tell I'm losing my grip and exit the room to head to the kitchen. Once in the hall, I exhale, trying to lock my shit down and move forward.

The table outside is set. The sun to set soon. I pull on my Jackie O sunglasses. Their large frames make me feel protected, like I will make it through this with my emotions intact.

Lucy has gone to announce dinner to Graham again. We take our usual seats around the table minus Becca and Matt. Ruth is to my right and Graham has arrived to take his seat across from me, next to Lucy. He's quiet.

The rest of the family is oblivious and buoyant in their conversation. I watch Ruth who winks at me. Jules sets a Diet Coke in front of me, and I expect push back from Graham. He doesn't say anything, nor does he acknowledge it.

He speaks when spoken to, as do I. I doubt the family is any wiser.

"I feel extra blessed to have each of you here today. My family," Ruth says squeezing my hand, and I bite my lip to keep it from quivering.

"Darling," she says to Ben, "We have so much love to be grateful for. Would you say a blessing?"

Ben studies his wife with love and admiration for a moment. His right hand reaches out to Jules and his left one to

Lucy. One by one we hold hands around the table. Adam squeezes my hand as he folds it into his. Ruth tightens her grip she already has. Ben says a prayer of blessing.

My eyes are on Graham. He knows I'm struggling to hold my emotions together. He nods slightly at me. I know it's his way of comforting and letting me know I can make it through this dinner. It's enough to undo me, and I am so grateful that my eyes are covered. Tears well but don't fall.

Adam pokes me each time he passes me food, causing me to punch him in the arm. It's like a usual family meal. Love and laughter and stories.

After dessert, I hand Ruth the gift I had been wrapping earlier.

"I wanted to give this to you and Ben before I leave to-morrow. I cannot thank you enough for your kindness this week. How much care you have shown me. It filled a place that has been void in me for a while now. It's just a little something to show you the gratitude I feel for you both."

I look back to Ruth, and she swipes away a single tear that has fallen down her cheek.

"Mom, you are so sappy," Lucy gently teases.

Ruth laughs, removing the wrapping. She stops when she sees the picture I framed of her and Ben. She stares at it before turning it to Ben for him to see.

"When did you take this? It's beautiful."

She turns it over to find the message I have written on the back.

Ben and Ruth, Words cannot express what y'all mean to me. Thank you for being the kind of people who make an impact on others. When I first saw this picture, I was mesmerized by the beauty of both of you. As I studied it longer, I realized it's the beauty of the love you have for each other that is shining through so boldly. May your love and family continue to be bold in the lives of others. With love, Emme.

"Emme. It's…" Tears begin to follow the single one that fell a moment ago. Ben moves to her end of the table placing a hand on her shoulder. Her hand coming up to rest on his. He reads the message I have written and kisses Ruth's head in a show of support of her emotions. Ruth never finishes her sentence, but leans over and kisses my cheek like only a mother can, laughing at her own tears.

She hands the frame to Adam and it makes its way around the table. I'm embarrassed and touched by the response to the note I've written. Graham reads it and excuses himself from the table.

The rest of us help in clearing the dishes and cleaning up, everyone expressing wishes I would stay another day. I make polite excuses of course and let them know that they will see me in the city.

"Adam or Jules, would you mind driving me to Jackson's? I was hoping to save them a trip in this direction."

"Sure thing," Adam studies me for a minute. His face softens and he kisses the top of my head. "I'll help you get your things."

Graham

Her hips sway and slide down over my rigid cock. My breath leaves my body in a rush of air. My hands rest on her thighs as she lifts and lowers herself on and off me.

Her chin is raised, her hair falling long and thick down her back. I watch as she takes her pleasure from me. Her hands knead her breasts, pinching her nipples when I direct her to.

She's a goddess. An enchantress.

She was meant for this. Meant to be mine. Meant to be possessed by me.

Her mouth parts and her tongue licks the plump curves of her lips, wetting them as her pace quickens. She's close. I know her body. I know every inch of her.

I want her.

I need her.

She is mine.

The tips of her fingers skim her skin as she slides her hands to her neck, lifting her hair onto her head. Sweat glistens between the globes of her breast. I move my hands to her hips, my grasp firm and possessive. I direct her movements, driving myself deeper inside of her, my hips meeting hers on each thrust.

"Graham." She breathes my name like it's music to her. She's close. Three, maybe four more thrusts and I know she will be coming over me.

"Come, Emelia." I command her body, pushing it over the precipice she has been perched on. Her hands fall to my chest and her beautiful large brown eyes open and spear my soul, making contact with mine. She sees me, all of me, and before I can control it, I'm coming long and hard inside her. Her eyes never leave mine. She doesn't back down.

She is mine.

I wake with an ache in my dick and semen in pools on my stomach. I haven't had a wet dream since I was a teenager. My breathing is long but shallow, and my cock is still hard, almost painful to touch. To finish what the dream started, to find some temporary release, I close my eyes and imagine it's Emelia's hand touching me, her lips wrapped around me. It's all that is needed to send me over the edge.

It's been two weeks since the Hamptons. Two weeks since she called me on my shit and walked away. Two weeks of this miserable abyss.

A woman has never had this effect on me before. My attention to business has been completely lacking. I've been snapping at my staff. My family. Everyone. I thought Adam was going to deck me yesterday when I snapped at Jules, Emelia's best friend.

The first week back from the Hamptons was difficult enough, but I survived it. The second week has been utter torture. Sitting across from her in meetings, watching her interact with other men. Watching them eye-fuck her. Christ. I nearly put my fist into that fucker's face yesterday.

And yet, she seems fine. Totally unaffected. Oblivious to the havoc she has caused in my structured life. The destruction she left in the wake of her storm.

I've never had to fight for a woman, much less a relationship. If I said ten words to the girls I fucked, it was a loquacious event. We both knew what we brought to the table: I brought money and connections, they brought sex. All I wanted. But Emme, she doesn't care about my money or connections and I want her around all the time. Not just for sex. I'm thirty. I have an organization to run. I still have things I want to accomplish. A relationship complicates that. I'm not sure I would even know how to have both at the same time.

The heat from the shower distracts me and I find a moment of peace without thoughts of her controlling my every breath. I can do this, I think. I can. As I rinse off the body wash she left at the beach house, I know. I know I'm lying to myself. Emelia is mine and today is the day I take charge. This will go much easier if I take control. If I had taken control at the beach, I wouldn't be so tormented. She's just so damn stubborn. I don't know that I have ever met anyone as obstinate as she is. It's fucking sexy.

No wonder she's all over the place, Taylor. You're sending her so many mixed signals.

Smith is waiting for me. He's kept his thoughts to himself, but I feel his frustration at how I have handled Emelia. It's irritating. Irritating because he's right and because I care. We ride in silence to the office, and when Smith stops at the front door, I take a moment to regain the composure I lost since I first sat next to her on that plane. Today, I will rectify that mistake. I'm taking control. I walk through the doors of the empire I've built, make my way to a pillar across from the elevators, and wait.

It's no time at all before I see her and *fuck me*. Her hair is pulled up, errant strands hanging loose framing her face. What little make-up she wears just accentuates how naturally stunning she is. Her hips sway seductively as she teeters on four-inch heels. Her sheer blouse shows a lace structured bodice underneath. Her skirt is what pinup dreams are made up of. Tight, the high waist lying flat over her stomach, the taper at the knee highlighting her curves. Very sexy secretary.

As she enters, she greets the staff by name, something some of my senior staff can't do after years of working here. She has been here a week and already she knows the people who work the door, the desk, and security. I hear her asking

Sarah about her daughter. Her genuine smile tugs at my heart, and whatever Sarah tells her makes her laugh. Her laugh is genuine and attentive.

She steps away from the crowded entrance to locate her badge. Adam made sure her card had access her first day in the building, but I already know she won't take the elevator reserved for me and my immediate family.

She locates her badge and Magda, one of my custodial staff, drops some supplies she is carrying. I watch several men's steps falter when Emelia smooths her hand down the back side of her skirt when she squats to help Magda pick up the supplies, addressing her by name. Duncan in legal stops to offer her a hand as she stands. Oblivious to his intentions, she says thank you and makes her way through security. He can't take his eyes off of her ass as she walks away. I make an unreasonable mental note to fire that fucker.

Troy discretely stops her after the security check and feeds her the line I gave him. She enters my private elevator. And so it begins...

ackn♥wledgments

Words really don't do justice for the love I have for each person that helped encourage me along the way. There is no way this would have happened without you!

Jess - From the beginning, you were the encouragement I needed to keep going. You were my first reader and the first one to tell me you needed more. We have built a sister bond without even meeting - a sign we were meant to be!

Anna – No way would I have made this without you. You are the perfect editor for me. Your honesty and feedback is exactly what I needed. Thank you for taking a girl with no knowledge of grammar and making me smart. A daunting task!

My Betas - Tracey, Amy, Kelly, Andrea, and Elizabeth – Your time is the best gift you could ever give me. Thank you for meeting deadlines, reading and re- reading and reading once again. Y'all coming along for this ride made it all the more fun. (Dinner and drinks helped too!)

Regina - Your patience and guidance in determining my brand was exactly what I needed. Thank you!

Amber - We are both new to this and I wouldn't have it any other way. Thank you for always being there to bounce ideas and questions off of and for working hard to make sure as many people as possible get to read Graham and Emme's story.

Kiki - Thanks for taking a chance on me when you didn't have to. Your desire for me to be my best means so much.

Alessandra – Your willingness to share your experience was invaluable and such a blessing.

Last but not least,

Kelly – You helped me find my inner Kj. No one else could have done that.

Rachel - I lost count of the ledges you talked me off of. Thank you for clothing me when I was ass naked in the middle of Times Square.

Ne - The true picture of encouragement and compassion. That you call me your best friend is one of the best gifts God ever gave me.

J- You know…

Most importantly,

You – I don't know how many of you there will be. I can only hope that each of you as readers love Graham and Emme as much as I do. I wrote this with only you in mind.

www.ingramcontent.com/pod-product-compliance
Lightning Source LLC
Chambersburg PA
CBHW020224180626
46810CB00006B/2043